The Urbana Free Library

To renew materials call
217-367-4057

DISCARDED BY THE
URBANA FREE LIBRARY

1-04

DATE DUE			
FEB 03 2004	APR 08 2004		
APR 0 2004	JUN 17 2004		
MAY 04 2004			
JUN 01 2004			
JUL 11 2004			
MAY 05 2012			

This special signed edition is limited to 600 numbered copies and 26 lettered copies.

This is copy 411.

Unintended Consequences

URBANA FREE LIBRARY

Subterranean Press • 2003

Unintended Consequences
Copyright © 2003 by Alex Irvine.
All rights reserved.

Dust jacket illustration
Copyright © 2003 by Patrick Arrasmith.
All rights reserved.

Interior design
Copyright © 2003 by Tim Holt.
All rights reserved.

FIRST EDITION

ISBN
1-931081-86-7

Subterranean Press
P.O. Box 190106
Burton, MI 48519

email:
subpress@earthlink.net

website:
www.subterraneanpress.com

Contents

Jimmy Guang's House of Gladmech   7

Akhenaten   37

Rossetti Song   51

The Sands of Iwo Jima   67

Intimations of Immortality   77

Chichén Itzá   113

The Sea Wind Offers Little Relief   135

Tato Chip, Tato Chip, Sing Me a Song   163

Down in the Fog-Shrouded City   177

Elegy for a Greenwiper   207

Agent Provocateur   221

Vandoise and the Bone Monster   235

A Peaceable Man   263

Jimmy Guang's House of Gladmech

Jimmy Guang Hamid smoked tobacco cigars until he found out that vat-grown lungs were still prone to immune-rejection problems and that the vat wranglers hadn't made much headway on what they called amongst themselves the Larynx Problem. Then he went over to herb-and-marijuana panatelas, anxious to maintain his image as a Golden Age wheeler-dealer, but not so anxious for a long convalescence or opportunistic infection following a double pulmonary.

But he was in Kyrgyzstan, anyway, a long way from organ vats, and the only people there who cared about his image were the Russians. The Russians were the only people who cared about lots of things in the brutalized city of Osh, a still-proud prominence in the tank-tracked, cluster-bombed, spider-mined, cruise-missiled ruins of what had once, a hundred years or so before, been the southern part of the Soviet Empire. Now Kyrgyzstan was a member of the Islamist Federation, a loose group of non-Arab Muslim states, and the Russians fought with the IF out of concern over concentration of power in Central Asia but mostly out of sheer terror of what would happen if their soldiers were ever allowed to come home.

Jimmy Guang was not a deeply religious man, although he'd been raised a Muslim and inhabited the belief the way he inhabited his tastes in food or music. He took no sides between the IF and the Russians and the Chinese, who hovered like a storm waiting to break from the East. He had come to these wars thinking he could make money.

He came to the city of Osh, on the flanks of the Ferghana Valley, a sliver of warm green pointing up into the windswept expanse of the Tien Shan ranges. Once Osh had been a major stop along the Silk Road. Alexander the Great had slept there. Mohammed had prayed there. Now there wasn't much left after sixty years of sporadic war, but it was close to Tashkent without being too close, and the last thing a foreign entrepreneur wanted was to be too close to Tashkent. Or, for that matter, Bishkek, the capital of Kyrgyzstan, which was still alive with bad, bad bugs the Russians had left during their previous visit.

Osh was no longer a major part of anything. It still had its legendary bazaar, and it was still warmer than just about anywhere else in K-stan, but even for war profiteering it didn't offer the potential of Karachi or Almaty or Yerevan. Still, Jimmy Guang came there with his cigars and his pinstriped suits and his silk ties, a good hundred years out of fashion, and he started making deals. He knew people in Singapore, his father was still living in Jaipur and an uncle in Xian, he'd gladhanded his way over the Khyber Pass and through the Karakoram, sneaking through the Muslim hinterlands of China on the strength of his gap-toothed grin and fragmentary bits of half a dozen languages he'd picked up around the house when he was a kid. Jimmy Guang Hamid could get things.

He set up quietly, in a bombed-out storefront on Lenin Street, not far from the bazaar but not too close either. Jimmy Guang was always careful about distance. For the first week he swept and cleaned and arranged, covered over holes in the walls and made himself a pallet behind a curtain. He would take his meals at restaurants, the better to be seen, but not expensive restaurants because behind his façade of leisure and comfort Jimmy Guang Hamid was desperately poor. He washed in the restrooms of the restaurants he patronized; he burned incense under his shirts so he could save the expense of cleaning them; he scavenged in the burned-out university campus for flaps of furniture vinyl to stitch onto his shoes. If he did not succeed here in Osh, there was a good chance that he would starve to death on his way back to India or China.

He was as piratical and polyglot a stereotype as had ever been encountered in those parts, and that's exactly how he wanted it. Let them think him a buffoon. Let them insult the many strains

Jimmy Guang's House of Gladmech

of his ethnicity, and the many colors of his ties. He would consider bargains.

It only took a few days for him to get to know people, and a few days after that to broker his first deal, between a Russian quartermaster suffering from an excess of toothpaste and an Uzbek merchant who had found himself awash in vodka straight from Kiev. The Uzbek traded mostly among the more fundamentalist IF brigades, who wouldn't drink the vodka anyway, and the Russian would make a killing from his alcoholic and lonely compatriots.

"Amazing thing, war," Jimmy Guang said in his creolized Russian to the quartermaster, whose name was Yevgeny. They clinked glasses. "Even in the midst of all this misery and misunderstanding, still there is commerce. Still we find ways to get what we need. Something grand about it."

Allahu akbar, thought Jimmy Guang, even though he wasn't particularly religious.

Yevgeny muttered a toast and drank. Jimmy Guang knew in that moment, early on a Thursday morning in May of 2083, with a fine sharp breeze shuddering down out of the Pamir range, that he would survive. He had been right to come to Osh.

The man who sold Jimmy Guang his first gladmechs reminded him of his father, and for that reason Jimmy Guang walked away from the deal certain that he had gotten the worse of it. No man could bargain with his father.

"I have no use for these," the old German trader said.

"Nor do I," Jimmy Guang said. He thought it odd that a German should remind him of his father Reza, a proud glowering Persian who claimed ancestry among the Mughal conquerors of India. He had already decided to buy the robots, six creaking Izmit general-services models. He knew he could put them to use, and he was beginning to have financial reserves sufficient to quiet his anxieties about the return voyage to India, should that become necessary.

"Put them in a pit, have them fight each other," said the Russian who had inspected the truck and pocketed three of Jimmy

Guang's cigars to ignore its doubtful papers. "That's what they do everywhere else."

"Is that so," said Jimmy Guang, and just like that his course was set.

On the edge of the university campus was a long row of corrugated-tin sheds. One, which judging from the deep oil stains in its concrete floor had once held heavy equipment, was still intact. It measured forty meters long by some twenty-five wide, which Jimmy Guang figured was big enough to cordon off an arena and still pack in something like a thousand spectators. He placed a call to the robots, and was surprised to see them all arrive in a Russian army truck driven by the beneficiary of Jimmy Guang's smoky baksheesh the day before.

"I was waiting for you to tell them where to go," the soldier said as he got down from the truck's cab. He was tall and heavy and blonde. Jimmy Guang could not imagine what it would be like to fight him when he was fully suited and armed. "Monitoring you. My name is Slava. You want these robots to fight, you're going to need them fixed up a little. I'll do it."

"There's no money for a mechanic," said Jimmy Guang, thinking that brushing Slava away would cost him more cigars. He resolved to get better encryption for his personal commlink.

"I'll do it free. Just to see them fight." A toothy grin split Slava's blunt face.

This was a deal Jimmy Guang could not refuse. He and Slava got the six Izmits off the truck and into the hangar, where they spent the rest of the day cleaning and cordoning off the arena space. Then Jimmy Guang gathered the mechs together.

"What we're going to do here is you're going to fight each other," he said.

"This is outside our parameters," one of the mechs said.

"We are not adaptive intelligences," added another.

Jimmy Guang had anticipated this. "The instructions are simple. A waste-management task. Each of you is to render the others fit for a standard industrial recyc. This requires separation of extremities from the trunk. Are you familiar with this protocol?"

"I am," each of the robots said.

After that, it was a matter of hanging posters, making sure there were enough pretty girls to run concession stands, and letting it be known that the house would take forty percent of all wagers. A few days later the six Izmits, painted different colors on Jimmy Guang's theory that this would promote audience identification and therefore wagering, banged and jerked each other to sparking pieces before an raucous and intensely partisan crowd of locals. By the end, the last surviving robot careened around the arena to thunderous cheers, missing one arm and trailing glittery strings of fiber-optic from holes punched in its trunk.

Jimmy Guang made enough on the evening that he didn't have to worry about hunger for two weeks. With some of what was left over he had his trousers hemmed and splurged on a box of tobacco cigars from Ankara, vat problems or no. That night he sat in his office listening to Russian rockets exploding in the hills, and he thought to himself: You can take your mind off anything. You can even take your mind off love. But you cannot take your mind off being hungry.

Of course the next day he fell in love.

———•◆•———

Marta was her name. Jimmy Guang met her while trying to sell her uncle Gregor razor blades and Sri Lankan pornography. She looked curiously at the porn disks, then crinkled around the eyes and looked at her feet when she saw him watching her. This combination of humor and modesty caught his attention, as did the fall of her hair across her eyes. She had his mother's eyes, thought Jimmy Guang, that sharp black gaze that missed nothing. "Marta is ruined," her uncle said. "The Russians did it. At least she fought."

She had three missing teeth, Gregor went on, where a Russian shoulder had hit her with a rifle butt to stop her fighting back. Gregor told the story like it had happened in a video. Jimmy Guang listened to it with growing embarrassment that made him look more closely at Marta. A crease of scar split her upper lip on the left side, and he thought about her missing teeth. He himself was missing a tooth, although he had no dramatic story other than gingivitis and an unsympathetic dentist.

And he had been ruined himself a time or two. He waited until Gregor was preoccupied with the finest filth Colombo could produce, and then he sidled up next to Marta and asked if she would like to take a trip to the Toktogul Reservoir.

No, she said. It was too heavily guarded.

Jimmy Guang knew a way in.

He smiled at her, made sure that the gap was visible between bicuspid and incisor on the upper right side of his mouth.

Marta glanced at him, then looked away. Her left hand rested at the corner of her mouth. It has been a long time since I went swimming, she said.

He didn't see her for nearly a week after their first meeting, but she was never far from his mind. The thought of her distracted him as he dickered with Yevgeny over another truckload of robots. When he'd paid too much for the robots and even absently agreed to take the stolen truck off Yevgeny's hands, he went back to his office and thought about how much he wanted to watch Marta swim. She would remove her vest and shoes, perhaps her top skirt. Maybe she would even track down a bathing suit, or he could present her with one. That was it. Yes. She would strip down to her bathing suit, every line and motion clean and wary as a cat's, and he would sit on the bank with a cigar while she stepped into the black water, disturbing the reflections of mountains, and swam, eyes closed and corners of her mouth relaxed into a faint smile. It struck him that he very badly wanted to see her happy, and he could not understand why.

Jimmy Guang's second evening as gladiatorial impresario teetered on the edge of debacle from the moment the grim cluster of Russian soldiers entered the arena. What had been a raucous crowd of several hundred fell nearly silent. Jimmy Guang heard muttered profanities in Kirghiz, Russian, Arabic.

The lone officer in the group of Russians approached Jimmy Guang. "You are fighting robots here," he said.

Jimmy Guang saw no way to plausibly deny this, so he nodded.

The officer nodded back. "How much to watch?"

A delicate situation, this. The officer might be leading Jimmy Guang into an admission of war privateering. He might simply expect Jimmy Guang to announce that he and his men could watch for free, which would of course remind everyone present of the inequities that had provoked the Islamic Federation's war in the first place.

Or, thought Jimmy Guang, he might be willing to pay.

"Rubles, dollars, or yen?" he said.

The Russian officer paid for himself and his men—in American dollars—and they sat together at one corner of the arena. Slava Butsayev was already there, and he came across the arena floor to join the other Russians. Jimmy Guang continued his introductory patter – he had already begun flamboyantly naming each of the robots and claiming an illustrious heritage of victory for most – until he was interrupted by a teenage Kirghiz boy who leaned forward as one of the Russian soldiers walked by and spat on the man's boots.

Jimmy Guang knew for the rest of his life that many people might have died in those next few seconds, and that he might have been one of them. But in the endless moment that stretched out after the boy's expectoration, he thought of only one thing: walking across the Khyber Pass to India, penniless and hungry with hundreds of kilometers of empty mountains between him and the nearest human who cared.

"No!" he shouted, and rushed to put himself between the soldier and the defiant boy. "No!" The soldier took a step, and Jimmy Guang, to his everlasting surprise, put a hand in the man's chest and nudged him back. "Not in here! Everyone pays the same here, everyone watches the same here. The war is outside! The war stops at the door!"

A long moment passed, and then the Russian officer touched him on the shoulder. Jimmy Guang shut his mouth and made himself ready to die.

"Tell the boy to clean up his mess," the officer said.

Jimmy Guang looked at the boy. He grew more acutely aware that he had saved a life. Perhaps more than one.

His bravado began to melt away, and as it did Jimmy Guang felt the enormity of what he was doing begin to impress itself on him. He drew his handkerchief from his breast pocket and passed it to the soldier, who wiped his boot and handed it back. Jimmy Guang, already regretting the loss of his only good silk handkerchief, held it out for the boy to take. A small voice in the back of his mind said, *Now you've done it. Now you'll always be stuck in between them.* At the edge of his field of vision he saw Slava Butsayev looking intently at him, as though he were one of the robots with unclear prospects in the ring.

When the cloth had disappeared into the boy's pocket, Jimmy Guang stepped back into the center of the arena and said, "In Jimmy Guang's House of Gladmech, everybody gets along."

He didn't find out until the next day that Marta had been in the audience that night. They were swimming, or at least she was. He, as he had in his fantasy, sat a little away from the water, hat low over his eyes against the glare and a fine macanudo between his fingers. She swam, sleek as a dolphin, out into the reservoir. Jimmy Guang saw a gleam from the dam: soldiers' binoculars. Anger swelled in his chest as he thought of Marta's missing teeth, what she had suffered. The marvelous strength of her. He was beginning to love that strength.

Later, as they ate supper back in Osh, she was distant, preoccupied, a bit cold. For twenty minutes he pried gently, and at last she came open.

"All the Russians in your audience."

"Russians, Kirghiz, Uzbeks," said Jimmy Guang. "They all pay the same, and they don't kill each other in the stands."

"They didn't this time," she said. "But if you keep doing this, it will happen. You can bet on it. And then you can bet on one other thing."

"What's that?"

Her face was to the window, her reflection a woman-shaped vacancy against a field of stars. "That the Russians will come after you, and I'll be alone again."

The next Tuesday, the Russian captain found Jimmy Guang drinking coffee on the patio of a restaurant called Fez that faced a broad square in one of the older parts of Osh. He introduced himself as Vasily Butsayev, and shook Jimmy Guang's hand. Jimmy Guang offered him a cigar, and Captain Butsayev politely declined.

He had come alone, which piqued Jimmy Guang's interest. Solitary Russian officers had a tendency to disappear in Osh, reappearing piece by piece in family mailboxes back in Petersburg or Komsomolsk. Either Captain Butsayev was more courageous than the average Russian, or he knew the right people in Osh and therefore had no reason to be afraid. It was this second possibility that had provoked Jimmy Guang's offer of a cigar.

"Is Slava Butsayev a relation of yours?"

A strange look passed across the captain's face. "He is my younger brother. I understand he is spending his spare time working on your robots."

"He is an energetic and knowledgeable young man," said Jimmy Guang. It was the truth. He had come to enjoy the young blonde Russian's company around the hangar, and without a doubt Slava kept the mechs in better condition than Jimmy would have been able to. "I am fortunate that he agreed to work for free."

"Better than some other things he could be doing," Butsayev said with a thin smile. The waiter appeared, and he ordered coffee. "A good show you put on last night," he said when it had arrived.

Jimmy Guang shrugged modestly. "Considering what I had to work with."

"This is why I am here. You are known to us as a broker of deals."

Those words opened up a huge pit in Jimmy Guang's stomach. He swallowed and said with great delicacy, "I seek only to make things a little more bearable for those who must spend much of their time amid the horrors of war."

Captain Butsayev smiled. He had good teeth. "Do not be afraid, Mr. Hamid. I'm not here to arrest anyone for profiteering, and if I were," he glanced at Jimmy Guang's threadbare suit, "there are others I would visit before you."

The pit closed, and Jimmy Guang breathed a little easier. Butsayev wanted to deal.

"If I can get you more robots," the captain went on, the tone of his voice lightening, "can you set up more matches?"

"If you get me more robots," said Jimmy Guang, "there would of course be more matches. But I am not certain that my finances are up to purchasing quantities of robots. These are hard times."

"They are," agreed Captain Butsayev. "But let us be clear about something. We know, and the Islamic Federation knows, and the Kirghiz militias up in the mountains know that this war solves nothing. The IF continues because fighting us keeps their donations flowing from the rich fundamentalists in Saudi Arabia and Indonesia. The Kirghiz fight us because they are always fighting someone. And we Russians, why are we here?" Butsayev looked pained. "I fear that the civilian government of Mother Russia is uneasy at the prospect of half a million discharged soldiers returning home at once."

Jimmy Guang thought of Marta. He tried not to let it show. Captain Butsayev studied him for a moment. The Russian had hard blue eyes and heavy bones in his face. It was the face of a man who knew that the war would leave him with bad dreams and loneliness in his old age.

"When I said you put on a good show last night," Butsayev said at last, "I didn't mean the robots."

Jimmy Guang's shoulders twitched. Even after a week, he could still feel the Russian soldier's gaze boring through him to the thin teenager with eyes hardened by privation. People walking through the square did not notice him, did not know how difficult and frightening it was to be talking to a Russian captain without knowing what the Russian captain wanted him to say. The collar of his shirt pinched under his chin when he opened his mouth.

Captain Vasily Butsayev held up a hand, and Jimmy Guang's mouth shut. "I am not a peacenik, Mr. Hamid. And I am not a soft man. But I do not love war for its own sake." He stood. "I believe you know Master Sergeant Yevgeny?"

Since there was no way to deny this, Jimmy Guang nodded.

"Good. Speak to him." With that, Captain Butsayev touched the brim of his hat and left Jimmy Guang trying not to hyperventilate at his sidewalk table that was suddenly not nearly far enough away from the war.

The next day, though, he talked to Yevgeny, and four days after that he staged another round of matches with Indian-made salvage mechs whose cutting torches glowed in the eyes of eight hundred Kirghiz and two hundred Russian spectators, none of

Jimmy Guang's House of Gladmech

whom killed or tortured or assaulted any of the others while within earshot of the old heavy-equipment shed. And the week after that was the same, only with two Chinese riveters pitted against a walking scrapheap of domestic-service units. This was such a success that Jimmy Guang went looking for a larger venue, and found a hangar outside the Russian security perimeter at Osh's airport. It was three or four times the size of the university shed, and Jimmy Guang made sure that his gladiator fans knew that there was now room to bring their friends, and he painted large signs to hang on all four of the hangar's walls. JIMMY GUANG'S HOUSE OF GLADMECH, the signs proclaimed, "gladmech" being Jimmy Guang's zippy coinage for the mayhem that occurred inside. And beneath that, NO VIOLENCE EXCEPT BETWEEN MECHS. Jimmy Guang had made it clear to Captain Butsayev, and to the local IF commander he knew only as Fouad, that the first killing or serious maiming that occurred at one of his matches would be the last. All agreed that the airport hangar should be a war-free zone.

And thus it was that Jimmy Guang's House of Gladmech became the only place in Kyrgyzstan where Russians and locals could meet without violence.

Things were going well for Jimmy Guang. He was making enough money to have his suit mended and take Marta for dinners at Fez and the odd German-Chinese restaurant near the destroyed municipal building, the Russians and the Kirghiz and the IF would all do business with him, and he was discovering that it in fact felt good to be doing a little good in the midst of so much misery. He imagined that somewhere, someday, militant robot-rights types would hear of his activities and pillory him as the worst kind of murderous slaver; but it seemed to him that if he could carve out a space wherein enemies could meet without killing, it was worth the loss of a bunch of mechs who would soon have been rusting in a boneyard anyway.

And he was falling deeply in love with Marta.

Wartime romances are odd things, Jimmy Guang considered one day after Marta had left his office in a smoldering fury. Lovers are hard to each other, as if angry words and bitter actions can test one's ability to weather war. As if one must worry not just about stray bullets or microorganisms, but about one's lover being emptied of humanity by the proximity of war.

Marta had been testing him, he thought. It was unclear whether he had passed.

Yevgeny had stopped into his office while she was visiting, and a long look had passed between him and Marta before she disappeared behind the curtain into his small personal space. "I've found some real prizes for you," Yevgeny said. "American seafloor mining mechs, complete with cutting torches and shaped charges."

"In the name of the Prophet," said Jimmy Guang, "I can't let shaped charges into my arena. What happens if one isn't aimed exactly at the opponent and I lose a whole section of spectators? I'd be ruined."

Yevgeny shrugged. "Okay, if you don't want them."

"No, I do want them. But take out anything explosive. Cutting torches, okay. Those aren't going to hurt anyone. But no bombs."

"Whatever you say. You Muslim?"

Jimmy Guang hesitated. Religion was not a topic he wanted to broach with Russian soldiers, even one he'd done business with. "My father," he said slowly.

Yevgeny looked more closely at him. "Right," he said, nodding. "Thought you were just Chinese, but I can see the Arab in you now." Another long look, then the Russian scratched his nose. "I'm surprised the captain does business with you."

Jimmy Guang waited. If Yevgeny couldn't tell Persian from Arab, Jimmy Guang wasn't going to give him a lesson.

"Not that Butsayev has anything against Muslims, but he's got a brother who," Yevgeny clicked his tongue, "isn't reasonable on the topic." Yevgeny grinned as if he was about to let Jimmy Guang in on a great private joke. "Captain's brother Slava, he collects the teeth of the women he catches alone on the street at night. He practically rattles, all the teeth in his pockets."

"When can I pick up these American robots, Yevgeny?" asked Jimmy Guang. Tomorrow, answered Yevgeny, and then he left the shop.

Jimmy Guang felt as if invisible tar had been poured over him. Blood roared in his ears, and every sound that came from the street—voices, the grinding of ancient transmissions, the coo of the pigeons that roosted under his waning—was subtly deformed. When Marta touched his shoulder, he was too thickly entangled to move.

"I know what you're thinking," she said softly. "But don't."

With great effort he turned his head. Marta's eyes spitted him, and he felt crushed between her terrible anger and the ferocity of his own hate for this Russian who collected women's teeth.

Slava Butsayev, he thought. Who fixes my robots. Who drinks my vodka and shares my cigars. Slava Butsayev whose company I have grown to enjoy.

"Don't," Marta said again.

He could not answer.

"Jimmy," Marta said. "Too many people are dying."

"Or perhaps the wrong people," he said, his voice barely above a whisper.

She held his gaze for another long moment, then looked away from him. "Do you ever think about what your gladiator robots really are?"

The change of topic threw him off balance. "They're robots," he said.

"They're stand-ins, Jimmy. The Russians look at them and see my brothers. The Kirghiz look at them and see Russians. The whole thing makes a sport of killing, makes it something to wager on."

Jimmy Guang checked his temper. He went to the window and spoke to it since he was for the moment too angry to speak to her. "Two men run into each other in the bush, up in the mountains. One is Russian, one Kirghiz, or Afghan, or Pakistani. Nobody else around. They sight down the barrels of their rifles at each other, and then they recognize each other. From where? From Jimmy Guang's House of Gladmech. And they lower their guns and walk on and they forget it ever happened, and when their superiors ask for a report, they lie." He turned to Marta. "If that happens just once, what do robots matter?"

"But you're just substituting death for death," she said, her voice rising. "You create this false oasis for people. It doesn't stop anyone wanting to kill, it just makes them want to kill for sport. The men in the hangar, don't you think that each of them imagines that it's his enemy dismembered and leaking into the sand?"

"What if they do?" he shouted. "What if they do? They're not killing each other right then, at that exact moment, and that's all. That exact moment."

Marta had withdrawn from him when he raised his voice. "Some of them don't deserve that, Jimmy," she said, shrunk deep into her coat. The cold fury in her voice frightened him because he could not tell whether he was its object. "They think about nothing but killing, and they deserve nothing but killing themselves."

She stormed out onto Lenin Street. Jimmy Guang straightened his tie and stood staring at the wall for a long time trying to pick apart Marta's knotty contradictions. His shop smelled like dust blown in from the street. Late that night he still hadn't decided whether she had left him with permission or a command, or which command.

The Russians' electronic surveillance was generally several generations more sophisticated than what most of the IF rebels in Kyrgyzstan had, but there were exceptions, and one of them was a thin, pigeon-toed young Afghan named Pavel, who had studied at Moscow University before becoming radicalized by the news that the Russians had exterminated his family in what became known as the Centennial Offensive, a bulldozing push through Kandahar in 2079. Like all large cities, Moscow had a carefully-disguised IF presence, and before long Pavel and his excellent education were on their way to the Tien Shan, where every night guerrillas set up remote rocket launchers and every morning the Russians came to destroy them. Picking through the rubble of launchers, automated Russian hunter-killers, and the occasional aircraft, Pavel put together an information-gathering apparatus that was without peer in the Ferghana Valley.

Jimmy Guang found Pavel in the city, deep in the sub-basement of the university's administration building. The building itself had long since collapsed, but the sub-basement was intact and the underground campus data network largely intact. From the sub-basement, Pavel could receive information safely from a number of remote sensing stations he had arranged in the foothills surrounding Osh. He could not broadcast for fear of detection, but he could transmit via the university network, which had surviving cable strung as far as the airport and an observatory some twenty kilometers to the east.

What a strange war this is, thought Jimmy Guang as he patiently endured the search inflicted by Pavel's guards. The Russians have satellites, infrared detection, missiles beyond counting, automated helicopters. The IF rebels have, by and large, weapons out of the twentieth century, except when their benefactors in Riyadh or Kuala Lumpur or Tripoli manage to sneak newer equipment through the Kashmir and over the Tien Shan. Still no one is going to win any time soon.

"Jimmy Guang," Pavel said. They had traded on several occasions, and Jimmy Guang had come to like this pallid fanatic who fought not because he believed that he could redress the wrongs done him, but because he did not know what else to do with his grief.

"Pavel." Next to Pavel's voice, Jimmy Guang's sounded like the croak of a crow. Pavel had a beautiful voice, rich and liquid. In another time, he would have been in a university sub-basement broadcasting on the college radio station. "I need you to track a Russian for me, Pavel. And I need a gun."

Pavel looked at him with new interest.

"An old gun. A Colt .45 automatic, or perhaps a Smith and Wesson. From before World War Two."

"I thought you were the man who could get things," said Pavel.

Jimmy Guang took off his belt, unzipped its interior pocket, and counted out three thousand American dollars in twenties and fifties. "I cannot be seen dealing with this item," he said. "Already I have put my life in your hands finding you things for your little electronic cerebellum here. You have done the same for me, and we Chinese have a saying: when you save a man's life, you become responsible for him. So we are responsible for each other."

"You are Chinese at your convenience," Pavel said. "Is your Islam so convenient?"

Jimmy Guang's hands began to tremble. But when he spoke, his voice did not. "'They scheme and scheme: and I, too, scheme and scheme. Therefore bear with the unbelievers, and let them be a while.'"

The verse was from the *surah* of the Koran called *The Nightly Visitant*. Jimmy Guang had read it when he was a small boy, and been horrified by it, by the way its patient hatred spoke to him across centuries. Quickly he turned to other, more comfortable passages, and he asked his father about the verse. "The Koran was written by men," Reza Hamid had said, "and it contains them at their worst as well as at their best. It is a human book that aspires toward God."

A small part of Reza Hamid's son was saddened that the verse no longer seemed so horrible to him.

Pavel looked at the money for as long as it took Jimmy Guang to get his heart rate under control. Then he picked up the bills, tapped them even like a deck of cards, and slipped them into his pocket.

"Why an old gun?" he asked.

"Pavel," said Jimmy Guang with grim humor. "Please. I do not ask you why you need to track satellites."

By the time he left the university campus, Jimmy Guang knew that after his patrol shift and time spent puttering among robots at the House of Gladmech, Slava Butsayev drank in a nameless bar near the bazaar, and that some nights he set out from there looking for solitary Kirghiz women. This last activity was said to be less and less frequent over the recent months, a fact that gave Jimmy Guang momentary pause. Something to think about.

That night, Jimmy Guang watched as the excellent American mining robots destroyed each other for the enjoyment of perhaps eighteen hundred windburned and war-hardened Russians, Kirghiz, Uzbeks, Afghans, and miscellaneous others, including a wary knot of sharply dressed Russians who could only be government observers. Captain Butsayev sat with them. These new mining mechs were sophisticated enough to improvise, and early in the evening one of them began taunting its opponents. Quickly it became the crowd favorite, and when it had survived the destruction of its fellows, Jimmy Guang realized he had his first returning champion.

This is like a license to print money, he thought. He spoke to this robot after the matches.

The conversation left him obscurely disappointed. Afterward, he supposed he had wanted the robot to demonstrate the kind of fire one expected of great athletes.

"You fought well," said Jimmy Guang. "Much better than any other mech we've had so far. And the crowds particularly appreciate the way you taunt the opposition."

Slava arrived and began spot-welding a patch onto the mech's back. Jimmy Guang congratulated himself for maintaining a cool exterior.

The robot's voice was a smooth baritone, its inflections nearly human. "I assumed they would, and as a strategy I had nothing to lose by it. If my opponents devote CPU time to analyzing my taunts and formulating retorts, that increases my chances of winning. Also, if the crowd begins to support me, I anticipate that you will be more forthcoming with necessary repairs and maintenance."

"You are a clever machine," said Jimmy Guang. "You use all tools to stay alive."

"No. I am programmed to maintain optimal functionality. Whatever action I take is directed to that end."

Jimmy Guang was storing this up as evidence against his imagined future robot-rights persecutors. "You don't care about staying alive?"

"My programming imbues a preference for awareness over oblivion," said the robot, "but I neither enjoy the first nor fear the second. You put me out on the arena floor to destroy the others. That is what I will do."

While these words were still rolling in his head, Jimmy Guang tried to avoid remembering the conversation he'd had with Marta the day before, but in his sleep that night he saw the surviving gladiator taunting Russian soldiers who surrounded it with railguns and rocket launchers, and in his sleep he was oppressed by a hope that it would survive.

The next morning, a ten-year-old boy staggered into his shop, bent under the weight of a bag of coffee beans. With a gasp of relief, he dropped the bag to the floor and stood expectantly until

Jimmy Guang fished in his pocket for whatever coins he had handy.

Once the boy had gone, Jimmy Guang took the bag into the curtained-off portion of the office. He slit it open, and his heart fluttered in his throat. He took a deep breath, smelling the coffee, and plunged his hands into the beans. At the bottom of the bag he found a canvas bundle. Inside the canvas bundle was a Colt .45 automatic that could have come from the hand of John Dillinger. It was cleaned, oiled, and loaded.

And here I am, thought Jimmy Guang. I have decided to kill a man, and here is the weapon I will use to do it.

Was he falling into the war? Had he lost his ability to stay apart from it, to keep it in its proper perspective? Surely there were IF soldiers who raped women, who committed atrocities.

Surely. But none of them had broken Marta.

He heard his door open. Stowing the gun in his desk, Jimmy Guang went out front, arranging the knot of his tie as he went. Captain Butsayev was waiting for him.

"Jimmy Guang," he said. "I fear there is going to be trouble. You noticed the delegation that sat with me last night."

Jimmy Guang nodded.

"They commented on the superlative show put on by the robots," said Captain Butsayev, "which is to your credit. But they also gave me to understand that they were gravely unsettled by the intermingling of Russian soldiers and locals. The lack of animosity disturbed them. They consider it inappropriate for a time of war, and they demanded that the performances be ended." Incredibly, Butsayev smiled. "But I stood up for you. I noted the effect of the House of Gladmech on morale, and argued—strenuously, I might add—that this benefit outweighed any possible detrimental effect of fraternization." The captain clapped Jimmy Guang on the shoulder. "Not to mention the fact that working on your robots helps to keep young Slava out of trouble. I believe that the delegation was swayed by my arguments. Your shows can go on."

All of this washed over Jimmy Guang like a surprise rainstorm. "Thank you," he said. The gun in his desk drawer loomed hugely in his mind, and he tried without success to inject some warmth into his tone of voice. "I believe that you are right about the benefit of the House of Gladmech, and I thank you for your courage in supporting me at what must have been some risk to your career."

"You're certainly welcome," Butsayev said. "I meant what I said." After a pause, he furrowed his brow and said, "Are you all right?"

Jimmy Guang was saved from having to answer by the entrance of Marta. She saw him before Butsayev, and she smiled at him. Out of the corner of his eye, Jimmy Guang saw Butsayev notice her missing teeth. The Russian's gaze flicked over to Jimmy Guang, who gave no sign that he had noticed.

So you know, he thought. You know about your brother, or at least you've heard rumors. But you protect him, of course. He's your brother. And after all, these aren't Russian girls.

"Captain Butsayev, this is my companion Marta Chu," he said, with what he thought was the right admixture of formality and warmth. "Marta, Captain Vasily Butsayev."

Butsayev snapped a shallow bow. "Miss Chu," he said.

Marta's hand darted to her mouth before she could stop it. Self-conscious, she returned it to her side and nodded at Butsayev. "Captain."

"Captain Butsayev has just informed me that my gladmech operation has ruffled the feathers of Russian bureaucrats," Jimmy Guang said with a too-broad smile. "He says that we should continue to ruffle, and not worry about their squawking."

Marta's answering smile looked tired and forced. "A little fortune," she said.

Butsayev, sensing the tension in the room, nodded to Jimmy Guang. "In the midst of war, one does what one can," he said, and shut the door softly behind him.

They went to Fez for lunch on the patio, and as the waiter was clearing away their soup bowls the top three floors of a building at the other end of the square blew away in a tremendous explosion. The concussion of the blast felt like a giant thumb jabbed into each of Jimmy Guang's ears. He leaped out of his chair to grasp Marta, but she was faster than he was and had already ducked into the restaurant. From there they watched as six Russians in full suits approached the burning building. As its surviving occupants emerged, the Russians rounded them up, directing them to a waiting flatbed truck.

With a flash one of the suited Russians blew apart. The sound, a flat crack compared to the deep boom of whatever had destroyed the building, nevertheless made Jimmy Guang flinch. The other five Russians turned as one and raked the doorway with railgun fire. The people coming out were obliterated, and part of the doorway caved in.

They stand there, thought Jimmy Guang, inside their shiny suits. Like robots themselves. Uplinked and shunted so they can move faster than I can think. It was difficult to imagine that a human being inhabited those suits.

Another Russian detonated, the shining green fragments of his suit clanging down on the stones of the square, and the remaining four abruptly changed their tactics. Backing away in an expanding arc, they poured railgun fire into the building and twenty seconds later another rocket destroyed it completely. Smoke hung in the square, and as the echoes died away the sounds of panicked voices formed a background to the creak and groan of shifting rubble.

He had seen it all before, but something in the horror of the moment provoked Jimmy Guang. "If you could get out of here," he asked Marta, "where would you go?"

"Today there is no out of here," she said. "Some days there is, but not today."

He was thinking about this as they walked in the square the next morning on their way to the bazaar in search of apples. The fires in the destroyed building were out, and shirtless laborers under the direction of Russian soldiers worked to clear the rubble. Fresh pockmarks pitted the pavement, and blood had sunk into the stones of the square like dirt in the creases of a hand. The workers called out and began digging a body free of the wreckage.

It's not working, Jimmy Guang thought. What if they do watch the matches without killing each other? What does it matter if later this happens?

"Marta," he said to distract her. She was looking at the body and the workmen and the soldiers too, and he wanted her to think of something else. He wanted her to think about him, to understand that he asked her questions to find out if his answers were the same as hers.

"I've never been to India. You grew up in India, didn't you?" she said.

"Also Hong Kong and Bangladesh. My father was an engineer. He met my mother in Shanghai while building a bridge, and married her before its span was complete. I am named for the nickname of an ancestor of hers who worked on railroads in the United States." Two hundred years ago, that had been. Jimmy Guang supposed he still had relatives in America, in San Francisco or New York maybe. For a fleeting moment he thought of asking Marta if she would go to America with him. He thought he had enough money to do it.

Marta smiled at him. "You with your American name," she said, "and your old-fashioned American clothes. I love you, Jimmy Guang Hamid. If I could ever get out of here I would go with you to Hong Kong or Bangladesh or Shanghai or anywhere."

His American mining-robot champion somehow acquired the name John Wayne. It continued to dispose of any opponents, and Jimmy Guang grew afraid that the monotony of its victories would cut into audience interest.

About a week after Marta's promise, though—which Jimmy Guang carried with him like a charm—a Russian army truck pulled up in front of the House of Gladmech. Jimmy Guang was there overseeing welders who were patching one of the hangar's walls, which had been partially shredded by a rocket attack from the mountains the night before. Slava Butsayev was elsewhere, which was good. Jimmy Guang hadn't worked up the nerve to kill him yet, and he didn't trust himself to keep up his friendly façade when other things were aggravating him.

Maniacs, he was thinking as the truck ground to a halt. Don't they know not to target this building by now?

A beefy and florid soldier hopped out of the truck's cab and came directly to Jimmy Guang. "You Jimmy Guang?" he said, pointing at the sign on the hangar.

"Yes," said Jimmy Guang.

"I have a robot in my truck there that will take your John Wayne apart," the Russian said.

Possibilities unfolded in Jimmy Guang's head. "I assume you're willing to wager on that," he said.

The big match took place the next night: John Wayne, the American seafloor miner, against Lokomotiv Lev, liberated from an abandoned factory in Bishkek and retooled by bored Russian combat engineers. Jimmy Guang had a feeling that John Wayne was about to meet an Indian he couldn't kill or outsmart.

The House of Gladmech was packed and sweaty. It had been a hot day, and even with the hangar doors open, a faint fog of perspiration hung in the cones of light from ceiling lamps. Lokomotiv Lev's partisans, a group of Russian perimeter guards from Bishkek, sat near the normal crowd of Butsayev's men from the Osh garrison. They formed an olive-green cluster amid the riot of Uzbek weaves and kaffiyeh worn by the locals. Jimmy Guang himself was wearing his suit, but he had gone to the only Western clothing store in Osh to buy a new tie for the occasion, and his shoes were polished to a quiet shine. The Colt automatic rested heavily in the small of his back. He wasn't sure why he'd brought it, but the night was fraught with uncertainty, and he hadn't wanted to feel unprepared.

He had a tremendous amount of money riding on the match. Fully three-quarters of the evening's receipts were at stake. If John Wayne suffered a defeat, Jimmy Guang would be without enough liquid cash to complete the purchase of tobacco and foot powder he had been negotiating with a Pakistani trader who would not return to Osh until spring. Without those goods, his income potential—and with it his dream of running to Shanghai or Delhi with Marta—would be severely injured.

If he won, though…and if the Russians paid up…he would have enough money to get them both anywhere. Berlin, perhaps. Sydney. San Francisco; he could look up relatives. Jimmy Guang's stomach fluttered.

Marta entered the hangar and took a place on a raised bench against one wall. He was glad to see her. She caught his eye and waved. Big night for her too, he thought. She knows what's at stake.

Then Slava Butsayev walked in, worked his way through the crowd, and sat next to his brother. Marta's face turned to stone. Jimmy Guang watched Captain Butsayev closely for the next few minutes. The officer greeted his brother, touched him on the shoulder, made space for him on the bench; but no pleasantries, no exchange of affection, took place. He knows, Jimmy Guang thought, just as he had thought days before in his office. He knows, and he despises his brother, but blood is blood.

Slava Butsayev never sat in the stands with the other Russians. Did he have friends among Lokomotiv Lev's crew? That seemed most likely. Jimmy Guang had a paranoid spasm; had Slava sabotaged John Wayne? Did he have some arrangement with the Lev's builders? The idea passed as quickly as it had arisen. Slava takes pride in his work on the mech, Jimmy Guang thought. He wouldn't throw a match.

Whatever the reason for Slava's action, his visibility gave the evening an entirely different flavor. Jimmy Guang looked back to where Marta sat near the wall.

She was getting up. She did not look in his direction as she left.

Angry and fearful, Jimmy Guang raced through his prematch patter, leaning heavily on the crowd to bet local, to show some pride in Osh. He played shamelessly on whatever regional animosities he could think of and channeled them into ferocious wagering. By the time the mechs themselves appeared, the floor was thrumming with the stomping of feet and dust was sifting down from the rafters.

John Wayne destroyed Lokomotiv Lev in less than ten minutes. The Russian robot lumbered to the center of the ring looking purely invincible: squat, barely human in shape, with customized steel plating welded around its sensing apparatus and most joints. It looked as if Lev's crew had scavenged the armor from a tank. They had also, it appeared, amped up the grasping power of the pincers that served Lev for hands and provided the robot with epoxy sprayers and other nozzles whose function Jimmy Guang couldn't begin to fathom. Still, John Wayne was quicker, and more importantly, he had adapted himself to the idea that he was fighting for his life—or, as he preferred it, optimal functionality. Lokomotiv Lev had been programmed to destroy John Wayne; John Wayne to survive. So, while Lev managed to glue shut John Wayne's primary torch, encouraged by the hoarse shouts of the Bishkek Russian contingent (and some of the more fundamentalist IF guerrillas, who hated modernity and blamed it on America). Then Lev caught and tore away a significant amount of John Wayne's external plating, and for a brief moment it looked as if the Bishkek mech would get its pincers into John Wayne's internals. The voice of the crowd grew constricted, frenzied. John Wayne's escape brought them back into full-throated roar, and the momentum of the match seemed to shift. Lev couldn't keep the American in one place for long enough to bring its full strength to bear. And while it tried, John Wayne danced to the side and slashed at Lev's joints with his remaining torch until, as a thundering cheer rose from the weave-and-kaffiyeh side of the arena, Lev's left leg failed entirely and it toppled to that side. Within a minute, John Wayne had disabled both of Lev's pincers, and shortly after that Lokomotiv Lev was fit only for Pavel to scavenge gyros and CPU space.

The room of the old hangar rattled with the fierce roars of the winning side. The uproar was deafening, and grew a sharp edge as the Russians from Bishkek got up and left, leaving their champion to leak hydraulic fluid into the sand. What an odd stew of rivalries here, thought Jimmy Guang: Russians and Kirghiz, different divisions of Russians, even a strange flavor of the old Russian-American Cold War. Money changed hands in thick handfuls, and parts of the crowd broke into spontaneous chants that reminded Jimmy Guang of the fenced-off portions of European soccer stadia. Look what I've done, he thought as John Wayne clanked and whirred toward him. He snapped the robot a mock salute, and John Wayne saluted back. Over the robot's shoulder Jimmy Guang saw Slava Butsayev get up and follow the Bishkek group, and he knew at that moment that he could wait no longer.

Butsayev and the Bishkek Russians found their way to his favorite bar, and there they drank until the sky was beginning to lighten. Meeting out on the street in front of the bar, they began shouting at each other. Jimmy Guang's Russian wasn't good enough to determine the source of the disagreement, but it grew heated, and after a sudden flurry of punches, the Bishkek group began walking in the direction of the airport. Slava Butsayev watched them go. After a moment, he called something after them, some Russian colloquialism Jimmy Guang had never heard before. Then Butsayev set off down a side street, wending his way toward the area of the bazaar.

Jimmy Guang was stiff and chilly from his vigil, which he had kept from the vantage of a second-floor balcony in an empty apartment house opposite the bar. He resisted the impulse to shoot Butsayev right then and there: apart from the difficulty of hitting someone with a pistol shot from that distance, there was the question of propriety. Jimmy Guang Hamid was a man who did things a certain way, as his mother had plotted graphs a certain way in her classrooms or his father held the pencil a certain way when drafting. He had never killed a man, had never fired a gun, and if he was to do it now it would have to be done in a certain way. So he followed Slava Butsayev through the twisting ancient streets near the bazaar, and it was not until Butsayev came upon a teenage girl sweeping a crooked concrete porch in front of a building honeycombed with darkened windows that Jimmy Guang removed the gun from the waistband of his trousers. The trousers immediately sank onto his hips, and he hoped that they did not sink any further to trip him up in what might follow.

Butsayev acted with the speed and decisiveness of a hunter, rather than the swagger of the torturer. He made as if to walk past the girl, who had stopped sweeping and dropped her eyes toward the street as he approached. He said something to her and reached out to curl her hair around his fingers. She flinched, and his hand clenched.

Now, thought Jimmy Guang. Before he can do anything.

"Corporal Butsayev," he said, and Butsayev froze.

When he saw who had addressed him, though, a sly grin split his face, which was like his brother's only in coloration. "Robot Guy," he said. "Want in on the fun?"

Jimmy Guang brought the gun up and pointed it at Butsayev's nose. "You are a despicable man," he said, "and you do despicable things."

He pulled the trigger, and the Colt went off with a tremendous bang. Jimmy Guang's arm leaped up, and his hand, numbed by the recoil, let go of the gun. The muzzle flash faded from his eyes, and he saw Slava Butsayev lying on his left side in the street.

There was a hole punched in Butsayev's face, just to the left of his nose and below his eye. The eye was rolled back, showing only white.

His fall had pulled the girl to the ground beside him. She was was streaked with blood. As if picking lice off herself, she removed the dead man's hand from her hair finger by finger. "You should go home," Jimmy Guang said, and she ran into the building whose porch she had been sweeping.

The sky in the east was pale blue. Jimmy Guang dropped the gun near Butsayev's head and squatted next to the corpse. He rummaged through Butsayev's pockets until he found a small drawstring bag. When he pulled it from Butsayev's coat, its seam split, and teeth fell to the stones of the street. Pinching the seam between his fingers, Jimmy Guang walked back toward Lenin Street as the first curious faces began to appear in the windows around him.

The angel said to Mohammed: *God has knowledge of all the good you do.* Jimmy Guang's father had often reminded his son of this. The verse comforted Jimmy Guang, made him feel as if he was important, noticed, his actions weighed fairly and with sympathy. That was a God he could believe in, take solace in. But as he walked slowly back to his office, the knowledge that God watched him filled Jimmy Guang with deep sadness and shame. He had killed a man. He had become part of the war, and something of him had been lost.

He went directly through the bazaar to Osh's ancient old quarter, the surviving Osh of Alexander the Great and Mohammed and, if you believed local traditions, King Solomon as well. And now Marta, who lived in a dusty stone building with her parents and sisters. All of her brothers were up in the mountains fighting the Russians.

Jimmy Guang stopped in the street before her house to straighten his tie and tighten his belt, which he had let out a notch to accommodate the gun. He ran his handkerchief quickly over his shoes, patted at his hair, and only then knocked on the front door of the Chu house.

Marta herself answered. Over her shoulder Jimmy Guang could see her parents. They were smaller than she was, and both beginning to be a bit hunchbacked. She was tall, taller than Jimmy Guang, with strong hands.

"It's early, Jimmy," she said.

He took her arm and led her out, shutting the door behind her and waving quickly at her parents. "I have something to show you," he said when they were outside. Traffic was just beginning to appear on the narrow street, bicycles and an oxcart or two. It struck Jimmy Guang that the year could be 1930 instead of 2083. Somewhere the Russians had satellites that could tell the color of your eyes, and somewhere there were aircraft guided by robots smarter than the recently-departed Lokomotiv Lev, and in the mountains Uplinked Russian soldiers patrolled with inhuman precision; but here on this street Osh was as Osh had always been. There was something quietly defiant about it.

Jimmy Guang removed the bag of teeth from his pocket and held it out to Marta. She took it, and teeth spilled from the open seam. Jimmy Guang had a moment of irrational fear that Russian soldiers would rise from the teeth, as in a story his father had read to him once. Instead, Marta let out a scream and flung the bag to the ground. She covered her face and began to sob. The teeth rattled like dice on the street.

"Marta," he said, wanting to touch her but afraid.

"It took you after all," Marta said through her hands. "The war, it took you."

For a long while he didn't know what to say. It was true.

"I thought that's what you wanted," he said at last.

She rubbed at her eyes, then closed the distance between them with a step. "We have to get out of here," she said. "Now. Come with me."

"Where are we going?" he asked.

"It doesn't matter where we go. The war is here. It's claiming you, Jimmy." She looked at him. Saw him hesitating, and knew why.

An impulse seized Jimmy Guang. He took all of the evening's winnings from his inside coat pocket. "Here," he said, and closed one of Marta's hands around the thick wad of dollars and rubles and euros and rupees and God only knew what else. "Take this and go to Pavel. Wait for me."

Her face grew still.

"Just until sundown," Jimmy Guang pleaded. "Just wait until sundown."

When he got back to the office, Russian soldiers were waiting for him.

"What do you expect of me?" Captain Vasily Butsayev asked Jimmy Guang Hamid.

They were standing in a field southwest of Osh. Distant thunder rolled down on them from a jet passing far overhead. Jimmy Guang listened, and he listened to the wind, and he watched the dry grass bend, and he smelled the mountains. Captain Butsayev was going to kill him, he was sure, and Jimmy Guang was saddened by this because it meant he had overestimated the captain from their first meeting.

About five hundred yards away stood the House of Gladmech. The wall facing them was patched with rusting rectangles of corrugated tin scavenged from other hangars destroyed in various assaults. One of the patches covered part of the sign on that wall, and Jimmy Guang pursed his lips in annoyance. If he survived the afternoon he would have that fixed.

Jimmy Guang realized that although he did not want to, he would have to speak. So he decided to speak truthfully.

"Your brother was an evil man who preyed on women," he said, looking Butsayev in the eye. "I am in love with one of those women, and because I love her I had to kill your brother. I had to try to heal her, and your brother's life was like an infection in her spirit. She could not live while he did, and I need her, Captain Butsayev. I need her very badly to live."

Butsayev looked toward the mountains. "You heal a woman by killing a man. You create an illusionary peace among men by making a spectacle of destroying robots. If I were close to you, Mr. Hamid, I would fear your impulses to do good deeds." Still speaking softly, Butsayev quoted: "'Do not walk proudly on the earth. You cannot cleave the earth, nor can you rival the mountains in stature.'"

A Russian officer quoting from the Koran. Jimmy Guang could not decide whether this was a good omen or bad.

"My actions were not meant to be prideful," he said, and almost said more, but stopped himself. "Captain Butsayev. I will no longer defend myself. I have done what I have done, and you shall do what you shall do. Given the same situation again, a thousand times, I would kill your brother a thousand times."

Butsayev waved an arm over his head, a gesture of some sort to someone Jimmy Guang couldn't see. A rocket tore through the air, and Jimmy Guang's House of Gladmech exploded in an expanding cloud of dirty smoke. Large pieces of its metal walls flew up into the air and came slanting crazily back down to embed themselves in the earth.

John Wayne was in there, Jimmy Guang thought.

"Nor do I do that out of pride, Mr. Hamid," said Butsayev. "Leave now. Go with your woman, go back where you came from. Leave war to those of us who have made it our profession. And remember: I am not a butcher like my brother. But neither am I a weak man. Go now."

Butsayev walked toward his waiting jeep, leaving Jimmy Guang alone in the field. A wave of sorrow overcame him. For the House of Gladmech, yes, but mostly for Vasily Butsayev, whose respect Jimmy Guang realized he had treasured.

When he got to Pavel's, Marta was no longer there. "She said she was going to find her brothers," Pavel said. "You were to follow her."

"Where are her brothers?"

Pavel looked at Jimmy Guang, a small quirk at the corner of his mouth. "Do you understand what I am telling you? She is going to the mountains. If she is going to the mountains, it is not up to me to tell you where to find her."

Another test, thought Jimmy Guang. He did not think she was leaving him, no. Pavel might smirk, but Jimmy Guang had been smirked at before. He knew what he knew. She feared the war in him, the way it had crept into the corners of his mind, and when he had followed her through the rocks and the snow and the privations of the Tien Shan, he would be purified again. She would see him and know that this was true, that what had drawn him to the war was gone in the blast of a rocket and that she herself had drawn him away from it again. Perhaps he would find her in the mountains, among the militias and the mujahideen. Perhaps she would have gone ahead of him to Shanghai, or Delhi, and he would find her waiting for him at his father's house with a cup of tea in her hand.

Akhenaten

She found him half-sunken in the Nile marshes, tangled in reeds and rushes like a shipwrecked sailor amid the wrack of his raft. Or, she would later think, as if the great river itself had birthed him from its banks, and whenever she had that thought as an old woman she would shiver and glance up expecting to see the hands of the sun reaching out for her. The sun: he claimed the sun for his own, he claimed all Egypt for the sun. When her bearers wiped the black mud from his face, there on the banks of the Nile before the city of Thebes, the sun blazed from his eyes. Blinded, she ordered him taken to the palace, hidden in the harem of her husband Amenhotep Nebmaetre, bathed and fed and hidden from the sun.

When next she saw him, he looked only as a slave might: spindly of arm and leg, shrunken of chest, his belly protuberant like a hungry child's. But he was not a child. Neither, perhaps, was he a man. His face tapered from high cheekbones to a jaw like an arrowhead; no hair grew on his chin, and his skull lay oblong on the silk cushion in her private chamber. His eyes opened, and she caught her breath.

With a gesture, she dismissed her Hebrew chambermaid Miryam, who left breathing prayers to that tribe's pagan gods. "I am Tiye," she said after a moment. "God-wife to the Pharaoh who is the third to bear the name Amenhotep."

He whispered in reply, and she bent close to hear his words. "Again," she commanded, and again he spoke, but she did not understand his words. Only then, with the strange sounds of his language in her ears, feeling as if from a distance her own lips haltingly repeat those opaque syllables, did she ask herself why she had brought him up from the marsh. One deception was rarely enough. How many was she prepared to undertake?

Amenhotep knew nothing of the stranger until his son Thutmose died and the question of succession was thrown open to debate. Viziers and eunuchs furrowed their brows; fishermen and scribes found themselves flinching at the passage of clouds across the face of the sun. Amenhotep himself worried, and spoke long to Tiye. Was the second son, Amenhotep IV, fit to bear the double crown of the Kingdom of the Nile? Tiye had no answer, and then that question too was swept away when Amenhotep the son followed his older brother through the gates of Anubis.

On the night of her second son's death, Tiye stood vigil with her husband. Egypt slept on the banks of the Nile, unaware that its future, docile as a kitten six days before, now crouched to pounce.

She found herself speaking before she had entirely decided what to say. "They must not know," she said. "The succession must not be questioned. How many of your generals, how many priests of Amen, are even now imagining their own accessions? A second death…"

Amenhotep nodded, his many chins rippling. He leaned heavily on a staff as he settled his bulk onto a raised platform of cushions. In him Tiye saw the cares of kingship, saw the way he had gorged his body as if the spread of his girth might set an example for the borders of his nation. He wheezed heavily as he sat, and for a moment could not get his breath to speak.

"They must not know," he agreed, "but they will. What are we to tell them?"

Tiye pitied him in that instant. His heir dead, dead too his second son who was not fit to follow him. Aging, obese, without male issue, knowing that the greater part of his days were surely behind him.

And sadder yet, she thought, because he knew that neither of his sons could have borne up under the weight of his legacy.

"There is a man," she said. Silence fell and she became aware again that her second son lay dead in the room with her, near enough to touch. She waited.

Amenhotep gazed long at the body of his second son. In his eyes Tiye saw the sickness of mortality, his and his sons', like a creeping Nile fog—or the crocodile that hid within. After a long silence of moonlight creeping across the stones of the floor, he spoke. "Would you have a coregent, then? What sort of a man?"

"No," Tiye said in answer to his first question. Then her mind began to stumble over the many things she wanted to say about the stranger sequestered in the harem. The stranger who had learned to speak the language of Egypt, who had become first her confidant, then her lover and now, if she had her last desire...

Who had spoken to her of Aten, of the sun. Who had spoken of the distance between stars, and the sources of life. Yes, Aten, she had said. Pharaoh worships Aten, and the people worship Aten in him. She had in mind a wall of the palace, carved with rays of the sun that ended in human hands bringing gifts to Pharaoh her husband and to the people of Egypt. The gods created the sun to give us life.

The stranger had shaken his head, his marvelous, elongated, shining head. You misunderstand, he said. Men of Egypt, he said, fed on the grain of the fields, and the grain fed where? Fish of the river fed on smaller fish, and those smaller fish on smaller still, until the smallest fed on what but the plants of marsh and bank, and those plants fed where? The wind, he said, like the man and woman of Egypt, rises in the morning and falls at evening—what does it follow?

She had gone to her brother Aanen, the high priest of Ra, and said to him, There is a man who asks questions I cannot answer. What would you have me say to him? Aanen asked, and his eyes widened as she whispered in his ear. Aanen left his vestments and put on simple linens, and she smuggled him past the eunuchs into the harem. To his credit, he betrayed no fear at meeting the stranger, did not even wait for introductions, but immediately began. You have spoken of suns and stars, he said, and fish and rivers and men. What of the gods?

Tiye had found herself suddenly mindful of the Hebrew maid with her brawling pantheon, and as if reading her mind the stranger had said, *From whence comes the light that you may carve these other gods?*

Aanen nodded and understood. He turned to her, his eyes bright as if the stranger's gaze had left sunlight there. He spoke, and in his words Tiye could hear the scorching heat of revelation.

She had begun to believe the stranger then, and to carry the priest her brother's words inside her like faith. And she believed him now, in this chamber with her dead son and dying husband, and her belief lent a quiet strength to her voice as she freed her brother's words once more.

"He has come from the Sun."

And thus it was that Amenhotep's second son did not die, but came forth from the palace at Thebes the next morning. If the viziers and eunuchs whispered, the keenness of Pharaoh's ears kept them from doing more. Amenhotep IV lived, and would succeed his father.

He stood sometimes, during that last year of his father's life, watching the sun set in the hills west of the great river, and then he stood watching the stars wheel across the sky. Tiye came to him, always, unable to help herself, and always he softly wished for solitude, and always she went away with her heart strangely broken and uplifted by the starlight caught in the depths of his eyes. It seemed to her at these times that he spoke in his old language, the language of the starving nameless man washed up on the banks of a river that had no beginning. And it seemed as well that she understood, and that in the silhouette of his head blocking the stars was written knowledge of things whose names she lacked the words to ask.

This and more she remembered, when during solitary nights of her own Tiye would chew over the errors of her life.

Amenhotep IV rose to power amid whispers. The sounds of the wind in stone, river in sand, leaf against stem, all began to sound tones of apprehension. The artists came to sculpt him, and showed him their heroic studies. "Destroy those," he said, and rose to his feet. With a flourish he swept his cloak off and unfastened his tunic. Naked he stood on his throne, and even the palace cats stopped in their tracks and averted their eyes. "The sun is as the sun is," he said, "and the body is as the body. The skies are full of suns and the worlds full of bodies." Amenhotep IV flung away his garments and raised his spindly arms to the shaft of sunlight that fell through the topmost window in his chamber.

"See me as I am," he commanded. "Carve what you see."

He turned then, and looked out the window into the square. "Bring me the most beautiful woman within sight of this window," he ordered, "except the ones in the shade. The most beautiful woman in sight of this window will be my wife in sight of the sun."

The sculptors ran from him, and the architects of the new monuments at Karnak looked at each other. What madness was this, to marry as monkeys might?

"Aten looks down," Amenhotep breathed as his soldiers spread through the plaza. "Aten sees, Aten gives. From Aten we have come."

Her name, when she came through the door dressed in simple linen, was Nefertiti. She was thin like him, and next to her he looked even more girlish than his advisers had thought. He caught her gaze and held it. "Aten has chosen well," he said, and the soldiers looked elsewhere as the greed in his eyes rose in his body. "Leave us," he said, and Nefertiti became his wife.

This much Tiye saw, but it wasn't until she heard the Hebrew maid gossiping that she heard of Nefertiti's naming. Neferneferuaten, Tiye thought. Is everything to be for Aten now? Shall we no longer remember the gods of our fathers, Isis and Anubis and Osiris and Amen-Ra who...

Who shines in the sun, she had been about to think. What was the truth now? Was Aten something outside the sun, something that used the sun as a means to spread his power to the Earth? This is what Amenhotep IV said, when she asked him, but what did it mean? Either a god was, or wasn't. What did it mean to say a god used the sun or the river, if it didn't mean that the sun or the river were the god? But Amenhotep IV said this was not so. "Look into the sky," he said, when Tiye found him out on the balcony at night. "How many stars are there?"

The astronomers said there were one hundred thousand, so that is what she said to him.

"Meaningless number," he said. "I have counted them. I have good eyes, and I can only count three thousand."

Tiye tried to imagine counting the stars. No, she tried to imagine not losing count. Counting was easy, if one could begin over and over again. But to move one's eyes across the sky, weaving every star into the fabric of memory and giving each its own number…this was impossible.

"Three thousand?" she said. "Is that all there are?"

"No. There are thousands of thousands of thousands. Some of them I have seen and you never will. Others neither of us will ever know except in the telling." He turned to her, ran a long finger down from the point of her chin to the hollow between her collarbones. "Tiye, you have been all that stood between me and the loneliness of the mad. Now I have taken a wife; will you not reprove me?"

"Pharaoh must take a wife," Tiye said. She was certain that his finger had left a blazing trace down her throat, and wondered before she mastered her silliness why she could not see its glow in the sloping hollows of his face. "A young woman will give you children, and a man with children need never worry about loneliness."

"A man with children," Amenhotep IV whispered. She tried to speak to him again, but he seemed not to hear.

He moved the capital upriver a year later. The priesthood of Ra pressured him not to, and he threw them from his chamber, screaming after them that Pharaoh was would move very Egypt if he chose. Did not the Sun move? And was not Pharaoh the Sun of his people?

The next morning he arose and came out of his chamber bearing papyrus scrawled with strange symbols. Nefertiti followed, her eyes strange as the shadow of current cast on the bottom of a pool. Her first daughter squirmed in her arms, a lively child with her father's elongated head and her father's habit of looking at the stars. Thebes was sick with the infestation of Amen and Mut, he declared to the early-morning servants sweeping the throne hall. He had been sickened by proximity. He sent them to gather the important figures attached to the court. When they arrived, heavy-eyed with sleep, Pharaoh gave them these words: "Amenhotep is dead."

They brought Tiye, and he said to her, "I am no longer named for the man who came before me, but for the god who comes before us all. I am the god walking on earth, I am He Who Is For Aten. I am Akhenaten."

Late that night, Tiye awakened with the aches of age. Stiffly she walked to him, mouth leaping with a question that had plagued her dreams for years before surfacing just this night. The way a dead man returns from the river, bringing with him the tales of his sojourn in the weedy depths of the dead, she brought Akhenaten the question of her dream and put it to him under the moonless sky.

"I found you in the reeds," she said. "Where did you come from?"

"Not so very far away," he answered, and it was no answer.

"Where?"

"When I was a boy," Akhenaten said, "I learned the stories of Egypt. I used to look across the waters of the sea and think, Egypt is there. Someday I will travel there."

Assyria? she wanted to know, and then, Canaan? Persia?

None of those, he said, but nearest Canaan. She thought about travelers' tales of Canaan, of its fine rivers and sweet olives. "Is it not on the ocean?"

"Yes," he said. "When I was a boy, we lived on the ocean, and the world was the blue of water and the white of stone. Now I see the black of night and what color are the stars?"

For a while Tiye had nothing to say. Then she asked him the question behind the question. "When I found you, were you fleeing the place you were born?"

"No."

"Why, then, do you wish to move upriver, away from the ocean?"

"Because," he said, "I want to travel through time."

Tiye had words to answer this. "All men and women travel through time," she said. "There is no other road."

"I want to travel back up that road." Akhenaten pointed at a gleaming streak on the river, where the reflection of a single star elongated into a shimmering ribbon on the water. "See; the river flows only one way until it reaches the sea. Time flows only one way as well, and no man knows what sea it fills. But there is a way to go against the current."

"Against the current to what?" she asked. "To yesterday? You are Pharaoh. Egypt cannot look always toward yesterday. I learned this the day you broke the sculptors' studies."

"All men can spend their lives looking toward yesterday," Akhenaten said.

They regarded the river in silence. Tiye knew she should withdraw, but she was old enough that Pharaoh's annoyance no longer frightened her, and she was still sleepless with the complaints of her body. "You said once that Aten is the light by which we can know the other gods. I heard you say this, and saw my brother Aanen. Did you look at his face as he began to believe? I think I would not want to see a face like that very often." Aanen had become militant in his priesthood of the new Aten, destroying temples to other gods. Three times he had killed a priest of Amun, and once a priest of Ra. His acolytes had begun hacking images of the other gods out of temples and stelae.

"Aanen believes in belief," Akhenaten said. "I believe in the search for it."

"Which of you believes in the gods?" Tiye said, and he had no answer.

"I have taken my name for Aten."

Tiye nodded. "And yet you spend your nights looking at the sky when he is not present to caress you with his rays. You worship the sun, but all your life you watch the stars."

"Every star is a sun," Akhenaten said.

"Is every star Aten?" she challenged him.

He chuckled then, a sound like the scraping of scarabs on stone. "Must old women blaspheme?" he wondered. "When men no longer come to your bed, must you throw your scorn at the gods?"

"Is every star Aten?" she asked again, with a rushing in her head that battered against her mind like a flood. Beginning to understand. Her eyes came back into focus and she saw him looking at her. Starlight streaked his eyes as it had the eternal surface of the river.

"You see," he said. "I do not know if every star is Aten, but I do know that he comes to me through the sun. If other eyes look up at other suns, Aten looks down at them as well."

Tiye thought of that night many years later, when while looking for her Hebrew maid she turned a corner and ran hard into another Hebrew, a young man. He looked at her and for a moment she felt as if she must be in two places at once, as if she had been overlaid onto herself. The stone corridor fell away and she smelled the salt marshes near the mouth of the Nile, saw the contorted body of the young man who lay in the mud looking up at her. This young Hebrew had the eyes of a fanatic, a gaze touched with knowledge of the infinite. A gaze like the one the man who would become Akhenaten had fixed upon Tiye, so many years ago.

"Who are you?" she asked, at once quavering and imperious.

He held her gaze as he walked around her at a respectful distance, but he did not answer her question, and when he walked away she did not follow.

Tiye found her maid Miryam in the washing room. "Who was that who was here just now?" she demanded.

Miryam ducked her head. "Please," she said. "I cannot tell."

Tiye slapped her hard on the ear. "It is that Moses, is it not? Who stirs up the Hebrews? He believes, does he not?"

"We all believe," Miryam said, crying only a little.

Tiye thought for a moment. A Hebrew named Moses was, incredibly, preaching Aten against the Egyptians. One of the priests said he was Miryam's younger brother; others said he had been born to Levite slaves. Akhenaten paid no attention. As long as Aten's name rang in the streets of his cities, Pharaoh paid little heed to what was said. Tiye softened. She had been harsh out of discomfiture from her encounter in the hall and the memories it provoked.

"You mustn't fear me," Tiye said, although fear was part of what she wanted. "I know how your tribe believes. It isn't so different from how we believed before Akhenaten. When I was a girl, every household had the gods it preferred. But now some of you are uncertain, aren't you? And some of you have become like this man Moses. He has found Aten."

Miryam touched the corner of her eye and flicked the tear away. "He has gone farther than that. He says now that even to name the god is to blaspheme. He says that if Aten is supposed to be a thing beyond the sun, an idea only, then how can it be named? This is foolishness. He says that Egypt is headed for the same doom that awaits all of the other peoples who know not the truth of the invisible god, the He Whose Name Must Not Be Spoken. He says that naming god Aten is like naming a man Worm."

"Where has he gone?"

"I beg you, Mother," Miryam said, tears springing once again from her eyes. "Let him speak his mind. Egypt is huge and Hebrews are so few. He hurts nothing."

"Pharaoh will judge," Tiye said, and Miryam slipped away down the corridor.

Tiye stood in the washing room, thinking. Perhaps she should have all of the Hebrews out of the palace, out of the harem. They were too quick to anger, too eager to seize on new ideas. What Egypt needed now was stability, and nothing could be stable as long as the royal household simmered with dissent and wild heresy.

But the look in the young Hebrew's eyes. She had seen that look in Akhenaten's eyes, so very long ago by the marshy banks of the Nile.

In the next year Akhenaten's daughters began to die. One after the other, as each of them approached the age at which she might have expected them to bleed for the first time, they began to complain of headaches. Strange fits followed, marked by a turning inward of the limbs as if the girls wished to swim back up the river of time until they found their mother's womb again. Then, just like fish that stop gasping bit by bit, they died.

Nefertiti bore sorrow as quietly as she had borne the children. Still her beauty stole the gazes of men, but it was the beauty now of sunset rather than sunrise. Still her voice charmed Pharaoh, but her spell was a shared dream of the past.

Akhenaten held each of his daughters as she gave up her body, stroking the beautiful long head and crying out in the language he still spoke in his sleep. As his children died, something in him broke. He paid less attention to Egypt, worried less about border incursions and trade difficulties, ignored completely the building program at his city Akhetaten. Even his tomb stood unfinished, its workmen idled to play dice outside the sculptor Thutmose's workshop. Only his nights remained constant. Shunning

Nefertiti's bed, he stood watching the stars from sunset until dawn, weeping to himself in his strange cold language that to Tiye seemed like the language a river would speak if it wished to be heard by men. She took it upon herself to approach him one night, walking slowly on knees that ground like mortar and pestle, touching the walls when her failing eyes lost the way. When she took her place next to him and looked up to see what he saw, she realized that all but the brightest stars now hid from her.

"I believed," he said softly, "that I would live in them."

Tiye touched his shoulder. "You yet might in two of them."

"I have no great faith," he said. In the darkness, she thought a corner of his mouth tensed in what might have been a smile. He turned to look at her. "You said once that a man with children would never know loneliness. But here I am. My daughters die, and I am lonely."

"Sorrow and loneliness are not the same thing," Tiye said.

"I tell you I am lonely. I knew children might die, but you were right. I believed that seeing myself in them, seeing them in myself, I could forget that once I came alone from the sun." He kept silent for some time then, and when he spoke again his voice was twisted. "Instead I killed them."

"Every father kills his child," Tiye said. "To have a child is to set it on the road of time."

"I killed my daughters," Akhenaten said again. "They were beautiful, and they loved me, and I killed them by giving them life." Something lit up within him then, and he straightened. The old language and the new spilled together from his mouth until with great finality he said, "The next generation. Yes." With that he left the terrace in great purposeful strides.

Tiye followed him, fearing the worst, and by the time he had reached the bedchambers she knew what he intended. "You must not," she begged, holding onto his arm with all of her old woman's strength. "They have not yet bled."

He threw her away as if shrugging off a robe and she fell to the stone floor. Her knees made twin sharp cracks and pain flooded from them. Tiye tried to stand, but her legs would not bear her. "Pharaoh!" she cried.

Strong hands bore her to her feet. "Hush now, mother," Nefertiti said softly into her ear. The quiet strength of the queen's voice checked Tiye's struggles, and seemed even to still her pain.

Nefertiti led her to the queen's bed and lay her there until the pain in her knees began to subside.

"How do you bear it?" Tiye said. "Is this not the first time?" She recalled his face, flashing suddenly with revelation, and thought, *Surely it is. Surely he has not done this before.*

"First time for these girls, yes," Nefertiti said. "Not for the others."

Egypt, Tiye thought. Turning inward, losing interest in the world just as its Pharaoh was turning inward, defiling his own family. Because of me, she thought. I raised him up from the mud and reeds, and now Egypt will fall with him. A desire to confess surged in her, reached as far as her mouth and stopped there, at her old woman's thin lips that would not pass the truth of her betrayal.

"He believes it will save them," Nefertiti said. "He believes that they were poisoned by his seed when it made them, and that they can only be saved by receiving it again. At other times he says that their children will live, and it is true. Tutankhaten is healthy."

This secret of Pharaoh's only son stopped Tiye's mouth more tightly. Tutankhaten, King's Bodily Son, begotten upon one of his sisters? It was a story one might have told about the old gods. It had no place in the modern Egypt of Aten.

The dam in Tiye's mouth broke. "What is he?"

"A man," came the reply, hushed almost to a whisper. "Only a man. But he says he has gone too far up the river, and looks different than those around him. He never explains." Nefertiti caught Tiye's chin, guided it around until they were facing. "Do you know what this means?"

"He said to me once that rivers only flow one way," Tiye said, and might have said more, but Akhenaten returned then, slick with sweat and his eyes alight. He brushed past Tiye and caught Nefertiti in his arms, burying his face in the swanlike curves of her neck. "I will save them," he said, and said it again, and said it again. Tiye got stiffly to her feet and left without a word.

Akhenaten's daughters, with their strange heads and their strange deaths, hung over Egypt like a plague of the mind. Tiye watched herself grow older, watched Akhenaten too begin to hunch and walk slowly. More and more rarely she met him on the terraces late at night.

The last time, she shuffled slowly along the route she had long since learned by touch of fingertip and echo of breath. She found him leaning against a statue of himself, and she imagined sculpture and subject training their gazes over Egypt and what lay beyond. "Once," she said, "you told me that every star is a sun."

She felt him nod.

"Which one is your home?"

He laughed softly, and his breath wheezed in his throat. "Aten is my home," he said.

Tiye jabbed him with a horny fingernail. "Which?"

"This one," Akhenaten said. "All the stars are the same star, and all the rivers are the same river, and all the directions are the same direction. But none of them lead home."

She was thinking about that the next year, a year in which Moses Miryam's brother killed a man and fled east to Midian, the year in which she died in Akhetaten with her Pharaoh, who had been her lover, who had once staggered her with a gaze that spoke of infinity.

Rossetti Song

Some people have always wanted to be President, or a baseball player, or a movie star or business tycoon. Me, I've always wanted to own a bar. Not some flaky franchised chicken-finger paradise for post-fraternity muscleboys and their bimbos; a real shot-and-a-beer kind of neighborhood joint. Pool table or two in the back, an old Wurlitzer by the bathroom doors, a long mirror behind the bar suitable for the sort of what's-he-got-that-I-ain't-got scrutiny that melancholy drunks love to subject themselves to. Tables with a topography of cigarette burns, water rings, dents of uncertain origin, all preserved under a quarter-inch layer of varnish. Beer signs on the walls, no bikinis or volleyballs allowed, just painted mirrors and classic flickering neon like the sign out front that says FRANK'S PLACE. Cab company numbers taped to the side of the phone. A blackboard leaning against the mirror advertising the day's special and a permanent addendum: HANGOVERS FREE OF CHARGE.

An old neighborhood bar, like I said, but it's hard to find a good one because fewer and fewer people live in the old neighborhoods anymore and the ones who are left don't talk to each other. Harder still to start one up, because any place that will support one already has one, but that's a defeatist attitude as Susan would have said. A real go-getter can-do type of person, that was my wife. She died the day after my small-business loan was approved. Car wreck. She wanted me to have the bar, though; ever since I'd known her she'd said I was born to be a bartender. How do people decide things like that?

Did you know that more Americans die every year in car wrecks than were killed in Vietnam? Or maybe it's every two years. Nine months ago I wouldn't have known that, but tending bar fills you up with more useless trivia than you would think any one brain could hold. I know that the Ambassador Bridge in Detroit runs south to Windsor, Canada, and that Wally Pipp is the name of the guy who lost his job to Lou Gehrig. Bar bets. There is nothing so esoteric or irrelevant that someone won't bet a beer over it.

I spent Susan's insurance policy on an antique Wurlitzer that plays real records. Limits my selection a bit, but the kind of crowd I draw has a certain collective taste and the guy who sold me the juke threw in about twelve hundred forty-fives that he'd been collecting since 1956. So I have Elvis and Patsy Cline, the Beatles and Marvin Gaye, Louis Armstrong and Johnny Cash, along with tons of stuff that I've never even played. And I take requests, got a sign over the Wurlitzer, so I find myself sorting through those boxes of forty-fives looking for something that I'm pretty sure I should have even though I've never actually seen it. It was because of one of those requests that I struck up an acquaintance with Milt Chrzanowski.

A guy—not Milt—sat down at the bar once in the early evening, not long after I'd opened, and said, "Beer."

I love people who order like that; to a bartender, it's an expression of trust. At least, I choose to look at it that way since the alternative is believing that people don't care what they drink, and that concept is unsettling and foreign to people such as myself. This guy looked at first inspection like a local-brew sort (not something I can explain), so I cracked open a Pike. After a second look, I set it down without a glass.

"Nice juke," he said, finding the beer without looking at either it or me. He took a long swig, glanced at the label, and dug a twenty out of his shirt pocket. "What's on it?"

People always ask me that when they see it's an antique, as if I'm only going to have some sort of theme music. It annoys me. The guy got up and walked over to the box, standing slightly bent in front of it as he examined the selections; he was taller than he'd looked sitting down. He stayed that way for a long time.

There were eight or ten people in the place, Boeing workers and fishermen killing time until their boats went back out. Two or three trickled in every time one or two wandered out. I lost track of the guy as I filled orders and shot the shit with regulars about the Sonics' postseason collapse and the continued influx of Californians into our fair city. Eventually my granola-punk waitress Donna came in and everything leveled off into an average Wednesday night. I was unloading the dishwasher when I looked up to see the tall guy back at the bar. He waggled his empty beer at me. As I set a fresh one in front of him (I'd guessed right about the glass), he dropped a five on the bar and walked off.

Donna sashayed up to the bar laden with empties. "You haven't even noticed my new tattoo," she said petulantly.

"I lose track," I said, flinging bottle caps all over the floor behind the bar. I have a trash can by the coolers, but some nights my aim is off.

"Do tattoos change color when you get a sunburn?"

The speaker was not the tall guy. He was a slight balding fortyish guy in a pinstripe suit that looked kind of crooked. Except for the suit he looked kind of like me. I looked around for Donna but she was gone, a faint odor of patchouli her only remnant.

"Dunno," I said. "I never had one."

"Neither have I," he said.

"Fine place you have here," he added, squinting into the narrow neck of his bottle. "The Wurlitzer is a lovely touch."

He gave me a funny look when he said that, like he expected it to mean something more, or at least other, than just what he said. I'm a bartender; when in doubt, I always agree. "Yup."

"You don't recognize me, do you?" he said, looking back into his bottle. I've heard many a man swear that they saw God in the bottom of a beer bottle. Myself, I just usually feel Him pounding on my head the next morning.

"'Fraid not."

"Ah well," he said, motioning for another beer. "I guess you wouldn't, but those of us in invisible occupations occasionally pine for recognition. We are the offensive linemen of the commercial banking world, the mid-level functionaries."

Lawyers and bankers, two kinds of people you never want to piss off. "I'm sorry, ah, Mister…"

"Chrzanowski."

"Oh, yeah," I nodded vigorously. "I remember talking to you now." It was actually true. He had called to reassure me that the loan was not in danger because of Susan's death. I had been worried because she made quite a bit more money as an engineer than I did as a local government reporter for the P-I, and I had quit my job to give the bar a go. So they could justifiably have worried about my ability to make the payments. But we had some money put away, and even after the funeral expenses and the Wurlitzer there was a bit of insurance money left over. I was a financially comfortable widower, at least as long as the bar broke even. "It's Milt, right?"

He brightened. "That's right, Mr. Sutter," he said, reaching for his wallet.

I shook my head. "On the house, Milt, as long as you never call me Mr. Sutter again." I caught myself just as I began to slide into smarmy-bartender mode. "The name's—"

"Frank, yes, I remember." We shook hands, me self-consciously wiping my hand on a towel first. He peered into the full bottle, wrinkled his forehead as if in disappointment, then drank anyway. "You know that this space was occupied by a bar before you leased it, don't you?"

I nodded. "Yeah, they left it a mess, too," I said. "Place was a dive."

He nodded, wistfully I thought. "It was that, at least in its last few years. But in the years before that, it was a place not unlike this one; not too rowdy, but not sanitized either."

I was surprised that my taste in bars had anything in common with that of a mid-level bank manager.

"I used to stop in fairly frequently when I worked out of the branch near here," Milt continued. "Ten years or more, until I transferred downtown in 'eighty-one, I came to this place to decompress after a busy day of climbing the corporate ladder." He chuckled and shook his head. "God, has it been seventeen years? Ambition; glad I've given that up. Middle management is the lubricant in the great engine of commerce," he said grandly, raising his bottle in a toast.

I returned the gesture with a dirty highball glass, and Milt fell silent as I filled Donna's orders. I never did ask her about the sunburn thing.

"They had one of those, too," he said suddenly. I looked up and he was gesturing at the juke with the now-nearly-empty bottle. "Splendid machines, those. Memories as pleasant as the music." He drained the bottle, waved it at me. He was getting lit pretty fast, and the more he drank, the more English he sounded. Not an accent, but choices of words and emphasis. Something.

I set another beer in front of him. He clinked the neck of his empty against its replacement, a sardonic little fare-thee-well. "Have you ever heard of a folk duo called Five and Dime?" he asked.

"Nope," I said. "I wasn't much of a folkie; earnestness makes me squirm."

"Well, you couldn't really be expected to know them if you weren't a native, either. Are you?" I shook my head; I'd grown up and gone to school in Michigan, then ended up in Seattle by way of Texas and Colorado. Susan had more to do with it than anything else. I've always been a sun-worshipper, and there are winters here when I'd willingly trade a week at the beach for melanoma. But love will make you do strange things.

"I didn't think so. Anyway, they were locals, students at the U-Dub." This is a strange local colloquialism; University of Washington, therefore U-W, therefore Yoo-Dub. "They never amounted to more than playing coffeehouses for tips, but they pooled all of their money once and recorded a single. It was 'Tangled Up In Blue,' as Simon and Garfunkel might have done it while on a sodium pentothal IV drip. Godawful song. But it was backed with the most amazing piece of pop music I think I've ever heard, a lovely ballad called 'Rossetti Song.'" He raised a questioning eyebrow at me; I shook my head again and looked at the clock.

Nearly ten. I cracked open my first of the night, cheating by only a few minutes. Since the accident, nostalgic people give me the jitters.

"'Rossetti Song,'" I said under my breath. The sound of the words out loud brought to mind 'Rosetta stone,' and it was in the grip of strange allusions that I went back to lean on the bar opposite Milt.

"The reason I ask all this," he continued, "is that your predecessor had that song on his jukebox. I was wondering if perhaps you hadn't acquired his collection as part of the lease or something."

"No, I got the spinner and the records from an ad. 'Actually plays records!' the copy said, like it was walking on water, and the guy who sold it to me referred to it as an antique. Shit, it's only two years older than I am."

I paused to drink my beer, get something in my mouth before I started some maudlin rant. "Helluva collection came with it, though; supposed to be twelve hundred, but I haven't counted."

"Twelve hundred," Milt repeated. He drummed his fingers on the bar for a moment, then added, "Did you get it around here?"

"Jesus, Milt," I said, rolling my eyes. "Yes, I'll look for you."

"It's called 'Rossetti Song.'"

"I know."

"Reminded me of the words 'Rosetta stone' the first time I saw the title; isn't that strange?"

I drained my beer. Slowly. "You don't say."

"I do, and you know what else? The word juke comes from Wolof, a West African tribal language. Their word *dzug* means 'to live wickedly.' How about that?" He knocked back the rest of his Pike. "Another, please?"

I got one for him and another for myself, and it still wasn't ten o'clock.

"Rosetta stone," I said, sitting cross-legged on the attic floor of the home Susan and I had bought 4 BC. Before Crash. Every event, every memory of mine was starting to orient itself around the accident, around the afternoon that I'd come in the front door shouting "I got it! I got it!" and heard the phone ringing. I picked it up and the voice on the other side identified itself as one Maura Yee from Swedish Hospital downtown. I didn't get there in time to say goodbye.

And that was it, really; I was a married newspaper columnist one day and the widowed proprietor of a drinking establishment the next. I wasn't able to either mourn my wife or exult in the realization of a lifelong ambition. They canceled each other out, and I trudged ahead in a sort of dazed equilibrium. No great epiphany, no sudden collapse; just a bit more beer than was really good for me and an aching vacant spot that I tried to pretend wasn't there. And every now and then I would wonder when I would begin to mourn, or stop mourning, or begin enjoying Frank's Place, and by the time I got done thinking about it I didn't know

Rossetti Song

what the hell was going on. And at that time it was nearly 1 AC, almost a whole year; when did everything start up again?

The streetlight across from my house flickered weakly, mortally wounded by neighborhood teenagers. It its sporadic pink-orange light I could just barely read the label of the forty-five that rested in my lap: FIVE AND DIME, it said at the top of the circular label, and on the bottom ROSSETTI SONG 3:47. And running along the outside edge was the legend SPARE CHANGE RECORDS. I'd never heard of the label.

Rossetti, I knew, was a poet. Two of them, as I discovered when I rooted out Susan's *Norton Anthologies* from her undergraduate English courses. I flipped through the wrinkly translucent Norton paper and found Christina Rossetti, younger sister of Dante Gabriel. The first two poems were simply titled "Song," and I put the book down. It was four o'clock in the morning; Milt would be happy and the poems could wait until tomorrow. I reached for my beer, remembered I'd left it upstairs next to the boxes of records. The book lay open in front of me, and I suddenly registered that the handwriting between lines and in margins was Susan's. Susan's from twenty years before, when the only Frank she was interested was Zappa.

"Yeah, well, he's dead too," I said, and stood up. I flipped the Five and Dime record over in my hands and laid it B-side-up on my ancient Garrand turntable. The soft crackle in the dim room as I laid the needle smoothly on the lip of the record gave me a shiver; it was a sound I loved, bringing a weight of anticipation that the tiny spark of a compact-disc laser cannot match, and the few seconds of not-quite-silence that follow it always flood me with memories of songs, and memories of Susan.

I sat on the floor in front of the couch and picked up the book as the music began, a melancholy call-and-response between two guitars with a faintly Celtic flavor and a definite tinny recorded-in-someone's-bathroom edge. One guitar dropped into a steady chorded dum dadadada dum dadum and the first voice came in, a half-chanted lyric baritone:

> I met my love and wooed her, overarched by cypress leaves
> She was so frail, her face so pale, I feared that soon I'd grieve.

> My love proved stronger than my fear, and her fair hand
>   I won
> Though we both knew her illness grew, our two lives we
>   made one.
>
> It was my wont to mourn her as we clasped our hands
>   together
> To slowly walk and hear the clock toll far across the
>   heather.
> I had but to caress her cheek; my touch bespoke my
>   fear
> "But I still live!" she'd say, and give this song to stop my
>   tears:

And now the second voice (was it Dime or Five, I wondered?) took over from the first, a sprightly tenor dancing a cappella except for a double knock on the guitars at the end of every phrase:

> When I am dead, my dearest, sing no sad songs for me;
> Plant thou no roses at my head, nor shady cypress tree:
> Be the green grass above me with showers and dewdrops
>   wet;
> And if thou wilt, remember, and if thou wilt, forget.
> I shall not see the shadows, I shall not feel the rain;
> I shall not hear the nightingale sing on, as if in pain:
> And dreaming through the twilight that doth not rise
>   nor set,
> Haply I may remember, and haply may forget.

At the second line, I recognized the second "Song" in Christina Rossetti's Norton entry. I followed along as that lovely tenor embraced her words and then soared into wordless arpeggiated harmonizing as the baritone and guitar leapt back in:

> One day she lay and could not sing, nor raise her lips to
>   mine
> Her breath was stilled, hard sorrow spilled my love upon
>   her dying.
> I laid no roses at her head, nor sang a dirge to mourn
> An oath I swore, to nevermore love any woman born.
>
> She was my Lady of Shalott, my belle dame sans merci,

> And when she died, I only cried to keep her memory.
> I walk the grass above her now, and every shady tree
> With her voice rings; I know she sings, and know she
>   welcomes me.

I sat very still, Susan's handwriting in the margins of the blocky book wavering in my teary gaze. There was a *pop* from the speakers as the needle kicked off the end of the runout groove, and a tear fell directly onto a note she had made next to "Song."

Expressions of mourning, it said. *Dead don't remember us, why should we them?*

The tear sat trembling in an auroral ring of dissolved black ink, smudging the word *don't*. I started to close the book. There was a touch on the back of my left hand, a familiar brushing across the backs of my fingers that started a quivering in my stomach as it paused briefly over the still-pale stripe on my ring finger. Then it was gone, and I was left alone in my house an hour before dawn, my only company the ticking of the runout groove and the crushing realization that she really wasn't ever coming back.

Milt didn't show up until the next Wednesday. I spent the week staring at the Five and Dime record peeking out from where I'd stashed it behind the cash register. I suppose I was convinced that if I stared at it long enough I would figure out whether what had happened was real. I was wearing my wedding ring again. Donna noticed right away and asked me if I'd been to Vegas and what was her name; after an inexplicable crippling wave of embarrassment, I threw a washcloth at her and went to open the doors. I mopped the floors, got deliveries, sparred with Donna, called cabs for laid-off Boeing riveters, and not once did I find myself suddenly destroyed by remembering that my wife was dead. *Well,* I found myself thinking at irregular intervals, *I guess I went and got over it.* The words wouldn't attach themselves to an emotion.

When I turned around from the register and saw Milt there, the first thing I noticed was that it was nearly twelve, much later than it had been the first time he came in. He was wearing the same crooked suit, wet from the misting rain. I wondered if he wore it every Wednesday. He was the kind of guy who might have a schedule like that.

"Whatever it was I was having last week, I'll have it again," he said, and damned if I could remember. I reasoned that if I couldn't, he couldn't either, though, and cracked him a Pike. "So," he said, and I cut him off.

"Got it," I said, pulling the disc out from behind the register. I returned to the bar and spun it on the polished wood in front of him. "It's been here a week, waiting for you to come back."

Milt seemed afraid to touch the record, afraid even to get near the corner of its plain paper sleeve that pointed at him. "That isn't funny," he said.

It happened to him, too, I thought, although what exactly I meant by *it* I wasn't sure. I looked at the clock again, suddenly in a hurry to chase everyone out and close up; I didn't want to play the song with people around. If whatever had happened in my living room happened again, the whole bar would be treated to the sight of my flipping out over a thirty-year-old garage-folk ballad.

A scan of the premises revealed only three bodies not in my employ, and one of those was Milt. The other two were down to the lukewarm dregs of a pitcher of Budweiser and showed no great promise of finishing it. "Call you a cab, fellas?" I asked, hardly raising my voice over Patsy Cline singing "I Fall to Pieces." The pair squinted up at me, then stubbed out cigarettes and rose to leave.

Donna had already put most of the chairs up. I called her over. "You can go early if you want," I said. "I'm coming in tomorrow morning anyway."

She shook her head. "Rent's going up. I need the hours."

"What, it's Wednesday; you'd be gone by one anyway—never mind, I'll pay you until two. Just go. Deal?"

She looked quizzically at Milt, then back at me. "You just put your wedding ring back on, Frank."

After she left, I turned out the neon signs in the windows and the hanging lights over the pool tables. Streetlights cast spiny shadows of chair legs on the floor, made wavy by the rain and crosshatched by the sharper shadows cast by the single light behind the bar. Across the street was a vacant factory building, most of its windows broken out, graffiti covering the padlocked doors and grimy brick walls. It was raining like hell.

I wondered if my place was going to turn into a sleazy dive the way my predecessor's had; I was on the edge of a vacant part of the city. But who knew? I was also on the edge of a perfectly healthy retail area, and in six months Frank's Place could be surrounded by a completely new trendy zone. Fashion was too capricious to be outguessed.

Milt was still staring at the record as if it was a booby-trapped memory. I walked by him and picked it up on my way over to the jukebox. I pulled the juke away from the wall and opened its case, removing the Supremes and dropping Five and Dime in their place. Milt hadn't moved; he was looking at me out of the corner of his eye and gripping his beer in two hands.

I dropped the canopy back into place and was pushing the Wurlitzer back against the wall when Milt said, "It's happened to you too, hasn't it?"

I stood slowly up and wiped my palms carefully on my towel until I was sure I could speak without making a fool of myself. "What exactly do you mean by 'it'?"

"Come on, Frank, you kick everyone out as soon as I get here, send your waitress—who obviously thinks I'm some sort of rough trade—home early, and you're wearing your wedding ring again. I hadn't noticed that until she brought it up, but I'd bet the contents of my branch safe that you played the song and something happened." He was looking at me greedily, practically begging me to admit to something. I wondered what he saw when the song was played. Or thought he saw; maybe I'd just been drunk and feeling guilty.

I dug a quarter out of my pocket. "Why is this song so important to you, Milt?" I asked.

He hesitated, but only for a second. "Because my wife died here while it was playing."

I was looking at the selection cards, and I saw number 126, "Baby Love" by the Supremes, but my hand wouldn't quite move to put the quarter in the slot. "I remember humming along with the tenor over the melody line," and Milt went on, and right at the words 'raise her lips to mine' she put a hand to her temple and just pitched over out of her seat. Her name was Petra and she would have been forty-six this September." He said all of this as if he was the Ancient Mariner, doomed to repeat his tale of woe. I saw that he still wore his wedding band as he pointed to a window table and said, "Right there, under the Mount Rainier sign. That's where it happened."

Milt slid off his stool and walked towards the front table, still pointing. "And now when I hear that song in this place, I can see her," he said, his voice beginning to tremble.

His arm fell back to his side as he approached the table and stood in front of it. "After I was transferred downtown, I found a copy of the song and took it home thinking that whenever I needed her I could play it there. But it didn't *work*," he choked, and I could see tears shining in the odd pink glare of the streetlights. "It didn't work, and then this place closed and it was years, *years* before you came along."

Milt paused, his fingers tracing the surface of the table. When he spoke again, he was calmer. "And when your wife died I was terribly afraid that you would refuse the loan and the space would remain vacant for longer than I could stand. A midlife crisis is difficult enough without the added complication of a dead wife you can't talk to, ha ha. So even though I had no idea what you would do with the space, I had to make sure your loan wasn't recalled. And after you actually had the place open, I came in just sort of—quixotic, you know, and saw the jukebox..." He shrugged miserably and produced a handkerchief.

I caught myself punching buttons and realized that I'd put the quarter into the jukebox. The selector arm reached up and plucked the Five and Dime single from the row and laid it on the turntable, and the sad, searching guitars began their once-upon-a-time.

The colors in the Wurlitzer's bubble-glass began to dance, and I could feel gentle vibrations in the palms of my hands as I leaned against the machine and watched Milt stand quietly for a moment, then pull out one chair and stand behind it. He smiled and went around to the other chair, sat down and leaned forward, spoke quietly and reached out, his hand moving like he was brushing his thumb lightly across invisible fingers. He stayed like that, smiling and talking, his eyes alight, and once I swear he laughed out loud and I couldn't hear it.

And I felt nothing.

The song ended, and Milt looked down and shrugged, then lifted his hand in a halfhearted wave. He looked up at me like a man beatified a long time after death.

I stalked across the room and flipped the door key onto his table. "Lock up when you leave," I said harshly, and charged out into the storm.

"You haven't slept," Milt chided, looking me up and down from the other side of my screen door the next morning.

"Your goddamn pounding on the door woke me up," I answered truculently, lying. Milt shifted nervously from foot to foot.

"The key," he said, almost as if reminding himself, and he lifted it wrapped in a handkerchief from his breast pocket. "I left the two dollars for the beer next to the register."

"Oh, for Christ's sake," I said, snatching the key from him. We stood there for a moment not looking at each other. "Well," he said, but I cut him off.

"You had coffee?"

"Well, no," he said. "Is that an invitation?"

Neither one of us spoke again until I'd gotten coffee and we'd both had the first scalding sip. Then the silence seemed more companionable, and finally Milt said, "You can tell they're not English, can't you?"

"What?"

"Five and Dime. Whatever their real names were. Are. I mean, heather and cypress trees don't even grow within a thousand miles of each other, I don't think."

"What's your point, Milt?"

"No point. It was an icebreakcr. Another middle-management skill." He sipped at his coffee. "As was accepting this coffee. It gives us a chance to talk. Communication is the first step towards a solution of any problem."

"How come I didn't feel anything last night?" I asked. I have no middle-management skills.

"Why do you expect me to know?" Milt answered.

"Goddammit, Milt. Answer the question."

He paused, and then spoke carefully. "There is a difference," he said, "between mourning and nostalgia. That's as simply as I can put it. And some people make the transition from one to the other invisibly, over a period of time. Invisibly. Ha. That's me," he said bitterly.

Then he shook it off and continued. "Others make it in a great terrifying epiphanic moment. You felt something the first time you played the song?" I nodded. "And where was this?"

"In my living room."

"But Susan didn't die there, did she?"

"No."

"Well." He rubbed at one eye. "Hm. There's an old saying, ancient really, to the effect that magic only works on those who believe in it. Now I don't necessarily believe that's true, but I do think—how to put this—that there are some things that can be used in unusual ways given the proper circumstances. Which wouldn't arise unless the person was aware of the object's capability, so there you have your 'magic only works' canard. And I suppose this record, or this song, is one of those things. What's it about, after all? Getting past mourning. Are you through mourning your wife?"

I thought about it. *My wife is dead,* I thought, and waited for the squeeze in my chest, the anger, the rotten ache of loss. It didn't come. In its place was a memory, almost a waking dream, an image of the way her fingers used to brush across the backs of mine and linger for a moment on my wedding band, like Piglet saying *I just wanted to be sure of you.* And then it was gone.

I found that my throat was tight, but I was smiling. "'Tis better to have loved and lost, right?" I said. "There's a canard for you."

"That's what I thought," Milt said.

Donna got used to it, I guess, but she always gave me an odd look when I let Milt stay past closing on Wednesday nights. I let it go; after all, it wasn't something that could be easily explained. Milt and I evolved our own set of rituals attendant only on Wednesdays: he brought a roll of quarters, I left the door key by the register. Usually when I came in the next morning, there were a few empties on the bar and a sawbuck on the register, and in return Milt drank free whenever I was there. It was a peculiar arrangement and it proved satisfactory for both of us, if not for Donna.

And after a dozen Wednesdays, I took a detour on the way home after leaving Milt to his visit. I sat with a six-pack on a park bench facing the Sound and drank slowly until I had to turn around to watch the sun came up. The colors of the dawn take on a certain enduring splendor when you've stayed up all night to see them, as if you've ridden the underworld, been swallowed by the wolf and come out the other side. And the sun, oh, the sun, leaping huge and molten from the Cascades and waxing into its full blinding brightness as the city began to wake up around me. I drove home accompanied by foreknowledge of nostalgia.

The next Wednesday was miserable, gray and drizzly, the sun a pale smudge. I spent the day running errands. The evening at the bar passed pretty much like it always did, and Milt showed up at quarter to twelve like he always did.

I stopped Donna before she could escape and handed her an envelope. "Don't read it before you get home," I said.

She shook her head and said, "Nothing you do surprises me anymore." I held the door for her as she left, thinking *Yeah. We'll see.*

Milt and I didn't usually talk on Wednesday nights, him being incoherent with anticipation and me likewise with exhaustion, but tonight I went over to his table after I'd shut everything down and said, "I put the key in an envelope tonight."

He looked at me quizzically. I'm the worst liar in the world, and I know my face was giving something away, but all he did was nod, God bless him, and I walked out the door. Outside it was still raining and I whistled all the way to my car. Then I whistled all the way home, and then I went through the list one more time. Accountant; check. Realtor; check. City clerk; check. Bank account; check.

Loan officer. "Check," I said, and laughed out loud.

I thought about it as I hummed down I-90 past the suburbs and the outlying communities and up into the mountain towns. Thought about the progression from mourning to nostalgia, and moments of epiphany. *Invisible, ha, that's me,* Milt had said, but what he hadn't figured out is that he didn't want it any other way. He'd opted out, settled into a comfortable mid-level job, saved my loan after Susan's death, done everything he could to keep everything the same. Or not even that; he'd gone back, recreated a previous sameness. Petra keeps coming to him because he wants her to.

And that was the one thing Susan was wrong about. The dead do remember us, and they do want to be mourned, and they will keep coming as long as we keep wanting to go to them. I didn't want to do that any more.

Frank's Place was a huge temple to Susan's memory, an everlasting flame hoping to draw her like an ectoplasmic moth. I threw everything I had into it after she died because it was her dream for me as well as my dream for myself. It was more than a year before I figured out that dreams you dream with someone die with them. Frank's Place was a dead woman's dream kept alive by the living.

And I couldn't keep it alive any longer, but Milt Chrzanowski could. He was on that invisible slow climb, that vision-dulling trudge through the bleak underground of loss and inadequacy and abandoned anger, and Frank's Place had been his dream for a dead woman before anyone had dreamed it for me.

Or maybe that's all bullshit. But Milt signed the quit-claim, and sent a letter to my accountant too. I don't think I want to read it just yet. I do hope Donna still works there, and I told her so in the letter I gave her that last night. There was a check in that envelope too, in case she thought she couldn't work for Milt, but my accountant says she hasn't cashed it. So maybe things are just going along there like they always were. Maybe Milt quit at the bank to take on the barkeep's life that was dreamed for him. Maybe not. I imagine I'll find out whenever I read his letter.

Meanwhile, the check from the realtor came, and due to the robust nature of the Seattle housing market I can afford to drive myself a bit further down this road or that, looking for a little sun to worship and a new, living dream instead of a monument to loss. I'm leaving the sad songs to Milt. Let him hear the nightingale. And let him rendezvous with the dead, too; I'll remember if I will.

And if I will, forget.

The Sands of Iwo Jima

Seventy-three years old, standing on the shore of Lake Mitchell, Harvey Sprewell felt like an explorer. The sky was blue enough to shatter like china, and so distant that it seemed impossible that snow could fall that far. It was October 10th, just past peak time for fall colors in northern Michigan and the anniversary of Mama's passing. The trees surrounding the lake blazed frantically against the rows of cottages as if trying to drown them out, to paint themselves over the uniform canvas of white-painted wood. *We will still be here,* the trees murmured in the clean fall breeze, *still here.* The rasp of their dying leaves recalled a rattlesnake Harvey had seen in Camp Pendleton before he left for the Pacific. A lance corporal with a neck like corned beef had cut it to pieces with a folding shovel, Harvey remembered, and the trees were losing their battle too. Every year, there were more houses around the lake and more fudgies from Grosse Pointe and Birmingham willing to pay an arm and a leg for them. The trees' war split along seasonal fronts; development was the warm-weather enemy, fighting from freeze to freeze before giving way to winter. The oranges and reds of the maple, the birch tree's bitter gold, the sumac's melancholy purple—all were challenges, every leaf a gauntlet thrown at the advancing feet of winter. *We will meet you,* the leaves whispered in the dry rustle of their fall. *We will meet you naked, shorn of beauty and breath, and when you have gone, we will still be here.*

Winter in Wexford County: clear, still January mornings, beautiful through frosted windows but cold enough to freeze your breath in your nose, cold enough that your eyes ached with the effort of blinking, cold enough to kill if you were old and stubborn and insisted on walking at dawn every morning. Oh Mama, Harvey thought, just once, one morning you could have been lazy. You could have made the coffee while I laid the fire and we could have sat looking out the back window at deer returning to their beds. How many deer do you see in seventy-two years in Wexford County? Never so many that you don't stop and take a second look. One morning, Mama, you could have slept in.

It was a heart attack that killed her, but Harvey'd sat down, laboring over the multiplication, and figured it out: fifty-two times three hundred and sixty-five was eighteen thousand, nine hundred and eighty, plus thirteen leap years made it nine hundred and ninety-three. October 10th was thirty-eight days after their anniversary, making for seventeen thousand five hundred and seventy-one days since they'd walked down the aisle in Tustin in 1940. Of all those days, what made one more deadly than the others?

Proximate causes and contributing factors, the doctors said, but Harvey knew it was winter that had taken her away from him. Winter had probed her defenses for fifty-two years, and finally found a weakness.

Mama took at least one walk every day, missing only three, nine days before Pearl Harbor when her only pregnancy ended and the stillborn baby nearly killed her. They hadn't tried again; Harvey was too afraid to lose her, and now it seemed to him that the stillbirth was a warning. Then it was the war, him in the Pacific and Mama gone downstate to Ypsilanti, building B-17s at Willow Run while he slogged through the mud on Tarawa and Saipan and every other Pacific lump of dirt big enough to fight across until his war had ended with a million-dollar wound on Iwo Jima. He'd called her Mama even then, never Estelle or Stella; when the funeral director asked him how he wanted her name at the service, Harvey had been confused for a moment before he remembered her name.

My story, Harvey thought, is typical. How many other old men with memories of wars and slim-fingered wives lived just around this lake? How many of them are telling themselves my story?

He went back into the house, checked to make sure the china was all still properly shelved even though he'd dusted it himself that morning, rubbing each piece until it shone blue and distant as the autumn sky. A single red maple leaf had followed him inside on the sole of his shoe, and it seemed to say to him *Winter isn't here yet.*

He sat heavily in the recliner facing the fireplace. Winter wasn't even there yet. With two fingers Harvey rubbed the sides of his nose, tracing the deep lines past the corners of his mouth to the line of his jaw. *It wasn't today,* he thought. *Not October tenth, it's never that cold in October. It's in January.* He squeezed his eyes shut and bent forward in the chair. *Isn't it?*

He tried to ignore the tears as he turned on the VCR, but the maple leaf stuck to his heel, reminding him.

The movie nears its climax. Private Conway is standing along the rail of the troop transport that is taking him and the rest of his platoon to Iwo Jima. He leans against the rail and says to Bob Duxxe, "It's hard to explain...I gotta feeling I'm not gonna come out of this operation."

Duxxe takes a drag on his cigarette. "Yeah?"

"It's like a voice in my ear. I can't shake the feeling off."

"Take my advice," Duxxe says. "Shake it off."

Conway shakes his head, and Harvey knows he is thinking about his new baby boy and the bride he left behind in Hawaii. Harvey knows this because he was thinking similar thoughts on his way to Iwo Jima, thinking about Mama back in Michigan and hearing that insistent little voice.

"No dice, Pollyanna." Conway shrugs. "When things like that get in you, it's no use trying to fight them."

Private Duxxe shakes his head and pops Conway on the shoulder. He mutters something meant to be reassuring and the scene cuts to a wide-angle shot of the Higgins boats churning toward the landing beach north of Mount Suribachi.

Harvey was in the Fifth Marines, and he remembers that landing, just like it is in the movie, hitting the beach and driving straight up the lumpy, ragged slopes of Suribachi to plant the Stars and Stripes on its crumbled summit. After that, the battle became a murderous game of paint-by-numbers; it would take another month, but Iwo Jima would be taken and held by the United States Marines. Harvey is glad he has the videotape of *The Sands of Iwo Jima*, because his memories are starting to fray at the edges, letting odors and images seep in that don't belong in his story, his ordinary-guy northern-Michigan dogface story. *It must be that I'm getting old,* he thinks. *I don't want to die because it won't be as clean, it won't be as good and honorable as it would have been on the sands of Iwo Jima.* He has been dreaming about Iwo lately, dreams that bear no resemblance to the movie's truth.

In his dream, Japanese artillery and machine-gun fire have blasted the entire beach into a haze of cordite and thin volcanic ash that thickens into quicksand around Harvey's knees, sucking at his feet. The island will not support him, he thinks; he will sink through the shifting sands to the bottom of the Pacific Ocean. The first advance is stopped dead on the open beach, huddling behind shattered bodies of amphtracs and even comrades for protection against the enfilading hail of bullets and shrapnel. *It isn't just me that will sink,* Harvey thinks as he vainly tries to dig a foxhole in the ashy sand. *The whole island, blasted to the bottom of the Marianas Trench and we'll all be nothing but bones.* He is surprised when his shovel strikes something solid. Rocking the blade back and forth to free it, he finds that he has thrust the shovel into the mouth of a Marine. Harvey jerks the blade out of the dead man's mouth, the motion tipping him over backwards into a warm flood of shock. He sits stunned on the beach, surrounded by dead indistinguishable save by the fabric of their pants, until a passing corpsman hauls him up by the collar and shouts into his face until Harvey's fingers will wrap around the stock of his rifle again. Then the corpsman slogs away down the beach. Harvey kicks away a tangle of ropy guts and struggles through the treacherous sand and gore to his platoon. They regroup and thrust inward, away from the blood-soaked sand and onto bare volcanic rock, aiming to isolate the Japanese stronghold on Mount Suribachi. They are Marines; what else can they do?

Harvey jerks awake. The VCR has stopped and the snow on the television screen is the only light in the room. He tries to find the remote, but he has been clenching his fists in his sleep again and his fingers are numb.

Consider a fish; Harvey did.

In many religions, a fish is a symbol for life. There was a time when people died for tattooing crude fish on their chests, a fact that struck Harvey as mildly ridiculous. Neither Mama nor he had ever been particularly religious. Why anyone would want to kill a bunch of harmless nuts with fish tattoos, and why anyone would get a fish tattoo if they knew it could get them killed…these things escaped him. He thought about it for a minute, and came to the conclusion that everyone has to have something that they're willing to die for. I went to war, Harvey thought. Guess I was willing to die. But all Mama did was go for a walk to see some deer.

Harvey sat on a overturned bucket inside his ice shanty on frozen Lake Mitchell, staring at his tip-up, which had yet to tip up that morning. Outside, the January wind shrieked down from Saskatchewan, toothy with spite. Harvey heard it, but he had heard it before. It had rattled the boards of dozens of shanties like the one he sat in, shanties betrayed by early springs and thinning ice whose bones now snagged his lines in the summer, tugging as if they missed his warmth. Winter and he were no longer strangers.

Imagine the deepest red paint dried into the darkest black paper; this was the color of the chimney of Harvey's Franklin stove after an afternoon spent chopping wood and stoking the fire until sweat soaked through his thermal undershirt and Pendleton flannel, chilling him as he stepped back to watch the condensation form on the inside of his windows. Harvey would not admit winter. He cleaned his eaves in January, changed the oil in the old F-150 when it was so cold his fingers couldn't grip the bolt on the oil pan. Winter was a Jap sniper crooning your dead best friend's name in the midnight jungle, a sneaking wretched killing sonofabitch, tricking your feet with ice and your eyes with stinging wind, lulling you with the lethal beauty of silent crystal mornings that sliced into your chest like a surgeon's futile blade. But, like the Japs, it could be licked. Harvey hated it, waged war against it with single-minded Marine intensity; the shanty itself was a challenge hurled into the teeth of the wind, its corrugated walls torn from the sides of the toolshed behind the garage. It was an extension of his house, of himself, standing on the lake in defiance of frigid air and short pale days.

Fishing over the bones, all year round, his lines catching on them in the summer as he trolled along the weedy dropoffs, his hooks bringing up a hammered square of tin that was once a patch on a shanty how many years ago or the red-painted end of a long-discarded tip-up. *Join us, Harvey,* the jealous bones cried. *Follow us down through the ice and lie among the weeds, here where you can see the sun but never feel its warmth, here where you can remember with us the time when we were tall and supple and winter was a war we always won, merely a promise of coming spring.*

Harvey jerked his line at the distant dead sound of the words, but the bones of lost things held on a moment longer, and he was in the old boat, his arms burned nearly dark enough to hide the blurred heart-and-rose tattoo on his forearm (CADILLAC MAMA, I'M COMING HOME, it said; he'd had it done in Manila but it had blurred and he could hardly read it anymore), sweat stinging in the sunburned creases on the back of his neck, and the dead bones spoke again. *Pike will glide through the eyes of your skull, Harvey—*

The line snapped, and Harvey fell backwards off the overturned bucket. The cold had settled in him as he slept, deeper than it would have a year ago, and the noises in his hips and knees as he stood up were the voices of bones, of dead leaves like rattlesnakes cut to pieces by shovels.

The tip-up stood erect, its red-painted handle quivering slightly at the level of Harvey's moaning knees. *Pulling back,* he thought, and the crackle in his shoulders as he reached for the tip-up was the dry distant laughter of bones. He saw his hands in the dim light, the knuckles knobbed by arthritis, chapped and split by the spiteful winds of seventy Michigan winters.

He pulled the line in and found a dead pike, its jaws slack around the line, the hook buried deep in its throat. How long had he been asleep, that a fish as stringy and vicious as a northern pike would die on the line? The hole hadn't even frozen.

He ripped the hook loose and dropped the northern back into the black water, seeing in his head the way it drifted grinning and gaping down among the weeds and the bones. He stood slowly and swayed on numbed feet. Outside, the sun was low across the

The Sands of Iwo Jima

lake and the air so cold and still it wouldn't have carried the sound of Mama calling him in to supper.

Sometimes the fish aren't biting, Harvey thought wearily, and went into the house.

───•◆•───

Sergeant Stryker, played by the one and only Duke, is sitting easily just below the summit of Mount Suribachi, watching the six Marines he has sent to raise the American flag over Iwo Jima. Private Conway drops down next to him and the old sergeant grins at him. "So, Conway, I see you made it."

Conway grins sheepishly. "Yeah, I guess that little voice was wrong." He relaxes; he will see his wife and infant son again, and the monkey of his father's reputation ("The finest man I ever served under," Stryker has proclaimed earlier) has been tumbled from his back. "I feel better."

"I feel a lot better too," Stryker says. "Matter of fact, I never felt so good in my life."

A single shot rings out, the bullet striking the Sergeant just above the second button of his khaki shirt. Another Marine leaps up and cuts the sniper down with a long burst from a BAR, then they all turn to the dead body of the man who made sure that they were well-trained enough to get this far. The wound starts Harvey thinking, as it always does, of March 21st, 1945, of his own wound, received in the narrow gorge in the northern part of the island where General Kuribayashi had built his bunker.

It was a single shot from an unseen sniper, and the impact of the bullet sent Harvey stumbling backwards to fall on the seat of his pants. He remembers it being a high wound, under his left collarbone, miraculously missing lung, heart, arteries and bones; a million-dollar wound, bad enough to get you sent Stateside to recuperate, not so bad that it wouldn't heal completely.

But lately Harvey has been having wicked dreams about that too, he can't remember any recuperation, just the hot high buzzing in his head and vague irritation that he can't find his balance. He blinks and when he opens his eyes again he is lying on his right side, his face half-buried in the fine ash that covers the trail and a weight pressing on his chest. Gunfire crackles from far away, there is shouting and the muffled grunt of grenades exploding underground. A nearby explosion brings tears to Harvey's eyes; when he blinks them clear he sees a teenage Marine lying in the trail facing him. At first it appears that a fragment of shrapnel has ripped through the kid's throat; another blink and Harvey realizes that the slim white missile lodged under the kid's jaw is a fragment of human bone. The kid reaches up and carefully works the sliver out, bright blood pumping over his fingers. He examines it, his mouth pursed in a frown of dizzy consternation. Finally he drops the bone splinter and shifts his weight so he is facing Harvey. *Wait up, Sprewell,* the kid mouths; Harvey's ears are ringing, he can't tell if the kid is making any sound or not, but he can see blood on the kid's teeth and seeping around the ribbed cartilage of his Adam's apple. *Wait up, I'm coming with you.*

Thinking back, Harvey can remember nothing between that moment and right now, sitting in the overstuffed vinyl chair in front of the television and the VCR he bought for Mama the year before she died, the china cabinet against the wall to his left. He hadn't gone wherever that kid had gone in the dream, he hadn't died, he'd heard about it when they finally got Kuribayashi, must have been from a nurse, must have been on the hospital ship that took him away from Iwo Jima and the rest of the war.

The Marines' Hymn starts playing as the final scene of *The Sands of Iwo Jima* fades into the Marine Corps emblem. THE END.

Harvey is watching a blank screen when he remembers that Mama didn't die in January at all. March 21st is the day Mama died.

First day of spring, my ass, Harvey thought as he hooked a wriggling minnow and dropped it into the black water. *Vernal equinox, my blue cheeks.* He thought of the Bible verse Ernie Harwell read on the radio every year on the Tigers' Opening Day; if the voices of any turtles were heard right then, he doubted very much that they would be rejoicing.

Harvey's tip-up tipped up and with a flick of his wrist he jerked a silvery perch, not a keeper, from the hole. The hook had caught in one of its gills, and the minnow's tail stuck out between the lacy red filaments.

The Sands of Iwo Jima

He worked hook and minnow loose, but the perch died. Harvey dropped it on the ice and the minnow turned to a sliver of bone in his fingers.

Wait up, the dead perch said.

It had been three days since he got any decent sleep. The nightmares were coming too thick and it got harder every time to wake up from the sand and the blood and the horrible look in the kid's eyes when he said *Wait up, Sprewell. Wait up, I'm coming with you.* The kid had looked at him like he knew Harvey was going to die.

His memory was failing him. He couldn't distinguish between memory and nightmare, and even though he watched *The Sands of Iwo Jima* every day, it had lost something. It seemed too clean—the line of landing vehicles too regular, too unscathed, men dying quickly with pictures of their sweethearts close at hand. The movie had become a mockery of itself, a mockery of him, and Harvey couldn't remember when it had happened. He had been there; shouldn't he know?

And he had forgotten to dust the china, Mama's china in the cabinet that he had refinished for her when he got back from the war. The dust on it had been heavy, heavier than it should have been, when he'd brushed it carefully that morning, the morning of March twenty-first, 1993, the forty-eighth anniversary of the sniper's bullet on Iwo Jima and the first anniversary of Mama's last morning walk. Suddenly it seemed to Harvey that only one of those events could really have happened, that there wasn't room for both of them on only one day.

He shivered, and realized that he'd forgotten also to put on a coat. For four days now it had been almost warm, over freezing, and while fishing Harvey had heard the distant boom of the ice sheet cracking. The shanty had sunk slightly into the ice during the infrequent thaws of the ending winter, its sun-warmed walls biting into the ice, and it had taken on a slight but noticeable tilt. The thaws would come more often now, and Harvey had decided he was partial to this shanty; soon he would have to pull it down and store it until next winter.

Another warm day and the ice would be unsafe and he could give up the fight against winter for another year, the sun and the wobble of the Earth on its axis would take care of that for him, but in the predawn darkness it was cold. The weathermen said it would warm up near forty by noon, but Harvey didn't believe it. Not on Mama's anniversary. Not on a day so cold it seemed like he had died instead of her.

As daylight began to show itself through the seams in the shanty's walls, Harvey's tip-up remained still. Mama's absence had acquired its own weight, the weight of cold days without sun, and now Harvey wished he had neighbors, someone to offer a kind word. But all of the houses on this side of the lake belonged to fudgies now, and they wouldn't be up until June, or Memorial Day at the earliest.

Memorial Day, Harvey thought, with no one to remember with. If the baby had lived, there would be a son or a daughter, grandchildren, someone to sit in the shanty with. But all I've got is memory, and I can't tell the difference between that and nightmares of Iwo Jima. He shifted his weight on the bucket and the slushy sound of it scraping on the ice reminded him of the predictions of the weathermen. *Winter is dead,* they were saying, and the gusty wind carried the brash agreement of the trees. *We have survived as we always do.*

We were once green and alive, the bones chimed in, and the tip-up quivered. *We remember. Just like you, Harvey, we were once alive.*

"No," Harvey whispered. It was not getting warm, not on this day, he could feel the chill in his feet on the ice, he could see it in his hands, reddened and split, the knuckles swollen with arthritis and frosted with chapped dead skin. He could feel it under his collarbone, where winter beat in the slow, careful rhythm of his heart.

Intimations of Immortality

Norman Campbell stood on a saddle of land between two mountain peaks on the Continental Divide and recited part of a poem.

> But there's a Tree, of many, one,
> A single Field which I have looked upon,
> Both of them speak of something that is gone:
> The Pansy at my feet
> Doth the same tale repeat:
> Whither is fled the visionary gleam?
> Where is it now, the glory and the dream?

Norman had once killed a man to avoid doing the very thing that he was going to do that morning. It was his son Sasha's eighteenth birthday. Nobody understood Wordsworth who hadn't read him aloud from the top of a mountain.

I must make the right decision, he said to himself.

"Dad," Sasha said when Norman came back to the camp they'd set up three days before. A stream, swollen with snowmelt, rushed past them on its way down what the maps still called Herman Gulch. Two miles downstream, Interstate 70 still split the Rocky Mountains; Norman's stomach rolled over at being so close to civilization. Sixteen years, he thought.

"Son." Norman sat by the campfire and spooned himself a bowl of stew. "Happy birthday."

Sasha squatted by the stream to rinse his own bowl. Norman could see the kid wanting to ask a question. He ate stew and waited for Sasha to work himself up to it.

"Are we going down the mountain today?"

The right decision, Norman thought again. "Yes," he said.

Sasha didn't look at him. "Will they arrest you when we get there?"

"I'd be real surprised if they didn't."

2

A little less than nineteen years before that morning, Norman Campbell had been, if not the happiest man in the world, certainly the most immediately content. It was Friday night. Norm's account was swollen with his week's wages, his head was perfectly fogged with Coors, and the balls on the scuffed and chalk-smeared pool table obeyed his every command. He was twenty-four years old, and there was no place in the world he would rather have been than the Valverde Country Club on West Alameda in Denver, Colorado.

"Hey, Crash," Terence called from the table. "You got this one?"

"I got 'em all," Norm said, and rolled the eight down the rail, slow and easy as a Cadillac in the mag-lane of the Valley Highway. It dropped into the corner and Norm came back to the table to pay the waitress for the fresh pitcher.

"Bet you wish you could drive like you shoot pool," Terence said. Beer foam clung to his bushy red Santa Claus-style beard.

"Shit," Norm said. The accident had been three months before, and he'd long since paid it off. "Bet you wish you could fuck like I shoot pool."

Matt and Bill Amidor, brothers who worked in the office-supply warehouse Norm and Terence drove out of, roared. Terrence wiped at his beard to hide the fact that he was grinning too, then he said, "Hey. Look what just walked in the door."

Intimations of Immortality

They all looked. Bill whistled. Norm overfilled his mug and stepped back from the table to let the foam run onto the floor. "Good impression you're making there, Crash," Terence said. "You clip rental trucks in the yard, spill your drink whenever a pretty girl walks in...what's next, you gonna spit on the boss's shoes? Quote Shakespeare at him while you do it?"

"Fucking boss needs his shoes spit on," Norm said, but his attention stuck to the woman who now stood at the bar. Tall, long black hair, long black coat that cost more than Norm made in a month, face crying out to have a poem written about it. "Bet she's on the T," Norm said.

"Mm," Bill said. "A little too perfect, isn't she?"

Matt lit a cigarette. "What's she doing here?" It was a good question. The Country Club wasn't exactly dangerous, but even Norm—since he'd never been in jail more than overnight and had a tendency to read books once in a while—was a bit out of place there. This woman was a walking pearl in a pigpen. And, unless they'd all missed something, she was alone.

Oh, no she wasn't. Here came her friends: three equally perfect, perfectly beautiful, and beautifully incongruous young women. Like vid models after a day shooting, Norm thought, but the only place around here that used live vids was the porn shack around the corner, and no woman who looked like these would come anywhere near that place.

"Slumming," Matt grumbled. He liked to go to upper-class bars and light cigarettes just to get kicked out, but he hated it when his favorite dives were invaded by people who normally wouldn't look at him on the street. "Go talk 'em up, Crash," he said. "Recite poems, take 'em home, and piss all over 'em."

"Bitter, bitter," Norm said, but Matt had gotten it two-thirds right. Recite poems, take 'em home. It worked if you weren't too smarmy about the poems.

His next opponent called out from the pool table and he went back to win number fifteen. He won easily enough, but he could tell that his invincibility was ebbing; too much time looking at that first woman out of the corner of his eye. Norm decided that she was on the T for sure. She looked about twenty-five, but she didn't carry herself like she was fresh out of college. There was an assurance, a...he didn't know how to pin it down, but he would have bet his job that she was quite a bit older than she looked.

Waiting for the next game to start, he debated asking the guys what they thought, but Matt would just start in on one of his eat-the-rich diatribes. Telomerase therapy was so expensive that practically nobody could afford it, and Matt wanted to be immortal as much as the next guy.

Except Norm. Live forever? Sounded like a nightmare to him. He'd probably see a hundred anyway, and that seemed like enough to him. As it was, he doubted he'd recognize the world in his old age.

But was that really true? Here it is, halfway through the twenty-first century, Norm thought, and all the old tensions are alive and well. It's amazing how nobody ever predicts that the future will be exactly like their present. He broke again, was lucky to sink a ball because of a rack loose enough that it sounded like maracas when he hit it, and was struck by the idea that a hundred years ago, bars were probably full of guys shooting pool after an evening of loading office furniture and paper onto box trucks. Like him, they probably didn't do their runs on Fridays, coming in on Sunday night instead when there were fewer drunks on the roads. It was snowing outside, and Norm was glad he didn't have to go to Cheyenne.

One difference, though, between the nineteen fifties and now— let alone desegregation, VR, electric cars, the Water Crisis, and whatever else—was that back then, young women who went slumming weren't immortal.

The Greek gods coming down to Earth, Norm thought. Zeus sowing his wild oats, Apollo chasing Daphne through the forest. He caught himself. Were they really that far apart, people on the T and the rest of the world?

The four women sat in a corner booth by the fire exit. They watched TV, joked with each other—probably sniggering about a bar that doesn't have terminals at every table, Norm thought. He missed his next shot, pool invincibility clearly slipping away, and realized that deep down he was more sympathetic to Matt Amidor than he'd thought. He looked at his three friends, laughing and waving their arms, finishing the pitcher he'd just bought. Well into a Friday night.

This is not so bad, Norm thought. I like my job, I like my friends, I make enough money to have some fun, and the world is full of pretty women. Who needs immortality?

Still, when the brunette immortal bought him a beer, Norm found himself as much curious as horny.

3

Sasha stayed a little ahead of Norman as they followed the stream down Herman Gulch. No wonder he's excited, Norman thought. Eighteen years old, and for the first time he's about to go into a town during daylight. Norman experienced a flush of pride, thinking that in twenty-first-century America, a nation of three hundred eighty million people, he'd managed to raise a son who was completely at home in the real world of trees, stone, and water.

Not that he'd stunted the boy. The battered terminal with its solar attachment and VR headgear had been a pain in the ass to haul around—at least until he'd destroyed it when Sasha was six—but Norman had done it so Sasha would be educated. So he would have some exposure to the world of cities and human society. So he would know about literature, history, government, politics. So he would be able to make an informed choice when the time came for the choice to be made.

They stopped at the last big bend in the trail before it terminated in a dirt parking lot. Sasha's eyes were wide like a deer's as he watched cars whirring up the slope to the Eisenhower Tunnel, and Norman wondered what he was feeling. I've created a real-life Victorian novel two hundred years late, Norman thought. The boy coming back to claim his birthright.

"There's a world up here, and a world down there," Norman said. "We're going back down there, but you have to take this world with you when you go. Cycles, Sasha. That's a world that's lost track of its cycles."

Sasha nodded, his eyes still on the line of cars.

"You know why I did this, don't you, son?" Norman wished he hadn't said it. They'd been over this a million times. But a man had to make sure his son knew…what? Why he'd had to pretend he was just out backpacking on the few occasions they'd met other people in the Rocky Mountain wilderness? Why he'd seen his father stab a man to death when he was six years old? Why he'd never been able to play on a soccer team, take a vacation to California or the Moon, date girls?

Norman forced himself to calm down. Never mind what Sasha's thinking, he thought. You'd better take care that you don't have a heart attack when you walk down into Georgetown.

But that was ridiculous. He was forty-three years old, and in better physical shape than most Olympic athletes half his age. What Norman Campbell had to worry about was his mind. In sixteen years of living in the wilderness, he'd developed an aversion to civilization so profound that to call it pathological would be charitable. Even now, before he'd spoken to a soul or set foot on concrete, it was all he could do not to turn around and disappear.

"I know why you say you did it," Sasha said.

Norman sat next to him. "Sounds like there's more you have to say," he said, and was suddenly afraid.

4

"I was wondering when you'd come over to say hi," the brunette said. "Do you always ignore women who buy you drinks?"

"Well, I was kind of on a streak there," Norm said.

"Mm," she said, the beginnings of a smile in her eyes. This is a woman who likes to play games, Norm thought. "Superstitious?"

"It's pool," Norm said. "You get it going, you don't want to do anything to screw it up. Thanks for the beers." She'd bought him three.

"You're welcome." The brunette put her chin in her hands and looked up at him. "What's your name, pool shooter?"

"Norm. What's yours?"

"Melinda. And these are Licia, Quincy, and Michelle."

"My pleasure." Norm raised his beer to them and finished it off by way of a toast.

"Are you going to invite your friends over?"

Norm considered. "Well, I could, but Matt there has a problem with rich girls on the T."

Melinda smiled, and her friends laughed out loud. "Is that so?"

"'Fraid it is. And I doubt Terence would be able to speak in your presence. He's a bit shy around people who aren't as ugly as he is." Well, now, that wasn't very friendly, was it? Norm said to himself. It was true, though; Terence had said as much himself. But there was a difference between being self-deprecating and having someone else do it for you.

Norm stepped back from the table. "I'll get them over here anyway."

"She gonna take you out in daddy's suborbital?" Matt said when Norm came back.

"She just might," Norm said with a grin. "And one of her friends might take you. Come on, the ladies desire company. If your principles permit."

"Shit," Matt said. "It's only the big head has principles." They dragged their table over in front of the fire door. The four immortals already had another pitcher waiting.

(5)

"What I mean to say, Dad," Sasha said, hesitating over every word, "is…okay. You talk and talk about wanting me to be able to make decisions for myself, but you basically made all of my decisions for me, didn't you? I mean, when you took me off into the mountains. I didn't decide that. My mother didn't decide that. You did. You took away sixteen years' worth of decisions, and you want me to believe that this one moment when I can choose is worth it."

Norman was silent for a while. "We've had this discussion before," he said, mostly to buy time to gather his thoughts.

"And you say the same thing every time. I know, you did what you thought was right."

"It *was* right," Norman said. He floundered, mouth open, wondering what he could say that hadn't already been said. What he could say that would convince Sasha once and for all.

Remember, he told himself. When you have to move a skid of paper, and it's so cold and icy that the pallet jack's wheels won't grip, you break the skid down and horse the paper two boxes per trip. No man can move a ton at once, but just about anyone can do it a hundred pounds at a time. Norman looked at his son, so like himself. A little taller, a little leaner, framed more like his mother but with Norman's blonde hair and Norman's face.

Sixteen years I've spent trying to teach you, he thought, and now the day my teaching stops, we're back to the very first lesson.

"Your mother," he began.

"No, Dad. I don't want to talk about her. I know her better than you do."

"You haven't—" Norman broke off, unable to speak the question. Had Sasha sent her a message, spoken to her? Left a note in some dumpster somewhere, during one of the winters when weather had forced them closer to the cities?

"No, I haven't talked to her. I haven't sent her Mother's Day cards. But I used to go back to places where you buried newspapers and dig them up to see if I could find the name MacTavish. You'd be surprised; it pops up a lot. I've kept up. I had to. Your only memories of her are older than I am."

"Okay. I see where this is going," Norman said. "You think I'm, what, poisoning your mind against your mother?"

Sasha said nothing.

"You think," Norman went on, growing angry as he always did when the conversation turned to Melinda MacTavish, "you think I would do that? Christ on crutches, kid, that's exactly the kind of thing that I did this to avoid. You better believe that if you'd grown up with her, she'd have made sure that you didn't even know who I was. She'd have had you believing that you were modeled in a lab and then turkey-basted into her, and your dear old dad would have gone on with his life not even knowing you existed."

Sasha was looking at him. Norman stopped. "See what I mean?" Sasha said.

Why doesn't he understand? Norman thought. He shrugged because it was either that or smack the kid down the hill, and after Ivan Klos he'd sworn never to lay a hand on his son. "Fine," he said. "You can't tell the difference between truth and sour grapes, there's nothing I can do for you. We might as well stroll on down into…" His voice caught, and Norman swallowed. "Into town. But understand this, Sasha my son: it was pure luck that I ever found out about you at all."

6

When the Country Club closed down, everyone paired off, Olympian woman with United Supply mortal. "Shall we head downtown?" Melinda said. "I know a place or two."

"Lead on," Matt said. Norm stifled a grin, knowing that wherever Melinda was going to take them at three in the morning, it wouldn't be a place where smoking cigarettes would cause an uproar. Like all the rich, Melinda and her friends knew places that tolerated vice, and tolerance aggravated Matt's sense of injustice more than anything else in the world.

They took the maglev downtown and ended up on the roof of the Republic Plaza, once Denver's tallest building but now just another in a double handful of glass-and-concrete fingers. Things unfolded pretty much the way Norm had figured. Everyone got a little more drunk, and Matt acted like an idiot while Bill tried to calm him down, and Terence sat in the corner all night watching Orion creep across the sky to impale himself on the invisible ridges of Mount Evans, and the girls passed around eyedroppers of something felonious and intensely pleasurable, no doubt formulated in the basement of some startup gentech concern. Norm rinsed his eyes but good, despite his normal reliance on alcohol and the occasional joint to improve his state of mind. After all, rich people could be counted on to have good drugs, couldn't they?

They could. Norm's sense of time, not to mention any and all misgivings he'd had about mingling with a crowd of immortals (everyone had heard the stories about them playing lethal jokes on those whom they'd come to call "short-timers," as if immortality was one long war and they were already envious about mortals' ability to get sent home, and even though you couldn't trust the Urban Legend nets Norm had no desire to wake up splattered on the pavement with parameds scraping him into a bag for transport to a T-therapy clinic to see just how good the process really was), evaporated like the predawn rain from Republic Plaza's rooftop dome.

"So," Norm said eventually, "what's it like knowing you'll never die?"

Melinda arched one of her perfect eyebrows. Reflected light from the holos playing across the dome glowed on her face. "What's it like knowing you will?"

Norm laughed. "Okay, right. I don't think about it all that much. But still, you must..." he waved one hand, and beer spilled into a potted yucca plant, blooming like crazy even though it was already September outside the dome.

"Come on, Norm, it's not forever. Nobody knows how long. It's not immortality." Melinda smiled over her drink. "And don't ask how old I am."

"Wouldn't dream of it," Norm said, but having brought the subject up, he couldn't let it go. "'Nothing was more difficult for me in childhood,'" he quoted, "'than to admit the notion of death as a state applicable to my own being.' Close enough, right?"

"Other than the fact that I'm not a child, sure. Who is it?"

"Wordsworth. He was—"

"Please, Norm. I went to college. I know who Wordsworth was, and I'll bet that isn't actually a poem you quoted. Sounds too prosey." Norm nodded. "I'd even be willing to bet," Melinda went on, "that he was talking about," she tapped a finger on the edge of her glass, "either the *Prelude* or the 'Intimations' ode, right?"

"A literary woman," Norm said, surprised. "It's the 'Intimations' ode." Most of the filthy rich college students he'd known had gone out of their way not to learn anything, relying instead on net tutors and Norton subliminals. It was nice to find an exception.

Of course, then Melinda had to squash his sudden magnanimity toward the rich. "I wouldn't have figured a truck driver would quote Wordsworth."

"I wouldn't have figured a rich girl on the T would take a guy out just to remind him that he drives a truck," Norm said slowly.

Melinda laughed. "Look at yourself, so defensive. Insult me if you want to, Norm, but remember this: if you could get on the T, you would. It's not my fault the therapy's expensive."

"Two things," Norm said, getting angry even as he reminded himself that he didn't want to be any more like Matt Amidor than he had to. "First, no I wouldn't. And second, I don't care whose fault it is that the T is expensive; it still pisses me off."

Melinda had stopped listening after the first. "You wouldn't?" she said incredulously. "Come on. Of course you would."

"No," Norm said stubbornly, "I wouldn't."

"Well, then." Melinda plucked a drink from a passing waiter's tray. "Nothing more to say about that, is there? I think you're in a minority, though. I don't know anyone who's had the chance to get on the T and turned it down. I sure wouldn't."

She produced an eyedropper, incredibly, from her cleavage, drawing out the motion to be sure that Norm's gaze followed her hand. "Your grin is looking a little strained, driver man. Look, we both know why we're here. Do you really want to bog everything down in arguments about social injustice?"

Norm forced his attention away from her breasts' perfect dusting of freckles—like a constellation really, or was her neckline a cipher drawing his attention down?—long enough to take the eyedropper. Don't want to be Matt, he thought, but he did wonder: why, he wanted to ask her, *are* we here? Really?

But there was no point, and my, those freckles. "You win," he said, tilting his head back. "Let's have a good time."

And so it was that around sunrise, Norm found himself fifty thousand meters above the Continental Divide in a robot suborbital, Melinda's heels bruising his lumbar vertebrae while they cruised over the San Juans. He laughed out loud, both from residual eyedropper goodwill and at the realization that Matt Amidor's sour prophecy had come to pass, from poetry quoting to suborb ride. Matty, he thought as Melinda laughed with him, I hope you're doing the same. Just don't piss on anybody.

By noon, he was sitting in the old White Spot just south of the Golden Triangle, watching cars whine down Broadway and suffering an eyedropper hangover of apocalyptic intensity. His head hurt; his balls hurt; the inside of his cheek hurt where she'd sampled him just as the suborb hit a little bumpy air; and he'd done something to his neck earlier, so even swallowing bites of *huevos rancheros* hurt. I never did get her last name, Norm thought, and chuckled. He couldn't decide whether that was a good thing or not.

⑦

Sasha didn't understand. Norman could see it in the boy's expression, in the rigidity of his shoulders, in the way he looked at the gravel surface of the parking lot instead of the mountains and sky as he usually did. He didn't look at Norman as they waited by the side of the freeway, thumbs out. After a while a car stopped and they got in, Norman awkwardly shoving the unstrung bow in ahead of him.

"I can take you as far as Idaho Springs," the driver said. He was young, midway between Norman's age and Sasha's. Probably not a sales rep; the car was too clean. Did he work for one of the ski resorts? Could just be visiting family, Norman thought. "Idaho Springs is great," he said.

"Name's Gavin Dix," the driver said. Sasha introduced himself and, when Norman didn't say anything, said, "Sorry. My dad gets carsick."

Well done, kid, Norman thought. He had to try very hard not to vomit once the car was moving. It was like you lost the skill of seeing the world go by so fast. He'd had Sasha take virtual rides in cars, trains, suburbs, whatever other machines moved people around the world, but Norman hadn't wanted to take them himself. When he'd left, he'd really left. And now, coming back, he fully expected his return to kill him. One way or another.

He closed his eyes and tried not to feel the concrete flying by under the car. Choices. I leave the mountains, Norman thought, for my son's sake. Just as I went to them for his sake. He remembered what Melinda had said to him, the last time they'd spoken: *Your son will live for hundreds of years. He'll be a piece of you in the world long after you're gone.* He hadn't been able to answer her then, eighteen years before, and the only solace he could find now was Wordsworth: *We will grieve not, rather find / Strength in what remains behind.* Wordsworth had been wrong about that, though. What was left behind didn't always give strength. After Idaho Springs was just Floyd Hill, and then the long slope down to Denver and the plains. Eyes closed, weakening, he whispered to himself as the car whirred past the Route 40 exit. *O, ye Fountains, Meadows, Hills, and Groves*, he whispered, his voice like the muffled sound of tires on pavement, *Forebode not any severing of our loves.*

Like Wordsworth, though, Norman knew that saying didn't make it true. It didn't even mean that the speaker believed it.

Gavin Dix pulled off at the western Idaho Springs interchange. "I'm headed up into the Mt. Evans Wilderness. Meeting my girlfriend." He winked. "How far you going, anyway?"

Norman opened his mouth, but Sasha jumped in. "Denver, eventually. But this is probably far enough for today, right, Dad?"

"You can get the maglev from here right downtown," Gavin said. "Here, I'll drop you off at the station." He eased the connector pedal down and the car rolled forward.

"No," Norman rasped. Gavin looked back at him and he raised one hand. Saw that it was shaking. "What I mean to say is thanks. But I think I need to walk for a bit." He saw the look that Gavin gave Sasha—*the old man all right there?*—but he didn't care. All he wanted to do was get out of the car. Get the whole business over with.

"Yeah," Sasha said. "Like I said, he gets carsick. Thanks for the ride."

Then they were out of the car watching Gavin Dix charge up the road toward Mount Evans. Not a Victorian novel, Norm thought. At least not for me. More like Rip Van Winkle, or—he chuckled bitterly—Tarzan dragged off to London. Once he'd lived in a city, but those memories now seemed to have happened to someone else. His eyes no longer knew how to look at bricks and concrete; his nose had forgotten how to smell paint, rubber, the occasional whiff of propane or gasoline. And the memories were no consolation.

"What's funny?" Sasha said.

Norman shook his head. "Let's head into town."

(8)

Six months after he'd spent the night in the company of immortals, Norm sat at the White Spot's counter just before five-thirty in the morning. It had been a long night, heavy snow from

Greeley all the way up to Cheyenne, and fatigue whined in his head as he paged through the *Denver Post*'s print edition. Strikes on the asteroid colonies, resettlement of Water Crisis refugees, Kasparov beating Capablanca in the Inter-Era AI chess championship, qualifying for the 2054 World Cup. Coming to the back of the entertainment section, he dropped a forkful of potatoes and chili on a picture, wiped it away, and saw Melinda's face looking back at him. Next to her, the other three women from the night at the Country Club smiled their best society-immortal smiles. "Huh," he said, grinning as he remembered her freckles, and read the caption. And dropped another forkful of food.

Pregnant? Norm looked back at the picture. "I'll be goddamned," he said.

She'd done it on purpose, had to've. Synchronized her period or something, and gone out to piss off her dad.

But why? What kind of perverse fucking immortals' game was this?

Despite energetic speculation about the father's identity, no clear candidates have emerged, the accompanying article read. *And Ms.—soon to be Mrs.?—MacTavish remains coy, saying only that she's giddy about prospective motherhood. Sources place the due date sometime in the middle of June, just in time to celebrate wedding vows if any are in the offing.*

"Unbelievable," Norm said. He counted back, and there it was. Arithmetic didn't lie.

He was going to be a father. Melinda MacTavish, of the MCT Research MacTavishes, the MCT Tower MacTavishes, the vids-taken-with-the-President MacTavishes, was going to bear his child.

Knowing her last name, Norm didn't have much trouble tracking Melinda down, and the next weekend he caught up with her outside a benefit for the Denver Dumb Friends League. "Hey," he said, and she looked right through him, walking on to a waiting limousine. He stepped in front of her, and a cluster of net stringers appeared from nowhere.

"Hey yourself," the limo driver said. He grabbed Norm's arm.

"It's okay, John," Melinda said. "Take a ride, Norm?"

Intimations of Immortality

The driver scowled at Norm, but stepped back and held the door while they got into the limo. Melinda moved carefully, scooting across the seat until she found a comfortable spot and sank back against the cushioned armrest. "How have you been?" she said.

Norm ignored the question. "Were you planning to tell me about this?" he asked, nodding at her belly.

"Why? So we could get married? Please, Norm." Melinda took a bottle of water from a small refrigerator set into the wall. "We had a good time. Leave it at that."

"That's—that's my child there," Norm sputtered. "You can't just ignore me. We did that together."

She drank, set the bottle down. "Norm, we need to get some things straight. First of all, you don't know the child is yours. How do you know what I did the night before we met, or the night after? How do you know I didn't just decide to bear a child and have something worked up in my dad's lab? I could, you know."

"Okay," Norm said. "Is it mine?"

"Yes, it is. Which brings us to the second thing. I can too ignore you, and I intend to do exactly that. You can make noise, go to the nets, do whatever your sense of injustice demands. But nothing will happen; you know that, don't you? Don't take this the wrong way, but my father is one of the richest men in the world. He decides who represents you in Congress, and he decides what the nets decide is news. You better believe they'll ask him whether or not to cover a truck driver's paternity claim against his only daughter. He'll make your claim disappear. He could make you disappear."

Sure, Norm thought. I won't take that the wrong way. They rode in silence for a while. Finally he said, "Why?"

"Why what? I should think you'd have lots of whys."

"Why did you do this? You go slumming for short-timers, working guys you normally wouldn't look at, that much I can understand. But why a kid?"

"What answer would satisfy you? Do you want me to say that it's some decadent experiment, the elite playing with your gene pool? Nature versus nurture?" Melinda drank more water. A frown crossed her face, then a smile. "He's moving," she said.

Norm gaped at her. He? A son. Norman Campbell's son. "Can I feel?" he said, his voice trembling.

Melinda looked at him for a long moment before nodding. "You deserve that much, don't you?" she said. She took his hand, placed it on the right side of her belly.

A small shift, then nothing, then a sharp kick. Norm made a small noise in the back of his throat, and realized he was about to cry. His son shifted again, then the motion subsided.

Melinda picked up his hand, put it in his lap. "Why are you taking this away from me?" Norm said.

She shook her head, the shadow of sadness on her face almost believable. "I'm not taking anything away from you, Norm. If you'd never found out, you wouldn't have known there was anything to take away."

Still staring at her belly, Norm said, "But I did find out."

"Yes. I'm sorry. Think of it this way. Your son will live for hundreds of years. He'll be a piece of you in the world long after you're gone. I thank you for giving him to me."

His son would live for hundreds of years, Norm thought. His son would be immortal.

Whether he wanted to or not.

The limo cruised to a halt. "I should let you off here," Melinda said. "I know you're angry, Norm, but Sasha will have the best of everything. Isn't that what every father wants, for his children to grow up in better circumstances than the father had? I didn't do this randomly, Norm. I looked for quite a long time before I chose you."

Sasha, Norm thought. His son's name was Sasha.

"You're right about one thing," Melinda went on. "Most of the people I know who are on the T, I wouldn't let them within ten feet of my uterus." Her forehead wrinkled. "Does that answer your question? At least in part?"

The driver opened the door. When Norm didn't move right away, he reached in and laid a hand, hard, on Norm's shoulder. Norm got out and the driver walked him firmly to the sidewalk, then went back to the limo and drove away.

Sasha. Not what he would have chosen, but a good name.

It was Saturday night. Terence and Bill and Matt would be at the Country Club. Norm stood on the downtown sidewalk for a long time as people walked by and thin clouds passed across the face of the moon. After a while he got on the maglev and went down to the warehouse, where his loaded truck was parked. Seven hours later, when he got back from his loop through Greeley and Cheyenne and Fort Collins, he went to the White Spot. When he paid for his *huevos rancheros,* he saw that the balance in his account had been multiplied by a factor of one hundred.

That was when he decided to kidnap his son.

⑨

They walked together over the freeway overpass, Norman's feet bewildered by the flatness of the road. At the first intersection in town, a service station faced a little café next to a ski and bike store. An old man in coveralls stood on a ladder screwing a sign into the wall over the service station's garage: WATER SEPARATORS SERVICED HERE. Water separators, Norman thought. The last time I was here, that station still had a gas pump at the end of a row of charging docks.

"Let's get something to eat," Norman said, hoping someplace in town still took cash.

"Yeah." Sasha's eyes were even wider than they had been looking over I-70 from the Herman Gulch trailhead, or down into Georgetown from the Guanella Pass road, wider even than the one afternoon they'd spent sneaking through Air Force holdings to look down at the city of Colorado Springs. Different looking down on a sight and suddenly finding yourself part of it. Sasha's whole face seemed to have expanded somehow, his nose twitching like a rabbit's, to accommodate the torrent of novelty from this one intersection in this one little town.

"Wait'll you get to Denver," Norman said, and they turned down Idaho Springs' main street.

The old BeauJo's pizza place was still there, still dark and open and woody, its walls festooned with customers' napkin artwork. Some things never change, Norman thought, and he fervently hoped it was true. "You take cash?" he asked the hostess.

"We'll take whatever you have," she said, and led them to a table near the old mine shaft in the main dining area. "Something to drink?"

"Water for me," Norman said. Sasha looked over the menu terminal, his eyes dancing as his fingers played over the display. He ordered a citrus soda.

The hostess disappeared into the kitchen. "Careful," Norman told his son. "The carbonation might be a little much."

Sasha shrugged. "If I don't like it, I'll get something else. What does orange juice really taste like?"

That's right, Norman thought. You've only tasted it on the VR. His taste buds stood at attention, remembering the sharp sweetness of fresh-squeezed OJ. "It's wonderful," he said. "Maybe you should try it instead of a soda."

Sasha changed his order when their waiter showed up with the drinks. Then he returned his attention to the menu terminal, asking Norman questions about this topping and that appetizer. They settled on a large Mountain Pie with ham, tomatoes, and fresh garlic—all things Sasha had never tasted. "Wow," Sasha said, tasting the orange juice. "Wow."

They ate until neither of them could move, their biggest meal since Norman had brought down an elk the previous winter and they'd spent three days gorging on steaks. Sasha was immediately smitten with cheese, picking it off the pizza slices and eating it by itself before going back to finish off the crust and sauce. Norm, too, found himself tasting the food as if he'd never had any of it before. Amazing, he thought. I used to eat pizza twice a week.

"If this is civilization, Dad," Sasha said with a grin, "I'm not going to mind it at all."

If this was all it was, Norman thought, I wouldn't either.

(10)

It took Norm two weeks to formulate his plan. At first he'd just had wild ideas about grabbing Sasha and heading for another city—Miami, maybe, where wave after wave of immigration had made South Florida into a patchwork of informal city-states. He could hide there. LA was the same way, but people in LA were crazy after the Water Crisis. Norm had no desire to get shot for using a public water fountain in the wrong neighborhood.

This was the MacTavishes he was talking about, though. If anyone had the resources to find him, they did. Could he get out of the country, head for Asia or South America? Norm didn't know Mandarin, and only had enough Spanish to follow soccer broadcasts when the Anglophone nets were preoccupied with baseball or hockey, but he thought he could get by long enough to land a job. Problem was, there was no way to get through the airports without leaving your name, and more importantly your retinal scans, in a database that Conrad MacTavish would crack open like a peanut shell, civil liberties be damned. Drive to Mexico, hire a coyote to get him south of the border? Possible, but all the charging stations refused cash, and if he got to the Rio Grande Norm didn't want to trust his son to coyote ethics. A dilemma.

So there was only one option, really. Fly in the grass. Go under radar. I will take my son, Norm thought, and disappear into the wilderness. There are plenty of places in the Rockies where a man can disappear, and Arizona's practically empty now. Southern Utah. Up in the Cascades.

The next morning, he spent two hundred dollars in a South Broadway used bookstore buying old wilderness-survival manuals, autobiographical narratives of people who had survived extended periods alone in the mountains, and biographies of the great nineteenth-century mountain men. That afternoon, he signed up for a Colorado Free University course on wilderness survival, spending three consecutive weekends in the mountains learning how to distinguish edible plants from poisonous, set snares, find or build shelter, and—most importantly—hunt using concealment and ambush. His job kept him fit, but he bought a bike and started riding back and forth to work instead of taking the maglev from his apartment in Edgewater. During the week, he read all day and ran his route at night, leaning out his truck's window to learn constellations and how they moved across the sky.

This would be a hell of a lot easier, he thought one night while wrestling a fire safe over the doorjamb of an office-supply store in Cheyenne, if I could take a gun. Not to mention GPS gear and two decades' worth of vitamin supplements. And oh yes, a babysitter. Norm had started lurking around new-mother net chats, and they'd given him nightmares about all the things that could go wrong with a baby.

It wouldn't work, though. Gunshots could be heard, vitamin supplements would just expire, and so on. The only way to do this, Norm thought, is to go completely native. Become Jedediah Smith or Jim Bridger. Wear skins, hunt and gather—and raise a son. He felt a deep stab of fear at the realization that his plan could very well kill the son he was trying to...what, save? Not quite. But if the boy grew up among people like Melinda MacTavish, what would he know of the world?

"Pretty thin rationalization, Crash," Norm said to himself. The truth of it was that he was doing this because Sasha was his son, and he deserved to be a part of his son's life. And if that meant he had to spend years wandering through mountains and deserts, well, Sacajawea had done it with Lewis and Clark.

Sasha was born on June 9, 2054. In the two years following his son's birth, Norm spent lots of time on the gossip and society nets, getting an idea of where Melinda went with and without him, looking for the time and place when she would leave him alone. The MacTavish estate was out of the question: they had photoelectrics, dogs, human sentries, the whole bit. Likewise one of the many benefits Melinda was taking the baby to; too many people, too many net stringers.

Norm finally settled on swimming lessons. Melinda took Sasha to the Cherry Creek Golf Club's gym once a week, starting when he was about a year old, and Norm took out a membership himself—gym only, no course privileges or AI trainer time. Then one day, when Melinda left Sasha in day care while she took a shower, Norm waited until the provider was preoccupied changing one of her charges and then simply walked in, picked Sasha up, waved at her, and left.

In later years, Norm would spend entire nights looking up at the sky, trying to remember what it had felt like to hold his son in his arms. He could never recapture the sensation, and as he grew older his meditations on that night came to be a sort of timekeeping. Instead of remembering the first time he held his son, Norm would stare up at Ursa Minor thinking of the last time he'd stayed up all night staring at Ursa Minor trying to remember the weight of a tiny child held against his chest.

At the time, though, Norm just walked. He did not run, and he didn't hurry out of the parking lot in his old converted-electric pickup truck. It wasn't until he'd gotten on the Sixth Avenue

Freeway that he floored it, and when he got to Grand Junction he walked into a garage run by Mexicans and let it be known in miserable Spanish that he had a truck to get rid of, cheap. They looked at Sasha, still squalling for his mother, and shook their heads. "All right, then," Norm said, and tossed his keys on the floor. "At least give me a lift somewhere." One of the mechanics gave him a ride back east a bit, into the national forest north of Rifle, and then he shouldered his backpack and compound bow, cradled his son in one arm, and struck out into the mountains. It was July 28, 2056, and he had two months to prepare for winter.

⑪

Sasha demolished the Mountain Pie in fifteen minutes, chasing it with orange juice. The Coke upset his stomach a little, Norman could tell; he left it alone except for a periodic experimental sip. "Careful there, kid," Norman said. "Too much processed food, you're going to spend your first civilized night in sixteen years puking into a real toilet." Sasha laughed and munched down the last of his crust.

Not him you have to worry about, Norman told himself. He's eighteen, invincible. You're past forty now. The wilderness made him tough, but it beat you down. He could feel those sixteen years in his knees, the soles of his feet, the small of his back. Even the Indians had known to stay out of the mountains in winter, and they'd all lived to be leathery and wise. Norman was leathery, but he didn't feel wise. He felt old. Should have known, he thought. Coming down the mountain to surrender my son. Childbirth and empty-nest syndrome all at once, plus this damn noise. Smells. It was true: you could forget how to live in a civilized society. Even if you remembered how to order a pizza.

"Let's go," he said. "I want to see if I remember something."

The bar was just named Red's. Two antique pinball machines stood against the rear wall by the bathroom doors, and two pool tables occupied a quarter of the floor space, and there was not a single terminal screen on the premises. Red's, Norman thought, made the Valverde Country Club—if it was still around—look sophisticated. The carpet smelled of long-ago spilled beer, and cigarette smoke burned his nostrils. Norman loved Red's immediately.

"Your first beer, kid," he said to Sasha, handing him a stubby brown bottle of Coors with a softly blinking logo. "If you don't like it, that's okay. The second's always better."

Sasha drank, grimaced. Drank again.

Norman drank too, the sharpness of the hops flooding up into his sinuses, making his eyes water, or was that just nostalgia? No way to tell. He set his bottle on a table, dug for change in his pockets and was almost able to forget that he had spent the past sixteen years hiding from the twenty-first century and that he would be in jail before the next sunset.

"Come on." He caught Sasha's arm. "Time you learned to shoot pool."

Sasha picked up the game quickly, and Norman's shooting eye had suffered from sixteen years' hiatus, but the older Campbell still whipped the younger easily. Sasha took it all in stride, intrigued by the challenge of the game and more often than not distracted by the occasional woman who walked in. After they'd been there for an hour or so, a group of young women clustered around the bar near the pool tables; Sasha quickly lost all of the pool skills he'd acquired. He asked Norman for another beer and they sat.

"So, font of wisdom," Sasha said, "what do I say?"

"What, to those girls?" Norman shrugged and the beer coarsened his speech. "Shit, boy, don't say anything. Last time I did, a chain of events ensued and I became a fugitive from justice."

It was the wrong thing to say. Sasha looked down at the table, his shoulders hunching defensively. What have I done? Norman asked himself, knowing that the answer was as obvious as the question was useless. Knowing that he had condemned his son to years of asking himself what to say, what to do, where to go—that he had made his son a stranger to his own time.

I did the right thing, Norman silently insisted. I did.

Intimations of Immortality

(12)

    Norm spent the first three winters, until Sasha was five, hiding out in the cliff dwellings that dotted southwestern Colorado and northern New Mexico. Other than the touristy little square of Mesa Verde National Park, the Four Corners was empty enough that a man could hide. Norm hid in the arroyos, shot deer and snared jackrabbits, learned how to sneak through Mancos and Cortez late at night, stealing from produce trucks when he could and dumpsters when he couldn't. He began to feel a strange empathy with the coyotes who sometimes accompanied him on his foragings.
    Sasha learned early on the necessity of silence. Too young to be left behind, he followed Norm through canyons and alleys, piggybacking until he could keep up on foot. Wide-eyed he pointed at the coyotes the way other boys his age were pointing out beagles and retrievers in Denver parks.
    Summers in the Four Corners were brutal and dry, forcing Norm back up into the high country. He worked his way from the San Juans to the Absarokas, moving every few days whether he'd seen anyone or not, staying under tree cover as much as possible, hiding from every overflying aircraft, worrying at night about the brigades of pursuit that must have been swarming up the slopes of the Rockies after him. The old ghost towns saved his life. Apple and pear trees, grapevines, wild corn; the gardens planted a hundred and eighty years before fed him and his son, and their dried fruits, cached in mineshafts and fault caves, kept them going through the winters after he'd abandoned his southern haunts. It was like living in a post-apocalypse world, having the ability to travel back in time and not doing it. Sasha learned to snowshoe before Norm had a chance to teach him how to read from newspapers stolen out of rest-stop trash cans.
    Occasionally, three or four times a year, Norm stumbled across a backpacker. As soon as Sasha was old enough to talk, Norm taught him to tell other people that his name was Billy and that they were from Louisiana. It became a game, and Sasha loved to put on the overbroad Southern accent Norm taught him. He grew disappointed and little-boy sulky when too many months passed

without encounters with other people, and during these sulks Norm's own self-interrogations grew more pointed. He's a little boy, Norm thought. He wants to see other little boys, wants to chase the girls around the playground.

Except Sasha had only seen little girls in a picture book stashed in a shelter cave south of Loveland Pass. Norm waited until his son was sleeping, and then he wept.

One morning after such a night, when Sasha was six years old and Norm was thirty, rain kept them from venturing too far from the rocky overhang under which they'd slept. Norm read to him from Shakespeare's sonnets, wishing he had more books in contemporary English. He could only carry so much, though; other than Shakespeare, he had small editions of Wordsworth and three novels: *The Hobbit, The Phantom Tollbooth,* and *Pynchon in Dreamland.* The first two had been favorites of Norm's father. Apparently, Norm often thought, along with taste in literature, he'd picked up some of the old man's resentment of the twenty-first century. *Pynchon in Dreamland* was the only exception, and even it was a time-travel novel dragging the great TwenCen novelist into the 2040s, where he disintegrated when confronted with the death of print.

Reading Shakespeare was good for the boy, though, since the dated language kept him asking questions and kept Norm answering them. Questions, Norm believed, were good. Better than hyperlinks that taught you only to select highlighted words. He limited Sasha's terminal time to one hour a day, and encouraged the boy only to use it when he wanted a specific question answered and Norm couldn't or wouldn't answer it. It was irrational, but Norm kept Sasha from reading the books in the terminal's library. He wanted Sasha to grow up believing that books were made of paper and questions were asked of other people before being surrendered to machines.

Questions taught. Questions were good.

Then Sasha looked up from the sonnets and said, "Who's my mother?"

Norm gently took the book from him and closed it. He had been waiting for this, but still was not looking forward to it. "Her name is Melinda," he said.

"Why didn't she come backpacking with us?"

"Sasha, buddy, can you do me a favor? Ask me that again when you're about ten."

"I want to know now, Dad."

"I can't tell you now, son." Norm took a deep breath. "If your mother found out about us up here, she'd take you away from me."

Sasha's forehead creased. He needed a haircut. "Why?"

This was the hard part. "I can't tell you that either, Sasha," Norm said. "Promise me you won't ask again until you're ten."

Sasha didn't like it, Norm could tell. He picked at his moccasins, already wearing through at the toe; scratched at the bridge of his nose, so much like his mother's, blew the hair away from his forehead. "Okay," he finally said.

"Thanks, buddy." Norm wanted to stop there, but with a flash he remembered Melinda saying *He could make you disappear*. "I took you because I love you, Sasha," he said. "If your mom finds out we're up here, I might be killed." He felt something die in himself as he said it, but the words went out into the air, found their way into his son's ears, then drifted away to be hammered to bits by the pounding rain.

⑬

On the maglev platform across I-70 from the Arapaho National Forest ranger station, Norman Campbell stepped up to the retinal scan to charge passage down to Denver. The invisible light played across his eyes, codified its findings, sent them off to the Transportation Department's central processor. Along the way, Norman guessed, the burst of information that represented Norman Campbell was noted by either the Colorado State Patrol or whatever private people were still working for the MacTavishes. Hello, forces of law and order, Norman thought. He stepped back. "Go ahead," he said Sasha. "Give it something to think about."

Sasha looked at him for a long time before approaching the scanner. Probably my accounts are long since seized and he doesn't have any, Norman thought. Either it'll let us on anyway, just so they know where to catch us, or it won't and I can buy some tickets.

It'll all turn out the same. Maybe in Golden, maybe in Lakewood, maybe at the Alameda station, they'll be waiting.

Sasha blinked, turned back to face Norman. "Dad—" he began.

"Too late, kid," Norman said. "Let's get on the train."

The maglev accelerated smoothly out of the Idaho Springs station and swept down Clear Creek Canyon. Twenty minutes later it coasted into the 19th Street station in Golden, where eight uniformed state patrolmen were waiting. They were polite and efficient, bonding Norman's wrists firmly but without malice while Sasha was led away by three men in suits. Norman was incongruously struck by how little fashion had changed. "Sasha," he called, "son."

Sasha was looking over his head, at the Denver skyline that towered to the east. He didn't appear to have heard.

14

It was less than three weeks after their rainy-day conversation that Norm and Sasha stumbled across the path of Ivan Klos.

"Howdy," he called, walking toward them on a ridge somewhere in the Mosquito Range. "Y'all don't have a map, do you? I am purely lost."

Warning prickles tracked up and down the back of Norm's neck. The Southern accent, he thought. It sounds as fake as the one I taught Sasha.

Sasha waved back. "Hi," he called. The man approached, dropped his pack, and sat next to them on the ridge, looking down a broad valley just beginning to lose its early-summer green. "Are you from Louisiana too?" Sasha asked.

"No, Texas. Casey Kenner," the stranger said, and shook Sasha's hand.

Later Norm would be unable to figure out what had set him off. Paranoia, maybe. Too many years, even then, without enough human contact. Maybe the fake-sounding accent. But what always came back to him was the sight of Sasha's tiny hand disappearing into Ivan Klos's knobby, tanned fingers.

Someone else holding onto his son.

Intimations of Immortality

Norm drew his knife, leaned forward, and drove it into the side of the stranger's neck just below the hinge of his jaw. Sasha screamed, an impossibly high-pitched and endless sound that lasted as long as it took Norm to jerk the knife out, as long as it took a bright arc of blood to splatter Sasha's arm from the hand that held the stranger's to the collar of his leather shirt, as long as it took for the stranger who was not Casey Kenner to topple over and try to get up again. Norm held him down, pried Sasha's hand out of his, leaned across him and listened to him die.

Sasha's screams subsided into hitching soundless whoops. Norm reached out to him, tried to wipe the blood away from his hand and the side of his neck but found that his own hands were also bloody. "Sasha, Sasha," he said, "breathe. You have to breathe, son." Sasha rocked forward into him and Norm held his son close, sshhing at him until his breath evened out and he started to relax. Norm stood and walked a mile or so down into the valley. He set Sasha down. "Wash your shirt, okay, buddy?" he said. "Wash yourself real good and stay here. I have to go get our stuff."

Back up on the ridge, flies were settling on the dead man. Norm took a deep breath and went through his pockets. The first thing he found was a compass and GPS locator with beacon.

"Purely lost," he said, and crushed the instrument with a rock. "How did you find us, you son of a bitch?" In the man's back pocket Norm found a wallet containing an investigator's license identifying him as one Ivan Klos. A holstered gun nestled in the small of Klos's back.

Norm sat back and his hands began to shake. The shakes spread up his arms, into his jaw, into his stomach. He turned away from the body and vomited on the delicate tundra flowers, heaving until threads of blood laced his bile. "I did the right thing," he choked each time he could draw breath. "The right thing."

Eventually his stomach settled and he went back to his search. Klos's backpack contained ordinary camping stuff—stove, dried food, clothing, sleeping bag—and one extraordinary thing as well.

I look like myself, Norm thought stupidly as he unfolded a laminated photograph. It was blown up and enhanced from a softball-team picture; in it twenty-three-year-old Norm Campbell grinned his third baseman's grin, beardless and without a care in the world. This is what I gave up, Norm thought. I threw this over so I could take my son away into the wilderness, so he could grow up not knowing the rest of his family, so he could never know his culture, so he could watch his father kill a man.

So he would know how to live in the world. So he would know what he was accepting, and what he was losing, if he decided to go on the T. So he would be a human being.

He gathered his and Sasha's possessions, set them to one side, and took out the solar-powered terminal he'd used to teach Sasha about governments and genomes. Using the same rock he'd used on Klos's GPS, he smashed it to fragments. When he realized that he'd been growling, "No more chances," with every blow, he dropped the rock and put both hands over his mouth. For a long time he stood like that. Then he gathered up the pieces, put them in Klos's backpack, hooked his elbows under the body's armpits, and dragged the dead Ivan Klos down into the valley. In a clearing he piled dry brush and tree limbs, threw the body on the pile, and burned everything that would burn, stoking the fire to keep it hot.

When nothing but ashes, bones, and metal remained, Norm sifted out the bones, wet and scattered the ashes, and buried everything that hadn't burned. The whole process took four hours, and Norm spent every second scouting the horizon for planes and helicopters. He wouldn't be able to see suborbitals, but it was cloudy and they wouldn't be able to see him either. Pray for rain, he thought grimly as he smoothed over Ivan Klos's unmarked grave. Rain and a little luck.

It was dusk before he'd recovered his gear from the ridge and found Sasha by the stream. "Hey, kid," he said, sitting down next to his son.

Nightfall was noticeably closer by the time Sasha responded. "Why'd you do that, Dad?"

"He was looking for us, buddy," Norm said. "Remember what I told you; if they catch us, they'll put me in jail for sure, and—and they might kill me." Norm tasted bile in his throat. *What right do I have to do this to him?*

A father's right. And he has a right to grow up and make his own decisions, not be Melinda MacTavish's damn trophy.

Again Sasha paused for a long time before answering. Night fell around them, recast the stream in moonlight. "Are we ever going to go back?" he asked.

The right thing, Norm told himself. I'm doing the right thing. "When you're eighteen, buddy, we'll go back. We'll go back together."

"Why not 'til then?"

"I can't tell you yet." Norm reached for his son, felt a teary wave of relief when the boy didn't jerk away. "Bear with me, Sasha. I'll tell you everything when I can."

15

On the vidscreen, people in Bangladesh tried to rescue a water buffalo from a rising river. Norman flipped the channel, found a soccer game, settled into his bunk. How easy it was to fall back into old habits.

Already forgetting: the feeling of strength as the right hand draws the bowstring. The peace of sleep in silence. The pure smell of nothing.

Someone scored a goal, and the quick succession of shots that followed—crowd, goalscorer, goalkeeper, crowd, ball in net, defenders standing with hanging heads, crowd, goalkeeper kicking ball back upfield—dizzied Norman. He closed his eyes and could see the purple ghost of the vidscreen scored into his retinas.

Already forgetting: the Milky Way in the dead of winter, seen from Guanella Pass. Sunrise over the Continental Divide. Sunset over the Continental Divide.

The look on Sasha's face when he caught his first fish, learned to swim, understood Shakespeare's hundred and twenty-seventh sonnet.

The purity of a poem composed at dawn on a mountaintop, remembered ten years later, taught to one's son on the same mountaintop.

Around him, three concrete walls and one made of steel bars. A low ceiling with a recessed fluorescent light, artificial and uncomfortable. A sink. A toilet. Five books in a corner. An electronic port set low near the door—net jack for prisoners? Or something for jailers? He got a little chill as the word *interrogation* whispered through his mind.

Stone walls do not a prison make, Norman quoted softly, "nor iron bars a cage." Not Wordsworth. Who? Forgetting, forgetting.

Jail, Norman thought. Prison. This is where they put kidnappers. This is where they put killers. He felt his strength ebbing away. I am a kidnapper. I am a killer, although they don't know that. He debated confessing, decided: *No. I did the right thing.*

16

When Sasha was twelve years old, he had enough confidence to claim that he could just run away back to civilization. It was a moment Norm had realized was approaching, and he'd spent months agonizing over whether to broach the subject himself or let Sasha do it. Ultimately he decided to leave the initiative to his son.

It was very sudden. "Rifle's just ten miles or so southwest of here, isn't it?" Sasha asked one day.

They were tanning a deerskin. Both of them needed moccasins. "Yeah, ten or twelve," Norm answered. In fact, they were even closer to the place where he'd first carried Sasha into the wilderness. "We'll have to head north a ways once we get this done."

"It would only take me one day to get there."

Norm stopped scraping.

A new look creased and tensed in the lines of Sasha's face. "I could do it," he said.

"Yes," Norm said. "You could." He started scraping again. He told himself that this was all normal, that testing of boundaries was part of human development, that Sasha was beginning to understand that he could exist without his father around and to desire that existence. Perfectly normal.

But he couldn't breathe through the cold squeeze his son's expression put on his gut. Are you afraid he's going to run off and die? Norm asked himself. Or are you afraid he'll run off and not die, that he'll run back to Melinda and tell her where you've been all these years?

Intimations of Immortality

If he was honest with himself, he had to admit both.

"Why shouldn't I go?" Sasha said. "Everyone lives in cities. Why are you so afraid?"

"I told you, kid, when I go back it's straight to the inside of a jail cell." Norm stopped scraping again. "I made you a deal. I'll go back when you're eighteen. Not before."

"You made me a deal when I was six, Dad. That isn't fair. I didn't know."

"Well, now you do."

"What are you afraid of? You can't just be a hermit."

"I'm not. I've got you."

Sasha's face darkened. "Well, I can't just be a hermit."

"Okay, kid," Norm said. "I'll tell you what I'm afraid of. I'm afraid that when I go back your mom's going to make sure I never see sunlight again. I'm afraid that I've forgotten how to live anywhere but here, and I'm afraid that if we go back—when we go back—you're going to forget everything I've tried to teach you. I'm afraid that the world I took you away from is still there, and I'm afraid that it isn't." He tossed his scraper to the ground. "I threw my life away for you, son. I don't expect you to return the favor, but I do expect you to respect the gift."

"What gift?" Sasha shouted, and just like that he was crying. "What gift? I don't know anyone but you. I don't remember ever sleeping in a house. I don't remember my mother. I want to have friends, Dad, I want to go to school, I want to eat chocolate and drink soda pop, I want to read a book that I pick myself, I want to watch vids and surf the nets, *I want to live like everyone else does*!"

"Like everyone else does?" Norm repeated. "What do you think would happen to the average person who had to spend a week in these mountains?"

Sasha was silent.

Norm knelt and picked a stem of flax. "Look at this flower. You know when it blooms, you know when it dies. You know where it grows and where it doesn't. All of them; you know which you can eat and which you can't. You know where to hunt for deer in April, and where they go in November. You know how to build a lean-to and live in a snow cave. You can smell a mountain lion from farther away than any of them," Norm waved in the general direction of the world, "can smell their own shit. You know the cycles here, *and you're part of them*. You want to live like everyone else? Everyone else has their senses scraped away by living in a place where there's light and noise twenty-four hours a day, where the air and water are full of chemicals you can't see. Everyone else spends their lives trying to make money and please their bosses. Everyone else experiences the world that the vids tell them to experience. You experience the world that is there. That's what I gave you, Sasha. You've got your whole life to be like everyone else. All I'm asking for is these first sixteen years."

Sasha walked away.

Norm sat up that night without a fire, counting shooting stars and trying not to admit that he was praying. Around sunrise, Sasha returned, and that day they struck north and didn't stop until they reached Montana.

17

When he'd been in jail for six days, Melinda came to visit. He'd been wondering if she would, wondering too how she would look. Did the T really work that well? Would she look like his memories?

She did. "You have to disappear, Norm," she said from the other side of the bars. "We'll send you to the colonies if you like. It's all been too embarrassing; the nets got hold of it and now it's everywhere."

"I know." He was following the stories, drinking in the images of his son, hating the images of his son that looked so little like the boy he remembered.

Remembered? he thought. It was only a week ago.

"You're a celebrity," Melinda said.

"I know," he said, and thought, oh God.

"I'll be honest with you, Norm. My father was hoping some of the people he'd sent after you would just kill you and bring Sasha back. Even now I'm holding him off."

"Why?"

Melinda sighed. "I don't know. There have been enough times when I'd have killed you myself."

Intimations of Immortality

"Spring me," Norman said. "I'll disappear. No more celebrity, no more embarrassment."

"Explain to me why I should do you any favors, Norm."

Norm paced quickly around his cell, returned to face her. "Is he going on the T?"

Melinda turned frosty. Norman could see her father in her gaze. "That's up to him now, isn't it?"

"If he does," Norman said, "you'll have him for how long, Melinda? How many centuries is the T good for? You'll have him forever. I just wanted him when he was a boy. He only got to be a child once, and I wanted to show him…I wanted him to know what was real."

"He only got to be a child once," Melinda said, "and you took that away from me."

(18)

After he'd destroyed the terminal, Norm worked harder to educate Sasha, teaching him the basics of math and science and trying to use unfamiliar words in conversation—*atmosphere, adjective, allele, atom, anthropology*—so the boy would have to ask what they meant. This activity had the desirable side effect of keeping Norm's memory sharp, and for that he was grateful. He'd reconciled himself to spending the rest of his life in prison, starting about six months from right then, but he didn't want to be an idiot too.

Most often, Norm's educational efforts showed up when he and Sasha got into an argument, and this was the case when, in December of 2071, Sasha exercised his vocabulary and called Norm a hypocrite.

They were cheating that winter, staying in the falling-down remains of a cabin deep in the Mount Evans wilderness. With only six months before Sasha's eighteenth birthday, Norm found he couldn't help letting his guard down. Part of him wanted to be captured so he wouldn't have to go and turn himself in. After protracted internal arguments, though, he concluded that being captured would tarnish his image as someone who had, out of principle and concern for his son, gone into the wilderness and then come back. If somebody tracked him down and dragged him back in handcuffs, he'd look like just another nut who kidnapped his son.

Which was, more or less, the offense of which Sasha was accusing him. "All this about saving me from civilization is bullshit, Dad," he said. "You were just pissed off at Mom and you used me to get back at her."

Norm counted to three, slowly. "Partly," he said, and stirred the fire. "If your mom had come to me and said, 'Hey, I'm pregnant, let's work something out,' this never would have happened." Saying it, he wondered if it was true. "But there's quite a bit you don't know about this, kid. Let me be blunt: are you going on the T when we get back?"

Resentment flashed in Sasha's eyes. Norm had only told him about telomerase therapy the year before, and Sasha was still angry about having it withheld for so long. It must sound like magic to the kid, Norm thought, not for the first time. He's only seen DNA in a model I built him. I wouldn't be surprised if he didn't believe in it.

"I don't have to tell you," Sasha said.

Norm remembered everything his parents had said about teenagers and tried not to get angry. "No, you don't," he agreed. "You don't owe me anything. I deprived you of a normal childhood, of all the girlfriends you would have had before now, of two whole years of driving and sucking in hydrocarbons..." He cut himself off before his sarcasm got too sharp.

"There you go again." Sasha pointed an accusing finger. "I say something, and you drop guilt on me because it's the only thing you have."

"That's where you're wrong, my boy," Norm said. "You are the only thing I have. This is not guilt. This is fact. I threw everything away to give you a chance."

"You threw everything away to give me a chance at something you didn't even know I'd want!" Sasha shouted. "This has been about you from the beginning!"

"Well then, tell me!" Norm snapped. "Did you want it? Do you see what it's worth? Tell me, Sasha. When you go down the hill next summer, and you have the rest of your life to do whatever you want to do, are you going to look back when you're fifty, or a hundred, or two hundred years old, and be angry at me because of the way you spent your childhood? Because if you are, boy, go ahead and put on your snowshoes and head right over that ridge to Chicago Lakes. There's a trail there that'll take you right down to a lodge. You leave in the morning, you can have dinner in Denver tomorrow night. I'll wait for the police here." He was shaking with anger, and also with fear that Sasha would go, fear that everything Norman Campbell had done these past sixteen years was not only worthless, but simply and ordinarily criminal.

He could see it all working in Sasha's face: fear of the city, desire for the city; fear of leaving his father, anger at his father; fear of what lay down the hill, fear that he would never see what lay down the hill. The war of the son with the father's shadow and the father's likeness in the mirror.

"You see?" Norm said, more softly. "You're all torn up about it because you've realized that there are alternatives. You can go on the T and live a thousand years, or you can not go on the T and when you're eighty your grandchildren will be able to see you for what you are. Don't you want to know what it's like to be old? Before the T, I never thought I did; now I know better, and I've tried to pass that along to you. God knows I've tried not to preach to you, son, but this is my last chance, so here it is: *you belong in this world*. You don't belong in the world out there where rich people outlive redwoods. Next year, you can either join them, or you can bring this world with you into that one. You can *choose*. Whatever else you might blame me for, son—and I'm sure you've got a list—you could at least thank me for that."

A pause stretched out, broken only by the whistling of wind on the peaks. Norm forgot to breathe. The entirety of the last sixteen years seemed to narrow down to a point that slowly thrust its way into his aging, mortal soul, driven by the weight of a childhood's accumulated guilt and misgivings.

⑲

The suborbital arced down out of the afternoon sky, ghosting to a landing at the base of the ridge encircling the upper Chicago

Lake. A couple of fishermen looked up, annoyed at the interruption, as Norm slowly got out, scratched at his cropped beard, and reached back into the suborb's hatch for a tall frame backpack and a compound bow.

He saw himself in the suborb's mirrored window and thought *Old. A man who has been left behind.* Norman Campbell in jail was a celebrity; Norman Campbell in the wilderness was just a hermit. Forgotten. A nut who kidnapped his son.

"Come out and have a visit sometime, son. You know where to look."

"Yeah," Sasha said. Norm looked at him, looked hard, burning him into memory. A line from Wordsworth floated through his head, from what poem he couldn't remember: "the little actor cons another part." Already Sasha looked somehow harder around the edges, his gaze a little less direct, his shoulders a little less straight. The city getting into him, Norm thought.

"You going to go on the T?" he asked. It was clumsy, but Norm was a little stunned by being outside again.

"Don't ask me, Dad. I don't know." Norman kept looking at his son, wanting to believe.

But there was no way to tell.

"Thanks, Dad," Sasha said.

"Thanks?"

Sasha shrugged. "You know," he said.

I wonder if I do, Norm thought. "I'm serious, son. Come find me sometime."

"I will." The suborbital's hatch slid shut and it lifted away. The fishermen went back to casting. Norman Campbell shouldered his pack and stood in the shadow of the mountain, looking back down the valley. After a long while, he turned to his left and began making his way slowly up the side of the mountain, a man without answers.

Chichén Itzá

Despite the sensors and pharm patches and the branching IV drip sprouting from the crook of his elbow, Brian's grandfather didn't look like he was dying. His face still held its color, his eyes shone, his hair was thick and bristly. The picture of health, save for the fact that he couldn't move; his nervous system had begun suffering rolling blackouts a month or so before, and now it was clear that the old man's power grid was fast approaching total failure. The doctor had offered Brian this metaphor by way of explaining a poorly understood viral syndrome that acted like an incredibly accelerated Lou Gehrig's disease, and Brian clutched at it, considering his grandfather as a sort of city whose inhabitants were being exiled by the coming blackout. It helped, somehow, to think of the old man as a collective instead of as an individual who would soon die.

"God damn comet," a tiny speaker in the wall said. The old man couldn't talk any more, but he retained enough muscular control to subvocalize and a speech processor took care of the rest. The words came through distinctly, a slight hesitation between them the only sign of the effort it took Grandpop even to move his tongue and palate.

"Yeah," Brian said. "Once it could have showed up six weeks early."

Grandpop tried to shrug. A vein popped out in the side of his neck. Through the hospice window Brian could see across the towns of Lafayette and Boulder to the Indian Peaks, lumpy and crooked under a May snow. Foothills spread green below them, and at the base of those foothills Brian could almost pick out the exact location of the stone house next to Boulder Creek that he shared with four other grad students. Kris was probably there, fiddling with the garden she kept in the back yard. She wouldn't move in, but she used the house as a surrogate garden/laundry/dog foster home, retreating to her apartment when Brian's roommates got too omnipresent.

He looked back at his grandfather, feeling suddenly beleaguered and in need of refuge. Grandpop was dying, his parents had been dead for years, Kris was fading away from him, he wasn't really close enough to any of his roommates to rely on them for support. He had no one to share the burden of the deathwatch, and Grandpop, who had always been Brian's sounding board in matters emotional, had stopped caring about love at roughly the time he stopped being able to speak.

The transformation in the old man was the worst part about the disease. Brian's mental image of his grandfather was leathery and obstinate, aggressively romantic, accidentally domineering, the kind of man whose presence automatically rearranged any space to center around him. Now, in the final stage of a terminal illness, Grandpop had withdrawn into a sort of dazed bitterness. *God damn comet* was about the extent of the speaker's transmissions the past few days. Brian understood, or thought he did, but the change was still hard to deal with.

"God damn comet," the speaker said again.

Before he got sick, Grandpop had planned a trip to Mexico to see Comet Halley from the top of one of the ruined buildings at Chichén Itzá. He'd been there in 1986 for the comet's previous rendezvous, on his first trip with the woman who later became Grandma Bruckner, and he'd intended the trip to commemorate Grandma and celebrate his own robust ninety-seven years. Now he lay paralyzed in a hospice in Lafayette, and every time Brian mentioned the trip—which he didn't do very often—the speaker growled, "Stupid sentimental idea."

It was sentimental, but it appealed to Brian anyway. Something romantic and committed about it reminded him of the way Grandpop had been when Brian was a kid. Then, the old man would have walked to Mexico.

He didn't know what to say. Grandpop wanted to see the comet, but he was going to die instead. What exactly did you say to that?

The old man was looking at him. "Grandpop, I have to go," Brian said. He stood. "I'll come back tomorrow, okay?"

"Tomorrow," the speaker said, and Brian closed the door softly behind him.

———•◆•———

The house was empty when he got home, but he heard Kris's voice muttering softly in the back yard. At first he couldn't make out the words, but as he passed through the kitchen, with its pawprinted floor and breakfast nook hung with copper pans, Brian's ears started to make sense of the speech.

It was a rapid-fire flow of Latin: *Cynodon dactylon, Eleusine indica, Trifolium repens.*

He stood on the back stoop watching her. Kris, on her knees in the garden, weeded around new tomato plants and among a cluster of nearly mature peas. *Pisum sativum, Lycopersicon esculentum.* Automatically as breathing, she murmured the name of each weed as she tossed it into a pile by the open driveway gate: *Ambrosia artemisiifolia, Convolvulus arvensis, Taraxacum officinale.* When she paused to brush a lock of black hair from her eyes, she said *papillapigmentfilamentepidermis,* all in one rushing word.

Post-Link fugue, Brian told himself, parroting a doctor again. Perfectly normal during the first couple of weeks after the retinal piggybacks were implanted. Still it scared the bejeezus out of him, like she was possessed, or channeling. Which in a way she was. Her freshly-Linked brain was still accommodating itself to the torrent of information that now surged through her whenever she focused her attention on anything. The natural outlet was speech, and the doctors had said that a mania for naming was a common but temporary post-Uplink distraction.

"*Leptinotarsa decemlineata,*" Kris said, and flicked a bug off one of the tomato plants. "Go away."

He walked toward the garden and said, "Kris."

She turned her head and Brian noticed that the two black eyes the implantation had given her were now faded to a dark yellow. "Hey, Brian," she said in her own voice, a throaty mezzo with just a little grain, and then she added *"Homo sapiens"* in the other voice, the unconscious automatic articulation of muscle. She smiled at him.

She doesn't even know she said that, he thought. He wanted to get on her bike, leaning there against the corner of the house, and ride away.

All of the doctors said it would pass, but Brian had an irrational feeling that it wouldn't, that the Kris he was seeing was the Kris he would always see, that she would go on with her savant-speech as long as he could stand to be around her. A little bit distant, a little bit preoccupied, part of her mind permanently drawn away to the volcanic flood of information that had become for her a dominant sixth sense. Doctors said what doctors said.

It hurt him that he could not share it. He had met Kris during a depression that seemed in retrospect to have been a bit self-indulgent but at the time had been like going through the day shrinkwrapped. Nothing touched him and he couldn't muster the strength to reach out. The depression had started to lift one summer afternoon as Brian was walking along Boulder Creek behind the public library. A hummingbird had appeared in front of his face: flash, there, bright red and hovering, one black gleam replacing another as it turned its head from side to side and looked at him. Then it was gone, and he'd stood there with the creek rippling by and a stupefied grin on his face. Speechless. Not a thought in his head. A little stoned by the intensity of the connection he'd felt, a little shaken by its evanescence.

Kris had blown into his life a few days after that, suffusing him with the kind of surprised joy he had felt at seeing that hummingbird. Only she had stayed.

Brian didn't believe in omens, exactly, but he had come to think of the hummingbird as a harbinger, if not of Kris then of his reawakening from isolation. The idea of her had become superimposed on the memory of the hummingbird, and whenever Brian thought about it he realized that she was inscribed in every pleasant memory he could think of from the past few years. He thought of her constantly. Something she'd said about Chaucer once that he'd ended up putting in an exam essay. Her recessed incisor. The taste of the skin behind her ears, the tingle of static electricity in her hair the one afternoon when they'd stayed up on South Boulder Peak a little too long. The noise she made in the back of her throat when she rolled over in the middle of the night.

Chichén Itzá

The intertwined scents of piñon pine needles and sexual musk. The color of the Flatirons before dawn, as they catch the hint of daybreak and glow while stars still speckle the sky: he remembered that because of the night he and Kris had spent lying in the grass at Chautauqua Park, following the triangle of Jupiter, Saturn, and the Pleiades across the sky and talking about going to Newfoundland or Ulan Bator or Mars. Going together. The sun had come up just as the moon was going down, and Brian would never forget watching the sky change color around the brilliant bone-white of the moon.

And now she had a sixth sense that drew her away from him.

Kris got up and walked over to kiss him. "How's your grandfather?"

"Other than the terminal illness, he's pretty much okay." Stupid fucking question, Brian thought, even though he knew she'd only spoken to leave him an opportunity for whatever he needed to vent. But Jesus: *How's your grandfather?*

Let it be, he told himself. This is hard on her too.

He started talking to distract himself from how pissed he was. "It's hard to be angry at someone who's going to die."

Kris rubbed dirt from her fingertips. "Why would you be angry at him?"

"I get in kind of a deterministic funk, you know, seeing how he's just going to die. Nothing anybody can do about it. We cure cancer, grow new hearts, regenerate severed spines—and Grandpop gets this brand-new disease that's going to kill him anyway." From the back yard, through a break in the trees, Brian could see the upended slabs of the Flatirons wearing their late-afternoon salmon pink. "Grandpop was a big mountain climber when he was younger. He got my dad into it."

"Oh," Kris said carefully.

"It's hard not to blame him."

"Brian, you might as well blame the freezing point of water," Kris said. "Your parents fell because of a rockslide, which happened because water expands and contracts when it freezes and melts and because gravity points toward the center of the Earth. Do you think your grandfather would have taken your father climbing if he'd known it would kill his only son?"

"No," Brian said. "No, of course I don't. But I'm discovering that this ahead-of-time grief is a post-hoc-fallacy kind of emotion.

Grandpop's dying. It doesn't make sense. I try to make it make sense by imposing patterns. This impulse to impose patterns spreads. I blame Grandpop for my mom and dad falling off a mountain. See?" He looked at Kris, trying very hard not to take his bottled-up anger out on her. "Self-analysis is easy, and I still feel shitty."

She just looked back at him, waiting for him to go on. So he did.

"And the thing is, he never once tried to force me into anything remotely hairy-chested or outdoorsy. I was kind of a strange being in my family; they all wanted to climb mountains and I got a bigger kick out of reading about someone else doing it. I don't think my dad ever really got comfortable with that. But after he died, Grandpop absolutely let me go my own way. He let me know that if I ever wanted to come hiking or ice-climbing or whatever, he was happy to take me along—he asked me every single time he went—but I also knew that he didn't look down on me for not going.

"So what do I do? I get mad at him for not pressing me. I start to think that if he thought I was a real male Bruckner, he'd want me to take up the old man's pastimes, carry on the family tradition of death-defying nature worship. That's what my father called it. Death-defying nature worship, like snowshoeing along the Continental Divide was religious. I never understood it. But I wanted Grandpop to want me to understand it, and I sort of got bitter at him for not trying harder. Put that together with what I feel now, as an adult, which is that I owe him something and don't know how to make it good, and..."

He realized that Kris had been muttering something under her breath for several seconds. When he stopped speaking, he could parse it: *ergo propter hoc ergo propter hoc ergo propter hoc. Primus inter pares. Pro bono publico.*

Piscem natare doces, she said, and her cheeks dimpled in a dreamer's smile. *Doctum cani antiquo dolos novos. Permitte canes dormitos sitos esse.*

"Jesus, Kris!" he shouted.

"What?" she said, taking a step away from him.

"You don't even know, do you? You don't hear yourself naming the goddamn weeds as you pull them, in *Latin;* you name *me* genus and species when I come out the door, now you finish my phrases to yourself while I'm trying to say something, what the fuck? Is *Wheelock's Latin* running all the time on one of the piggybacks?"

"The doctors explained this, Brian," she said, keeping her voice steady. Her fingertips rubbed against each other, bits of dirt falling from them into the grass. "Fugues. All subconscious. You know I'm listening to you."

"Part of you. I know part of you is. The rest is I don't know where. Up there." Brian swiped an arm at the sky, coloring with Rocky Mountain sunset. "Communing with a fucking satellite. Sure as hell isn't here."

One of Kris's hands went to her mouth, and Brian could see her making a focused effort not to cry. When she spoke, her voice had more stone than sadness in it. "You're upset about your grandfather," she said. "We've had this argument before, and I sure don't want to have it again right now. I just want to tell you one thing, Brian: don't take it out on me. You're better than that, and I don't deserve it."

She turned around, jerked her bicycle upright, and pedaled away without another word.

He visited Grandpop the next day, and the one after that, and each of the next sixteen days until the old man died quietly—as if he could have died any other way—on the thirtieth of May, 2061. A doctor came into the room when the Code Blue alarm started its insistent beep. He shut off the alarm and noted the time of death at the wall terminal, right under the speaker that Brian half-expected to mutter something angry and inarticulate. Brian witnessed the death statement and authorized another form attesting to the hospice's compliance with state and federal palliative-care guidelines.

"My sympathies for your loss, Brian," the doctor said with complete sincerity before leaving Brian alone with Grandpop's body.

Brian looked at the old man's face, trying to see if he could discern some difference between the stillness of death and the inert mask of paralysis Grandpop had worn for the last five or six days he'd been alive. If anything had changed, though, Brian couldn't see it. He'd been so surrounded, so permeated by the knowledge of Grandpop's death that the event itself came only as a kind of fulfillment.

"All right, Grandpop," he said, because he had to say something.

It had rained earlier that day, and through broken clouds the setting sun cast the shadows of the Indian Peaks up into the sky. In another hour Comet Halley would be visible through telescopes.

So damn mundane, Brian thought. Grandpop got old and died. He thought the haze that seemed to hang around him must be grief, but it didn't feel like grief. Grandpop got old and died.

Just like that he made the decision.

"I'll go for you, Grandpop," he said.

He caught himself waiting for the speaker to answer. Before Grandpop had fallen silent six days before, he'd gotten single-minded on the topic of memorials. Nothing, he said. Don't do anything. Let me be dead. Only the deterioration of his nerves had overwhelmed the speech processor's ingenuity, and what came out was *Uh-ing. Oan oo eng. Eh ee ee eh.*

It struck Brian then how creepily similar the speaker's cryptic cadences seemed to Kris's sleeping murmurs. He shivered, physically shaking the thought away.

Oan oo eng.

"I have to, Grandpop," he said. "It's for me, all right? I have to."

He lifted the crisp white bedsheet over Grandpop's face and let it settle. "Okay," he said, and went into the hall. On his way out he passed an orderly coming to prepare Grandpop's body for cremation.

"I'm going to go to Mexico in a couple of weeks," he told Kris when she came for dinner the next night. After twenty-four hours behind drawn shades trying to figure out how to mourn, Brian had wanted to go out, but Kris was jittery about the fugues, didn't want people staring in restaurants.

She put her fork down and dabbed at her mouth with a napkin. "I thought your grandfather didn't want you to do anything like that."

"For seventy-six years he planned to go back there the next time the comet came around," Brian said. "After Grandma died he got even more determined about it. Then he got sick and I think it was easier for him to reject things he'd wanted to do than admit he'd never be able to do them. Call it a rationalization if you want to. I think he was trying to make dying easier on himself."

Kris waited for him to continue, eyes steady and focused, and Brian lost his train of thought for a minute when he realized how long it had been since he'd had her direct attention. "Um," he said. "So." Maybe the doctors were right, and she'd just taken a little while to arrange the piggybacked information flow.

"It's for me really," Brian went on. "I miss the old man, and I want to do something for him. Some kind of goofy symbolic romantic sentimental thing that's exactly what he might have done before he got sick. I'm going to scatter his ashes at Chichén Itzá the day Comet Halley looks best from Earth."

"Wow," Kris said, "hope it doesn't rain," and that was when Brian really knew she was there, completely there, and he was laughing with her and it was like the piggybacks had never happened.

Late, late that night, after they'd made love and fallen asleep and he'd woken up when she'd come back from the bathroom, Brian lay listening to the creek and watching Kris sleep. He felt a little jittery, as if she'd be angry if she caught him looking at her, and he figured she would if she knew why he was watching her.

He'd been reading up on the Uplink, its effects. Like any new and possibly revolutionary medical procedure, it was wreathed in hyperbole both positive and negative. From one side hosannas, from the other sackcloth gnashings. Either humanity was entering into a new age of absolute availability of information, or the fundamental incompleteness that made each human distinct was being thoughtlessly and irreversibly erased. Technoprophets heralded the advent of practical telepathy, the shared knowledge of human civilization; New Humanists deplored the headlong rush away from unmediated experience of the world. Moderate voices couldn't even hear themselves reason.

Brian wanted to be moderate. The procedure itself was safe, had been tested for years on a variety of first lower mammals and then primates: the retinal piggybacks tracked whatever the eyes focused on, and a custom-grown genetic processor framed on the patient's own bone cells and powered by body heat identified the physical objects and selected key words from the patient's speech. These objects and words became topic searches on a satellite network that would achieve global coverage by the end of 2062, and the resultant spray of information squirted along a private frequency to a receiver drilled into the mastoid part of the skull. Implantation generally caused temporary light sensitivity and some maxillary or malar bruising. There was a risk of blindness, but you could always get new eyes, and—at least according to Kris's doctors—the risk of psychological dysfunction due to the brain's inability to handle its radically expanded informational vistas had been wildly overstated by hostile manipulations of study data.

Kris herself had shrugged off Brian's worries: "Everything new brings alarmists out of the woodwork. In the eighteenth century people thought that vaccinations would turn you into a cow." There was no good way to answer that. And the procedure was very expensive, but Kris had money and none of it was technically challenging anymore, and anyway technical obstacles hadn't kept Brian lying awake watching the woman he loved sleep under moonlight. He wanted to see if what he had read about Uplinked dreaming was true.

Kris's breathing slowed and deepened. Brian couldn't see for sure, but he thought her eyes were moving. Then she started to talk.

At first he couldn't make out any words; after a moment he figured out that she wasn't speaking English. *"Matay nipagesh?"* she said, quite clearly, followed by a rush of indistinguishable syllables, and then, again plain as day, "Chichén Itzá. June. *Sivan.*" All of the clarity faded from her speech again, and gradually she fell silent. Had she said something like *Halley*? Sure sounded like it, but that could have been associations in Brian's own sleep-deprived brain. He wanted to shake Kris awake, find out what she'd been dreaming, what language she'd spoken, what it had been like.

"I'll be damned," he whispered. It was true. The piggybacks even tracked dream-visions. The dreams of the Uplinked were open for anyone to see. Brian wondered how many dream addicts were already out there immersing themselves in slumbering Uplinked reveries.

He lay awake for a long time after that, wondering what else he had read was true.

"Did you dream about Chichén Itzá last night?" he asked her in the morning, to see if she remembered.

"Um," Kris said. "Yeah, I guess I did."

"Don't you ever think it's weird that people could hack your Link and see your dreams?"

Her mug banged on the breakfast-nook table and she said, "Not this early, Brian. Please."

Brian set down the spatula he'd held hovering over scrambled eggs. "I didn't mean it like that. Not trying to be combative. Just a question. Doesn't that seem weird?"

"No mood to be persecuted," she grumbled into the steam rising from her tea.

"Kris, come on. It's been less than a month. I still have questions. Don't you still have questions? Does everything make sense for you that fast?" Brian served the eggs onto two plates, added a liberal portion of salsa to each, and sat across from her. "I'm trying to reach an accommodation with this, okay? Help me out a little."

Later that afternoon, Brian scrolled through airfares to Merida, Mexico. Kris was putting in library time, planning to come over for dinner. Without her around, Brian had to repress a recurrent urge to turn off the terminal and walk over to the travel agency on Canyon Boulevard next to the liquor store.

It wasn't that Brian hated computers; he'd just absorbed from his grandfather an abiding belief in the fundamental importance of human contact. Computers were faster, more efficient, et cetera and so on, but their eyes didn't light up when you walked in and said, "I'd like to look into airfares to Chichén Itzá." It was possible to get a video link to one of the travel-and-tourism nets, but why would anyone do that when they could just walk around the corner onto Canyon Boulevard and talk to the fearsomely brisk and smiling young women at Canyon Travel? Brian was old-fashioned, so old-fashioned in fact that it was old-fashioned to be old-fashioned like he was. He knew this, and it changed nothing except for his teeth-gritted determination to get the damned reservation on the computer so there would be one less thing for him and Kris to argue about. If he went to Canyon Travel now, she would doubtless misconstrue it as a gesture of sublimated disdain for her piggybacks, and that was the last thing in the world Brian wanted.

So he scrolled through menus. As it turned out, it was easier to fly into Cozumel than Merida, and the park-service maglev shuttle from Cozumel was faster than the bus from Merida. Brian bought plane and maglev tickets, then started thinking about a place to stay. Grandpop would have camped, even at ninety-seven, but Brian felt that undertaking a journey to Mexico was gesture enough. He didn't need to sleep in the mud too.

There was a hotel, though, where he and Grandma had stayed after a downpour...

Brian pulled up a fresh screen and dug around in Grandpop's photo album. Names and places skated across the screen: Annapurna and Allagash, Gizeh and Gobi, Yosemite and Yucatan. Aha. The Piramide Inn, starting place of Chichén Itzá tourists since time immemorial, or at least since the nineteen-seventies. There was Grandpop with his new girlfriend Eliza Millett, later Grandma Liza, grinning for an anonymous photographer who hadn't quite managed the focus on Grandpop's old 35-millimeter Pentax. Grandpop was hiding a cigarette behind his back, and Grandma was trying not to laugh out loud at something someone had just said. Had the photographer made a joke? In English or Spanish?

"Hm," Brian said, and ran a search for the Piramide Inn. It popped up immediately, almost obscured by a phalanx of aggressive bubblescreen ad-links. Brian patiently waited for those to pop, and then he set about making reservations at the Piramide. The symmetry of it appealed to him. Continuity.

He'd heard the back door slam, but he didn't really register Kris's arrival until she was in the bedroom with him, looking over his shoulder at the overlapping screens. "Brian," she said.

"Just a second."

"Brian, look at me."

He did. She was practically jumping in place, a wide and excited smile lighting up her face. "I want to go with you," she said.

This was more of a surprise than, in retrospect, Brian thought it should have been. "You do?"

"Yeah, I do." She nodded and smiled, waiting for him.

He found himself nodding and smiling too. "Great," he said. "Yeah, excellent. This'll be good for us. Time together, in a strange place. Yeah. This'll be good."

They kissed. Kris was a little sweaty, and Brian could feel her heartbeat where his fingers traced the hollow of her throat.

The Cenote de Sacrificios gaped at his feet before he was really ready for it, a perfectly cylindrical hole in the ground fifty meters across and twenty deep, with still green water at the bottom like the pupil of a blind eye reflecting the scattered clouds of the Yucatan sky. Omphalos, Brian thought. Next to him Kris said, very softly, "The lugubrious associations attaching to it fill the imagination with indescribable melancholy."

"What?"

She looked at him for the first time since they'd left the Piramide Inn. "It's what Desiree Charnay said when he wrote about the Cenote. He explored the whole area in the eighteen eighties." Her nose wrinkled, ever so slightly, and she looked back down into the water. "They dredged it in 1904 because Spanish records said that the Maya threw gems in with sacrificial victims, honoring the rain god. Edward Herbert Thompson did that. He found skeletons and all kinds of jade, archaeological treasures…" Kris trailed off and smiled self-consciously. "Right. Ugly American."

That was a response, Brian thought. And I didn't say anything.

"Oh my God," Kris said, suddenly delighted. "Did you know he once wrote an essay suggesting that the Maya were survivors of Atlantis?" Her laughter rang bright from the Cenote's bare stone walls. She was no longer speaking to Brian.

"Chichén," he said, to distract himself. *Mouth of the well.* He knew that much just from the tour guide's theatrically convivial Spanglish introduction. To the Maya, the Cenote was a passage between worlds, a spirit gate. Grandpop would have called it superstitious bullshit, but his tone of voice would have been tinctured with admiration.

Brian worked his way around to the other side of the Cenote, away from the concrete apron at the end of the causeway that led back to the main plaza of Chichén Itzá. He didn't speak to Kris before he went, and he was glad to see that she was following. It meant she still knew he was there.

Several times since they'd gotten off the maglev shuttle, she'd fugued out on him, standing still but not rigid and looking at nothing in particular, her mouth moving but only drifting snatches of sound coming out. Brian wasn't sure whether this was an improvement on the unconscious logorrhea or not. She always came back after a few seconds, but the spaces of her absence were deeply unnerving.

"Time," Brian said to her when she caught up with him. He'd come two hundred degrees or so counterclockwise from the end of the causeway. A thick stand of brush had survived the tourist onslaught long enough to disguise his intent.

"I think he would appreciate this," Kris said as Brian took an aluminum vial about the size of a cigar tube from the thigh pocket of his shorts.

"Yeah," he said. "I think so too."

With that he unstoppered the vial, leaned out as far as he safely could, and tipped a long plume of ash into the shadowed depths of the Cenote de Sacrificios. Kris watched him, and when he'd returned the tube to his pocket, she laid a hand gently on the back of his neck.

"Nobody believed they died," she said. "They were supposed to be carried away by the *chacs,* rain gods who lived in the earth."

Brian considered this for a while, then shook his head. "They died," he said.

Hunger followed with impolite quickness on the heels of Brian's moment of mourning. He and Kris walked slowly back up the causeway, looking at the people who, like them but unlike them, had come to Chichén Itzá from wherever they had come from. It was, Brian figured, a pretty typical traveler's moment, but that didn't change its impact on him. Take several thousand people, he thought. Remove them from familiar surroundings and lump them together in a place they've all always wanted to see, and you find out just where similarities refract into differences.

Me, Brian Bruckner, I'm different from them. But I want to be different from them in some way that makes my similarities with Kristine Albritton meaningful. I want to see us as a united pair in the midst of this anonymous throng.

As soon as he'd finished that thought, lust ran right up the back of hunger and trampled it out of his mind.

"Hey," he said to Kris, trying not to grin the way he wanted to grin, "let's find us a little secluded place."

She played it cool, only quirking an eyebrow and letting a smile play at the corners of her mouth. "My goodness," she said. "It's true what they say about funerals."

Somewhere near the boundary of the park, they found a secluded little overgrown test trench and made love with much suppression of giggles and awkward slapping at opportunistic mosquitoes. Nobody bothered them, and once Brian had located the bug spray in one pocket of his shorts (ignoring Kris's arch joke about the aluminum tube riding against his thigh), things went more smoothly. So smoothly, in fact, that afterward they nestled into a hollow and fell asleep.

That was just broadcast worldwide to anyone who knew where to look, Brian thought distantly, stupefied by sex and the afternoon heat. Sweat trickled down his belly into his navel. The ground was soft and much cooler than the air.

But heck, what a rugged guy I am, rolling around in the Yucatan jungle. Let 'em watch.

As he fell asleep, he was thinking about Edward Herbert Thompson, one more Ugly American digging trenches in search of lost Atlantis.

By the time Brian stirred again, the light under the forest canopy had purpled into something like dusk. Kris was nowhere to be seen.

Brian got dressed and clambered out of the trench onto a trail. Not seeing Kris anywhere nearby, he headed back into the center of the park. Two thoughts competed for attention in his head: he was hungry (*ravenousstarvinginsatiable,* he thought in a crude parody of Kris) and he was worried about Kris. The worry was wrapped around a core of anger.

Between El Mercado, the excavated marketplace, and the Grupo de las Mil Columnas, some kind of memorial building with an altar attached to the Templo de los Guerreros, a new marketplace had sprung into being. The rows of vendor carts weren't technically legal on park grounds, but like many other things in turbocapitalized Mexico, technicalities were easily smoothed over with the proper application of pesos. Smells of fruit, cooking meat, spices, peppers, and beer fractured Brian's attention. He hesitated, then plunged on through the market in search of Kris.

Just at the thinning fringe of the market crowds, he thought he heard her voice. Brian ducked behind a tamale stand, nearly had a heart attack when a small hairless dog scrambled up to sniff him, then found Kris under a tree, deep in animated conversation with a tall, angular woman wearing cutoff army fatigue pants and a Toluca soccer jersey. "Jesus, Kris," he said, throwing his arms up as he approached them. "You couldn't leave a note?"

As the words left his mouth, Brian became aware of an incongruity between his speech and theirs. Discerning exactly where the difference lay absorbed his entire mind for what seemed like a long time, but Kris and the other woman had barely turned their heads toward him when he realized that they hadn't been speaking English. Kris's dream, Brian thought. He looked at the other woman, olive-skinned and black-haired.

"What—" he began.

Kris said, "Brian. Yael. Yael, Brian."

"You met here," Brian said, or asked. He wasn't sure.

They exchanged a glance. Yael said something to Kris, who grinned and repeated the phrase, then for Brian's benefit said, "Not exactly."

"Your dream," he said. "Kris, were you talking to her in your dream?"

"Speaking Hebrew," Kris said, "and I didn't even know I was speaking, and I didn't even know I knew Hebrew, and I didn't really know we'd met until I ran into her here." She blinked and said, *"Ivrit, Hebreo, Hebreu, Hebraisch."*

"Ran into," Brian said. Something was starting to come together in his head. He started to pursue it, but just then another man approached them, flinging up his hands almost exactly as Brian had. "Yael, where have you been?" he asked, his voice just a shade below a shout. "You can't just walk away like that, this is Mexico, what are you doing?" He glared suspiciously at Kris and Brian. Brian couldn't help but crack a smile.

"I was just doing the same thing," he said, and stuck out his hand. "Brian Bruckner."

"Nathan ben-Zvi," the other man introduced himself, and then they all stood looking at each other for a long moment.

"This is Kris," Brian said. "I just found out she speaks Hebrew."

Yael said something to Kris, who reached to clasp Brian's hand. "I'll be back," she said, and went with Yael across the plaza toward the ancient observatory, El Caracol.

"What did she say?" Brian asked Nathan.

"She said she wanted Kris to meet someone," Nathan answered. He shook his head. "It's like they're at a reunion."

This comment provoked a relieved feeling of fellowship in Brian. Yes, he thought. That's right. Nathan felt just like he did. They gazed at the spot in the crowd where Kris and Yael had disappeared.

"I read that there are babies who get Uplinked *in utero,* and never bother to learn to talk," Nathan said after a time. "They could, but they never bother."

This idea staggered Brian. To be Uplinked before you had any direct, unmediated experience of the world...were these babies picking up language from their links, or were they, dear God, forming their own language, a baby-language with a million words for mother? What did they say to each other?

"Before long," Nathan said, "they won't even notice the rest of us."

"Sure they will."

Nathan turned to him, a deep crease between his eyebrows. "Why? Why would they? Even now, Yael has an entire social, intellectual, emotional sphere that I know nothing about. That I *can* know nothing about. That I have no access to. And she was twenty-six when she Uplinked. A baby...what use does a baby have for the world when it has its Link before it's ever taken a breath?" He fell silent.

Brian wanted to disagree. Nathan's perspective seemed alarmist, wild-eyed, irrational. But when Brian remembered Kris naming the weeds in the back yard and then saying *Homo sapiens* to him without knowing it, he had to ask himself: *How much else is going on that neither one of us consciously knows about? What bridges are we building in other directions?*

El Caracol loomed to the south, crowds gathering on its observatory deck, more people streaming up its stairways that faced the cardinal directions. Brian wondered who Kris and Yael were meeting there, wondered too why they needed to meet at all if they'd already lived in each other's dreams through Uplink. Must be because they were adults, he decided. The Uplink is laid over the top of a deep matrix of impulses to connect physically, to get close to other humans. But the babies, Jesus. Was Nathan right? Against his better judgment, Brian caught himself mimicking Kris again: El Caracol, the snail, *die Schnecke. Escargot?*

It was a Spanish name anyway. What had the Maya called it? Now that Brian thought of it, Chichén Itzá was a bizarre melange of Spanish and Mayan names: Tzompantli stood next to the Juego de Pelota, the Cenote Xtoloc next to El Caracol, Chichén Itzá itself in the state of Yucatan between Merida and Valladolid. Different histories coming together, Brian thought, and only one really survived. The Spaniards won; the Maya are a curiosity. But they were right about this place: *Chichén,* mouth of the well. Gateway from this world to the next.

Looking over his shoulder, Brian saw the massive pyramid called El Castillo, the Castle, its eastern side in deep shadow. The sun was setting. Pyramid before me, he thought, and pyramid behind, and time like two pyramids aimed toward each other, the invisible point of their meeting the fulcrum of the present. Gateways. Into the Uplinked world.

His mind ran in circles like this for several minutes as the sun fell behind the treeline. "You here for the comet?" Nathan asked.

Brian nodded. "It's kind of a commemorative thing. For my grandfather."

"Ah," Nathan said, a little uncomfortable. "We're honeymooning. Yael's idea. If you don't want to see the comet, don't look to the south. It'll be clear any minute."

"You think they're here to see it?" Brian asked, and from the look on Nathan's face he knew that Nathan understood who he meant by *they*. Already the Uplinked were taking on a collective identity.

"Yeah," Nathan said. "It's a bithead thing, like some kind of organizational meeting or something. I heard Yael muttering about it."

"She dreams too," Brian said, and Nathan nodded.

Bithead, Brian thought, offended by the term despite a strong desire to use it himself. Pejorative slang was a powerfully comforting thing.

"I was thinking how strange it is that they even need to get together," Brian said. His objectivity surprised him; apart from the consequences to human culture, he was already beginning to figure out that Kris was lost to him, and still he talked about it like it was happening in a movie. He had an urge to blame even that on the Uplink: even thinking about it robbed him of the ability to experience anything immediately, in itself.

But that was bullshit. He'd known Kris was receding from him for a while, and this distance was his way of accepting what he'd prepared for.

He tried to joke his way out of it. "Man, I used to think I didn't understand women. But guys like you and me, this is something different."

Nathan smiled, but just barely. Brian could see that he too knew that coming to Chichén Itzá, he'd lost the woman in his life, and apparently Nathan hadn't been prepared the way Brian had. Of course, Brian hadn't known he'd been prepared until just then.

"It's mostly men, actually," Nathan said. "I read that only about thirty percent of Uplinks are performed on women."

"Well, aren't we lucky," Brian said.

Kris and Yael materialized out of the crowd and the dusk. Yael took Nathan's hands and said something softly in Hebrew. Brian heard Kris in his head: *Ivrit, Hebreo, Hebreu, Hebraisch.*

She walked up to him, made no move to touch him. Didn't really look at him, even; her face stayed turned toward the southwest, where El Caracol nestled dark against the last glow of sunset.

"They're here, aren't they?" Brian said to her. "The ones who could come."

"Yes. They're here," she said. To him but not really to him. Brian, not wanting to see the comet yet, cupped a hand around the orbit of his left eye and followed her line of sight to the flat top of El Caracol, dense with people looking up at the sky. A hundred, perhaps. Two hundred. He didn't know. They spilled onto the upper terraces below the observatory deck. He felt an almost gravitational tug on his hand, the night-before-Christmas desire to see, but he resisted it.

"This is why you wanted to come," he said, meaning it as a question, but it didn't come out that way even though he'd wanted to give her the chance to deny it. The possibility of reconciliation, snatched from a depth of separation he hadn't understood until just right then, arose and passed in her silent averted gaze. She saw the crowd, knew without asking which of them were speaking to her, and did not at that moment consciously count him among their number. It did not occur to her to deny what was so obviously and axiomatically and dispassionately true.

The long moment on the rim of the Cenote de Sacrificios replayed itself in Brian's mind: the spread of ash on dark water, yes, and the touch of her fingers on the back of his neck, but mostly the moment when those fingers had lifted away and the last real possibility of contact between them had drifted like a sunlit plume of ash down into the gateway between worlds. A twist of regret caught Brian's breath, and he thought *I wish I'd known.*

Kris was murmuring again, almost subvocalizing the way Grandpop in his extremity had ghosted words into the speaker by his bed. On top of El Caracol, an answering murmur rippled in the damp night air, the accidental voicings of a newborn human symphony.

She started climbing the steps, her pace slow and certain, her face lifted to the sky. Brian followed her to the first platform and stopped as she continued up the worn stone steps. Yael was a step ahead of her. When Kris reached the observatory platform he almost said something. Instead he allowed his gaze to be drawn at last to the southern sky.

Comet Halley was past perihelion, moving past Earth back into the vasty deeps at the edge of the Solar System, its tail leading it into its final sojourn. It had given too much of itself this time and it would never return, but in compensation it blazed in elegiac brilliance across an arm's length of the early summer sky. "Hey there, hairy star," Brian breathed in greeting, forgetting for a moment everything but the comet's beautiful dying fall into his eyes that were only his.

When he looked away from it, Kris was gone. The dome of El Caracol stood above a tableau of still figures with heads tilted back like Easter Island monoliths and mouths unconsciously forming words that blended into what almost but not quite ever became a kind of chant. Somehow the extended topography of heads and shoulders, black against the faintest light still in the sky, reminded Brian of the Indian Peaks, shouldering each other aside to look down into his grandfather's hospice room. Another gravitational urge drew him, this time to join, and Brian took three slow steps up toward the observatory platform, feeling for each step with his gaze locked on the rows of starlit silhouettes. Looking for Kris, knowing what he had to do to really find her. Acquiescing.

Almost imperceptibly, people began to move. Small groups slowly flowed toward the edges of the platform, began to drip down the stairway in twos and threes. Two women passed Brian, not meeting his eyes, glancing over their shoulders at the remaining figures scattered erect and murmuring around the observatory dome. Others followed, nudging Brian to the edge of the stair. On each face he saw a variant of the same expression: awestruck, fearful, uncomprehending wonder. None of them spoke, as if the undulating drone of the Uplinked watchers had made them fearful of speech.

They passed, and Brian stood alone on the terraced flank of El Caracol. At the edge of his field of vision, Comet Halley shone like an incandescent veil. In its light he could make out faces on the stone summit.

He stopped himself before he could find Kris. Acquiesce to that, he told himself. Eyes closed, he listened to the crest and fall of sound, wanting at least to pick her voice from the aural palimpsest that surrounded him. He soaked it in, felt again the tidal urge to join, to find a way through the noise to emergent understanding. Time slipped by, and he began to parse single voices, most of them male. He ignored them, concentrating on the women, moving his mouth silently to get a sense of their cadence and inflection, knowing he'd recognize Kris from that even if her voice was already altering the way it had in the garden, before he'd even decided to come to Chichén Itzá on a stupid romantic memorial pilgrimage, *alone without any idea of how alone...*

The sound of his own voice snapped him back into himself. Parroting again. Picking sounds, syllables, running words over his own tongue without knowing or, in the end, really caring what they meant. He couldn't even remember what he'd been saying, or in which language.

"Hey," someone said, and tapped him on the shoulder.

Brian blinked and started away from the contact. On the step below him stood Nathan ben-Zvi. They looked at each other for a long silent moment before Nathan said, "Don't you think...I mean, we should go, right? Come on."

Nathan's face looked like it might fly apart at any second. A muscle spasmed in his jaw, his eyes stared beneath a deeply-etched frown on his forehead, and the skin around his mouth was tight and pebbled with tension. His voice stayed remarkably steady, though, steadier in fact that Brian's when Brian swallowed and said, "Yeah."

Do I look like that? Brian thought. Nathan's wife is up there. It's worse for him. His wife. At least Kris and I hadn't made each other any promises.

Still he came back to get me.

He let Nathan stay a step ahead of him, no more, as they descended the steps and walked away from the newborn unity of the voices on El Caracol.

> # The Sea Wind
> # Offers Little Relief

He looked up when his jailers entered the cell, imagining the aether pouring in around them, lifted in Coriolis swirls by the passage of their bodies. It was a moment of fantasy; the aether had been there before their entrance, monitoring him, streaming into his lungs with each steady inhalation, transmitting information about his vital functions. He imagined despite this a purity in his solitude, a purity at least partially real, and the presence of the jailers fractured this dear illusion. Their entrance bludgeoned him with the Assimilated world that had excommunicated him at his sentencing, one hundred and forty-seven years ago. One hundred forty-seven years. He had become an old man.

The first jailer spoke to him, and he discovered again that solitary years had not inured him to shame. To be spoken to was to feel the impact not only of sound wave against tympanum but of one's own exile against the memory of choices wrongly taken. The aether conducted thoughts to everyone but him.

I should be comfortable. My space is my own, and I am surrounded by furniture and possessions of my own choosing. I am alone, but that too is my choice, and I have had many years to acquiesce to its consequences. Alone in my room—my cell—I find the virtue of contemplation.

In contemplation, though, and in comfort, I find sadness.

I write by hand, to place myself within a matrix of relationships available to me only through mimicry. The words I produce inspire joy and gratitude, and these emotions in turn inspire my attempt at reconstruction. Reading: what must it have been like for him? I imagine and I write, a scholar of languages sketching himself into the experience of a scholar of languages. Allow me this latitude; without it I would be stifled. The story will not be told the way it happened, but if I separate myself from time to time…please. Allow me this latitude. The Assimilation is centuries past, but because I cannot fear it I fear its memory instead, the history-spanning shadow of its occurrence, and this fear provokes inopportune utterances. From time to time I must assert myself. My self.

He bit back his shame and listened to the words. They came quickly, in an unfamiliar accent, and it took him several moments to piece together what had been said. Like bright light after long darkness, they dazzled his mind.

"You are required to read," the first jailer had said to him.

He breathed steadily, imagining the aether streaming in and out, binding to the dead receptors in his brain. He tried to calm the sudden spasming of his heart.

"Am I not," he began, and his voice failed him. Eyes closed, he sipped water and spoke again. "Am I not imprisoned for reading?" A rhetorical question. Words without information, run across his tongue to remind it how to speak.

"Come with us," the first jailer said. Something shifted in the scholar's head and he understood that the jailer did not know how to speak the language he was using. He was reciting, a parrot-jailer squawking out words. So, the scholar thought. They have lost the habit of speech.

As, for other reasons, have I.

An image of religious intensity presented itself: the aether as a visible, faintly shining presence, inscribed with sounds. The Assimilated jailer had only to wonder how to say a thing, and his tongue would begin to form the words. Without the natural cadence of a practiced speaker, though, the words did not fall together naturally into sentences.

The Sea Wind Offers Little Relief

Understanding this, the scholar rose and followed the jailers out into the white corridor. He shuffled, and his hips ached. Through his memory passed fragmentary sensations of youth: running. Leaning with a long-dead friend into the sting of a sea wind. The ecstatic exertion of making love.

The white corridor curved gently to the left. At regular intervals the smoothness of the walls gave way to recessed doorways. Other cells, he supposed, incarcerating other prisoners much like himself. His crime was not rare.

The jailers stopped, and a door opened on their right. "Enter," the first jailer said.

The room was the same size and shape as his cell. The scholar was comforted by the sameness of the room's shape and color, but agitated by the difference of its furnishings. No bed; no toilet; no sink; no point-source of light. A chair and table, and diffuse whiteness radiating from the walls. The table occupied the greater part of its floor space, and a jailer stood between him and the table. She was blind.

"Read," said the blind jailer. The vowel went on a little too long, the final consonant punched a little too harshly between tongue and alveolar ridge.

A cruel joke, thought the scholar. It was not unheard of. Prison duty eroded guards' humanity just as imprisonment gradually reduced inmates to automata; sometimes the only release for either was displacement of frustration and self-loathing onto the other. But to read: to track one's eyes across a field of symbols, parsing and connecting, inferring and interpreting, recreating symbol as idea, as emotion, as experience. He had no idea how long since he had done it, no idea in fact if he still could. At times he dreamed of reading, but upon waking could never be certain that his dream had authentically rendered the reality. What persisted beyond waking was a sense that the readingness of reading survived, somewhere in the dream hemisphere of his brain.

They were telling him to read. He had been imprisoned, many years ago, for his literacy. These two facts refused to accommodate each other.

Avarice overcame him, flooding from a reservoir of desire his silence had kept dammed. His hands trembled; his breath whistled in his throat; something fluttered in his stomach and he was aware that he had not moved his bowels in several days. They were telling him to read. He stepped around the blind jailer, approached the table, saw on the live part of its surface: words.

The scholar covered his face with his hands and fell to the ground. When the blind jailer touched him, he began to scream. His voice, frail from disuse, soon gave out, and by the time the jailers had taken him back to his cell, his screams lacked even the power to keep him awake. He slept as if stricken by catatonia, and his last thought was to remember his name, emerging by some graphological alchemy from the field of letters that had etched itself into his mind.

I know that he did in fact suffer a brief episode upon his first viewing of the text. This much is established in the records of the time, recovered from the aether at the end of Assimilation. What I do not know are his thoughts, but it seems to me that seeing text for the first time in one hundred and forty-seven years must have brought Edmar de Carvalho's identity crashing catastrophically down upon him. I think that he broke down not so much from seeing the words as from seeing what the loss of the words had done to him. Indeed the first question of the poem seems specifically designed to provoke such a reaction.

What is memory? The question like a low cloud
Settles in the sunset, beyond the hero's reach,
Who stands on deck, bright helm held and gray head bowed.

Again he asks. Sea mocks, he thinks, when it should teach.
But it is not up to him, who chases after
Horizons, whose quests bring him back to that same beach

On which he was born, on which the sea-goddess spread
Her legs and left him to dry in the sun until
Neyaus came upon him,

The Sea Wind Offers Little Relief

Edmar de Carvalho looked up from the words. "Neyaus?"

"Nomenclature indigenous to the planet of origin," said the blind jailer, after a pause perceptible only because he knew to expect it. The phrase rolled metronomically from her tongue, carefully memorized and prepared. They knew, then, more than they were willing to tell him; else they would not have taken such care to rehearse for his questions. *Planet of origin,* he thought. Around these bits of information, a plan began to accrete.

Historians of language note at least two independent occurrences of the name Edmar, in German and Anglo-Saxon. Possibly Portuguese offers a third. Unlike its German homophone, a demotic form of the name Ottmar, the Anglo-Saxon name Edmar means "rich sea," or "richness of the sea." To my knowledge, Edmar de Carvalho never knew of this. Even more than irony, I prize this bit of information: it is the one thing I know that I am sure he did not.

---

took him in, soaked his bread

In goat's milk, brushed the sand from his back, and laughing
Taught him to speak, to desire his name, crave knowledge
Of all that was forgotten. This is memory

Under whose whip rhyme falters.

"Read it aloud," the blind jailer said. Edmar de Carvalho began to speak. His recitation fell into the cadence of the poem. At the last line, his voice faltered, and he bent his head to hide his tears from the aether and those who attended to its transmissions.

"Explain," said the jailer, and Edmar de Carvalho's head snapped up. His tears dried and with burning eyes he said, "I will not. You demanded reading. I have provided it." A joke after all, he thought. They probe at my desires, coerce me into a vain exercise of the talents in which I once took such pride.

Unmoved by his anger, the blind jailer said, "The poem goes on. As you explain each portion, more will be made available. The choice is yours."

It was no choice at all. Even the single fact that more lines existed was more than Edmar de Carvalho could resist. Behind it, something else: the jailers, and whoever controlled them, needed to know something, and they thought he could tell them.

Leverage. He did not yet know what it was, or how it might be exercised, but he would find out. For the first time since his imprisonment, his desire and his guilt channeled themselves into the exercise of will.

"I must think," he said, and stood to return to his cell.

In his cell he thought, and when he was done thinking, he forgot. Edmar de Carvalho had the talent of forgetting. It had kept him free as long as anything could have.

It is a talent I wish I had.

He sat in his cell. I sit in mine. He was a prisoner, looking ahead. I am imprisoned only by the specter of him: a collaborator, a traitor. The most unlikely of ancestors.

"It's an imitative epic," said Edmar de Carvalho. He looked up from the text. Its words scrolled through his mind, perfect on the table display. He wondered about the handwriting of the man who had set it down. Certainly a man, something about the language already had told him that, or perhaps just the preconceptions of one too long by himself, who recreates the world in his own image. "I would be better able to contextualize it if I could see the original manuscript artifact."

"Imitative epic," his interrogator said. "The connotation of this phrase is unclear."

"Epic in that it's a poetic story of foundations, or so I would assume from what I've read so far. A story of a hero. Generally a story of origins, of nation-building. Imitative in that it's written in hexameter *terza rima*. Hexameter means a line of twelve syllables, with a number of possible stress counts; *terza rima* describes the poem's rhyme scheme. Greek and Roman epics employed hexameters, and Dante's *Commedia* is the first epic-scale poem written in *terza rima*. The schemes occur throughout the history of European and American poetry, with various embellishments. Perhaps the last significant poet to ring changes on these structures was the Transmillennial Derek Walcott, who combined hexameter and *terza rima* as this poet has, albeit more skillfully." Edmar de Carvalho did not add that Walcott was the last because less than fifty years after his death, dactylic hexameter and poetry itself had drowned in Assimilation. And he had been a scholar of Greek plays, his knowledge of Walcott and Dante conjured from undergraduate seminars two hundred years gone. "Walcott's intent was to explore the utility of epic in constructing stories of culture and perpetuating cultural myths..."

"Enough." The interrogator pivoted to meet the opening door.

―――・●・―――

There is material for a digressive footnote here, one that I shall probably never write, delving into the reflexive nature of any text executed as an inquiry into the nature of understanding text. Words speaking of words, a scholar of languages imagining the predicament of a scholar of languages: I take my place in what seems an endlessly receding spiral of inter-reflecting intelligence. Minds gazing back at what other minds have thought, and leaning forward to imagine what later minds might make of their ruminations. An imitative epic.

―――・●・―――

                                      The hero has a name
That rhymes with nothing, but even now, approaching
The beach of his birth on the sea-wind of his fame

Memories of his name are whales at night, broaching
Amid a moon-shocked glow of foam that hides their shape
From the searching eyes of his mind. Blind reproaching

Of sea-goddess mocking: I am named like seascape,
The hero thinks, a word that slides over many scenes
Like moon-shocked foam, connotation leaving mind agape

At these tricks of meaning. Mind's grasping only gleans
Certainty of difference: Seascapes no more the same
Than sunrise and sunset. Heroic deeds are means

To the end of finding one's name. The end of fame,
The final forgetting. The mind slackens, must forgo
Futures.

I have said that I thought Edmar de Carvalho's identity must have collapsed upon him when, for the first time in a century and more, his gaze was allowed to fall upon written language. It may seem at this point that, like any number of scholars before me, I am confusing, conflating, mistaking the text for the reader, the reader for the author. Edmar de Carvalho did not write the poem; he only read it. But removed from both text and reader as I am, I can no longer just read either. I must write them. This is the majesty of writing, its wonder and its danger. It maps itself onto the topology of our breathing interaction with the universe.

You may assume that I am recovering a bit too much from textual and biographical associations that are less fruitful than I wish to make them. Whether this is true has no bearing on the relevance of my story. Believe it if you wish.

In fact I ask you to. Please. Read me into Edmar de Carvalho, read my reading of him into his reading of the poem.

Deeds beget memories, the hero taking aim

At enemies remembers that moments ago
He was a babe on a beach. And then, the next day,
Anonymous on an anonymous sea he goes

Crying aloud, "Enough thoughts! Ocean, I will say

The Sea Wind Offers Little Relief

What I have done, not said, what my hands have wrought
Not my mind's eye bred. Nameless, I will not stay

So, but will speak myself though it be life's last lot
Like low clouds to see my name written on seascape.
My name, the name I would have chosen and would

Write anew, just as the sea-goddess once wrote me
In her blood on a beach for a goatherd to read.
My blood is the ocean, and on its flood I see

Mother mocking when she should teach. She knows my need,"
The hero cried to banded birds circling his mast,
"I will know hers, and show it her, and on it feed."

Thus saying, the hero leaned into the sea's blast
Closed his eyes, tasted salt, commanded memory
To open her doors, to show him both first and last

Of his actions that like celestial jewelry
Hung shining around the starry neck of renown.
She obeyed,

"This is fairly typical of a certain kind of hero," said Edmar de Carvalho. "A venerable strain of criticism would have it that any hero's journey is every hero's journey, and every hero's journey is undertaken in search of self. The hero here commands the ocean from whence he has come, asserting his control over both elements and origins. The rhetorical trope maps neatly onto the concern with identity. In addition, although I don't think much of the whole, some of the lines are quite fine as poetry."

"Aesthetic judgments are of no interest to us," said the blind jailer. She always stood between Edmar and the door while he read. A routine had established itself over the previous days, whether from administrative directives or the simple inertia of habit he did not know. Every day at the same time—as nearly as he, deprived of aether, timepieces, and natural light, could estimate—his jailers brought him to this room. He was more certain of the room than the time, having counted his steps on the way to it once the jailers had deemed him fit to examine the text again. Every day since then, he had taken approximately the same number of steps, and turned at approximately the same points along the way. Edmar de Carvalho was not prone to compulsive actions, but he remembered the overwhelming shock of seeing words, and he was afraid not only that it would happen again, but that if it did happen again he would be prevented from examining the words again. To exist—not live, exist—for one hundred forty-seven years without reading was horror enough; to weaken at the moment when the lexical exile was ending…unforgivable. Counting alleviated the worst of his nerves. He walked, counted evenly, inhaled evenly through his nose, exhaled evenly through his mouth. Did not think about what lay this or that number of steps beyond the walls of his prison.

"Aesthetic judgments," he said today, holding his voice level, "are part and parcel of the scholar's evaluative process." How to explain that each word of a poem—of any expression—demands an aesthetic response, depends for its meaning and answer on such responses? How to explain that for this ideal he had sacrificed his friends and the best part of himself?

Edmar de Carvalho did not speak. He turned to the poem's next line.

---

and the hero saw the scullery

Where as a stripling boy he broke the knobby crown
Of a leering giant lifting the red-shingled roof
Of the noble house where the goatherd bowed low down

In fealty to a mighty lord, whose flaw was proof
That men given dominion only deserve
Such respect as demands their remaining aloof.

It did not happen overnight. Networks proliferated, absorbed each other; nanotechnology liberated them from the constraints

The Sea Wind Offers Little Relief

of node and conduit; the aether began to coalesce. A slow accretion led eventually to a critical mass, and intercortical information transfer—Uplink, in the argot of its twenty-first-century innovators—destroyed a literate culture that had persisted for seven thousand years. Whatever the benefits, and benefits there were, this fact cannot be gainsaid. But the aether had no moral valence itself; its existence did not demand the legislative and cultural currents that churned in its wake. No teleology demanded the abolition, for security reasons, of non-aetheric communication. The Assimilation could not have happened without aether, but aether did not predetermine Assimilation.

Still, what happened, happened—and how grateful I am to be writing those words twenty-five hundred years after the events I recount (two thousand five hundred years: the distance, in another direction, between Edmar de Carvalho and the Greek plays to which he had devoted his working life). Never imprisoned, I can be objective, or at least dispassionate. I can speak of memories erased, cultures ground to blankness; but my telling assumes the hollow tone of a lecture delivered only to oneself. Edmar de Carvalho at least had auditors. This was his unmaking and his redemption.

He memorized, of course. At the end of each day, he had committed every line to memory. In a strange way, though, he had not read those lines. One hundred forty-seven years of incarceration develops peculiar properties of the mind, one of which is a dissociative sort of compartmentalization, and Edmar de Carvalho had escaped prosecution for so long because he had already possessed this faculty before his arrest.

The Assimilated Powers outlawed writing because it could be hidden, passed around to a select few friends—or conspirators. An incredible metamorphosis: writing, historically a means of disseminating information, became a tool of secrecy when employed by people who knew how to forget. Secrecy itself became treason in a civilization rebuilt upon the universal availability of human knowledge but still beholden to pre-Assimilation ideas of authority and power.

Every technological innovation is used both to consolidate power and to subvert it. The aether, sustained as it was by fantastic technological exertion, could be subverted by equally ingenious technological interference. It could be avoided, though only locally and never for very long. Thoughts could be thought and then forgotten. Even forgotten thoughts hide somewhere in the brain, but Edmar de Carvalho had developed the talent of forgetting things in places where the aether did not look. He became a node in a network of individuals, all born since the first Uplink in 2062, who quietly fought to restore the sanctity of the mind, who rejected the Assimilated axiom that all thought, because it could be shared, must be.

Each of us knows, through anecdote or experience, the power of the mind to suppress trauma, horror, even simple embarrassment. Learning to control this power, to make it an act of will instead of an infantile response, took a certain perversion of aetheric technology as well as a formidable strength. Learning to remember took still more technical and psychological acuity, and surviving for the thirty years and more of their conspiracy demanded an heroic arsenal of aetheric countermeasures in addition to an unswerving commitment: not to anything so trivial as the value of art or the beauty of beauty, but to the incorrigible truth that self and world are incomprehensible without the action of the aesthetic mind. They communicated through poetry, each verse a manifesto declaring the rebellion of the aesthetic living mind against the sublimely anaesthetic power of Assimilation. The aesthetic, perhaps, of revolution.

It was the methodology of every conspiracy in recorded history: each of them knew only what they required to advance the cause one step further. They allowed themselves to forget that they had even forgotten this information until they were called upon to use it again. In honing this skill, they developed an odd sense of distance from themselves, a consciousness that by constructing artificial barriers between parts of their minds, they were cutting themselves into pieces. Estranging themselves from themselves. They did not become precisely insane, but they sailed close enough to insanity's shore that—had there been language for it—they might have been able to speak of its contours.

They were caught, as they knew they would be, and tried, and their jury was every sentient mind on Earth. They were few enough that, after conviction, their memories were spared and their literacy called into service: at evidentiary hearings, primarily, where the apprehended literate acted as witness and defendant, one clamping down on shameful memories, the other anticipating, hoping to survive with mind intact even if the cost was witnessing at the ongoing purge of one's fellows and one's ideals. Edmar de Carvalho was one of those spared. Gradually his role as evidentiary witness had diminished, and after some decades he was left alone in his cell to ponder his betrayals. To keep his mind working, he remembered. He burnished his ability to memorize until it shone, but also until it grew dangerously thin, and he felt that he could see the glow of forgetting behind it.

Edmar de Carvalho had been a scholar of ancient literatures before he had become a conspirator, and the jailers' poem reinvigorated his mind. He knew every word of it long before he had read it carefully, and he forgot it in the way that he had nearly forgotten how to forget. It became a part of him that he did not notice, like a bone in the inner ear. He stored the poem against the possibility that it would be taken away from him, and he doled it out to himself only when he was in the presence of his jailers. At night his lips moved over stanzas he'd examined during the day, making notes on form, alliteration, allusion. His memory reawakened and grew distended with words and images; his tongue formed words, he translated stanzas of the poem into languages he hadn't spoken in more than a century.

Perhaps more importantly, he read himself the way he read the poem: a Brazilian, emigrated as a boy to Australia; a failed conspirator, son of a professor of literatures who named him for an athlete; an amateur astronomer who once wanted to marry a woman from Michigan. Slowly the feeling came over him that after a long stasis, an enforced senescence, he was living again. Thinking again. He began to fantasize escape, to imagine atonement.

"A fairly typical hero's first action," he said to the blind jailer. She did not answer. "Killing giants, rescuing women, and so on. No real surprises." He considered. "The juxtaposition of the young hero and the flawed overlord, though, is interesting, particularly if the lord's downfall is, as it seems, sexually motivated. In some traditions heroes are quite promiscuous; in others chastity and a fanatical hygiene are intrinsic to heroic bearing. I shall be interested to see how this turns out."

As shall I. I am not Edmar de Carvalho, as much as I wish I could be. I try to forget as he learned to forget, but what I wish to banish from my mind is the simple mundanity of my cell, and of my self within it. I try to forget the poem, though like him I have committed it to memory. With you I read it, as I first read it with him; with you I write it, as I first wrote it into my ideas of him, as I first wrote it into my ideas of myself. Each time, the newness of it brings me near his experience of one hundred forty-seven years' absence, ended at last in the presence of words. It is a glorious tale, and alone in my room I find a wild and fierce joy in the telling.

Lusts of his body weakened his noble reserve
He preyed on the women of his house. Wolflike
He came in the night to the quarters, the preserve

Of women. At last his debauches burst the dike
They meekly tried to maintain, and angered they turned
To the giants for help. Our lord's head on a spike,

They begged; his body on a pyre; his son exiled.
These giants stood astride the women's wrathful flood
Grinning and stroking their beards, their senses beguiled

By the scent of angry women's fiery blood.
We will come, they said as one, and free you; but first
We will have the noble seed that forms in the mud

Of your wombs. Each of the six women nearly burst
With the shame, but in turn they nodded and agreed
That their bodies' fruit should slake the giants' thirst.

The agreement thus struck, the six women took heed
That the lord should not visit them until children
Could be birthed, fed and weaned, and sent on goatherd's steed

To the shore where tall giants threw stones at the sky
In spiteful hope of bringing down the distant stars
And forcing the gods to yield their steely secrets.

"Why am I reading this?" Edmar de Carvalho asked finally.

I must stop at this question, to consider the moment at which it was asked. How long did it take him to ask? I do not know. What fears coursed through his mind, what uncertainties? They had told him to read, and he read; but they had not told him what for, and for all he knew, that was the one question he would not be permitted to ask. That he asked it tells more of his fortitude than I possibly could, and so I let pass my impulse to embellish, to filigree with detail and imagined emotion. Edmar de Carvalho considered the possible consequences, and he asked the question. I am cowed by his bravery.

"Why am I reading this?"

"Surely," said the blind jailer, "the balance of power in this situation is clear to you."

Clearer, thought Edmar de Carvalho, than perhaps it is to you. "You brought this from another planet," he said. "An artifact of a failed colony, I assume."

He had waited, and waited, and waited before making this assertion, being fairly sure that he was meant to know that much. The jailer's words *planet of origin* had clearly been intended to channel his thoughts in that direction.

"A reasonable assumption," the jailer said, as he had anticipated she would.

"A record," said Edmar de Carvalho. "Encoded, no doubt, by a literate outlaw as a last futile gesture." Emboldened by intuition, he guessed further. "The only record left."

A twitch at the corner of her mouth. Did she know the game he was (they were?) playing? The jailer said nothing. Edmar de Carvalho kept reading, certain she would have contradicted him if she thought he'd been wrong.

The women, all six, withdrew behind iron bars
They contrived a story of dreadful plague, called down
On women; made the lord believe they blamed his wars

Against their chastity; hid themselves in brown
Cloth and shaded rooms. Discord grew, and ugly words
Began to be spoken about six women's gowns

That grew looser as the lord's hands like vengeful birds
Pecked and tore his servants' hides. Still giggling gossip
Flew faster than the lord's blows; windy rumors whirred

Through rooms grown colder than a dead man's silver lips
Quieter than the last breath before winter dawn.
Six women whispered groans, six women arched their hips

And six children came, and as quickly six were gone.

I have no children. Of all the consequences of solitude, this is the most painful to contemplate. Edmar de Carvalho had children, if not of his body then of his deeds; I myself am among this issue. My solitude, conceived as an homage to him, becomes in this light yet one more instance of my inadequacy to his example. Like all who are grateful to live but do not bear children, I suffer the pain of not being able to reciprocate the gift given to me. Regrets are one of my few indulgences, and to palliate my regret I keep and continue this story. Each of us must accommodate our errors, and in spite of them find happiness.

The lord's guest alone knew, the stripling foreign boy
Washed up by a storm, amid weeds, like monsters' spawn

Or windburned remains of a god's forgotten toy.
Finding generosity in that house of secrets
The boy who was not yet a hero knew the ploy

And when the giants came, and cooling freshets
Of loyal blood flowed over flagstone floors
He lay in wait with stolen sword, and his regrets

Mounted with the number of bodies blocking doors.
At last a curious giant peered in, at last
The boy could act, and killing the giant make some poor

Recompense for the fallen house's noble past
That now blood-soaked began to burn, timbers
Fueled by giant's blood in a fiery blast.

The boy fled choking smoke, flames, falling embers.
Bodies caught like candles. Six women he found
Forgotten behind iron bars, and with them he clambered

Free of that falling house. Outside, they looked around
Hoping that other survivors would join them there.

"Telling, the ambiguity of the giants' portrayal," said Edmar de Carvalho.
"Explain."
"Are there giants on this planet? Physically large humanoids?"
The blind jailer did not answer him, and short seconds later the first interrogator entered the room. Edmar de Carvalho waited, savoring the forgotten sensation of being awaited. One hundred forty-seven years of speaking only to himself had taught him something about outlasting the patience of an interlocutor.

The interrogator would speak soon enough, and Edmar de Carvalho soon enough would answer.

The interrogator's posture shifted, ever so slightly. "Of what value is this information to your task?"

Edmar de Carvalho nodded slightly. Understanding glimmered.

"If there are in fact giants on this planet, particularly giants who interact with the other sentient species who I assume form the basis for this noble house, then the poem must be read in a particular way. If there are not, or you are uncertain, other readings obtain. It will be useful to me to know whether the giants are meant figuratively or as a literal representation of real biological entities." His mouth dry, Edmar de Carvalho reached for the cup of water he kept by his left hand.

Again the interrogator did not immediately respond. Edmar de Carvalho imagined the interrogator's words propagating through the aether: *How much do I tell him?* It took longer than he would have imagined for the answer to arrive, or perhaps his concentration was such that its ferocity simply curved time around the gravid silence in the white cell.

"It is reasonable to infer," the interrogator said, "that the giants here are representative of another culture, and that their physical stature figuratively represents an imbalance in relations of power."

In the pause following this pronouncement, Edmar de Carvalho realized that he had, however inadvertently, been teaching. Already the jailers—or whoever spoke through them—began to grasp figuration. He wondered if this recovered knowledge would propagate.

"Then you see," he said. "Clearly this culture has brought much of value to the people whom the heroic speaker has adopted as his own. Just as clearly, though, this bounty has come at an intolerable price. Extending the symbolic framework, one might understand the children as manifestations of a worry that the other culture has compromised the future of the civilization represented by the lord's household."

They lifted him away from the table, and sent him back to his cell.

The Sea Wind Offers Little Relief

My admiration for Edmar de Carvalho perhaps reaches its apex here, when with so much to say he is able to say so little. He must have known then.

I say *must have,* and I fall back into the speculating, deifying mob, and—you must understand this—*I enjoy the fall.* Indeed, at this moment fidelity to scholarly disinterest becomes impossibly difficult, something like Christian purity of spirit in a fallen world. Reading of Edmar de Carvalho, writing about him, I become preterite. Salvation recedes to the faintest horizons of abstraction.

In Purgatory, then, or even the outer rings of the Hell of hagiography, I tell the story the way it must be told. Like Edmar de Carvalho, I hold the rest of it away while I focus on those few moments in which I see cruxes, tangled matrices of desire and fear and dawning hope. Every fall is a forgetting, and at times such as this, when I feel his presence in the room—when I can even imagine his body, bony like mine, with rounded shoulders—I think I have forgotten properly. Perhaps, like him, I am learning to forget things in the way they must be forgotten in order to feel the connection that sustains us when the distance between bodies grows so great.

Something like the scene I have set down must have occurred, and Edmar de Carvalho, whose name I whisper like a charm under my breath, must have known. He must have seen the poem for what it was, and seen as well how close he skirted the edge of telling too much. In my room, so unlike his, I write, and am unworthy. It is a marvelous abasement.

Ash-faced, the lord's son, knees pressed into cold ground

And his eyes with hate reflecting the hellish glare
Cursed the boy: "You knew the giants would come. You
Knew the bargain these women made, knew that they would
    tear

The heart from this house whose beginnings memory
Cannot discern. I condemn you to wander with one
Of these women, and to watch the other five die.

Thus may you have regrets enough to sustain you
And divided love, since I have no family
Among whom to divide my own." With that, the son

Turned his broad back on them and left that land behind.
Six women and one boy wandered forsaken:
Such are giants' oaths, such the hero's first lesson.

Rolling from round horizons, bearing memories
Of his birth, the sea wind offers little relief.

These words too I say to myself: *The sea wind offers little relief.* Their truth, which is a function of the truth of the poem, aches in my memory, in my sense of duty to him. The line carries a meaning to me only because of the meaning it carried for Edmar de Carvalho; my reading of it is always, always a reading of him. At the end of these lines, the poet—the privilege of naming him belongs of course to Edmar de Carvalho—speaks for himself and for his hero. He doubles himself the way I must refrain from doubling myself. He is his own hero, while I can look on mine only from a great distance, squinting to make out a resemblance.

"It ends here?" Edmar de Carvalho looked up at the blind jailer, knowing the answer. The evidence of the last line proved what he had surmised before, and the knowledge hurt him.

Without turning her head she answered. "There is no more."

He mused. "The rhyme breaks apart at the end. I think he lost interest. He must have known the end was coming."

"The end of what?"

"Your speech is improving," he said, allowing amusement to distract him, to mask his thoughts. This close to escape, to atonement, he could not let his guard down. "That was the first time you've spoken that it hasn't sounded unnatural."

The next day a different blind jailer had taken her place. This was Edmar de Carvalho's latest lesson in the precariousness of

The Sea Wind Offers Little Relief

his position, the proximity of telling too much, the cost of acting to preserve oneself. Unable to talk about the poem, he went back to his room and lay sleepless and tormented. What would they do to her, a young woman already blinded to perform her duties? Had she anticipated the moment when she would learn to speak too well, spent the hours listening to him mutter knowing that every communication, every unconscious absorption of his inflections and cadences, brought her closer to the end of her assignment? Of her life? Edmar de Carvalho wept, imagining his words like radiation, building up within her until she gave forth her toxicity as clear and beautiful speech.

When the jailers came for him the next morning he said to them, "I know what happened to your colony."

"Tell us," they commanded.

"I will not," he said. "And you cannot force me. We will trade."

The first jailer spoke. Edmar de Carvalho wondered if he was deliberately keeping his speech patterns rough, his vowels and diphthongs disproportionate. Perhaps he had learned from the fate of the blind woman who had guarded the text. Fresh guilt arose in Edmar de Carvalho, a feeling grown loathsome from long familiarity. He squeezed it ruthlessly back into the airless den of his conscience.

"What do you offer?" the first jailer said.

"I have your answer," answered Edmar de Carvalho. "I will deliver it to you when I am set down on the world where the poem was written. I am old, and I do not wish to die in this prison."

"What assurance do we have?"

"Neyaus is the name of a culture, is it not? Perhaps a race's name for itself. Certainly not imposed from without. It is not simply a female figure as it is represented in this poem."

They shut the door, and never again did Edmar de Carvalho look upon the text, save when he conjured it from its nook in the forgetting-place of his exemplary mind.

The sea wind offers little relief. The words recalled to him a conversation, one hundred and fifty years old. A disconsolate group of five, barefoot on a beach, escaping an academic conference, breathing fearfully the South Pacific air. Behind them the Sydney

Opera House and the harbor, nothing like Rio's harbor; before them ocean, so much like Rio's ocean. The particulars of the conversation have escaped him, but Edmar de Carvalho remembers one of his co-conspirators saying something: *This, too, shall pass,* or some other weary sentiment born of resignation. The Assimilation has taken their sixth member, and the five know that their time has run out.

No, another says. *What if it doesn't?*

It is an argument they have had before, and the third joins. *Take the long view. The ocean is as close to eternity as a human can understand,* he says. *It will survive Assimilation. Something else will too, even if it's not us.*

Someone—Edmar de Carvalho himself? he does not remember—says: *True; but it does not help.*

A pause, a look out, away from land, a bearded chin lifted and then dropping again. Words freighted with despondency. That they form the last line in the poem seems too improbable a coincidence; that the line recalls Edmar de Carvalho's name removes all possibility of accident.

It was more than exegesis. Edmar de Carvalho had experienced deprivation, and he had borne as best he could the anguish of treason and the sorrow of unfulfilled hope. The words on the table resonated in his mind, permeated his memories of what he had done before being imprisoned: *to wander with one, and watch five die.* Close enough. So completely did he drown in them that he concluded that they could mirror no experience other than his. A rigorous scholar might laugh at this conclusion, at the exercise of intuition unfettered by judgment and seemly disinterest; Edmar de Carvalho had, however, during his decades in prison lost the trick of scholarly rigor. In the words on the page he saw the speech and cipher of a life he had left one hundred forty-seven years before, the rebuke and exhortation of a friend long betrayed and dead. Even without the last line, he saw this.

It was his fortune, too, to be wrong about Neyaus in exactly the right way.

"Now you will tell us," the first interrogator said to him. Edmar de Carvalho looked at him, saw deprivation in the harsh lines of his face. Away from the aether's influence, the jailers began to look human to him again. He began to notice their faces.

This is why they did not search more thoroughly, he thought. Being neither convicts nor fanatics, they had no reason to suffer separation from the aether, and they could not bear the loneliness of themselves any more than a child in its amniotic ocean can withstand the stillness of its mother's heart. He thought he understood. Colonizing exile existed as an option because the Assimilated Worlds—Earth, Luna, Mars—were just civilized enough to renounce capital punishment, and just vindictive enough to demand a form of permanent sanction. No organized and Assimilated body had any intent of making a permanent foray beyond the insulating murmur of the aether to build on the foundations laid by spacefaring felons, and the aetheric infrastructure could not reach across interstellar distances.

Still, they had to monitor. Assumptions propagated through the aether, reinforced each other until they acquired the weight of fact, and became part of the collective axiomatic underpinnings of the Assimilated Worlds. One of those assumptions, rarely articulated, concerned the necessity of monitoring the exiled colonists. If it was perceived that they were allowed to simply disappear, much of the threat of exile disappeared; the possibility of surveillance and further exile, more than the reality of either, maintained the punitive illusion. Thus this pointless mission to investigate the ruins of a failed colony.

"Yes," said Edmar de Carvalho. "Now I will."

But he did not. Not exactly. He knew that the perfunctory surveillance would last only as long as Assimilation, and he did not believe that Assimilation could survive itself. Among the survivors on this world he would spread that belief. He would uproot Earth from the colonists' past and place it before them, within the grasp of their future.

"They have all died," he said. "I will stay here. I will discover for you the rest of the story."

It is the oldest choice: death or exile.

Every culture knows it and has enshrined it in myth, mortared it into the stalwart arches of literature. In this telling, it shapes itself thus:

A man fights for justice, which is always for this man the right to be only himself. He gathers about him a group of like-minded rebels, and their existence is their first disobedience. Secrecy is the next.

The group is caught, branded treasonous, made through guile to implicate each other. Convicted, they are offered the choice: death or exile. All choose exile, and are cut off from their peers as swiftly and surely as if their senses had been stricken from them and their bodies abandoned on a shore of brackish water and stinging flies.

Here is where this story is different. Some of this group choose to suffer their separation in the enforced solitude of incarceration. Others undertake a second exile, traversing the space between stars as if in the completion of that voyage lies the possibility of returning across the space between minds. Those who remain never learn which of their fellows stay, and which depart.

No records, save an elliptical fragment of epic poetry—a cryptic and desperate message—survive of the dispute that led to the collapse of the exile colony. It must have been another old story, told for the first time under this new sky: the story of powerful strangers, breasting the horizon with a cargo of knowledge and arrogance, failing to understand their impact on the place where they come to rest—and failing to understand the place's impact on them. The colonists suffered tremendous hardship. Each was cut off from the aether, and each carried the knowledge that this separation was his or her own fault, and most of them, unlike Edmar de Carvalho's co-conspirator, wanted nothing more than to return to its subsuming grace before they died. They knew, though, that this would never happen; they voyaged to lay the groundwork for a civilization that would never even arrive to excommunicate them again. Perhaps the stress of this is what finally, after decades of gradual differentiation, broke them apart into the two factions whose conflict survives in the poem.

Scholarly equilibrium reasserts itself. Dispassionate and careful, I tease possibilities from a stubbornly reticent record. I offer what follows as conjecture, untainted by the bias which has unfortunately colored so much of what has come before.

Perhaps the advance party, devastated by the conflict narrated in the poem, fell back on the paleolithic springs of tenacity that enabled humanity's survival. They had enough resources not to lapse into barbarity, but too few to attach any importance to their conscripted mission. They survived, and in the totalizing immersion of the impulse to survive, they forgot why they had fought amongst each other. They forgot, too, how deeply they had once desired to re-Assimilate.

Perhaps when the scout ships returned, they had simply learned how to let the planet forget them.

Perhaps it was some years after this forgetting that Edmar de Carvalho appeared.

"Which of them was it?" asks Edmar de Carvalho, as a last gesture to his charade of innocence. He is not free yet. They offer him the name he has expected. Stricken, he realizes that he has forgotten the face that went with it. He murmurs the name under his breath in a broken voice, the failure of his memory more, at last, than he can bear. *I should have gone,* he thinks to himself. *I was afraid, but I should have gone.*

Resolve gathers in him. He looks out at the desolate shore, the disorienting hues of sky and flower and stone. *I was unequal to this task,* he thinks. *I will be no longer.*

Somewhere are six women, and six children, and a lord's son poisoned by hate.

These sixes are of course myth. But the numbers may also be accurate. The same can be said of the account of Edmar de Carvalho's actions once the jailers left him to his sojourn: what persists are stories which may be true.

He found the colonists in small groups, violently divided and flung away from the remains of their first settlement where

Assimilated scouts had recovered the poem. According to the descendants of these colonists, there were in fact six groups, but twenty-five centuries is ample time for redaction, for the revision of history to conform with myth.

Let us say there were six. Over the course of years, his body steadily failing, Edmar de Carvalho traveled between these groups. He sailed a jungle archipelago, trekked over mountains and along the coasts of three oceans. Where he found people, he listened to their stories and their grievances; then, gradually, he began to tell his own story. Some chose to listen. Others reviled him and drove him away. Still he persisted in his telling, allowing the force of his presence, his stature as witness and penitent and survivor, to work slow changes his words alone could not.

He asked after the poet, and found a gravesite—found, too, that mourning cleansed him of the worst of his guilt. *I have done what I have done,* he said to himself, and went on.

Then, finally, someone asked him if they might someday return.

Beneath rubble, lights still blink, powered by distant sources of energy. Under a regrown canopy of jungle, near an arc of red sandy beach and a limitless expanse of green and restless ocean, a sealed spacecraft performs minimal maintenance, keeping its siphons clear and manufacturing what it needs to continue functioning. Scored by hand into the ceramic cowling near its bay door, the name NEYAUS is obscured by creeping vines and opportunistic mosses.

Neyaus has not found Edmar de Carvalho. He has found her. This is the literal, denotative truth.

The poem, though, found him, and through the poem Neyaus has found her unformed hero. This is the exegetical truth, the truth of the aesthetic mind.

Etched under the word NEYAUS is a careful outline of Australia. Edmar de Carvalho understands: Sydney, Australia. Ney-Aus. Close after this understanding comes a burst of relieved laughter. A survivor's laugh, startling strange winged creatures out of the trees. *How very close I came,* he thinks as leaves fall around him. *If I had noticed sooner, would I have given it away?* Wrong in exactly the right way.

Edmar de Carvalho is not home. He will never be home again. He is not Adam, he seeks no Eve, this world is not an Eden. Here, though, he will find minds that have fallen far enough to desire, yet not too far to listen, and he will tell them what has befallen him. Already some few have asked the right questions, and more are listening to his answers. He will tell them why he made the choices he made. He will be frank about his failures, his betrayals, his fiery reawakening. From him they will learn the value of what he preserved within himself.

In the meantime, the three Assimilated Worlds will, unwittingly and each at its own pace, prepare themselves for his return.

He will not live to see it. Already he is old, and away from the Assimilated Worlds he will age more quickly. But one hundred forty-seven years of solitude has taught him something about turning inward. He knows the difference between an inner space that maintains the shape of the thinking self, and the greedy infinitude of Assimilation. Desiring a mind without horizon, Assimilated humanity created a negative space which drains them away from the world they no longer desire to inhabit, and when this negative space has absorbed a critical mass of human energy and intellect and desire, the inward spiral will be too tight and steep to arrest. When at last this space collapses upon them…

As it must…

Only then will the world be enough again.

Only then will the mind suffice.

Again I lose myself.

Again I forget that I write more than an exegesis of a poem, or a biographical meditation on a figure of historical importance. I write family history, and must not lose sight of that responsibility or the privilege that comes with it. Even so, I imagine Edmar de Carvalho tearing vines away from that name painstakingly etched into the cowling of an old spacecraft. I imagine him imagining the poet—the poet who had once been his friend, whose face he had forgotten. I imagine him imagining the poet who had been his friend dying after having written a history that had not happened yet, a poem chronicling a hero as yet unborn, an epic of the future rather than the past, of hope rather than nostalgic regret. An act of aesthetic revolution, yes—but more importantly an act of faith, as every poem must be.

I imagine Edmar de Carvalho imagining this, and I begin to know what it is to put oneself in the place of another.

Edmar de Carvalho disappeared into the ribonucleic white noise of the exile colony he adopted as his own. But first he brought them out of their forgetting. He found them, brought them together, held out before them the possibility of redemption and return he had seen in the fragment of a poem. I write because he left them both his wisdom and his dogged will, both learned too late in life to bring him anything but regret and forlorn hope, and because they survived to return, and because they stepped among the shards of Assimilated Worlds and rebuilt a human civilization. His legacy is no less titanic than that. Writing about it, safely ensconced in my pocket of history, I feel like a parasitic speck on his memory. I am ashamed of my luxury of introspection. I sorrow that I do not live in a time of heroes.

Another perspective exists, though. In the face of this sorrow, this shame, this clinging sense of unworthiness, I take a pleasure from this tale that I can only call transcendent. This pleasure, this sense that *from the absence of heroes emerges the beauty of my life's work,* far outweighs the deprivations of loneliness. It gives me what happiness I find, and that is enough. Perhaps the scholars are right that each hero's search is every hero's search, and that every hero's search is for himself. Abrogating my scholarly responsibility, writing myself into my ancestor Edmar de Carvalho, reading myself into the poem that has become the cornerstone of my culture, I fully understood—for the first time—what it meant to search for my name.

I have written this history, here on a planet, humankind's oldest planet, a palimpsest of suffering and ecstasy. Here there are oceans, and I have had occasion to feel the sea wind. It seems to gentle me, and in its briny breath I scent the real distance between the experience of my life and the experience of writing about, and trying to understand, Edmar de Carvalho. On a strip of sand separating thousands of miles of land from thousands of miles of water, I understand distance.

> Tato Chip, Tato Chip,
> Sing Me a Song

Alfred hunched intently over the bag of potato chips, his skin pale and slick with sweat, colorless hair plastered to his forehead by the metal brim of his new hat. A soft humming floated indistinctly from slack, heavy lips as he opened the bag, reverently observing the seam. Swaying slightly (the hat sang, that's how he found it, it sang to him and he told it everything), he removed the chips from the bag in delicate handfuls and separated them into a dozen or so short stacks. Then he upended the bag and carefully sorted the crumbs by shape. The bag he added to a three-foot stack next to his stool, parts of meaningless brand names canceling each other out until all he saw was CHIP.

"Tato chip, tato chip, sing me a song," he sang.

"See here, now," said General Tunisia Martino. He stood ramrod-straight behind his half-acre desk, the medals on his breast tilting him perceptibly to the left. Peeking between them were row upon row of ribbons, punctuated by pins in the shapes of airplanes and rifles. Fingering one of the medals, General Martino noticed the price tag was still attached. Lieutenant Ezekiel would hear about that.

Forcing himself to let go of the medal, he tried to remember what it was he'd been talking about. Suddenly he very much wanted a potato chip. No, more than one; an entire bag. And a beer, a beer would be just the thing too, perhaps a few beers. Maybe after lunch. Better yet, *for* lunch, but potato chips—

"General?"

Martino started, clearing his throat and wiping his mouth. He looked around the room, deciding whom he'd been speaking to. It wasn't either of the bulky crewcuts flanking the doorway; he didn't know their names, but was fairly certain that they were his bodyguards. That left the three people seated in chairs on the other side of his desk. Two were in lab coats, a man and a woman, must be scientists, and one was wearing a uniform that was a poor imitation of his own, even if he did say so himself. *Lieutenant Ezekiel,* he thought suddenly. *You are on The List.* Martino tried to remember who else was on The List. It seemed that someone else must be. A List of one was no List at all, unfit to bear the appellation.

A man thinks better when he has something to munch on, Martino mused, absently stroking his broad belly. He saw himself in the full-length mirror opposite his desk and stopped, noting his fine figure in the uniform, noble ebony features, stern brow. He was getting a little thin, the stresses of command, he needed to eat better. Potato chips, for example—

"Ah, General?"

Martino snapped to attention, his medals jingling. "See here, now!" he barked. "I can't have you people coming in here and telling me it's lost! It's stolen, fine, or even broken, but not lost! Who's to blame? None of you can find it, none of you remembers the last time you saw it..." He sputtered. "Gah! Don't bring me situations for which I can assign no blame! Is that clear?" Three heads bobbed; the crewcuts remained still.

"Well then. Er, find it. If you can't find it, provide me with someone to chastise. We have to maintain some sort of order and tradition around here. Always remember, tradition is the backbone of any government. Each of us has a function, a place in our hierarchy. Mine is to assign blame. All of you are responsible for finding things for me to blame you for. If you are incapable of that, you must find someone else for me to blame your mistakes on. This is how things have always worked, and they aren't changing now. Understood?" Everyone nodded, including the crewcuts. "Dismissed."

The two scientists exchanged a puzzled glance, the man's beard bunching as he frowned. They stood and left, one of the crewcuts holding the door for them. Definitely a suspicious action, indicative of a subversive attitude. Martino resolved to do something about it. But it could wait; at the moment he had more important things to attend to.

"Lieutenant?"

Ezekiel stopped and pivoted in the doorway, coming to attention. "Sir?"

"We have something to discuss," the general began ominously. What was it?

Ezekiel stood perfectly still, his hat held in both hands. Martino squinted at him, awaiting revelation.

"Of course!" he said, just as Ezekiel had begun to sweat. "Lieutenant, pull the car around. We're going to the grocery store."

"Grocery stores are so much cooler when you're stoned," opined Jake Stukey. He passed the joint to his cousin Buddy.

"What you said," agreed Buddy, accepting the joint. He hit it and sank farther into the passenger seat of the ancient Volvo P-1800. It was hot, and he was sweating rivers in the closed car with the windows rolled up.

"I am baked," Jake announced.

Buddy didn't think he was baked; he felt like he was being boiled in oil. He felt like a damn potato chip.

"Hey, Jake, you wanna get some chips?" Jake didn't answer. He was staring out the window towards the front of the Shop-Rite, where a long black limo had just eased to a stop in the loading zone. The guy who got out of the front was at least six-seven and couldn't have weighed more than a hundred and eighty pounds. His Adam's apple preceded him as he rounded the back of the limo.

"Jake."

"What? Yeah, sure we're gonna get some chips, the hell you think we came for?"

"Well geez, Jake, I know that—"

"Shut up." Jake still wasn't looking at Buddy. He was looking at the fat black guy who got out of the back of the limo. The guy was wearing some kind of, like, Mattel version of a military uniform, and his driver had to steady him as all the fruit salad (Jake had been in the army for a month, and enjoyed using terms like fruit salad) nearly tipped him over. They left the limousine in the loading zone and went into the store.

"Buddy." Jake turned to look at him. He was slouched against the door, sulking. "Buddy, did you see who that was?"

"Don't care." Buddy fixed his attention on the dome light, haloed by the smoke, and tried to whistle. Jake always got weird when he was stoned. Buddy wished he'd get over it so they could take out their munchies on a bag of chips. Kettle chips maybe, or the frooey organic kind with sea salt.

"That was fucking Idi Amin, Buddy. Idi Amin just went into the grocery store."

Buddy stared and whistled, ignoring his cousin. Jake decided to ignore him back; he returned his attention to the limousine. What a cool gig it must be to be Idi Amin, he thought. Everyone thinks you're dead while you're cruising around in this block-long limo. What did he do? Jake knew one thing: if that was his limo, there wouldn't be any six-foot-seven stork-looking geek driving him around. No sir, the back of that limo would be full of Cindy Crawford and Cameron Diaz would be driving and serving from the bar wearing her Charlie's Angels Underoos. However Idi Amin had gotten out of Upper Volta or Timbuktu or wherever it was he'd eaten everyone, he had some serious cake to be driving a limo in broad daylight with all those people looking for him.

Jake suddenly thought about potato chips, thinly sliced and salted to perfection.

It occurred to him to wonder how much this Idi Amin guy would be worth to the people who were looking for him. Probably a lot, if he had the dough to be riding in that limo all the time. That dough would buy a lot of potato chips.

"Hey, Buddy," he said.

Buddy ignored him.

"Buddy, come on, shut the hell up and listen."

The President of the United States was worried. His approval ratings were in the toilet, former girlfriends couldn't seem to stay off morning talk shows, and now there was this Martino nut thinking he was a general and planning some sort of half-assed coup. With a, what, how did the CIA report put it, a "cranial-framework-type device purportedly able to project the wearer's thoughts into the mind of his chosen target." The chosen target would obviously be him, the President thought nervously. He wrapped himself in the Stars and Bars that stood next to his desk and waited for the phone to ring, trying manfully not to suck his thumb. The CIA men would be calling any minute with details of Captain America decoder rings and whatever else they found in the raid on Martino's house, out in one of the older white-trash suburbs. In the meantime, what he needed was to calm down. A snack would be good right now. Maybe some potato chips.

There were probably some in the kitchen. He nodded at the Secret Service on his way out the door and was already down the stairs when the phone rang.

Scott Brightwell was feeling put-upon, and justifiably so. It was bad enough that Ring-Dings were disappearing during the midnight shift, but the cleaning crew didn't even have the decency to rat out whoever was doing it. This was a serious challenge to his authority as Assistant Manager, and it wasn't helping things that the entire daytime cashier staff had thus far failed to return from their lunch breaks. As soon as he could get off the register, he intended to check the break room, and if they were back there slacking, heads would roll.

He looked up from putting a new roll of tape in the register and saw an immensely fat black man in some kind of military uniform, complete with sidearm, standing behind a shopping cart stacked high with bags of potato chips. Behind him stood a man his exact opposite in every way except the uniform—tall, skinny, pale, frowning—eyeing the cart and nervously twisting his hat in large-knuckled hands.

The black guy appeared to shift his eyes away from the piled bags with some effort. He looked at Scott, who smiled in his most professional way.

"Having a picnic over at the base, gents?" he said as he leaned over the conveyor belt to count the bags. They shifted their weight from one foot to the other and didn't reply. Scott allowed himself a little chuckle at his joke.

Thirty-eight two-pounders, various brands. Some organic, some not. Scott Brightwell stored information like that against the time he was sure was coming, when he would be asked for his input about the store's selection and clientele. Upscale, he would say. Go upscale. Organic, imported, little tins with strange pictures. Posole. Caviar. Haggis.

He picked one of the bags of chips up and ran it across the scanner, thinking that as soon as one of his cashiers came back, he'd go to lunch himself. Those chips—onion and cheddar, rippled, not upscale but attractive in a homely school-picnic kind of way—looked awful good.

"That'll be one thirty-five fifty-two," he said as he began loading the chips into grocery bags. Where had all the baggers gone?

The tall skinny white guy handed him two hundreds, licking his lips and jingling his car keys in his other hand. Scott squinted carefully at the bills, letting everyone who cared to notice know that Scott Brightwell was not someone you could pass counterfeit bills on. Satisfied that he'd made his point, he turned the smile on again and made their change.

As they wheeled the cart toward the sliding doors, Scott took a quick look at the camera behind the Customer Service desk. The store was vacant except for one old lady eating grapes in the produce section. He had a minute at least.

He was straightening his tie and clearing his throat as he thrust open the swinging door to the employee break room, feeling like Gary Cooper about to draw down on the black hats. The entire morning shift of J and J's Shop-Rite looked up in unison, the corners of every mouth decorated with crumbs and grease, chins gleaming and flecked with very upscale rosemary and ordinary black pepper. Scott opened his mouth and someone stuck a potato chip in it.

Jake and Buddy jumped the skinny stork guy as the grocery store's front doors slid open. Buddy knocked him down and Jake aimed a kick at his stomach, missing and hitting his sidearm

Tato Chip, Tato Chip, Sing Me a Song

instead. The keys skittered across the concrete and the gun went off, the bullet shearing off the tip of the stork's right shoe.

"Medic! Medic!" the stork screamed, his eyes screwed tightly shut and both hands wrapped around his toes. Jake scooped up the keys, ran to the limo, and had it started before he noticed Buddy and Idi Amin weren't with him.

He leaned out the door and stood up, one hand still on the steering wheel, and saw Buddy and Idi Amin wrestling over the pushbar of the shopping cart. Bags of potato chips spilled out of their grocery sacks onto the sidewalk, and both combatants leaped around like frogs on a griddle to avoid them.

Jake sprinted around the front of the car and grabbed as much of Idi Amin as he could, dragging him toward the limousine. The shopping cart tipped sideways and Buddy tripped over the mass of bags. Idi Amin struggled, his fingers flailing after a bag that had fallen just beyond his grasp.

"Buddy!" shouted Jake. "Open the goddamn door!"

Buddy grabbed two grocery bags under one arm and jerked the limo's front passenger door open with his other hand. Jake shoved Idi Amin into the limousine and pushed Buddy in after him.

"Medic!" screamed the stork.

Jake ran back to the open driver's-side door and jumped in. Slamming the door, he threw the limo into gear.

"Sure am glad you guys showed up," a voice said from behind him.

The rearview mirror showed two guys wearing dark suits and crewcuts helping themselves to Buddy's bags of chips. Idi Amin had a bag of his own, and Buddy was tipping the last crumbs out of his.

"Aaah!" Jake slammed on the brakes, dumping the crewcuts in a pile on the floor. Shoving the gearshift into park, he dragged Idi Amin with him through the driver's-side door and across the parking lot to the Volvo. Idi Amin followed contentedly along, munching potato chips by the handful.

"Buddy, come on!" Jake ripped open the passenger door of the P-1800.

Idi Amin would not fit in the back seat. No way, no how.

Pounding the seat back into its original position, Jake thrust the agreeable Idi Amin into the front, locked the door for no good reason, and hurdled across the hood.

"These chips sure are good," said Idi Amin as they screeched out of the parking lot. As the sound of the Volvo's engine faded, cars began streaming into the lot.

"Medic!" screamed the stork.

Alfred compared two potato chips. He found a difference visible only to the trained eye and discarded one. The other he ate.

Boy, are these good, he thought.

"Boy, are these good," said the President. The Secret Service men, the First Lady, and the head of the CIA were sitting on the floor in a loose circle. Nobody could politely respond with their mouths full, but everyone nodded vigorously.

Doctor Wilma Ziegfeld looked at the six CIA men eating potato chips in her laboratory and nodding at each other, in agreement over what she couldn't tell. She was mildly surprised at the morning's turn of events. First the General had postponed action to recover their primary weapon so he could go to the store for junk food. Then her colleague Doctor Elliott had been overcome with the same insatiable craving. The CIA had arrived just after the General left. One of the operatives had held up a bag of potato chips and said, "You are hereby charged with treason and conspiracy to overthrow the lawful government of the United States of America." He had then ripped open the bag and offered it to her. She had accepted before she could think about it, and the eight of them had been munching merrily ever since. Doctor Elliott lay stretched out on the Formica top of a lab table, overcome by some preservative or another. His bushy red beard was seeded with rippled and cheesy fragments, the corners of his mouth clotted with congealed grease.

She wondered when the General would return so she could ask him what he intended to do about the crisis. Then she wondered briefly what the crisis was. Then she opened another bag of chips and forgot all about it.

"I am General Tunisia Martino," said Martino, "and I feel obligated to inform you that not only is this kidnapping outrageous and misguided, it was carried out with a degree of incompetence heretofore only seen in my adjutant Lieutenant Ezekiel." He crunched a handful of chips and handed the bag to Jake.

Jake took the bag and settled it in his lap. "No way, pal," he said through a mouthful. "You're Idi Amin and I know it. You ate a bunch of women and kids in Zimbabwe or someplace and I just bet there are a few people who would be very interested in the fact that you're alive." Jake was a little confused. The munchies had long since passed, but he couldn't seem to stop eating these damn chips. At least they weren't Pringles. Jake had gotten mighty sick of potato chips in general recently, but he'd always hated those processed little turds.

"Idi Amin is dead, you fool," Martino said. He took the bag back with his free arm. "He was a despot. I am a revolutionary, and I know that you are merely a government stooge, sent by the fascist bourgeoisie to inconvenience my ordained rise to greatness." He smugly ate a chip.

"Aha!" cried Jake as he leapt from the couch opposite the chair he'd tied Idi Amin to with clothesline. He dashed into the kitchen looking for the Yellow Pages, taking the bag of chips with him.

Fabric shops, farmer's markets, fashion designers…shit. There was no listing for a Fascist Booshwahzee, or a fascist anything else. Shit, shit, shit. What else might it be listed under? Jake tried to formulate the ransom speech he'd make, but he was distracted by Idi Amin caterwauling for potato chips. He finished the bag, crumpled it and dropped it on the kitchen floor.

"That was it," Jake called into the living room. He was answered with a despairing wail. "Oh, hold your water," he said, and went down into the basement.

In the aisles of J and J's Shop-Rite, people committed mayhem for the privilege of the last Ruffle. Outside in the parking lot, a middle-aged Senate aide wearing a Brooks Brothers tie and cordova wingtips was run down with predatory efficiency by a pack of teenage baggers. Left beaten and divested of his chips, he lay on the baked concrete and cried out his frustration as they fought each other over the crumbs.

Tortilla chips and Cheez-Pufs remained untouched.

The smells of vegetable oil and closed-in sweat almost overwhelmed Jake as he went down the stairs. "Alfred?" he said, speaking in the tone one might take with a strange dog. "I'm gonna take out your garbage, okay?"

"Almost out, Jake," came the reply.

"Okay, Alfred," Jake said. Jesus. Old people, especially old women, who had seen Alfred's vacant stare, his obsessive interest in minutiae, had pronounced him "tetched"; Jake thought Alfred was just a hell of a lot more idiot than savant. Day after day he sat there in the same clothes doing stupid shit, and dear dead Mom's will had handsomely provided for Jake—as long as he kept handsomely providing for Alfred. Jake had bought more potato chips in the last week or so than he could remember. There was a chest-high pile of them in the back yard to show the lawyer when he made his next twice-monthly visit, and next week it would be something else. Some people just had rotten luck with siblings.

"You go wandering last night, Alfred?" Alfred had a tendency to go out in the middle of the night and just pick up anything he found interesting. The basement was full of curios found in dumpsters and alleyways, most forgotten the next day. And unlocked doors didn't stop him, either: Jake had lost count of how many times he'd gone out in the middle of the night to get Alfred from some random kitchen he'd wandered into. *My brother the crow,* he thought to himself as he crunched across the floor to the old worktable where Alfred sat. Alfred ignored him, scrutinizing two fragments of crispy potato.

Fine then, Jake thought. *I don't want to talk to you either.* He picked up the thirty-five-gallon garbage can and started humping it up the stairs, thinking *Where the hell did he get that stupid hat?*

"Here you go, freak," Jake said. He set the garbage can down in front of Idi Amin. Potato chips tumbled over the rim and littered the living room carpet. The guy dug into them like they were his last meal and Jake took a handful himself.

Simultaneously they said, "They're stale."

"Ah, shit." Jake threw the handful back into the garbage can. He stood, suddenly on the verge of tears, cursing the damp basement air.

"We have to go to the store," Idi Amin said. Jake could only be amazed at how quickly Idi Amin cut to the chase. That was the kind of decisiveness people looked for in a despot.

Alfred heard the door slam upstairs. Slowly he counted up through the first hundred numbers of the Fibonacci series, then back down, his eyes never leaving the two crumbs held between thumb and forefinger of each hand. He blinked and set them down. It was very hard to tell, especially when he had to pee. He stood up and stretched, then took his hat off. He laid it on the table and scratched his head as he went up the stairs.

Scott Brightwell dropped the empty bag of potato chips and gaped. Shelves were torn from their fixtures, the products they had displayed scattered across discolored linoleum that just that morning had been white. Ruined, Scott thought. I spend my life making sure everything is in its place, Ocean Spray next to Cheerios next to Chicken of the Sea, and now it's ruined, crushed together in a big messy intestinal sludge. People relaxed out of tableaux of life-and-death struggle, blinking and staring at the greasy shreds of plastic bag all of them held in aching fingers. Scott watched as a prominent congressman looked furtively around and bolted for the door. He slipped on the greasy floor and skidded into the grille of a pickup truck that sat, engine idling, in the doorway, the frames of the mechanical doors bent across its hood.

The President of the United States looked at the First Lady, who looked at the head of the CIA. There was a sudden, frenzied scramble for the phones.

Buddy crumpled up the last empty bag, rolled down the tinted window, and tossed it out, feeling sated and complacent. He smiled into the back seat and noticed that the crewcuts weren't smiling back.

Lieutenant Ezekiel stood up from behind the row of newspaper machines in front of J and J's Shop-Rite. The last careening minivan had nearly finished him off. He took off at a run for Headquarters, virile and heroic despite his grievous injury.

Jake was turning into the parking lot of J and J's Shop-Rite when he suddenly remembered Buddy. Simultaneously, the cartoon freak wedged into the passenger seat began screaming at the top of his lungs and pointing out the window, causing Jake to miss the turn and plow the P-1800 into the concrete base of the J and J's Shop-Rite sign. Dazedly he watched as the stork came sprinting out of nowhere, tearing down the street as Idi Amin leaped from the car and thundered after him.

Doctor Wilma Ziegfeld was shocked out of a stupor by the sound of six CIA men systematically tearing her lab apart. "General!" she shouted before she was fully awake. "The telepathy helmet!"

Six pairs of mirrored sunglasses swiveled her way.

Alfred waddled back down the stairs, settled in his chair and carefully replaced his hat on top of his head. He liked it because it looked like a beanie you could see in a cartoon, only with an antenna instead of a propeller, and because it had an extension that fit into his ear, and because it sang to him. He liked his hat very much.

He swept the table clear of chips and crumbs and picked up a bag, reverently breaking the seal as his shoulders hunched and his lips fell slackly open, leaking snatches of soft music. He sorted the chips into piles and began sifting through them, hoping that Jake would come back from the store soon. This was the last bag.

"Tato chip, tato chip, sing me a song," he sang.

Down in the Fog-Shrouded City

It happens more often than I, as a representative of the Agency, would like to admit. Most often the cause is an amateurish mistake made by an operative with more vigor than sense, and most often the result is unconscionable suffering for everyone but the author of the mistake. I was in love with a woman. I spent time loving her. I began to see that a great many things that had once dominated my waking consciousness became insignificant next to the calling of loving her. In the clear light of this understanding I began to be able to rest.

Someone made a mistake, and the Agency took her from me, and I could not remember who she was.

The Agency is immense, tentacled, so vast and penetrating that it often mistakes itself for the world. And it might as well be the world—but its reason for existence is to hold itself apart from the world for which it often mistakes itself, and this vital distinction is enforced with brutality and inexplicable caprice. To avow allegiance to the Agency is, often as not, to set in motion exclusion from it; open avowals make the Agency part of the world from which it wishes to distinguish itself. It is far too big to know whether such avowals are even true—too big to be centralized, so big in fact that there are several people who believe themselves to be the central locus of power.

When I saw the magician catching peanuts between his teeth at a back table of McGuirk's Tavern, I knew eyes were on me.

Magicians have to do little tricks like that all the time. They don't know how to stop, or maybe it's that they don't know how they would start again. I used to have the same problem.

My primary job for the Agency is to carry Monkey-prose from the Warehouse to the Refinery. This is what I was doing when I found out that my love had been taken from me. This is why I was in McGuirk's Tavern, and why I had to talk to the wizard, and why I knew eyes were on me. Magic does its own things to the senses, and the people in the bar, wizards or not, could no more have looked away from me than they could have picked out which stars were missing from one City night to the next. We forget about the stars, we City-dwellers.

This wizard was named Wink, for a tic at the corner of his left eye. His razored salt-and-pepper hair formed a sharp widow's-peak, and he dressed like the miners and railroad workers who frequented McGuirk's. He threw peanuts into the air, and some of them hung there until a passerby on the way to the restroom plucked them out of the air. Others organized themselves into miniature solar systems, or gathered into formations that moved with a smooth unison like players in a soccer match or minnows twitching together in unanticipated directions. Some of them just fell back to his mouth, to crack between his molars. Wizards cannot stop.

"I need a spell," I said to Wink. "There's this to trade."

The satchel I dropped on the table in front of him whispered, blinked, stank, vibrated with magic. Magic crept from it and sank into the grain of the wood. Every peanut in Wink's constellation spiraled down to it and clung trembling to the leather flap. Magic has its own gravity.

Wink's habitual smirk wavered. "You're making me unpopular."

"With certain elements, sure. Others are casting your statue already." I wanted to sit, but didn't want to give Wink the ease. "I need a spell."

"Can't trade raw magic for finished spells," Wink said.

I knew Wink. I had never asked him to do something like this before, but if I hadn't been certain he'd assent, I would never have taken the risk. He would find some way to refine the raw spellemes in the satchel, and he would find some way to hide the excess product from the Agency. Whichever branch of the Agency he worked for.

Most of the wizards I knew earned their living in the Refinery. Each bit of Monkey-prose that produced a sensible effect in the Warehouse became a potential spell, a spelleme to be vetted and polished by magicians. Spells diverged into oeuvres, imprinted with the personalities of their wizards, idiosyncratic as accents or neighborhood pidgins. Different phyla of spells came to identify various adversarial offshoots of the Agency. Wink and I were in theory cohorts, accomplices. The fact of the situation, though, was that neither he nor I knew whether the Agency thought we were cohorts, and what the Agency thought was generally all that mattered. This day, though, I was hunting for myself. The Agency had kidnapped my beloved, and by doing so transformed my loyalty into implacable hostility. Do not mistake me, though; the moment a reunion was engineered, I would slip back into my previous loyal mold, and the Agency would let me. In its vastness, the Agency lost track of small duplicities; the fact that a small duplicity had first riven my beloved away from me does not contradict that general truth.

Wink grinned. Like all wizards, he had excellent teeth, and he had a wily exuberance that suffused the spells he created. I thought I would need it. "Where do you suppose I can take this raw stuff, assuming? I haven't heard what you want."

"I want a spell. What's here is more than enough to create it and leave you enough left over to fly to the moon."

"I'd want to be able to get back," he said.

"Let's go to the Refinery," I said. "They'll expect us there anyway."

The Refinery, a facility as ornate and luxurious as the Monkey Warehouse is forbidding and austere, occupied a gentle brushy slope on the mountain side of the river. The view out its windows was never less than spectacular, even when the City was cloaked in fog. Everything seemed a little clearer, a little nearer, seen from the windows of the Refinery. Magic had long ago seeped into its timbers and beams, saturated the glass of its windows and the slate of its roof, polished the marble of its floors until one's reflection became a window to the soul.

From the Refinery's genteel perspective, the Warehouse squatted in a sooty district northeast of the City's clustered downtown. A steady stream of traffic traveled between the two, primarily couriers like myself carrying raw magic in one direction and experimental results in the other; the wizards never quite trusted the Spotters to look out for the correct new manifestations. None of this laborious exchange would have been needed if the Refinery and Warehouse had been located nearer each other, but long practice had demonstrated that it was unhealthy to test spells too close to the pool of chaos defined by the Warehouse's walls. Spells, too, failed to thrive and acquire a distinctive power unless they were given room to breathe away from the crude forms in which they first appeared.

On one side of the City a mountain range leaps up. On the other yellow plains stretch out. In between, a river flows. The City is prone to fogs. At the change of seasons it rains, and the river strains against its banks. The reservoirs have to release water. Below the spillways, forgotten debris is churned up from the river bottom. When the weather has cleared, the garbage of the City—which in one way is its only memory—has returned to the riverbanks. Whatever you throw away, if the fish don't eat it and the hoboes don't steal it, finds a new life on the riverbanks after the rains.

Money circulates through the City, and magic. One is blood, one is lymph. If you think of the City as a body, you become amazed that it has survived its diseases and the depravity of its history.

Sometimes at night the City's buildings block stars where, standing in the same location, I remember stars shining on other nights. From this I deduce that the City's changes are not always zoned, financed, backed by bonds. Sometimes during the day I find myself in unfamiliar streets, when at other times I knew every street between the snaking tracks that wind tortuously out of the mountains and the ruler-straight country roads that reach that more distant horizon behind the plains.

I've traveled in all six directions, seen oceans and mountains, the stars and the shining phosphorescence of animals that live underground, arctic emptiness and the overwhelming presence

Down in the Fog-Shrouded City

of jungle. But I always return to the City, and often as not I have no memory of where I've been, or why, or what I did there. Agency Amnesia: we try to laugh about it. This is part of the deal when you work for the Agency. Many things leave your memory. At first it upsets you. Later you become upset at the things you still remember, standing tall in what seems like a limitless ocean of featureless past. Agency Amnesia is selective, a little unpredictable. I have never yet forgotten my name, but they had effaced the name of my beloved. I had not forgotten the *delight* I took in her face, but that face itself was obscured. *Indelible,* I told myself. Her face is *indelible.* Something covers it only.

To resist the effects of the amnesia, I recited to myself a singsongy phrase: *If I am who I am, this is what I'll do.* The rhythm of it comforted me, and I swear there are times when muttering this phrase over and over again under my breath brought back a memory. A simple assertion of Self, I guess, in a place where everything and everyone is so easily forgotten.

I've traveled within the City as well, from its wealthy suburbs to the railyard menace lit only when the moon breaks through the clouds. By trade I was a courier, and by avocation a wanderer. In my work, my natural inclinations found expression. Because of this I imagined myself to be happy.

I worked for the Agency. Often the Agency forgot this. I was usually able to remind them, but even when I could not, they recognized that I carry things. A thing carried is a thing valued, and the Agency values every thing that is valued. In this way the Agency was constantly forgetting me and then being reminded. In me it—they—saw. See. Sees. No longer in their employ, I am to the Agency a reminder, an abrupt and demanding recollection of the desires it has forgotten in the particularities of its immensity.

In the Monkey Warehouse, the chatter of typewriter keys drowns out all other sound. Up close, each keystroke sounds distinct and harsh. From farther away, the strokes merge together into a kind of clacking roar, and behind that is the white noise pouring in from the dim reaches of the building, beyond the range at which the eye can distinguish figure from machine. Those three levels of sound are constantly present, and when speaking with someone else, I often find that certain sounds leap out from the background, silhouetted as it were against the aural vanishing point, that conceptual space into which all of the levels of sound collapse. The monkeys never talk. They harvest language, these monkeys with cigarettes and glasses of whiskey, bad posture and the perpetual squint of disillusionment. They seem to hear the aural vanishing point, but they locate it in a different space than I do. There are howlers and spider monkeys, great mandrills and tiny marmosets, capuchins and colobuses.

People walk up and down the aisles between banks of typewriters. Their footfalls create a jagged and hesitant counterpoint to the chatter, the drone, the whicker of typewriter keys. Some of them walk in absolute silence, assassin's silence. Others wear shoes with heavy heels, to startle the monkeys with sudden booming footsteps precipitating out of the infinite background rattle. Every one of them wears some sort of apparatus to correct and enhance vision—monocles, eyeglasses, loupes, sometimes all three. At first this seems strange, since their job is often as not to hear, but among the Spotters superstition is more important than the perceptions of Blinks, which is what they call anyone who isn't a Spotter. Each of these Spotters is responsible for a certain carefully demarcated area of the Monkey Warehouse. Within that area, an individual Spotter bears the responsibility of noticing when a monkey has created a disturbance that might be magic. In the Monkey Warehouse, the monkeys type and magic happens.

From minuscule causes great events arise. I read that somewhere.

On the way to the Refinery, I remembered: I had known how to read. I hoped to know again, when the tides of amnesia slackened.

Once, breaking every relevant Agency rule, I escorted my beloved into the Warehouse when she was off duty. Off-duty Spotters are prohibited from the Warehouse, on the grounds that they might identify with one or more of the monkeys as a spectator, and that this identification will interfere with their ability to dispassionately perform their evaluative function. While we were there, one of the monkeys typed something that spread in a fine mist above it, a gauzy prism. Filaments of this mist wafted over the monkeys' heads, touching them the way one might rest one's hand on the head of a dog, and as one the entire section of monkeys threw up their hands and screamed ecstatically, leaping from their chairs as if forgetting for a moment that they were cut off from the sun by concrete on five sides and steel on the sixth, many miles and more generations from the jungles whose images they still held behind their faces. She stood with shining eyes, watching their joy.

Sometimes magic is like that.

Like always, a brace of goons flanked the Refinery gate. They eyeballed me after letting Wink go on through. "Careful hanging around with wizards," one of them said.

I looked at his bald head, the thick fold of flesh under the line of his jaw. The pinstripes on his suit were too far apart. "Good thing I have you around to warn me," I said. I get irritated when goons think they know my business. I get more irritated when I find out they're right.

"Courier," the goon said as I brushed past him. "People are watching. Eyes on you."

"Nothing to hide," I said, and waited for him to take his hand off my shoulder. When he did, I slipped a bill into his cuff. It pays to have the goons looking out for you. Not that I mistrusted Wink, but it rarely pays to have too much riding on the reliability of wizards.

Wink led me into his laboratory. He drew the shutters, lit a lamp, and spilled the magic from the satchel onto a granite-topped table. Most raw magic is inert when in contact with granite.

Refining spells to attack igneous rock has been an intensive ongoing project of the Agency, and of its rebellious splinters.

The magic on the table lay in a jumble of creased corners and strikethroughs. Wink selected one spelleme and carried it to a burnished copper basin large enough to comfortably bathe in. Copper's electrical conductivity is surpassed only by its superlative suitability to magical propagation. In the basin, the spelleme began to spark, to throw off eyeball-sized orbs of plasma that left glowing oblong smears on the marble floor.

"Energy," Wink said. "Physical. A useful spell to the trades, with a little polish." He turned back to the table, leaving the spelleme to spit and crackle in the copper basin. I edged away from it, anxious to get moving, to be doing rather than waiting.

"Wink," I said.

"What sort of spell do you need?" He was using a pair of tongs to separate the sheaves of spellemes.

"I don't know," I said. "But once I do, I'll need it fast."

On the way out, the bald goon muttered a single word: *Haven.*

So the spell had to do with monkeys. Okay. Before I went back to the Refinery, though, I had to circulate through the expected channels.

Most Spotters are women. My beloved was a Spotter when I first saw her, and a Spotter until the Agency took her from me. This is the only thing I could remember about her. She roamed her area intently, stopping often to peer through a loupe at the air above a particular typewriter or the texture of a certain monkey's fur. When she reached to slip the paper from a carriage, she offered the monkey a piece of fruit in exchange. The monkeys, who have nothing else, grow possessive of their typewriters, their paper, their ashtrays and their melancholy. Like them, I who had only her—and the unstable benison of Agency employment—became desperately possessive of her. She withstood this, and saw me through it. In her I was able to find the strength to not wander, to look upon my surroundings and find them good.

Down in the Fog-Shrouded City

Driving through the City, I kept to streets I was certain I knew. Too much flux already, without me straying to add to it. I stopped at a diner, walked in the door and left again thinking *Deli. Deli. Deli.* The word would not leave my head. I wanted eggs and toast, but the word *deli* drove me to a counter on the other side of the city, where I tried to remember to sit up straight while I worked my way through corned beef. *Delicious.* Bad posture bothers many Couriers, who spend too many hours slumped in broken-down seats. It takes a conscious effort for me to keep it out of my stable of problems, an effort I was glad to make since it reminded me of how my beloved would make sure I kept my chin up and shoulders back.

To stay awake, I started driving again. Sleep makes the amnesia worse, and I had gained enough memory that day to know I didn't want to lose any of it.

At the Prison I spoke to the Warden. "Let her go," I said without preamble. "I didn't do anything. Neither did she."

"We have reason," said the Warden, "to believe differently." He sat at a granite desk. I imagined all kinds of counterspells etched into the arms of his chair, the handset of his telephone, the soles of his shoes. The granite desk was a natural precaution, given the Warden's constantly growing number of enemies. He'd certainly added me to the list.

"Your reasons are wrong. Let her go."

"Courier," said the Warden, "there is one thing you can say that will induce me to free her. I suggest you figure out what it is during the next twenty-four hours."

The Warden had let slip more than he realized. I chewed over the implications as I crawled across town to the University to drop a package I'd picked up at the Prison. I had to keep working; the Agency would only tolerate my freelance investigations if I kept up my normal volume of deliveries.

What I figured out was this: the Warden wasn't sure whether I had done what he'd been told I'd done. He'd been told by someone higher up what he had to do. Perhaps he even felt whatever sympathy a Warden is capable of feeling. When he told me I had twenty-four hours to figure out what to say, he was telling me I had twenty-four hours to convince him that he'd been right in waiting twenty-four hours before doing whatever the higher-ups had told him to do.

It was clear that I also had twenty-four hours before the Agency cut their losses and disposed of both my beloved and me.

When I sneaked my beloved into the Monkey Warehouse, she did in fact point out one of the monkeys. "Look at him," she said. "He's got something figured out."

"He's in your area," I joked. "You're trying to make yourself look good."

"Is that so hard?" she said, flirting with me.

This monkey, her favorite, a small and stringy capuchin with bald patches on the back of its head, was the one I stole from the Monkey Haven that night, a night clear and glittering as an act of faith, a night that made me afraid to look at the stars. Stealing the monkey was a hunch born of careful paranoia, and I played it. I assumed that I'd been watched at the times when the Agency should have been watching, and I assumed that this monkey was at the center of whatever misunderstanding had led me to my extremity. I assumed, too, that they were watching me take it from its comfortable cage. The bald goon had heard something and passed it along to me; I hoped he hadn't been overheard in the hearing, or in the transmission of his single-word message.

Agency shadows were following me, then, as I made my meandering way to the Offices and took the capuchin through the front doors, feeling the air pressure shift against my eardrums. Then I'm sure they waited for me to come out. Even the slickest shadows are afraid to go into the Offices. In the Offices, where the Agency is most powerful and most densely concentrated, slips of memory are common. If you're forgotten there, nobody in the City can remember you again.

Once, in the mountains, from an overlook where I sat picnicking with my beloved, I looked down on the City and thought: I could get away. The Agency mistakes itself for the world, but it isn't. It can't be.

I was unable to make myself act on that moment, and after some time I stopped believing that there was any difference between the Agency and the world. Only when I remembered her, mouth open in unconscious mimicry of the monkeys' ecstatic forgetfulness, did I realize how wrong that was. I defied the Agency, and all of the methods I had learned to accommodate and avoid its irrationalities, at least partially to tell her that. If I had not been able to tell her that, I told myself, I would have had to believe that the Agency, in its violently paradoxical interaction with the world that both is and is not itself, had at last stumbled on the truth.

Since people use it to kill each other, magic is big business in the City, and its manufacturers and distillers enjoy the sort of deference accorded to economic linchpins. Numerologists, graphologists, mathematicians, statisticians, linguists—the production of magic employs all of these, and still no one knows exactly how it works except one monkey who isn't telling. One of the supervising Spotters in the warehouse once shouted to me over the clacking din, "It all happens here. The rest of it...you take them, the wizards tinker, the Agency shoots it out with whoever. Epiphenomena. The real event is here. Monkeys, typewriters, Spotters to find the magic."

"Right," I shouted back. I think he was disappointed when I didn't ask him to define *epiphenomena.*

I was on the periphery of all this. As a courier of spellemes, and occasionally of finished spells to prominent citizens, I stood in the penumbra of the magiconomy. That was more or less how I liked it. When too many people start paying attention to you, one of them is bound to get jealous. Or envious, it doesn't matter. Too much attention means some of it will be bad. I didn't know for sure, but I was pretty sure that was why they had taken my beloved from me. Too many people had noticed me, or noticed her, or noticed the monkey I would name Mudflap, or noticed her noticing it. Something. Eyes on me. Eyes on her.

In the mountains, I remember thinking during this time, people would not watch us.

The air of the Offices sickens people who are accustomed to being outside. The reverse is true for the Office workers, who spend their lives within the Office Building's walls and gradually develop a powerful aversion to whatever lies without those stone and glass barriers. The monkey sagged in my arms as I waited for the elevator to take me—us—to the top floor, where the higher-ups were. Officials or Officers, I could never decide. Either was deducible from the fact of the Office.

I was sure that the shadows had let me go. The only danger I faced was a challenge from one of the mid-level Officials. Officers. One of the ones who seemed to demand the term Functionary. If challenged, I would have to muster all of my resolve not to answer the challenge as directly as it was put to me; I had a gun, but using it in the office would be tantamount to a prayer for bodily dissolution. The only path of any safety lay in being as oblique and absurd in my answers as my prosecutor was in his accusations.

"You there."

So at least I wouldn't have to wait. I turned, shifting the drooping monkey's weight in my arms, and looked into the bearded face of a Functionary. He was officious without being an Officer.

"What?" I said.

"Your business here? You can't come in here."

I saw on the other side of the lobby several goons. Among them was the watchful goon who had passed on the word *Haven* to me as I left the Refinery.

"This monkey is very sick," I said. I wasn't feeling so well myself.

The Functionary drew himself up and stuck out his beard. "You can't just come in here," he said, his voice like the grinding of worn gears. "Do you know where you are? You could get lost."

He meant it as a threat. "A Courier is never lost," I said.

The elevator door opened. When the Functionary didn't summon goons, I got on it and pressed the button for the top floor. The monkey lost consciousness on the way up, and I started to hallucinate. It seemed at one point that the elevator shaft was transparent, and so was the building around it. People, hundreds of them, thousands perhaps, walked on invisible floors, leaned against invisible doorjambs, slipped notes over invisible transoms and plotted into invisible telephones. Beyond them, all of the stars were in exactly their correct places, and the mountains were just silhouetted against the last fading radiance of evening. Afraid, I looked between my feet, and saw the base of the elevator shaft receding faster than I could have imagined moving. At its bottom, her face half-lit by an emergency bulb set into the side of the shaft, my beloved looked up at me.

My finger stabbed into the Stop Elevator button before it had registered in my mind that I could see the button again. The elevator lurched to a halt, its pulleys squealing. Everything was visible again.

"Come on, monkey," I said. "Snap out of it."

The monkey's head lolled in the crook of my left arm.

"Come on, monkey!" I slapped the side of its face. Its eyes opened. I reached up and popped the elevator car's emergency hatch. The monkey made a half-hearted attempt to hold on when I thrust it toward the opening.

I shook it. Shrieking, it tried to bite me. I lifted it up again, and this time it hoisted itself up onto the roof of the car. I managed to wedge myself through after it.

A groove cut into one side of the elevator shaft, with curved iron rungs bolted into the recessed part of the wall. I let myself down over the edge of the dangling car and looked for the monkey. It was lying flat on the roof, mouth open and tongue hanging. I hauled it closer and draped it over my shoulder, where it hung drooling down my back. Strength started to leave my arms and legs, and I realized that the monkey was just demonstrating what would sooner or later happen to me.

Before it did, though, I had to get to the bottom and pick up the trail of my beloved.

To call the climb down arduous.... My fingers grew clumsy, barely able to hook over each successive rung, and after a while it seemed like even the soles of my shoes were tiring, slipping a little more with each step.

When this is over, I resolved, I will take her and we will leave the City and we will not come back. We will leave the Agency to its own internecine devices. I had just completed the thought when my fingers loosened and I fell down the elevator shaft, holding the monkey with one arm and reaching out with the other as if someone might throw me a lifeline.

Either the building was shorter than it looked from inside or I'd been descending faster than I'd thought. Whichever was the case, the fall didn't kill me.

Monkeys, as a general rule, hate Spotters. They even go to such extremes as to stage shit-throwing battles amongst themselves just so they can catch a particularly despised Spotter in the crossfire. The monkeys recognize that every Spotter is only a Spotter until she or he picks out something important and gets whisked away to the Offices, never to return to the foul-smelling dimness of the Warehouse. Knowing that the Spotters use them in this way, the monkeys grow resentful. Violence is not unknown.

Alone among Spotters, my beloved made herself welcome in that key-clacking immensity. This, I think, was what made me realize her transcendent worthiness. If the monkeys could shower her with affection instead of effluvium, what greater emotional heroism could I achieve?

This was before it became clear to me how very similar I was to many of the monkeys.

The fall did knock me unconscious, but I didn't realize that right away. At some point I had been struggling against the steady depletion of strength and coordination; at some later point I opened my eyes and squinted at the bottom of the elevator car that descended toward me with remarkable speed. I rolled over, noticed grinding pain in every joint on the right side of my body, and banged into a block and tackle bolted into the cement floor. Hanging onto the monkey, I scrambled to a crouch and looked for a way out.

A door, thoughtfully labeled EXIT, glowed in the cone of light from an emergency bulb. The same light, I realized as I limped to the door, that had cast the planes of my beloved's face into their moonscape palette of light and dark. I opened it and stepped through as the elevator groaned to a halt.

Then I stepped back, read the sign again. I could read. Getting closer, I thought.

The door opened into an office. The monkey stirred, whined, urinated down my left leg. "Hey," I said, and held it away from my body. It was heavy, and my right arm ached with the effort. Its eyes opened, and I said, "That's more like it. Which way did she go?" I wasn't actually asking the monkey, but it seemed to understand. It pointed over my shoulder and made typing motions with its fingers.

On the office desk, covered in dust, stood a typewriter. I put the monkey down, and it leapt onto the desk and typed *I have been here before.*

So that's what its spell had been.

"Holy smokes, monkey," I said, a little awed.

It looked at me with an expression of aggrieved patience. What a cruel imbecile I was for not recognizing its radical individuality.

"Don't be such a pansy," I said. "Where'd she go?" This time I was asking it, and it started typing an answer. It occurred to me that I should name the monkey, and the first word that presented itself was *mudflap*. "Hurry up, Mudflap," I said.

The way I knew what was going on went something like this: the Agency had rules. The Agency broke the rules. The Agency was generally predictable, but sporadically responsible for actions that beggared belief. Putting all of this together with the knowledge that Mudflap was my beloved's favorite monkey, and that she was its favorite Spotter, and that she had been kidnapped out of a misunderstanding begun by a junior Agency Functionary and perpetuated throughout the Agency hierarchy, I could only assume that my beloved and Mudflap the monkey had at some earlier time been present in the basement of the Office Building. Whatever had happened during this previous visit had somehow precipitated the misunderstanding that had brought events to the juncture where they now stood.

Simple deduction, possible even though I didn't really know a thing.

"Wait, Mudflap," I said. "Who is she?"

Mudflap had already begun typing. He (I had started thinking of him as male) shot me a poisonous glance, hit his carriage return twice, and typed five letters.

I looked: *They took her,* he had started, and when I'd revised the question he had typed *Delia.*

It felt like breathing didn't work any more. I could expand my lungs, but no oxygen made it into my brain. The venomous air of the Office, yes; but even more than that, it was the overpressure of returning memory that squeezed my diaphragm, stole the breath from my throat.

Delia. Yes. Delia.

Her face swam before me, diaphanous, her black hair falling out of her severe Spotter's braid. Something in her eyes frightened me, and I closed my own. At that moment another memory reawakened, and I realized that something in her eyes had always frightened me. Her mouth was slightly open, as if in this image—which must, I thought, be memory—she was drawing breath to speak.

Mudflap typed again, while I gaped like a fish at the mirage of my beloved Delia. When I did not respond to him, he pinched me hard on the earlobe.

"Dammit, monkey," I growled, slapping his fingers away. Mudflap waved a sheet of paper before me: *You took her to the Flats yesterday.*

"I," I said. "I took her?"

I tried to remember the previous day, but in my mind there was no sense of previous and next. A jumble of days piled on one another, and each of them caught my attention only if I could find Delia in my recollections of them. Delia laughing, Delia shining faintly, I imagined, in the light of my adoration. Each memory of her more comical in its caricature of devotion than the last. I began to wonder if she was real at all, or if the Agency had created her in my mind; I had heard of spells, had in fact transported spellemes, that could do exactly that, and it would be just like them to make me suffer transports of love for a magical apparition.

But no, not if Mudflap too remembered her. Monkeys were notoriously resistant to magic. If they were not, their crude typings would too often grow into real (and uncontrollable) spells, exhausting their energy before the Refinery had any chance to exert its influence. If Mudflap remembered Delia in my company, then in my company she had been.

It is a strange thing to place your trust in an ensorcelled capuchin.

"Why the Flats?" I asked Mudflap, although I knew before he had typed his first word.

The Flats lie between the Refinery and the Warehouse, somewhat downriver of the Offices. The Monkey Haven itself is just across the street from the Flats' outer boundary. In the Flats live those denizens of the City whose collective voice is not loud or persuasive enough to lift them from the river's floodplain. Light falls strangely there. The garbage left by the river's seasonal flood clutters the porches and, if they are unlucky, the basements of Flatplainers. As the river passes through the Flats, it grows broad and oxbowed, shallow and reedy and mucky of bank. The detritus of the City stands out of the muck and cattails like public art that has survived the ruin of civilization.

The only reason anyone ever takes anyone else to the Flats, unless one or the other of them lives there, is to commit murder. The squalor of the Flats suits the tableau of the kneeling victim and the single spell to the back of the head. Beatings, sex crimes, extortionate assignations all take place in other neighborhoods. In the Flats, people live and people die. Nothing in between.

But there I was, not killing anyone.

"Wink," I called to the wizard when I saw him leaning against the corner of a low cinder-block house. He looked up and down the potholed street as I pulled the car to a stop. In the Flatlight his face seemed pallid and unevenly whiskered.

He got into the car. "You didn't kill her," he said.

I had known that, but the confirmation came as a relief. "What are you doing down here?"

"Figured the monkey would talk sooner or later." In the back seat, Mudflap looked a little bleary. Carsick, I figured; I knew I hadn't completely shaken the effects of the Office air. "And," Wink finished, "I knew you'd come looking for her."

"But she's not here. I didn't kill her."

I'd been shifting the car in and out of gear, feeling the thump in its transmission and hoping that my mind would clunk into drive soon. "We need to go to the Refinery," Wink said. "The spell you need is there." Grateful for the direction, I roared away from the curb and out of the Flats where I had not killed my beloved.

The Refinery steamed and groaned like it always did, and lights prismed in its many windows. But no goons waited at the door. Wink looked at me, and I made sure I had my gun. It was loaded with spells he himself had refined.

I left the car parked a short distance from the Refinery, in an open Courier space in the circular part of the driveway, with Mudflap hiding under the rear seat. He'd been there since we left the Flats; I didn't know whether the Agency had been observing since I picked up Wink, and I wanted them a little uncertain about Mudflap's whereabouts.

Wink went into the building first, and I followed him up the stairs to his second-floor laboratory. Red light flared in the heating ducts as we walked down the hall, and I wondered what had gone wrong in the basement. The Refinery wasn't always a safe place to be.

Gunfire erupted as soon as we opened the door. I flinched and ducked behind the frame, but Wink had thrown up counterspells and each of the goons' shots deflected away from us. Several burned or broke through the walls on either side of the door; others left behind effects more subtle and frightening. An eye appeared in the laboratory wall near Wink's head, squinting as if the person it belonged to was peering into a microscope, and a rain of iridescent fish scales scattered about our feet.

I fired several shots around the door frame and heard a variety of sounds as a result. One of the goons wailed; smoke whooshed out through the doorway with a sound like falling water; glass broke; Wink coughed and disappeared into the room; an odd flat buzzing tickled my ears and there was a smell of cilantro.

The truth is, even wizards don't have a clear idea about what many spells do. When I duckwalked into the room, hiding in the smoke, I had no idea whether I had hit either of the goons or what any possible hits might have done to them. By the time the smoke had cleared, it was abundantly clear that both of them were dead. One lay on the floor, knees drawn in and both hands over his face. I couldn't tell what had happened to him. The other goon was gone, and appeared to have been replaced by a loose group of soap bubbles that drifted in the breeze from the broken window.

"Damn," said Wink. "I wish I knew which one that was." I guessed he had an idea. Wizards and their false modesty.

I should have worried about killing Agency goons, but I didn't, first of all because they were trying to kill me and second because I knew that if the Agency decided I was more valuable than the goons the killings wouldn't cause any trouble. And right then I was worried about getting my beloved out of the Offices where, despite my conversation with the Warden, I was sure she was hidden. To do that, though, I needed the spell Wink had saved for me here in his laboratory. I asked him where it was.

He opened a drawer. "Right here."

The spell looked like a feather, one of those long ones from the tails of bright tropical birds. I tucked it in my pocket.

"Damn, I wish I knew which one that was," Wink said from the window.

"What does it do?" I asked him.

"If you're going to get her," he said, "it'll do what you need."

I held my hand over the pocket where I'd secreted the spell. "Thanks."

"Welcome," Wink said. "But you know it's not free."

"What do you want, Wink?"

"They took your girl to get at me."

For the second time that day, I reeled under a volcanic flow of returning memories. Delia and Wink, together on the floor of the Monkey Warehouse, a place as forbidden to wizards as the Refinery was to Spotters. Why had they met?

There was only one answer. Delia was giving Wink a spelleme she'd gotten from a monkey, probably Mudflap. I was one of very few people in the Warehouse who would have recognized Wink, so I must have been the only one who knew he shouldn't have been there. I knew Wink embezzled spells; I had funneled a few his way myself. But what had been so important that he needed to violate Agency directive by going to the Warehouse to pinch it?

"You know that spell the monkey cast on itself?" Wink winked at me. "It was working on a special typewriter that day, if you get my meaning."

Another door in my mind burst open. The Warehouse, silent. In wavering cantrip-light Wink puts a typewriter on Mudflap's desk. I stand behind him holding Mudflap's old typewriter. I take it up to Delia's office; she will replace it later and I will return Wink's enchanted machine to him. *Take me to the Flats,* she says. *It will throw them off the track if they think you might have killed me.*

And if they catch you, she goes on, *tell them you know you've lost, tell them we just want one last moment of us alone together.* She catches my wrist. *Remember,* she says. *Remember.*

"Yours?" I stammered. "Your spell?"

Wink nodded. "I figured it out. I prepared it. I can cast it on a human now. On myself. On you. On anyone. I just had to see if it would work on a monkey first."

"What would it do to a human?" I asked. "We can already talk."

"You'd remember everything, Courier," he answered, looking me dead in the eye. "The monkey remembers the spell, so it keeps working on him. You'd remember all the things you've forgotten that you've forgotten. Anyone could remember anything. You tell me: what would that do to the Agency?"

It would do to everyone in the City, I thought, exactly what Wink is doing to me now. Everybody would know who their friends and enemies were. What the Agency was, where it began and ended. Everybody would know who they were.

"Who made me forget all this, Wink?"

"Delia had to protect you, Courier. She couldn't have you remembering that you'd seen us together. At least not until she knew if it would work."

Delia had taken my memories. She had taken my memories even of dropping her in the Flats. And she had taken my memory of her name, her face. I suffered with this knowledge. It hurt me so profoundly that it almost obscured the more basic truth that she had done it so I could rediscover her, and so that after that

Down in the Fog-Shrouded City

rediscovery I would never again be made to forget. She had risked clandestine interactions with a wizard. She had plotted the misappropriation of spellemes and, much more dangerously, tinkered with the monkeys' generation of those spellemes. And when Mudflap had brought down Wink's spell upon himself, she must have been standing right there not knowing until the event whether things would go off as planned. Anything could have gone wrong. Anything.

Magic is like that sometimes.

"If it would work, if it would work, if it would work," Wink was muttering to himself.

"It did work," I said.

He looked at me. "You remember everything?"

"Not yet. That's not what I mean."

What I meant was, I knew what to say to the Warden now. I knew how to play the wounded bird, fluttering my wing so they wouldn't notice Wink stealing away through the rushes with the memories of the citizens. I knew what the Agency had done to me, and I hated them for it, and I began to believe in the possibility that Wink might bring wholeness.

I had been abased so that I could be made whole. Unknowing, I had been transformed by love.

"Sure is a nice car," Wink said, looking out the broken window. "Too bad we'll have to hide behind it while they shoot at us." He was absently spinning a pen around his thumb and index finger while his counterspells foamed and sizzled around the doorjamb. The copper basins in which he analyzed spellemes had begun to glow a strange green-orange. Abruptly Wink flipped the pen over his shoulder and said, "Time to go. Best hit the ground running."

I didn't ask questions. When Wink went out the window, I did too. When he hit and rolled, I did too. And when he came to a panting halt against my car, leaning against the passenger door but not getting in, I squatted next to him and waited.

"Car's spelled," he wheezed. "Can't drive it now."

"They were here?" He nodded. "Shit," I said. "Mudflap."

Wink shook his head. "Magic can't find monkeys unless they cast it themselves. Even then it usually doesn't work. My spell wouldn't even have worked unless I'd calibrated the typewriter perfectly. No way some random goon with generic spells is going to find your monkey."

"So he's in there."

"He's in there."

"Let's get him then."

Just then a huge white burst of energy shattered every window on the second floor. Bits of glass and brick rained down around us. I jerked open the car's passenger door and hauled Mudflap up from the floorboards. He bit my arm and I belted him against the dashboard. "Goddammit, Mudflap! It's me!"

Gunshots crackled like miniature echoes of the explosion. I could hear something hitting the other side of the car, and the usual unpredictable side effects of large-scale magical discharge manifested themselves. Snow fell. A palm tree grew suddenly out of the car's engine compartment. The tires melted, reconstituted themselves as gaskets, galoshes, rubber bands.

"We need to get out of here," Wink said.

"So it would appear." I looked back toward the building, expecting more goons from that direction, but they must have cleared out in anticipation of the explosion. Soon, I figured, they'd be circling around.

"Go," Wink said. "Into the brush."

I did what he said. Spells came my way, one close enough to leave a trail of poison oak on the back of my leg. Then I was in the brush, Mudflap clinging to my back. I thrashed my way down to the shady flats along the river and waited for Wink to catch up.

He didn't.

I swore, made as if to go on, hesitated at the tug of my conscience. "Damn," I said. "Damn all magicians." I set Mudflap at the base of a tree. "Stay here," I said. He scampered up the tree and peered down at me. "Don't you go anywhere, monkey," I said.

When I got back to the edge of the Refinery's lawn, I saw that Wink was alive and surrounded by goons. One of them was the bald goon who had said *Haven* to me and then watched impassively as the Functionary in the Office nearly erased me from the City's memory.

In hindsight, of course, I knew nothing could have happened to me there. The Agency needed me, and in the Office there were no miscommunications. The bald goon had given me just enough information to make me lead the Agency to Wink—and through him to my beloved Delia. Only she knew which monkey had been enchanted, and only I knew which was her favorite. But the Agency would only know what the bald goon told them.

There would only be one chance. I gripped my gun in both hands, breathed deeply, and fired at the bald goon in the pause at the end of my exhalation.

The spell struck him just under the left collarbone. I was expecting something grand and eerie: I thought he might burst into flame, turn inside out, disappear entirely. Instead he stumbled backwards and sat down hard. There was no blood. Slowly he leaned to his left, and then he must have lost his balance. He fell onto his side and lay there. I was too far away to see if he was still breathing.

"Go, Courier!" Wink shouted. One of the goons kicked him to the ground, but still he shouted. "Go, go, go!"

I hesitated. Spells began to flicker and stink in the brush around me. I shot twice more, high, and then leaped back down the hillside toward the river.

In the Flats I stole a car and drove toward the Office. "Okay, Mudflap. Where is she? You were there. Help me out."

Mudflap shook his head. He pantomimed typing.

"Goddammit, monkey," I said. "Do not fool around. I just left an ally to die if he is lucky. I could just kill you and deal with the rest of it later. Tell me. Write it on a napkin or something." I found a parking ticket, threw it into the back seat with a pencil I had in my coat pocket.

Mudflap pantomimed typing. I came to a squealing halt in front of a real estate office and dragged him inside. "You are not seeing this," I said to the receptionist as I grabbed the back of her chair and wheeled her away from her desk. "Repeat what I just said to you."

"I am not seeing this," she said, her shadowed eyes riveted on Mudflap, who climbed up onto the desk and painstakingly typed FIRST WE FREE THE MONKEYS FROM HAVEN.

When I could speak I said, as calmly as I could, "You spring this on me now?"

FREE THE MONKEYS, Mudflap typed again. With a growl, I tore the sheet from the typewriter.

"Shit shit shit shit," I said, and dragged him out of the office. In this way I became liberator of monkeys when all I wanted was to swashbuckle just enough to rescue my beloved Delia.

"How we do this," I said to him, "is simple. I go in with you on my back. You got lost and I'm returning you. If we're lucky, the guard loans me his keys. If not, I blast the locks and you screech in monkey-lingo. Fast, get it? I shoot, you yell jailbreak, and we're gone. Then you owe me. Clear?"

Mudflap nodded and pissed on the seat. I took that to mean that his anticipation had gotten the better of him. With him hanging on my back, I crept from the idling car around to the front door of the Monkey Haven. It was late at night, and the Warehouse was shut down. All of the Monkeys had been bused back to the Haven, fed, and separated into peaceful groups.

"Hey, Courier," the guard said as I entered. "Some important package you got there."

"Last time I take one," I groused. "You should see the inside of my car."

The guard got up. "No, take a load off," I said. "I'll put him back. Just tell me where."

He looked at Mudflap. "Capuchins are all on the right-hand side, about two-thirds of the way down. Make sure you don't put him in with the baboons."

It occurred to me right then that I didn't want to still be in the building when the baboons were freed. I took the guard's keys and made sure to shut the outer door tightly behind me when I went into the kennel corridor. Right away I started opening doors. Mudflap was smart enough not to scream right away, and most of the monkeys were asleep, so I got most of the way down the hall without much of a racket. At the first capuchin cage, though, Mudflap lost all of his self-restraint and started screeching. "Shit," I said, as the chorus of answers began to echo up and down the hall. I started unlocking faster.

The outer door opened and the guard appeared, silhouetted in the bright office light. "What the hell," he said, and then he was overwhelmed by a surging tide of monkeys. The marmosets scampered under him, spider monkeys leaped over and around him, and when he saw the baboons coming he turned and fled out into the night.

I finished unlocking cages and found the door at the other end of the hall chained shut. Mudflap was still screeching, but something in his tone had changed, and when I looked over my shoulder I saw what seemed like every mandrill in the world rushing fang-first in my direction. They're monkeys, I thought to myself. They don't know the door doesn't open.

Before I could think about it I leveled my gun at the door and began firing. Spells clashed, and before my eyes the door rusted, started leaking water, played a strange kind of string music, and—just as the band of mandrills got within biting distance—turned to flour. Most of the rear wall collapsed in a great white cloud, and I lunged through it along with the frenzied mass of my primate brethren. Somewhere along the way I tripped and fell, skinning my palms on the sidewalk, and I looked up to see what must have been hundreds of monkeys dusted with white, disappearing into the quiet City night.

Mudflap cringed as we approached the front doors of the great Office tower. "Strength," I said. "One way or another, we won't be in there long." I took several deep breaths before entering.

"It's you," a Functionary said. I could not tell if it was the same one who had accosted me earlier. They all seem to have the same beard and the same voice.

"It is," I said. "Where is the Warden?"

"He won't see you."

"Well, he'll see this monkey," I said. "Where is he?"

"The Warden works at the Prison," sneered the Functionary.

"But he's here," I said. "Where?"

The Functionary glared. His beard trembled. His hands thrashed in his pockets.

"The elevator will take you," he spat at last, and turned away.

I got on the first elevator that opened its doors and didn't bother to push a button. When the doors opened again, I stepped out holding Mudflap in the crook of my arm. The Warden sat at a desk in a grandly featureless white room. I thought it was the same desk I'd seen in the Prison earlier in the day.

"One thing, right?" I said to him.

"One," he answered.

"All right. Here it is. I just want a minute with her. Just us. To understand. I know there's no more than that."

For a long moment he stared unblinking into my face. Then he gave Mudflap the same treatment. "So you do know where you stand," he said.

I nodded.

"You do know you were already forgotten when you came here this morning."

I nodded again. This was the moment when I discovered whether Delia had been right, whether Wink still survived, whether I had been forgotten permanently or only for a moment, the time it takes for a city to stir and shake Agency cobwebs from its mind.

"Get in the elevator," the Warden said. "It will go up. She will be there. In a few minutes others will arrive to keep you company." The Warden showed his teeth. "The Agency is not cruel."

In the elevator I grew dizzy, and Mudflap began to sag in my grasp. The Office miasma. I was glad to step out onto the roof. Even though I knew that my life would either end in the next few minutes or be transformed into something unrecognizable to me, I was glad. Wind blew the Office air out of my nose, and I looked out over the magnificent nighttime City, cottoned with fog made translucent by the corpuscular glow of headlights on the streets. Beyond the City the mountains were a vast absence of stars.

And Delia was there.

Neither of us spoke for several breaths. I looked into her face and saw that she knew me, and something loosened in my stomach. I had been afraid that while I was remembering, she—like the rest of the City—would be forgetting. But perhaps the Agency hadn't wanted to waste the magic on amnesia for an ex-Spotter who was already forgotten by the City. She knew me, and she smiled.

"Did it work?" she said.

"I think it did," I answered. "I remember our meeting with Wink, the typewriter, all the rest. And here's Mudflap."

She laughed at the name.

"I couldn't save Wink, though," I said sadly. "I had to leave him at the Refinery. There was nothing I could do."

"Don't worry," Delia said. "They can't touch Wink."
"What?"
"Who do you think brews up their amnesia for them?"
Another wrench, I thought. Another surprise. And so late in the day. Wink, brewer of amnesia, tinkerer with typewriters to give capuchins the gift of clacking speech. I began to believe everything might work, but my mouth, tired and City-cynical, contested the point. "But the goons don't know that."

"The Warden does. They need Wink for amnesia, but they don't know he's crafted memory as well. Wink will be okay. He is the downfall of the Agency, and he has made himself indispensable to it."

The elevator chimed. Delia turned to me. "Now we find out," she said, "if he came through for us."

I took the feather from my pocket.

In every spell is an element of pure wishfulness. This is why the numerologists and graphologists, statisticians and linguists have been unable to fathom magic's mysteries. At its heart the spell is an expression of desire for that which cannot be. What separates it from most such desires is that the spell makes the impossible ephemerally real.

Mountains, I thought. Mountains and Delia and never return, *and you forget us.*

Before the Agency took her from me, I said my beloved's name with great joy. Now I fear that the mention of her name will call their attention to her again. I remember to fear them; and I remember to love her, nameless and eyes shining, looking down at the fog-shrouded City. Sometimes we skirt close enough to the City that we can smell its musk of money and magic. Generally we keep a more careful distance. We make jokes about the imbecility and ineptitude of the Agency, but I still refrain from calling her by name. We have evolved a flirtatious matrix of nicknames.

Wink brings us news and supplies, occasionally spells. He has forgiven me, I think, for the damage I did to his laboratory. I said before that wizards cannot stop. This means that they have great difficulty holding grudges, and in any case my beloved was right. Wink alone can make the City forget, and for this the Agency needs him.

But there is an Awakening in the City. Fewer people are forgetting, Wink tells us with a glitter in his crow-footed eye. More are aware of themselves. There are still typewriters in the Warehouse and wizards in the Refinery, but more magic flows outside the Agency's field of vision. Wink believes that he has set in motion irreversible change. I think he is right.

New monkeys have replaced the old, who fled to the mountains and now populate the sloping forests. They fling shit on my beloved and me whenever we startle them. Even Mudflap, who I see now and again gazing at the towers of the City with what must be simian longing, joins in the flinging of excrement. Let it never be said that monkeys are grateful.

Their screaming and flinging is not limited to our intrusions, though. Every human is treated much the same. From time to time I hear a ruckus in one of the valleys below the cabin I share with my beloved. Invariably it is the monkeys, joined in pitched battle against interlopers who must, I think, be Agency Operatives. The Agency perpetuates itself and its spurious distinctions. Despite my faith in Wink's magic, the threat of the Agency denies me peace.

"Relax," Delia says. "We're out here. Leave them down there." And she is right.

Out here my memory is intact. I remember everything of my last day in the City, and every moment since, making allowances of course for normal frailty. That, and my reunion with the woman I love, makes me complete. I no longer wander as an avocation, and no longer need to. Love drove me to recapture my memory, and in my memory I find love. I am myself again. No, I am myself at last.

If I worry about the Agency, I hope it is only in the nature of reflex self-preservation. The truth of it is that I have enough of Wink's spells stockpiled to repel an armed expeditionary force— or to simply go somewhere else. As I said, I no longer wander as

Down in the Fog-Shrouded City

an avocation, but I haven't completely lost the desire to see new horizons, and with Delia…

Sometimes I slip. Thus far there have been no consequences. She assures me there will be none, and I believe she is right. The rest is superstition, an irrational persistence of Agency paranoia. But she is right. Leave them down in the fog-shrouded City. We are out here.

Whenever there is no work to be done and I tire of the stars and the plummeting slopes of the valley we have made our home, I put each sense to work absorbing and reveling in her presence. I am Delia-tropic. We learn how to provide for our needs, how not to fear the tendrils of the Agency. We watch, but we do not spend our lives watching, and we rely on Wink's Awakening, as we have begun to call it. It is good to be clear-eyed and have faith and be in love.

Elegy for a Greenwiper

Orbital sensors detected the nanobloom just after sunrise. Within seconds, automated plasma burns had cauterized the site, less than one hundred kilometers from Hancock Dome. Overflying puffballs poured forth a stream of scrubbers designed to lock in on hydrocarbons and free oxygen. Maps of Kindred IV were redrawn to include the bloom as a warning to prospectors and surveyors.

Ten seconds later, greenwipers were called in.

The suborbital burn squeezed a headache from Krzysztof Nowak's sinuses. He closed his eyes, let his suit's autodoc equalize pressure and goose the humidity up a few percent. By the time the transport had crested its parabolic course and begun its accelerated fall back to the rocks of Kindred IV, the rebellion in his sinuses had been successfully quelled.

A smooth pattern of retros guided the transport in a sharp curve through a sandstorm. Clear of the storm, the pilot set out the circular quarantine course. Krz checked his filaments: clear to the left, clear to the right, clear to the apex that would drop from the transport's belly once all of the greenwipers had made their jumps.

His suit's subliminals, keyed to reinforce and focus, purred in his ear: *Humanity has proved that it cannot live in the green.*

Domes save both us and what we would destroy. A taste of green is the first taste of mortality.

GO, flashed the light above his bay, and Krzysztof jumped.

Thirty seconds to ground. Krzysztof's heads-up displayed the unfolding filaments of the containment hemi, anchored every hundred meters by a greenwiper in full dress. Bezel to his left, Morgan to his right, and in front and below the seared rock and sand that marked the area of the bloom.

Nobody had told Krzysztof what to expect. Any one of a dozen organized groups could pull off a terraforming bloom; the suit's processors had categorized more than a million separate nanos and attributed them to different cells. He had time to wonder which signature would light up in the heads-up retinal display, time to wonder why the greenies kept trying, time to think about the end of his shift, time to savor the whiskey he would drink and visualize the face of the woman who would keep him company that night.

His boots punched through Kindred's crust of frozen sand, settling shin-deep in the ashy lithosphere. The filaments began to grow, thickening and twining into an invisible spiderweb designed to catch molecular flies. Krzysztof released the flight locks and engaged his suit's joint servos. He deployed his plasma nozzle. Samplers darted into the thin carbon-dioxide atmosphere and returned with captured nanos, invisible enemy soldiers that under scanning would yield their secrets. Processors profiled the interlopers, came back with the verdict:

Viriditas.

"Big leagues," Krzysztof breathed. Confirmation came from Bezel and Morgan even as puffballs settled into the gaps between filaments, clouding the atmosphere with scrubbers known to be effective against Viriditas nanos.

Forty seconds after touchdown, the containment hemi was complete. Krzysztof stepped back from the gleaming surface. The storm cell loomed to the north, rolling down on them from the Kellerman Massif. Krzysztof blew his distributed network, surrounding himself with a ten-thousand-cubic-meter fog of sensors. A few stray Viriditas nanos showed up on the screens and were quickly annihilated by scrubbers.

All according to plan, Krzysztof thought. He tongued his mike. "Hemi complete. Fog deployed. Nowak on station. Report counter-clock."

The litany of names settled his nerves: Morgan, Greenwell, Bemelman, Ukafor, on around the circle until Zeke Bezel completed the two-kilometer perimeter of greenwipers. All fogged, all on station. Command back in the Dome would have a hard time finding something to bitch about.

Off to Krz's right, plasma flared. "Who?" he barked.

His heads-up turned orange. Lemelin's position flared green, and at the same time Tig Okafor's voice burst across the link.

"Green outside the hemi!"

A dozen voices at once: "Burn!"

"Can't!" Tig's voice too high, wavering. "It's inside Reggie's suit!"

Krz slaved Tig's camera. He could not credit what he saw.

Leaves were curling from the faceplate of Rejean Lemelin's suit.

"Burn, Tig," he said steadily. "Burn now."

Plasma flared, and the sandstorm was on them.

Thirty-six hours later, Krzysztof read the reports from his pallet in the Dome hospital. The foam treatments were doing wonders for his lungs; in another week he'd be able to resume his duties. Lemelin, Okafor, Bemelman, and Ross wouldn't be so lucky.

Four lost, Krz thought. Bloomed.

This was a new tactic for Viriditas. They had never before attacked greenwipers, never encoded anything that would be a threat to human life of any political persuasion. Had it been a mistake? Had one of their nanos errored, locked on the wrong target? There were other groups of greenies that wouldn't shed any tears over four greenwipers, but Viriditas professed a love of all life and demanded that life be given a chance to flourish wherever ingenuity or technology could give it root. If they had undertaken an attack like this, they weren't Viriditas anymore.

He tapped the terminal, flitting past a relief map of Kindred IV, pocked with containment hemis that varied in size from a hundred meters to nearly seven kilometers. Thirty-seven times Krzysztof Nowak had been part of the team that stabilized those hemis, which would hold their seal for ten years in good weather. By that time, isolation from light and heat would have killed off the greenie nanos inside, and mopup teams could go through with plasmas again to make sure.

Thirty-seven times. He'd seen tiny plants blooming in hundred-degree-below-zero temperatures; huge flowers vainly turning toward the dim disk of Kindred, four hundred million kilometers away, before flaring into ash in the glare of plasma discharge; a dozen varieties of lichen and algae creeping their inevitable ways over gray rocks that had never known the touch of life. Every time Krzysztof had stood firm, had burned and fogged and sealed, had made sure that the only green on Kindred IV grew in hydroponic vats and artistic mantelpiece vases.

He believed in the Paradox: Green gave life, but the first taste of green was the first taste of mortality. Man had been cast out of the Garden, and to build another Garden was to foreordain another Fall.

Doctor Grello entered Krzysztof's room. "Officer Nowak," he said. "Breathing the local gases again, I see."

"Well enough," Krz said. "I can get out of here."

Grello perused the display connected to Krz's monitors. "So it seems," he said eventually. "We'll keep a colony working in your lungs, cleaning scar tissue out of your alveoli, and before you leave the hospital you'll need to be green-screened."

"How's the rest of the detail?" Krz asked. When Grello hesitated, he added, "I already know four of my people were bloomed. Give me some good news about the ones who survived."

"I wish I had good news." Grello made a notation on Krz's monitor. "The truth is, you're the only one who has survived this long."

Nineteen? Nineteen greenwipers, bloomed by Viriditas nanos? Why wasn't this on the nets?

"Every other member of your detail suffered fatal blooms within twenty-four hours of your deployment. Apparently this new nano can break the sampler containment. Either it attacks the sampler's wiring or," the doctor cleared his throat, "or it propagates itself as information along a suit's processor circuits and, er, reinstantiates in the human epidermis."

Krz couldn't speak. A nano that could write itself into information and transform back into matter?

"That last bit is speculation," Grello said, as if saying that would make Krz forget he'd said it.

"Was it Viriditas? This new bug?"

"All of the signatures recovered were of Viriditas bugs," Grello said. "To this point, however, we haven't been able to type the fatal. It rewrites itself faster than our processors can track, and we can't crack its propagation algorithm."

Krz took a few moments to absorb all this. He sat up, looked at himself. Wondered when he would see the first patches of green on his skin.

"How long do I have?" he asked Grello.

Grello could only shrug. "I don't even know how long I have," he said evenly. "We can't tell if the nano is propagating in the hospital, or in any of the staff who treated members of your detail. It appears to be completely gone, but normal quarantine procedures clearly wouldn't work with a bug that can propagate as pure information. For this reason, the loss of your detail and news of this new nano have been withheld."

"Nobody knows?"

"Nobody who isn't a Greenwiper or military authority, except for a very few people in this hospital." Grello poked at Krz's monitor again, then turned it off. "You can go. Like I said, there's not point in quarantining you if this nano propagates the way we think it does. You've been placed on paid leave until this is resolved. Be informed that your discretion is of paramount importance in maintaining order in Hancock Dome. You will be physically restrained if you speak of this to anyone."

It was an open secret in Hancock Dome that a small percentage of its population held heretical views. In an ostentatious display of respect for individual rights, this group's greenie sympathies were tolerated as long as they remained purely sentiment. To ensure that belief could not translate into action, suspected greenies were prevented from any occupations that brought them into controlling contact with nanotech. Periodically, too, their homes were searched and all technical gear more sophisticated than the average twentieth-century microchip confiscated. No great outrage accompanied this abrogation of civil liberties: greenie sympathies, the popular thinking went, had as a natural consequence technological deprivation. Possession of unlicensed nanoengineering equipment was grounds for transportation to Kindred VI-17, a tiny asteroid nearly two billion kilometers from its star.

In this way, the Hermetic divines who governed Hancock Dome provided an outlet for the inevitable greenie yearnings that arose in a domed population. Human beings' sinful urges, they reasoned, were not limited to sexual license and blasphemy, and just as a certain number of venereal and verbal transgressions had to be tolerated in the name of civil order, a degree of understanding was called for when considering greenies. Scarcely three generations removed from the colonizing voyage, Hancock's nineteen thousand citizens were prone to fits of nostalgia for such features of Earth as sky, ocean, and prairie. To unsympathetically crush such impulses would display a certain lack of mercy, especially since Earth itself was no longer fit for anything but domed habitation. The greenies' dreams were doomed to be just that.

Thus it was that Krzysztof Nowak, veteran greenwiper and citizen of Hermetic Society-founded Hancock Dome, could find himself in a tavern whose walls were adorned with sky- and seascapes, with animated frescoes of animal herds and mountain climbers, with detailed portraits of wildflowers and flying birds. *What am I doing here?* He had to close his eyes and weather a wave of doorframe-clutching agoraphobia before he could find a seat at the bar and order whiskey and beer.

The whiskey hit him like a slow-motion orgasm, the beer like the chill of sweat evaporating from his skin. He'd had nothing to drink in nearly three days. The bartender set him up again, and Krz took a discreet look around, avoiding the nauseating pictures and settling briefly on each of the tavern's other patrons. The left corner of his mouth curled into a wry half-grin: none of the greenie women were likely to give him the hero treatment every greenwiper became accustomed to from the female population at large. But he wasn't here to be treated like a hero. He was here because someone here had answers to questions he couldn't ask anywhere else. Krz downed the second whiskey and waited.

It took longer than he'd expected, but after twenty minutes or so a long-jawed woman with bruise-colored eyes and a vidstar cascade of curly hair sat down at his left. "Hey, greenwiper," she said.

Krz nodded. He lifted a hand and the bartender refilled his glass. "Whatever she wants, too," Krz said, inclining his head toward his new companion.

"Funny thing," the woman said.

Krz looked at her, drank beer. "What's your name?" he asked.

"Alice. You're Krzysztof."

"The joy of reputation," Krz said.

Alice smiled slightly. "Funny thing," she said again.

Krz raised an eyebrow.

"Well, six blooms in the past twenty-four hours. That's a lot, isn't it?"

Krz's eyebrow stayed raised. Six was a lot, if it was true.

"And one of Hancock's finest greenwipers drinking in a greenie bar while blooms mar the surface of our dear dead Kindred IV. That seems odd," Alice mused.

You don't know the half of it, Krz wanted to say. You could be a bloom waiting to happen, and the nanos that would do it might be just electrical impulses in your brain. I suppose that is odd.

He killed the third whiskey, chased it with what was left of the second beer. The bartender appeared again, and as Krz sipped at the fresh beer he had a sudden urge to go to church. I shouldn't be here with greenies, he thought. I got the answer I was looking for.

"I have to go," he said.

He thought she'd protest, but she stood. "Thanks for the beer," she said. "I'll be around when you come back."

———•·●·•———

He needed a dose of reassurance, a dose of uncomplicated belief. There was a church offering hourly teaching near the puffball staging hangars. Krz arrived just as a gowned Hermetic divine was beginning her homily.

"Humankind," she began, her freckled face young and earnest, "was given dominion over the Earth. No; we were commanded to dominion. And on Earth we tried to assume it. What happened? We equated knowledge with dominion, and because of knowledge we fell.

"Now, you can believe that literally happened, or you can believe that it's a parable. Either way, we realize that at some point in human history we left off ensuring our own survival and set about endangering the survival of every other living thing. And what did we discover? Only that we depended on those things for our own survival, and that when we began bringing Earth's ecosystem down around our ambitious ears we began the process of our own destruction as well.

"But we were commanded to dominion! Whether the command was divine or just our genome finding its voice, we responded. We strove to dominate until we destroyed everything that was intended as our dominion. So what is the lesson? What are we to understand from the collapse of the Earth that gave us life? The lesson is that life will not be dominated. Life demands slippage, variation, rebellion, and if we examine ourselves we will understand that the urge to dominion is as much a part of us as the urge to feed and the urge to procreate. From this comes the Paradox: green gave us life, but it also commanded our deaths because our urge to dominion inevitably entailed our own destruction. Man has been cast out of the Garden, and to build another Garden is to foreordain another Fall. The first taste of green is the first taste of mortality.

"And so we came here. Kindred IV had never known life when we arrived, and outside the Dome it still does not. Here we can live as humans were meant to live; here we can spread and command our environment; here we can fill a vacuum, not destabilize a system that requires our absence for its survival.

"Here we can obey the command we have been given."

The divine stopped, and smiled beatifically. Krzysztof realized he was the sole member of her audience. A moment later he realized she was a holo.

"You look troubled," the holodivine said, her smile fading into an expression of tender concern.

All Krz could do was repeat her words: "Life will not be dominated," he said. "How do we know that we won't wake up one morning and find out that the grapevines in the vats can live outside the dome?"

"There's no atmosphere on Kindred IV," the divine said comfortingly. "No soil, no water. Nothing can survive here without us. This is dominion. Here we can achieve dominion without extinction."

Life will not be dominated, Krz thought. The Viriditas nanos that he was sure he carried, were they alive? "This is my problem," he said. "If the greenies can create life on this planet, isn't that the purest form of dominion? To create life where there was none? To demand life in a lifeless world?"

"But this is to demand self-destruction," she countered. "What if the greenies were to terraform Kindred IV? Wouldn't we then set about destroying it just as we did Earth? Have we changed so much from our great-great-great-great-grandparents? Are we not human, and does not to be human mean to seek dominion?"

Thirty-seven times I have sought dominion over greenie nanos, Krz thought. Thirty-seven times I eradicated them. Creation and destruction: this is dominion.

And if all creation is self-destruction, then all we can do is destroy.

Krzysztof Nowak walked with ferrocrete under the soles of his boots, artificial light in his eyes, steel and glass walling him off from vacuum. Hancock Dome was nine kilometers across and two hundred meters high at its apex. Half a dozen smaller hemispheres surrounded it, nearly as high but much smaller in diameter. He walked past the subterranean passages that led to these outer domes, with their manufacturing, energy, and maintenance facilities; he walked past the long blocks of greenhouses and hydroponic farms; he walked past chapels and offices and apartment blocks and training facilities and when Kindred's pallid disk was just breaking the horizon he walked through the door of the greenie bar he'd left the night before.

"Explain something to me," he said to Alice, who was still sitting at the bar. She was alone except for the bartender, who had a shot and a beer waiting when Krz sat down.

Alice shifted on her stool, facing him. "I'll explain what I can."

"Was it part of the plan to have me wander in here?"

"Well, there aren't that many places you could have gone," she said.

"Did you know I would go to chapel?"

The whiskey made Krz's eyes water. Alice reached out, touched him on the shoulder.

"We know nothing," she said. "But we are guessing right more and more often."

Krz worked on his beer for a minute or so.

"When will I bloom?" he asked her. Like Doctor Grello, all she could do was shrug.

Greenwipers enjoyed the same forbearance that characterized the old Vatican's attitude towards Crusaders. They defended civilization, and their excesses were glossed over. So when Dome authorities discovered Krzysztof Nowak stupidly drunk near a puffball hangar, they put him in an autotaxi home rather than charging him with conduct unbecoming or disorderly. His supervisors, although surprised that he'd been drinking in a greenie bar, wrote it off after the bartender reported that he hadn't said anything to anybody he shouldn't have. Alice they already knew about, and were waiting for her to disclose connections, allegiances, covert machinations.

The greenwiper authorities did not know how far the nanos circulating in Krz's system had propagated. They had debated eliminating him and the entire hospital staff, but had come to the conclusion that such action would likely endanger Hancock Dome's ability to sustain itself. Then they had debated eliminating only Krzysztof, but decided against partial quarantine measures since the more radical course of action was so uncertain. If Officer Nowak was alive, he might teach them something. Dead, he was only muck for the hydroponic vats.

What Doctor Grello had speculated, his superiors knew without having to learn it from Krzysztof. The Viriditas nanos were unlike any they had seen before. They could write themselves into pure information, employing neurons and inorganic circuitry with equal facility, and reinstantiate on command.

They were organic.

And they would bloom.

"After what you told me last night," Krz said to Alice, "I tried to steal a puffball."

"You shouldn't drink so much," she said.

He looked up through the dome at the stars. Where was Earth? I need a sense of origins, Krz thought. "They probably know I'm talking to you," he said.

She nodded. "But they don't know what the nanos will do. They're expecting me to give away something, but I don't know either, so they're waiting for me to find out something I shouldn't."

"I haven't really changed my mind, you know," he said. "I still believe in the Paradox."

"You can believe what you want. That won't change what's true."

"What is true?"

"We can't close ourselves off. We're strangling in here, Krz. Humans need to be out in air and light and heat and moisture. We need green things that don't do what we tell them. You know what happens in a closed system, and it doesn't get any more closed than Hancock Dome."

Entropy, Krz thought. And these nanos, pure information, are at war with it. So easy to believe. I carry information. Information will kill me. Entropy will kill me. To build another Garden is to preordain another Fall. All creation is destruction.

That night he did not drink.

When Krzysztof Nowak succeeded in stealing a puffball, he streaked along Kindred IV's equator. The Viriditas nanos leaped from his brain to the puffball's processors, instructing them to manufacture and deploy a fogged array. Some of these immediately began breaking down the puffball's exhaust, freeing oxygen and bonding the complex molecules into heavy groups that fell to Kindred's surface. There other nanos were at work: freeing still more oxygen and nitrogen, creating hydrocarbon chains from minerals in Kindred's rocky crust, constructing anaerobic bacteria that would begin grinding rocks into soil. Crystals began to form on the surface, glittering weakly in Kindred's distant glow.

Krzysztof's theft had been anticipated. The Hermetic authorities in Hancock Dome, knowing the battle lost, waited sixty seconds in the hope that Krzysztof would contact the greenie traitor who had doomed the Hermetic community on Kindred IV. If that traitor could be rooted out, the discovery would be worth the sacrifice of Hancock, indeed of Kindred IV itself. During that sixty seconds, Krzysztof traveled thirty-three kilometers, trailing nanos in a widening plume across Kindred IV's lithosphere. When that time had elapsed with no signal being sent, plasma strikes vaporized the stolen puffball and sterilized the surface half a kilometer on either side of the puffball's flight path. Every greenwiper in Hancock Dome was deployed without being told what they were up against, and every one of them bloomed within ninety seconds of sampling the distributed nanos. The puffballs accompanying them began distributing Viriditas nanos rather than scrubbers; another forty-seven square kilometers was contaminated before plasma strikes destroyed the nanojacked puffballs and dying greenwipers.

While authorities in Hancock Dome debated courses of action, nanos quietly attacked Krz's ashes, breaking the oxygen free and rearranging the carbon and hydrogen left behind.

Alice grieved. For Krzysztof, certainly, but more for an ideal. No, ideals: hers and those of the Hermetics who had founded Hancock Dome. Four hundred and twenty greenwipers dead. They bloomed with new life, but.

Viriditas had sworn itself to life. Alice had known about these new nanos, about the breakthrough that allowed the nano to remember its identity as it transcribed itself into information. She had agreed that such a development was the logical manifestation of the dual principle that information was fundamental to the universe, and that the ultimate goal of the universe was life. She had agreed that the deployment of the new nanos was necessary to counter the living death of Hermeticism.

But she had never agreed that the projected loss of life was justified. How could she, when Viriditas had been founded on the principle that life must be propagated, that life was the single invaluable thing in the universe and that it must never be sacrificed?

She had once received a message that offered a rationale for this action. It referred to an old Christian story, the parable of the sower. Some seeds fall on rocky ground, some among weeds, some where it is too hot. These were the nineteen greenwipers in Krz's detail. Each bloomed too early. But Krzysztof Nowak was fertile, and grew, and was fruitful and multiplied.

On the scale of history, what did it matter that one colony failed? What would it matter if a terraformed Kindred IV failed as well? What mattered was that some day it would succeed. Some day humankind would find a way to taste the green, and that taste would not curdle with mortality on the tongue.

But four hundred and twenty greenwipers dead today, she thought. History does not matter today. What matters today is that the Hermets were right. Viriditas tasted green and sowed death.

She was thinking this when the Hermetic authorities arrested her.

"Life will not be dominated," she told her accusers. "You're right about that."

Was this nano designed on Kindred IV? they asked her.

She did not know.

Was Viriditas behind the nano, or had someone else used their known signatures as a screen?

The question gave her pause. Having never actually met or spoken with the designers, she did not know.

If we survive the bloom, they told her, you will be transported.

She understood. "I have a statement," she said.

They indicated that she was to proceed.

"The greenwipers, dedicated to the eradication of life, have themselves been eradicated," she began, the words already feeling dead on her tongue. "This is a great tragedy because human lives were lost, but in this loss a balance has begun to be restored. I do not know who created this nano, and I do not know what their ultimate goals are, but I believe that this nano embodies the pure principle of life. Life respects no boundaries. It travels across oceans and across space; why should it not traverse the boundary between matter and energy? Why should life not be information instead of only transmit it?

"Life respects no ideals. Viriditas' ideals lie in the ashes of dead greenwipers, and Hermetic ideals failed when life escaped their containment domes."

Enough, they said.

Outside Hancock Dome, nanos worked their way into Kindred IV's crust. They extracted and isolated, purified and combined. They propagated, and Kindred IV came to life.

Agent Provocateur

It's July in Detroit, a Thursday afternoon in 1940. I am twelve years old. From my seat in the left-field grandstand at Briggs Stadium I can look over my shoulder and see the General Motors Building towering over Woodward Avenue. Cars stream up and down Michigan Avenue, Fords and Chevrolets and Buicks and the occasional Nash, many driven by the same hands that built them. I look at my hands and imagine that they will become autoworkers' hands, large-knuckled and scarred, grime worked so deep into the wrinkles that even Lava soap will never get it out.

My father's shadow falls across me. He sits on my right and balances three mustard-slathered hot dogs on his lap. I look at his hands and try to count the dozens of pale round pinhole scars that mark his wrists and forearms. My father works for the Ford Motor Company as a welder. He is thirty-one years old and seems to me to contain all the knowledge in the world.

I take a hot dog and devour it in three bites, then reach for another. "Christ, kid," my father says around a mouthful. "You and Babe Ruth. Tell you what, why don't we flip for this one and I'll go get another at the seventh-inning stretch?"

On the field, Schoolboy Rowe is warming up before the fourth and the Boston Red Sox are milling around the steps of their dugout. Rowe is throwing well and the Bosox are in a bit of a slump; three innings will probably take forty minutes. I am twelve years old. I could starve to death in forty minutes.

"Deal," I say.

Dad flips a quarter.

Heisenberg's Uncertainty Principle states that the act of observing an object displaces that object, so that its true position and direction cannot both be determined at once. Or so we were taught in high school.

The Baseball Encyclopedia states that Moe Berg hit six home runs in a major-league career spanning parts of thirteen seasons with four teams. It was said of him that he could speak twelve languages, but couldn't hit in any of them; Berg was the most scholarly of baseball players, and he made joking notes about Heisenberg's Uncertainty Principle while he watched the man himself lecture in Switzerland during World War Two, all the while deciding whether or not to kill him. I think Moe Berg would understand the subtle shifts my memories of him undergo every time I dredge them up from my seventy years' worth of neurochemical silt.

I was Moe Berg's biggest fan in 1940, even though he'd sort of officially retired at the end of the '39 season. Like him, I loved baseball, and like him, I loved to read—a combination unusual among twelve-year-olds as it is in major-league clubhouses. I even went so far as to adopt some of his eccentricities. When I found out that he wouldn't read a newspaper that someone else had touched, I demanded that I be the first in our house to get the *Free Press* off the porch. Nobody else could touch the sports section until I'd gotten a look at the box scores. Only virgin agate type for this devotee of the national pastime.

Berg stayed on with the Red Sox as a warmup catcher and a kind of team guru, but never played a game after 1939, and by the time the war rolled around, he was Agent Berg of the OSS. His photographs of Tokyo, taken on a goodwill tour of American baseball players just before the war, guided Jimmy Doolittle's bombers, and his good sense saved Werner Heisenberg's life.

At least, that's what the history books say. I remember things a little differently.

I remember, for example, Moe Berg's seventh home run.

Agent Provocateur

I call tails. The quarter glitters through its arc over my dad's hand, looking like any number of slow-motion coin flips I've seen in fifty years of movies since then. Dad catches it in his right hand, slaps it onto the back of his left. "You sure?"

I nod. He takes away his hand. It's tails.

"Here you go," Dad says. The last hot dog is gone before Rowe has taken his eighth warmup.

And then, would you believe it, Moe Berg steps to the plate. The Tigers' public-address announcer sounds like he can't believe it either; his voice hesitates, and is momentarily lost in the echoes of his last word. "Sox, sox, ox, ox, ox." The crowd stirs, and people look up from their scorecards to see if it could actually be Moe Berg taking a last practice cut and scuffing dirt away from the back of the batter's box. Baseball fans are always alert to the possibility of history being made.

For me, Berg's appearance is better than a ticket to the World Series. I take off my Tiger cap and look at his autograph, scrawled across the underside of the bill. I'd had to fight my way through the crowd around Ted Williams to get near the dugout, and Berg was just sitting on the corner of the dugout steps, rolling a quarter across the backs of his fingers and watching the crowd for pretty girls. When I'd leaned over the railing to hand him my cap, he'd cracked a smile at the Old English D. "You know what an agent provocateur is, kid?"

"No sir," I said, "but I'll go home and look it up after the game."

His smile broadened just a bit, and he scribbled his name on my cap and tossed it back to me.

Now he stands in, and Rowe fires a dipping fastball at the knees. Berg watches it go by, shakes his head, waits on the next pitch.

And smokes it out to left-center.

I'm on my feet cheering even before it occurs to me that the ball might have home-run distance. The ball reaches the peak of its arc, and the two Tiger outfielders slow to a jog, watching it head for the fence. Head for me. I remember thinking that: it's heading right for me. I reach up, watching the ball curve a bit as it sails down out of the sky and worrying that it'll go over my head. I don't have my glove, but otherwise for the longest second of my life it's just like Little League practice, watching the ball and hearing my dad's voice in my head. Keep your eye on it, look it in. Two hands.

The sound of the ball hitting my palms is almost exactly like the sound of my dad smacking the quarter onto the back of his hand. Someone bumps into me and I fall between the rows of seats. On the way down I bang my head, hard, on a seat or someone's knee, and fold up like Max Schmeling. But I'm not completely out, I'm still cradling the ball like one of the eggs the high-school girls have to carry around for their home-ec projects. My dad hauls me to my feet, and the knot of fans around me disperses as quickly as it converged. A few people slap me on the back and say, "Nice catch."

"Look at you, Avery my boy," Dad says. "You eat all my hot dogs and catch a home run."

"A Moe Berg home run," I say, looking at the ball. An oblong smudge covers part of the Spalding logo. Moe Berg's bat was there, I think. It's almost as good as shaking hands with him. I look up and he's rounding third, two of him, accepting a laughing double handshake from the twinned third-base coach.

It's like a dream. Berg starts to get blurry, and there is a roaring in my ears, and my father says something else but I'm too busy falling down to hear him.

And then it is a dream, or anyway it's different. Avery isn't in the ballpark any more, and his father isn't around; in fact, nobody is. He's alone in a room that seems to have walls, a ceiling, and a floor, but when he looks at them he can't quite tell whether or not they're there.

No, he's not alone. There's a man in the room. Like the walls, his face is indistinct, but Avery can tell he's wearing a tuxedo like the one in his parents' wedding picture.

"What just happened didn't really happen," the man says.

Avery is twelve years old. "Sure it did," he says. "I was there."

"Where was there?"

"Briggs Stadium, at the ballgame. I caught this ball," Avery says, holding it up to him so the man will have to believe him. He has the ball, therefore there was a home run.

Agent Provocateur   **225**

    Only the ball is a quarter, like the one Avery's dad flipped for the hot dog. A 1936 quarter, with three short parallel gouges across the eagle's right wing.
    "Where's my ball?" Avery looks around the room.
    "There is no ball. What you have is what you caught."
    "Come on," Avery says scornfully. "Ted Williams couldn't hit a quarter out of the park. Hank Greenberg couldn't. Jimmie Foxx couldn't. You expect me to believe Moe Berg did?"
    "What do you have in your hand?"
    "A quarter."
    "Then that must be what you caught."
    "No way. You stole it, didn't you? You stole my ball."
    "Avery. Listen to me. There's a reason it's a quarter."
    "Sure there is. It's a quarter because you stole my ball and you're such a cheapskate you only gave me a quarter for it." Avery throws the quarter at the man, but it stops halfway between them, spinning in the air just as it did on its way through the summer air in Briggs Stadium.
    "Now you've done it," the man says.

    Where am I going, where have I been, how do I know both at once? I'm seventy-two years old, retired from the GM Proving Grounds in Milford, Michigan to a seaside cottage in Seal Harbor, Maine. The Tigers have won three World Series since the day I saw (or didn't see) Moe Berg's home run—in '45, '68, and '84. The Red Sox haven't won any. They went once, in 1986, but after Mookie Wilson's seeing-eye grounder found its way through Bill Buckner's legs, it would almost have been better if the Angels had beaten the Sox in the AL playoffs. At least then…but if, if, if. "If chickens had lips," my dad used to say, "they would whistle." No use speculating on ifs. It wasn't easy growing up a Red Sox fan in Detroit, but I managed, mostly because, like Moe Berg's autograph under the bill of my Tiger cap, I kept my allegiance carefully hidden.
    In summer, I take a radio out on my porch and listen to the Sox while watching the waves come in from the North Atlantic. Waves crash on every shore, and I wonder every single day if there's some kind of middle point from which waves radiate in

every direction. The still point of the turning world, as Eliot put it. The place where choices resolve into certainties.

If there is such a place, I would like very much to see it, to know it exists. I would like very much to know whether or not my choice killed my father.

"Done what?" Avery says.

"The quarter's in the air. Now you'll have to make a call before it comes down."

"Why?" Avery looks at the man again, and he's sitting in a chair that wasn't there a minute ago. The quarter spins at his eye level.

"To decide what happens."

"What am I deciding?"

"You have two choices to make, Avery. Only one depends on the coin, so we'll deal with the other one first. Let me tell you a story." The man shifts in the chair, getting comfortable. "In a year and a half, America will be at war with Germany and Japan."

"No we won't," Avery says. "Roosevelt said we were staying out of it."

"Yes, he did. But it will happen anyway."

"How do you know?"

"Because that's what I do. I know. In fact, you might say that's what I am. Someone who knows."

Avery squints at the man, trying to make his face stay still long enough to get a look at it. "Someone who knows, huh? Well, do you know what you look like?"

"You're misunderstanding. Avery, I only look like this because that's the easiest way for you to see me."

"It'd be easier if you had a face," Avery says.

"Fine," the man says. "Give me one."

"It's that easy?" The man nods. "Okay." And the man has Avery's father's face.

"Are you more comfortable now?" the man says.

"Tell me what you mean, 'someone who knows.'"

"I mean that I didn't exist until a particular thing had to be known. When I know what needs to be known, then I will no longer exist."

Agent Provocateur

Avery is catching on. "So you only exist as long as you don't know what you need to know?"

The man with Avery's father's face nods.

"Tell me the story," Avery says.

It is easy to be retired in the nineties, especially when you've had the career I did. You collect your retirement and your Social Security. You try to make day lilies grow on the Maine seacoast. You take morning hikes with your wife in Acadia National Park. If you get bored, you do consulting for people in the automotive industry.

I cannot get bored, because when I get bored I start thinking about Moe Berg, quarters, afternoons in July when my father would use a personal day and take me to ballgames.

I have earned a lot of money from consulting work.

My wife's name is Donna. She's a little taller than I am, and a lot thinner, and her hair is exactly the color of a full moon high in a winter sky. We've been married for thirty-seven years, and I don't think I know how to love another woman anymore. She wants me to slow down a little, enjoy the golden years. She wants to know why I don't want to go to Europe. We are happy together, and our children haven't turned up on any talk shows to claim abuse or neglect.

I wish I could tell Donna why I don't want to go to Europe, but I've hidden that away like an enemy autograph under the bill of a sweat-stained Detroit Tigers baseball cap.

Moe Berg died in New York in 1972, outliving my father by twenty-eight years. After his death, Donna and I went to New York for the first time.

"There is a scientist named Werner Heisenberg," the man with Avery's father's face says.

"Is he German?" The man nods. "So we'll be at war with him," Avery says.

"Yes. Heisenberg is already very famous as a scientist, and when the war starts, he will work for the Nazis trying to split the atom and develop an atomic bomb. Here is the choice you must make: does Moe Berg kill this man Heisenberg or not?"

"Moe Berg kill somebody? He's a baseball player."

"Presently, yes. But when the war breaks out, he will join the Office of Strategic Services and act as a spy for the United States. One of his assignments, in 1944, will be to attend a lecture given by Heisenberg. Berg will have been instructed to shoot Heisenberg if he believes that the Nazis are nearly able to construct an atomic bomb."

"You're crazy," Avery says. "I read about atomic bombs in *Astounding*. There's no such thing."

"There will be."

Still dubious, Avery says, "Even if there is, what's that got to do with my ball?"

"If Moe Berg hits another home run, he will play more often this season. Being a little old for the Army, he will play next season as well, and the OSS will hire someone in his place. The man that they hire and send to Heisenberg's lecture will kill Heisenberg."

"Big deal," Avery says. "If there is such a thing as an atomic bomb, we sure don't want Hitler to have it."

"But what if killing Heisenberg has no influence on the Nazis' ability to build an atomic bomb before the United States does? Then a brilliant scientist will have been assassinated for no gain." Avery doesn't say anything, and the man continues. "If Heisenberg's assassination is successful, other German physicists will be targeted. The result of this will be that the men who would have built America's space program will either be dead or frightened into going to Russia when the war ends."

"Space program?" Avery is suddenly excited. He's just read H.G. Wells' *The First Men in the Moon* a month ago, and if atomic bombs, why not men on the moon? "Are we going to the moon?" His mind fills with images of sleek, silvery rockets, blasting off into space. With him aboard. He will be an astronaut.

"That depends, Avery. There are many possibilities, but this much is certain: if Heisenberg is killed, the people who first set foot on the moon will not be American. And perhaps no one will at all."

Agent Provocateur

Avery is silent, staring at the floor that wasn't quite a floor. More like a lot of different floors, each of which was almost there but not quite. "How do you know all this?" he asks.

"I don't know. Before you arrived here, I didn't exist. When you leave, I won't exist. But as long as this particular uncertainty persists, so do I."

"Does it matter who lands on the moon?" Avery asks.

"Perhaps not. But it might matter very much who has the first atomic bomb."

Avery watches the quarter spinning. If he moves a bit to one side or the other, he can make it look like the man with his father's face has quarters for eyes. A Moe Berg home-run ball; something to tell the guys about. He thinks.

"Okay," Avery says after a while. "You can have the ball."

Sometimes the moon looks like a coin, its endless maria spreading their eagle wings across the landscape. On summer nights I wait for it to rise above the distortion near the horizon, and then I sit up late thinking that the moon spins just like that quarter did. Full, gibbous, half, fingernail, new. After a summer of late nights I have a time-lapse movie in my head, and sometimes when I dream the man with my father's face has moons for eyes. They flicker like film that isn't moving quite fast enough to fool the eye.

Heads or tails. Fifty-fifty. Position or velocity. The cat is alive, the cat is dead. But if you flip a coin ten times, you don't often get five of each. I flip coins a lot, especially when it's summer and I'm up late and there's a fingernail moon.

Werner Heisenberg: Nazi or good citizen doing what he thought was right? Fifty-fifty. Most of his biographers and all of his friends say that he was simply a German, and when his country was at war he was duty-bound to build them an atomic pile. I wonder sometimes how much thought he gave to what Hitler would do with an atomic bomb.

On December 15, 1944, Heisenberg gave a lecture on S-matrix theory at ETH in Zurich. Moe Berg was there, posing as a Swiss student, an Arab businessman, or a French merchant, depending on whose account you believe. This is uncertainty: you can know that Moe Berg was in a place, but not how he got there. Were there Saudi businessmen or Dijonnese merchants? Certainly there were Swiss students. And certainly there was Moe Berg, agent provocateur.

I imagine the scene. Heisenberg, red-haired, balding, gnomish, looking older than his years, paces in front of a blackboard as he speaks. His left hand never leaves his pocket. In the audience, Berg listens attentively, taking notes. *As I listen,* Berg writes, *I am uncertain—see: Heisenberg's uncertainty principle—what to do to H.* He jokes with himself: discussing math while Rome burns. An automatic pistol weighs down Berg's coat pocket, and a cyanide capsule rolls back and forth in the watch pocket of his trousers when he shifts his weight.

Heisenberg speaks, Berg watches, and a coin spins in the air.

"Does that stop the war?" Avery asks. "If I give the ball back?"

"No, the war will happen. But your choice can change the way it ends, and what happens after."

Avery has been thinking. "Why?" he asks. "Just because I caught a ball?"

"Partially." The man shifts, and his right eye becomes a spinning quarter. "Think of ripples. A stone falls in water; how far do the ripples go?"

"Until they hit something else," Avery says. He thinks of his grandfather's cottage up north, near Traverse City. There is a pond in the woods near the cottage, and Avery catches frogs there. He is seeing the ripples the frogs make when they escape him into the brown water.

"The ball you caught is a stone thrown into the frog pond of history, if you'll pardon my borrowing your image," the man says. "The ripples thrown out by its fall come into contact with a sequence of other events."

"How do you know what I'm thinking?" Avery asks.

"In one sense," the man says, "I am what you're thinking. Or, more precisely, what you would be thinking if you had more information than you possessed at the game."

Avery pauses for a long time, watching the quarter spin. "Are you me?"

"You'll have to forgive me, Avery," the man says. The expression on his face reminds Avery of the time he asked his father how eyelashes knew when to stop growing. "I only know so much."

"But you know about this war that hasn't happened, and you're telling me about atomic bombs and going to the moon," Avery protests. "How do you know one thing and not something else?"

"Because some things haven't been decided yet. Call the toss, Avery."

"Not until you tell me where I am. Where we are."

"We aren't anywhere. For us to be somewhere, you would have to have made a decision. And when you've made a decision, I won't be here. I won't be anywhere. I only exist in the space of your uncertainty."

"Who are you, then? Are you God or something?"

The man shakes his head.

"Did God send you? Is there a God? How come He doesn't decide this instead of leaving it to me?"

Still shaking his head, the man says, "I can't answer any of those questions. I have told you all I can. You've already ensured that Moe Berg will attend Heisenberg's lecture; now you decide what will happen when he does."

"No," Avery says. "All I'm doing is calling a coin toss. I gave you the ball. That was a decision. This isn't."

"True. It has to happen this way, though. Conservation of information. I violated causality by telling you what would happen as a result of your last choice. Now you have to choose without knowing, even though I could tell you, so it balances out." Something flickers on his face, Avery's father's face. It looks like guilt.

"What am I deciding?"

"Whether Moe Berg kills Werner Heisenberg."

"It's not fair," Avery says. "That's why I gave you the ball, so Heisenberg wouldn't get killed. Stupid German. I should have kept the ball. Why couldn't I keep the ball and call the toss?"

"I already explained that. Call the toss, Avery. Collapse the wave function," the man says. "Either it happens or it doesn't."

"Tails," Avery says. And it is.

And I am back in Briggs Stadium with Bobby Doerr leading off the fourth inning, and my father holding me up with his scarred welder's hands. "Avery," he says. "You okay, son?"

"Yeah, Dad. I'm okay." I look around at Briggs Stadium, at the worn patches in the outfield, the flakes of rust on the bolts that hold the seats in the concrete floors. I have done something, I realize. It is all the same, but it will be different.

My father looks closely at me, concern in his eyes. "I'm okay, Dad," I insist.

"Okay, bud," he says. "That was your last hot dog for the day, though."

I feel the back of my head. No lump, no sore spot, no nothing. The Tigers lose, there are no home runs hit to left-center, and the next time I read a newspaper article about Moe Berg, it says he hit six home runs over the course of a major-league career that ended in 1939.

And Werner Heisenberg dies in Munich at the ripe old age of seventy-five, and atomic bombs fall on Hiroshima and Nagasaki, and Neil Armstrong lands on the moon instead of a man named Yevgeny or Sergei or Yuri.

And my father dies in World War Two, on December 11, 1944, when a plane that had recently carried Moe Berg to France crashes in the English Channel.

I was forty-one years old, watching on television from my new house in Farmington Hills, when Neil Armstrong spoke from the surface of the moon. The Tigers had won the World Series the year before, salving the wounds from the '67 riots that prompted me, like so many other white folks, to leave for the suburbs. I had long since given up on being an astronaut.

My father had been dead for nearly twenty-five years.

Ripples, the man with my father's face had said. Ripples propagate until they run into something, or until entropy robs them of their energy and they subside back into the flat surface of the water. I caught a ball once, at Briggs Stadium in the summer of 1940, and my father helped me up and said, "Look at you, Avery my boy."

Look at me, Dad. Briggs Stadium is Tiger Stadium now, and the welder's son from East Detroit became an executive with a custom-built home in the suburbs, and I saved Werner Heisenberg's life, and maybe I cost you yours.

I sit on the porch of my house in Maine, watching the waves come in and wondering where they come from. I wonder where the still point is, the place where waves are born and decisions hang between heads and tails.

Sometimes I talk to myself. More often I fall asleep and the sea breeze brings me dreams of men who are almost my father.

When I talk to myself, this is the question: If you had called heads, would your father be alive? If Moe Berg had never gone to France with Werner Heisenberg's life in his hands, a different plane would have been waiting for Dad at the cratered airstrip outside of Lyon.

Would that other plane have crashed?

I was twelve years old. I thought I did the right thing.

Would Moe Berg's seventh home run have put my father on a different plane?

The cat is alive. The cat is dead.

The Red Sox are playing a twinight doubleheader tonight. Donna comes outside and sits next to me in the Adirondack chair I built for her the year I retired. She touches me on the back of the neck, then reads in the waning afternoon. I watch the shadow of my chimney crawl down the sloping lawn into the quiet surf, for just this moment content to know where I am, for just this moment content to believe in where I have been. The still point of the turning world. Waves come in like epicycles rippling through the larger cycles of tides, and the moon's revolution around the earth, and the earth's revolution around the sun.

Coins spinning, waiting for someone to call the toss.

Vandoise and the Bone Monster

They were going to have to leave Colorado and go back East in the fall, and before they did, Jeff was determined that Cindy would see the old fort. And she wanted to, so one Sunday afternoon in August they hopped in the car and drove up I-25 almost to Wyoming. They passed it on the way, a huge, lumpy, toothlike clump of pale sandstone jutting up out of the yellow grass on the east side of the freeway. At the next exit Jeff doubled back on a dirt access road. "Excellent," he said. "I couldn't let you leave Colorado without seeing this."

Cindy looked out the window as they got closer to it. Tall spires of wind-carved rock formed rough walls, and inside what looked like towers loomed above the outer barrier.

"Did you bring a girlfriend here before?" she said, to tease him. She knew perfectly well that he'd first come here on his way to Montana for a backpacking trip through the Absarokas with his college friend Drew, but she liked to poke fun at him about previous girlfriends. He'd lived in Colorado for a few years before meeting her during a trip to Florida to go cave diving at Ichetucknee Springs, and Jeff had a tendency to point out places he'd gone with other girlfriends before he could think better of it. Lucky for him Cindy had a sense of humor.

As they pulled into the parking lot – just a wide spot in the road, really – Jeff saw an older man wearing a highway worker's orange vest loading the historical marker into the back of a green

Department of Transportation pickup truck. They got out and walked over to him.

"Excuse me," Jeff said. "Getting a new marker?"

"No, huh-uh," the CDOT guy said as he looked up at them. His eyes were a pale gray in the deeply seamed and creased angles of his face, and bristle-brush gray hair stood up from his high forehead. Seeing him, Jeff thought of Depression-era photographs of Civilian Conservation Corps workers. "Just taking this one down. Shutting the whole site down."

"You're kidding me," Jeff said.

"Too many people. That sandstone erodes right away, you know. State decided they had to shut it down until they could figure out some way to limit access. I'm just up here finishing with the sign, then I'm going to lock that gate back up the road a ways. You passed it on your way in." He settled a tarp over the historical marker and cinched it down.

"Man." Jeff was saddened by this. He'd told Cindy about this place ever since they'd first come back to Colorado together. It was a natural fort, and had been the site of a tremendous massacre sometime in the nineteenth century, or maybe earlier. After a harsh winter, a Blackfeet hunting party came down out of the mountains, trespassing on Crow land. The marker hadn't said whether their hunt was successful, but it did say that the Crow caught wind of the incursion and chased the Blackfeet to these rocks, where the Blackfeet holed up and fought until they were slaughtered to the last man. Nobody knew how many of them had been killed, but it was likely in the hundreds.

The place had always seemed to Jeff to capture something essential about the Old West, the pre-pioneer West, before it had industrialized and grown crisscrossed with railroads and reservations: the iconic rocks rearing up from the prairie, a battle between peoples who believed themselves enemies, and now the process of making it into history. It was different in the East, where suburban children had swimming lessons in Walden Pond and all that remained of the Boston Tea Party was a plaque on a building near the waterfront. Out here, the past hadn't yet been buried under brick and concrete, and history was as real as an arrowhead scuffed up from the side of the road. There might still be living people who had talked to men and women who had heard about this massacre when it happened. It was close enough to touch.

He'd spun it all out for Cindy before, and was about to do it again since the marker was under a tarp on its way to a warehouse in Denver somewhere, but before he could she asked the CDOT guy, "Are you sure we can't look around before you go?"

"Sorry, I can't let you do that. Site's closed."

"Please," she said. "We're moving to Pennsylvania next week, and who knows when we'll get out here again?"

"Can't do it."

She cocked her head and the wind blew her hair across her face. "What's your name?"

"Jarrett Bigelow." He stuck out his hand and watched her closely as she shook. Jeff watched both of them, knowing that some kind of negotiation was taking place but unable to quite figure out how. Bigelow had calluses the color of the dust that blew over the road.

"Mister Bigelow," she said, "I'm Cindy Gellner, and this is Jeff Loville. Jeff and I have been together for a year and a half. I'm going to med school at Penn starting in two weeks, and we're probably going to get married as soon as he finds a teaching job around Philadelphia. Then it's kids and careers, and by the time we're able to get back out here this whole thing might have blown away, you know what I mean? And besides," she pointed at Jeff without taking her eyes off Bigelow's face, "he's been here before. Do you want me to have to suffer through a lifetime of him saying, 'Geez, Cindy, I sure wish you could have seen that old natural fort back when we in Colorado'? You're a nice man; you don't want me to suffer like that, do you?"

He looked from her to Jeff and back. Then he sighed. "Tell you what. You go on up to Cheyenne, buy yourself a cheeseburger, kill the afternoon. Come on back down here around seven, and park off the side of the road by the gate. I reckon no one will know the difference."

She beamed at him, and Jeff found himself grinning too. "Thanks," he said.

"If I ever come back here and find your names carved in these rocks," Bigelow said, "I'm going to come looking for you all the way in Philadelphia."

"We just want to see it," Jeff said.

"Seven o'clock," Bigelow said by way of an answer. He got into his truck and sat pointedly waiting for them to leave.

It was about ten after seven when they pulled up to the locked gate. CLOSED BY ORDER OF STATE OF COLORADO. NO TRESPASSING.

"Trespassing on state property," Jeff said.

Cindy got out of the car. "As far as the Indians are concerned, the people who put up the fence are trespassers too. Come on."

They walked the hundred yards or so down the road on the other side of the gate, Jeff with a strange jumpy feeling the whole time on the back of his neck. He'd done his share of sneaking into places he wasn't supposed to be, but it was different when you were stepping onto a mass grave, the site of a massacre. The story, like so many others from the Old West, lay thinly buried, needing only a scuffing footstep to jar it loose.

In the evening light, with hardly any traffic on I-25 and the nearest house two or three miles away on a ridge to the east, the old rocks looked like they might just have thrust up through the ground the day before. A wind from the mountains ruffled the tall prairie grass, blowing hard enough to drown out the sounds of wheels on pavement from the interstate.

A seam in the side of the near wall, with worn hand-width grooves at waist level and a sprinkling of initials scattered around it like warning sigils, led them into the interior. Inside, the air was dead still and the sandy floor mostly empty of grass. The walls were scored with decades of initials and pledges, and charred stubs of firewood stuck out of the sand. Broken glass crunched under their feet. The rocks were laid out almost exactly like the plan of a castle: an external ring with towers spaced around it, a sandy courtyard just inside, and a central keep. *If I'd lived around here when I was a kid,* Jeff thought, *you wouldn't have been able to keep me out of this place. Wonder why the local Renaissance festival hasn't tried to take it over.*

Cindy climbed part of the way up one of the internal pillars and found herself a hollowed-out place to sit. Jeff climbed up next to her, and they looked out over the rolling plain to the east. On the other side of the dirt road, a barbed-wire fence ran north and south as far as they could see; at the crest of a ridge to the east, a low house looked out over a few head of cattle. If they turned around, they could see I-25, and on the other side of it more yellow grass and barbed wire, and a long way off the upthrust grays and greens of the Rocky Mountains. Longs Peak loomed huge in the southwest, its shoulders snowy even in August. The sun was low over the mountains; in another half-hour or so the sky would flood, slowly, from east to west, with that brilliant cobalt that existed nowhere in the world but the Front Range of Colorado, during a few minutes of a few evenings in the summer.

"Take away the freeway and you step back a hundred years," Cindy said wistfully.

Jeff imagined fleeing here and taking up positions along the walls, looking down the shafts of your arrows at the enemy you knew would kill you sooner or later. Below him, on that sand, men had fought and died because some of them were hungry. "Ghosts," he said. "This place is full of them."

"Ghosts are just history," Cindy said. "That's what this place is full of. Ghosts are what you feel when you realize how much bigger and older everything is."

"Okay," Jeff said, and thought she was probably right. But it still felt like ghosts to him. They sat for a while listening to the wind in the rocky spires and feeling the rock warm around them with their body heat. Jeff kept wanting to tell her things that he remembered from the historical marker, but he was smart enough not to. If she wanted to know, she'd ask, and if she didn't he would just be ruining the moment by spouting. This is the kind of moment that you remember, he thought. Sneaking into a historic massacre site just to sit with your girlfriend and listen to the wind in the old, old, worn-down rocks.

Then they heard footsteps, and looked down to see Jarrett Bigelow at the base of the formation where they were sitting. "Believe you're trespassing," he said.

"But you said—" Jeff began before Bigelow cut him off.

"A little joke, son. Relax. Didn't you see my headlights?"

Jeff and Cindy looked at each other. "Some lookout you'd make," she said.

Bigelow chuckled. "I just checked back to see if you'd actually come back. Since you did, I thought I'd drop in and tell you a little story about this place." He looked at Jeff. "Did you tell her what's on the marker?"

"Everything I could remember," Jeff said. "It's been awhile since I was here."

"But you got the Blackfeet and the Crow and the massacre, right?"

"He did," Cindy said.

"Okay." Bigelow paused. "There room for a third up there?"

"Sure," they said, and he climbed up and sat next to Jeff, who although not the jealous type was glad that he hadn't sat on Cindy's side of the rock.

"It seems a damn shame to close this place down," Bigelow said. "I used to come here when I was a boy. Found arrowheads all over the place back then, in the thirties." He shifted a little to point back toward the freeway. "See over there?"

Following his gesture, Jeff and Cindy saw another cluster of sandstone rocks, lower and more broken down than the one that offered them their vantage. "That one there used to be as big as this one," Bigelow said. "And there used to be a whole long series of walls and towers between them. This whole formation was huge back then, before they put the expressway in." He paused and gave first Cindy and then Jeff a long appraising look. "I'm retiring from CDOT next week," he said. "I asked them if I could come up and take the marker down, since they were doing it anyway and I hadn't been back here in forty years. I live down in Castle Rock now, and don't have any reason to come up this way.

"But I have a story about this place, and I've been carrying it around for about as long as I care to, and since you decided to come traipsing on in here, you're the ones I'm going to tell it to. Fair enough?"

"Sounds great," Cindy said, and Jeff was nodding with her. Bigelow nodded, ground out his cigarette, and stuck the butt in his shirt pocket. Then Jeff and Cindy leaned against the crooked spire next to a carved heart, and they listened to wind and passing traffic as Jarrett Bigelow told his story.

2

I was working on the road crew when they built the highway through here in the Fifties. Now the environmentalists would make 'em figure some way to cut it around, but back then they saw that it was a straight line on the map from Denver to Cheyenne and figured it might as well be a straight line on the prairie too. Course that meant we had to blast the middle out of the old fort here, but nobody cared about that except a bunch of dead Indians, and they didn't drive cars.

So we were out here one morning, and I was wiring up some dynamite in this old cave that used to be under there, and I heard some scuffing near the entrance. I looked up and this old boy out of the damn Wild West came skulking in. "Don't talk," he said, "until you've heard what I have to say."

"All right," I said. "I'm listening."

He held out a canvas bag and I took it. "Look inside," he said.

I did, and saw gold. Some coins, some nuggets, even some little oilcloth bags I figured must have been full of dust. I'm not sure what I would have said if I could have made my mouth work, but it didn't matter because I couldn't.

"All yours," the old boy said, "if you do one thing for me."

"What's that?"

"When you blow this cave," he said, "I need to be in it."

Just for a split second, I thought about it. Before the foreman blew the cave, he'd send someone through to make sure the coast was clear. I could probably make sure it was me, but then I'd have to come on back out and tell my boss that there was nobody down in the cave and stand there while he buried this crazy old man under a million tons of sandstone.

"You know I can't do that," I said.

"I know you can. Listen to me, boy. How old do you think I am?"

I shone my flashlight on him. He had that kind of seamed face and bristly hair you get when you've spent your life outside, but his eyes were bright and there were still hard lines around his jaw. "Sixty," I said.

"Hell," he said, "I spent more than sixty years collecting the gold in that bag. You know how many abandoned mining camps there still are up in those mountains? My name is Vandoise Castleton, and I am one hundred and four years old. Born in St. Charles, Missouri, in eighteen hundred and fifty-one. My father was a trapper who lost a foot in one of his own traps and my mother always meant to be a schoolteacher but had me instead. And I am ready to die."

My breath sort of caught in my throat, and I looked around the cave. It was kind of a windy seam with a big bubble in the middle, and in that bubble was a little pond full of the blackest water you ever saw. The floor was all covered with tin cans and burnt ends of sticks. An old shirt wadded up on a rock. I was a young man. I wanted to marry a girl named Charlotte Cassidy whose father was a professor at the university in Fort Collins. I'd never killed anyone, or thought of it.

There was a damned lot of gold in that sack.

"Why did you have to bring this to me?"

"I brought this to these rocks, boy, and the ghosts of all them dead redskins," he said. "Don't have nothing to do with you."

"Well now it does," I said. "You're asking me to kill you."

He reached out a hand and caught my shirt. "No. I am asking you to let me die."

Something in his voice caught me up short. I wasn't sure what to say, and finally I stammered out, "You don't look that old, mister. Why do you want to die?"

"There's something following me that takes death into itself," he said. "It'll kill me if it ever finds me, but until then it keeps me young. It eats death, I think. Every time it gets close to me, it eats a little bit of the death I have coming."

"Well, if you want to die, why don't you just let it find you?"

In the darkness I saw an odd gleam in his eye. "Cause I aim to take it with me."

I tried to look away from him and couldn't. Finally I said, "You get out of here, old man. I can't let you blow up in the cave. I'd lose my job."

For a long, drawn-out minute he just looked at me. "This thing won't let me alone," he said, "and I won't leave you alone either. You wait and see."

"You get out of here," I said again, braver than I felt.

He did, and I finished up wiring the charge and came up out of the cave.

At lunch, old Skyler Vasquez came over to me. He'd been working the road crew since before I was born. "What did that old boy want?"

"You saw him?" I said. "You wouldn't believe it if I told you."

"Oh, I might," he said, "if that was Vandoise."

Skyler's answer caught me by surprise. "You know him?"

"Let me tell you a story," Skyler said. "Then we'll see who has trouble believing who."

3

I was working in the Union Pacific freightyards back in the twenties, before the Depression. One of the things we done in those days on weekends was head down to the old fort to drink beer up on the rocks and swim in the pool down in that cave. Me and them other fellows on the freightyard crew tried every way we could think of to get some girls to come down with us and swim in that pool. Most of 'em wouldn't do it. Either they was scared of the old Indian legends or they was just a little too goody two-shoes to be out on the prairie with us rough old boys. But some would. Especially some nights.

This one afternoon, I remember it was a Saturday because I had the next morning off unless I wanted to go to church, which I wouldn't unless I did something especially sinful with Inez Fuentes, who was my steady girl. Me and Inez had been swimming. She made me turn around when she got out of the pool and while I was trying to peek so she wouldn't notice, that was when I saw the wires poking out from under a rock.

I followed them and found a dozen sticks of dynamite wedged into a crack in the wall, and I don't have to tell you that took the starch right out of me. I went running up and out of the cave in just my skivvies and caught sight of them wires curling around the edge of this big formation we called the Castle. At the end of them, up on one of the Castle's ledges, was a plunger, and both wires was wrapped around its terminals.

Well I didn't have nothing to cut with so I set to work unwrapping them wires as fast as I could, and I had just got the first one off when a shadow fell across me and I looked up to see old Vandoise.

"Why do you have to do that?" he said.

I hopped up and socked him in the mouth. He went down and stayed down, and if he'd gotten up I was ready to give him another one. "What the hell are you doing?" I shouted. If I'd had shoes on I'd have kicked him.

See, Vandoise was no stranger to the old fort. All the girls was afraid of him because of the way he hung around there and I'll admit I didn't like him much either. We'd been seeing him off and on for about a year then, mostly in the middle of the day, and he'd asked around about the old fort. All them Blackfeet slaughtered because they'd come too far down out of the mountains.

"I'm trying to save myself," he said. Lying on the ground with blood on his teeth.

I thought he was a religious nut. One of them Carry Nation types who went around busting up saloons. I got my old preacher's voice in my head, from when I was a boy: *dens of iniquity,* he always used to say. Maybe old Vandoise was blowing up the cave because he thought it was a den of iniquity. "Jesus don't want you to blow us up in that cave, you crazy old bastard," I told him.

Vandoise smiled. The late-afternoon sun caught the blood in his mouth. "Jesus forgot about me a long time ago, kid. I'm on my own."

"What for do you want to blow up the cave?" I shouted. He wasn't making any sense. I still wanted to kick him.

"I'll tell you," he said. "I'll tell you, and then you won't think I'm so crazy."

4

I was working for Professor O.C. Marsh in 1870, when we went out from Fort Wallace to dig along the banks of the Smoky Hill River. This was in Kansas. We found mosasaurs, great fishlike things with long bony jaws, and all kind of other things we'd seen before, but we also found a hollow bone like a bird's, and when we came back the next year we found enough more of those hollow bones to put them together into a flying dinosaur. A dragon! we all said. Dragons in America! I always thought of Red Cloud and Crazy Horse and them, or their ancestors, fighting against these monsters come out of the sky. I didn't know so much about how long ago the dinosaurs had been there.

Anyway, a few years later I happened to be working for Marsh again, this time keeping an eye on E.D. Cope, who was a Quaker and another paleontologist. He and Marsh hated each other. It didn't start out that way, but by the time I'm talking about, they'd developed a good healthy dislike, and they'd started sending folks like me around to the other's camp to see what could be done, if you take my meaning.

Well, in science publication means priority. We learned that early on, working for either Marsh or Cope. Both of 'em were mad to publish. In such a hurry that they weren't always able to check things out the way they might've in less pressing circumstances.

So one of the things that they hired fellows like me to do was maybe find a sample and tinker with it just a little bit. Move a bone that was here over there, maybe, or take away the middle toe from all four feet. If I was working for Marsh and I did this, then we'd leave sign all around the bones so Cope would come across them. He'd dig 'em out and publish with what he had, and then as soon as he'd done that Marsh'd come back with another publication that explained all of the things that Cope had gotten wrong. They did this to each other more'n once.

It happened once over in Morrison, Colorado, that I came across a site that bore unmistakable signs that Cope's men had been digging around. Marks on the rock, tracks everywhere, piles of sifted dirt. So I looked a little closer and damned if I didn't find a fossil, most of a *Dryptosaurus*. The one that Cope called *Laelaps* his whole life even after Marsh told him that was already the name of a spider. *Dryptosaurus* was a mean, jumpy-looking critter, all teeth and claws, and this one was in real good shape, practically all there except for Cope's boys had given it new anklebones that made it look like the extra toes they'd added belonged there.

I was perhaps a little too proud of having spotted this, even though I'd been in the dinosaur business fifteen years by that time—this was 1884—and if I'd missed something like that Marsh would never have hired me again. So I decided I would let Cope's boys know that I was onto them. I was traveling with a wagon full of bones that we had all seen before, we being Marsh's boys, and I thought I could add a few of those into that old *Dryptosaurus* and have a fine time, and maybe add a little humor to the situation, which it could sorely use. Nobody was ever killed over them bones, but guns were drawn, I can tell you that, and there were plenty of fights.

What I had in the wagon were a whole lot of ribs from some damn thing I couldn't remember, most of a sail from a *Dimetrodon,* and a near-complete set of wings off a *Pterodactyl*. Nearly sixteen feet across.

The sun went down and I took them wingbones back to Drypto's resting place there. There was a big waxing moon, almost full, and I spent the night nipping a bottle of whiskey and adding a fine-looking pair of wings to Mister *Dryptosaurus*. I made them a little more substantial with some *Dimetrodon* spines, and just for fun I took out all Drypto's teeth and stuck in a few from a *Hadrosaurus* that were rattling around under the seat of my wagon.

Right before sunrise, I laid some dirt over him, stood up to brush off my hands, and nearly pissed myself when I saw the man on the ridge sighting down the barrel of his rifle at me.

"You step on back from there," he said, and I knew him right away.

"There's no call to bring guns into it, Farley Sheets," I said. "You left him there for me to see, after all, and I was just going along with your joke."

"No joke this time, Vandoise," Farley said. The rifle barrel never moved. "Step on back."

I did, and five or six other men came creeping out of the brush. "What did you do to it?" Farley asked me.

Well, there was no way I was going to tell him after he pointed a damn rifle at me. "Took a look to see what was what," I said, "but those new anklebones of yours wouldn't have fooled a blind man."

He kept looking at me, and there was a time there when I though he was going to shoot. I don't mind telling you, that hurt my feelings; Farley and I went back a long way in the Bone Wars, and we had always kept it professional. Then he said, "Step on back," and I said, "I heard you," and I stepped further back, and saw that one of the men in Farley's party was an Indian.

The Indian was decked out like for a dance or a powwow, beads and furs and everything. His church clothes. It was a mystery to me what would get him out in the middle of the night wearing his finest. Eagle feathers in his hair, paint on his forehead, and something I'd never seen before: little bones woven into a braid that hung down over his ear.

Farley called down. "Should we check it out?"

Another of his men repeated the question to the Indian. It wasn't any Indian language I knew, and by that time I knew bits of quite a few. The Indian shook his head and said something back.

"He says no, the cover can't be disturbed when the sun's about to come up. We're gonna have to try it as is."

Hearing that, Farley looked like he might shoot me again. I stood real still beside my wagon and kept my mouth shut, discretion being – as the poet said – the better part of staying alive.

"Well, do it, then," Farley said. He looked over his shoulder. "The sun's about up."

Farley's man said something to the Indian, who put a drum under his arm and a kind of little wooden flute in his mouth. He started to sing around the flute while tapping on the drum, which had some kind of bangles hanging from it so it thumped and clinked at the same time, and then once in a while he quit singing and blew into the flute, which seemed like it changed notes even if he didn't finger the stops.

I was so busy watching him that I didn't even see the bone monster come up out of the ground. One minute he was singing, the next he was dropping the flute out of his mouth.

I looked where he was looking, and there was Mister Drypto.

It was improved by the wings, I must say. Claw-footed and taller than a man, with pterodactyl wings that I'd added some meat to with spines from a *Dimetrodon*. And little peg teeth from a *Hadrosaur*. It was at the same time the most ridiculous animal contraption you ever saw, and a sight out of a fossil hunter's bad dreams. A bone monster.

It cocked its head like a bird, spread its wings, and flew. It had no flesh, but it flew.

The Indian was closest, and the first to die. It fell on him like an eagle on a rabbit, hooked its claws into him, and pulled him up into the air. When it bit down on him, those peg teeth crunched his skull like hard candy.

Right then everyone else started to run, and it caught every last one of them, not even flying really. It took long soaring bounds, caught them in its claws, and killed them.

Except me and Farley. We stood still, and when it had killed the other six men, it looked around, craning its neck and clacking the bones of its wings. Looking for us, but it couldn't see us when we weren't moving. Farley and I looked at each other, moving only our eyes, and I saw him understanding the same thing I was.

At that moment sunrise broke over the ridge and, I swear to the Lord, the bone monster disappeared. Sunlight struck it, and sort of shined through it, and then it faded away and was gone.

It was a long time before Farley or I moved, though, and when I finally spoke I was half-expecting to hear it invisibly leaping onto me.

"I am damned glad you didn't shoot me, Farley," I said.

"I will never forgive myself," he replied. "You put wings and peg teeth on my dinosaur I was going to sell to P.T. Barnum."

"Is that what you had your medicine man there for?"

"You bet it is. He said he did this all the time, raised earth spirits and whatnot, and I said could you do it so it would listen to me, and he said he could, and I offered him ten percent of what Barnum was going to offer me." Farley gave me the fish-eye. "And if you don't think Barnum would pay for a walking dinosaur skeleton, you ain't got the sense God gave a mule."

"He might have," I agreed. "But not if it turned invisible and disappeared."

The rattle of bones shut us both up. It was closer to me now, much closer, and I thought how foolish I had been for assuming it was gone just because I couldn't see it. If those were the rules, it never would have come out of the ground in the first place. I froze and waited to feel its claws hooking around my ribs.

Another rattle, and another, and I figured out that it was still standing more or less where it had been when it disappeared.

Vandoise and the Bone Monster 249

Could it hear us? Why wasn't it coming after us? Did the sunlight blind it? I could see all the same questions running through Farley's head.

"Farley," I said, "I don't think it can move right now, and I'm not waiting until it can."

"You go on ahead," he said, "and I'll see if you're right."

I did, and Mister Drypto the Bone Monster didn't come after me, and I didn't see Farley again until 1906.

He surprised me in a saloon behind the post office in Vermilion, in the Dakota Territory. I was slouched at the bar—you get to slouching when there's an invisible bone monster chasing you for twenty-two years, it is a frost of cares, as the poet says—and he walked right up, sat down, and ordered a whiskey before I could even notice who he was.

I had always figured on having to kill Farley the next time we crossed paths, since I had ruined his plan to strike it rich with what by 1906 had become Barnum and Bailey, but he didn't seem to have held a grudge. He sipped his whiskey as cool as can be, turned to me, and said, "Vandoise, I have beat that damn monster for twenty-two years. Know why?"

"If I were to guess, I'd say because it's been chasing me," I said.

"Hell, no," he said, and sipped his whiskey again. That particular saloon wasn't known for the quality of its mash, and it was odd behavior coming from a man like Farley. I had difficulty picturing myself killing a man who sipped his whiskey. "I know what makes it hunt," Farley said between sips.

"Do tell," I said.

I had my own theory about that, which was that Mister Drypto was distracted by the presence of mass death. Because of this theory, for which my only evidence was the fact that I hadn't been dismembered that first day and had maintained possession of all four limbs during the years since, I had spent the years between 1884 and 1906 wandering from battlefield to battlefield, massacre site to massacre site, relying on intuition and what the poet calls man's inhumanity to man to keep the bone monster far enough off my trail that I could live. I had been to Wounded Knee and Tippecanoe, Shiloh and Little Big Horn, Sand Creek and every other place of misery I could think of, and somewhere in that time spent among the dead I had stopped living myself. I decided right then, with bad whiskey on my tongue and Farley Sheets hardly getting his mustache wet, that I had to get rid of that damned bone monster once and for all. Fare thee well, Mister Drypto. Back to the ground for you.

But I was right about it being distracted by death. Once in Wyoming I had fallen asleep under a scaffold, and when I woke up I could hear its weight on the planks over my head. Close enough to touch. Through the gaps I watched the bone monster become visible as the sun went down, and I saw it nuzzling the beam where the nooses were tied every Friday. The problem was, once it got used to a place, all the death didn't distract it any more, so I had to keep leading it around until it started to forget places and I could start the whole route over again.

"During the day, when it's invisible," Farley said, "we're invisible to it too. It can't see the world, really, so it has to move real slow. Same thing at night, I think, only at night I think it sees a little better. It's gotten close to me then, but during the day if I'm moving fast, I can't ever tell it's around."

He looked like he was afraid to let go the next words on his tongue, so I did it for him. "But dawn and dusk."

His eyes locked onto mine. We understood each other. "Dawn and dusk," he said, and sipped at his whiskey. Then he had a thought. "That shaman. You know what he did to make that spell work?"

"Can't say I know too much about shaman spells," I said.

"There's a place down south of Cheyenne, a big natural stone fort. Long time ago, I'm not sure exactly when, a whole mess of Blackfeet Indians got themselves massacred there by the Crow."

Another massacre site. Another place where Mister Drypto could be distracted. I was grateful to Farley for letting me know about it. When he went on, though, I started to be more than grateful.

"This old shaman told me he was there when it happened. He said he lay among those dead redskins while the Crow had their fun, and this is what he told me. 'I felt all of their deaths, one by one, going into me and settling there,' he said. 'How many hundred dead men I carry around inside me.' We found him up in Montana when we was looking for someone who we heard could raise up the dead. One of the boys, I can't take credit for it myself, said 'Hell, we should raise up one of them dinosaurs and sell it to

Barnum's show,' and once I'd heard that I couldn't think about anything else. So we went looking, and we found this shaman, and while we were riding down through Casper I got him drunk and he told me about all them dead Blackfeet he had inside him, how he thought he could pour them into the dinosaur bones and finally be rid of them. I thought that was fine, if it took a couple of hundred dead Indians so I could sell a dinosaur to Barnum's circus that was okay with me." He looked up at me with bleary gray eyes. "Then you had to come along with your damned joke."

I wanted to say something to distract him, to get him to stop thinking about this place down south of Cheyenne where the shaman had breathed death in. I was afraid that if he thought about it for too long he'd start thinking exactly what I was thinking, and I was thinking that if I could get Mister Drypto there and distract him, maybe I could be rid of him once and for all. He had come from there, really, or at least the infernal energies that gave him his horrible life had, and it seemed just that he should end there too.

Then I reconsidered. What if Farley and I could work together to trick Mister Drypto?

"Farley," I said. "We have to go to this old fort, you and I."

His eyes grew big as platters and he looked around like the bone monster might be under the piano. "You're crazy," he said. "Go back there where its power came from?"

"It's always distracted with massacres. We could get the drop on it. End it where it began."

"What if that massacre don't distract it, though? What if it gets stronger? What if we go there thinking it's going to do what it always does and find out that all of a sudden it can see us in the daytime? You want to take that chance?"

I looked at him for a long time, watching the little tremble at the corner of his mouth, the way the pupils of his eyes didn't seem like they were quite the same size. "I think I do," I said. "I think I would risk quite a damned lot to be rid of that bone monster once and for all."

"Well, you go ahead then," he said, and took another dainty sip of whiskey. "I'll notify your people when it gets you."

"Goddammit, Farley," I said, "I'll stand you another one if you'll just drink that one like a man."

"Don't mind if I do," he said, and drained his glass, and at that moment I figured out that Farley Sheets was churchmouse poor. And even though he had tried to leave me to be eaten by a bone monster that his own Indian shaman has brought to life, I felt sorry for the man. As it says in the Good Book, let him drink, and forget his poverty.

A man reads the Bible some when he's being pursued by a bone monster.

When I left Farley Sheets in that saloon, I made a beeline for the old fort with Mister Drypto hot on my heels. Death is thick around here, and he's very much interested. Rattles his wings and sniffs around like a bloodhound tracking Jesse James. I looked everything over well enough to have an inkling of a plan and then got out of there while I still could. I knew Mister Drypto would follow, and I knew that eventually he would forget that place and I could lure him back.

I was right, but it took me nearly twenty years, and at some point during those years the bone monster got Farley Sheets.

The bartender at a saloon in Deadwood told me, and I'm man enough to say I cried a little bit, and mine own tears did scald, as the poet says. I cried not so much for drunken double-crossing Farley Sheets as for myself. It was just Mister Drypto and me now. It had taken him thirty-five years to get Farley, and now he had just me to concentrate on before he would have killed everyone who was there when he rose up out of the ground.

Through years of being chased and watching the landscape of the West grow crisscrossed with fences and speckled with cities, I had developed certain ambitions. Most of them I have never realized. At one point I thought of killing Farley Sheets myself, but then I figured out that without him, Mister Drypto would be able to focus all of his attention on me. Then I wanted to kill that medicine man, but I remembered that Mister Drypto had already done for him, and I had to admit that if Farley Sheets had offered me a handful of gold to raise up a dinosaur, and I knew how, I would have done exactly as he did.

Gradually my desires pared themselves down to a few bare essentials. I wanted Mister Drypto not to be around anymore. I

Vandoise and the Bone Monster

wanted to settle down in one place. Get married. Be able to wake up in the morning without listening for the sound of that damned rattling, that clacking. I haven't had a good night's sleep in more than forty years, and just once I want to lie down at night without worrying that I'll die when the sun rises next. A frost of cares.

That bone monster is around here right now. I've lured him back. And if I'm in that cave come sundown, he will be too, and I can end it for the both of us. That's all I want to do. He's been chasing me for so long, and I've been running from him for so long. It must stop.

Clear the girls out of there and just leave me alone tonight. Please. That's all I'm asking.

(5)

Well, I couldn't believe that story, and I was still half-convinced that this old man was just a pervert come sniffing after the girls that was swimming down in the cave. And I didn't much like the way he'd said *redskin*. There's Indians in my family on my mother's side.

So I said, "You get out of here, old-timer, or you're going to find more trouble than some bone monster. Go on. Get."

He looked at me and I realized how I was talking to him. I wasn't no angel when I was a boy, but my parents still brought me up right, and here I was shaming this old man like he was a stray dog. "You can't just blow up the cave," I said, trying to make amends a bit. "You just can't."

"I wouldn't have blown it up with you or the girls in it," he said. "I wouldn't."

"I know," I said.

He sighed, long and kind of shuddery, like he was trying not to cry. "It's a long time before I can come back here," he said. "It takes Mister Drypto a long time to forget a place, and I can't bring him back here until he has forgotten. What if it takes another twenty years? What if he kills me before then?"

There wasn't much I could say to that. "I'm real sorry."

The sun touched the mountains right then and I heard a whirring, rattling kind of noise that had my balls creeping right up into my collar. Over on the wall of the old fort, the one that faces out toward the mountains, I saw something silhouetted against the setting sun. The light was too bright for me to get a good look at it.

"Don't move," old Vandoise said. "Don't even breathe if you can help it."

I didn't. I shut my eyes and held my breath and waited.

When I couldn't hold my breath any longer, I opened my eyes. The sun was nearly gone and I couldn't see no bone monster. Vandoise was gone too.

Now I'm a bit of an amateur historian and I did some checking over the years, but I never found anyone named Vandoise in any records. So I figured this old boy was just pulling my leg. The thing wouldn't let go of me, though, and a few years ago, 1950 I think it was, I heard of an old collection of newspapers at an estate sale up in Edgemont, South Dakota. I went up to check it out. And I'll be damned if I didn't find an article clipped out of the *Black Hills Prospector* talking about a man named Farley Sheets who was found dead on the banks of a creek out in Buffalo Gap. The article decided wolves or mountain lions must have done it even though it was 1919 and there weren't many of either left in those parts any more. My eye was caught by a particular detail: wedged behind the hinge of Farley Sheets's jaw was a fossilized brontosaurus tooth. The reporter speculated that it had been tied on a cord around his neck and was crushed in there by the force of whatever bit him.

On the same page there was an article about Eisenhower going across the country to scout out ways to move armies or some such. He spent a few days in Wyoming before arriving on the West Coast on September fifth that year. Just thought it was a little odd because we're both working for Eisenhower building the interstates. A historical coincidence. That newspaper connects us to Farley Sheets. And old Vandoise.

(6)

It was about time to get back to work, and I wadded up my lunch bag and threw it in the ditch. "A fossilized brontosaurus tooth, huh?"

Skyler nodded. "That's what it said."

"That old boy was crazy."

"You would be too. Anyway, that's why he came up to you today. I'll give you dollars to pesos that he wants you to kill him, and don't be surprised if he comes back."

Skyler paused like he was about to admit to something shameful. Then he said, "I thought about that old boy being chased by that bone monster, and I felt a little bad that I didn't blow him up the way he wanted me to." Then he looked up at me and bared his teeth. "I stood right over there and waited for that monster to come for me, Jarrett Bigelow. You watch out what you let old Vandoise get you into."

I nodded at him, but I didn't tell him about the gold.

Two weeks later, everything was different. It had rained a bit so the blasting was rescheduled, and we hadn't set off the charges I'd laid in the cave. And Charlotte was late, if you take my meaning. It looked like I was going to be a father. I wanted to marry her before her father found out – not that I was worried he'd do anything, since it never occurred to me to worry about being shot by a history professor, but still I wanted him to think of me as a man who would do the right thing by his daughter. And this was all begging the question of what my mother would think. No sir, it was best to marry Charlotte right away, run off and do it and then fudge the math on the other end when the baby came due. She was all for it; the only problem was I didn't have any money, and neither one of us wanted to live with a set of in-laws.

What with all this, when Vandoise showed up next to me while I was taking a leak out on the other side of the old fort one day, I was a little more ready to listen to what he had to say.

"You look me in the eye and tell me you want to die," I said.

He looked me dead in the eye and said, "More than I have ever wanted to live, I want to die tonight."

"Now tell me something else. Do you have family? I won't do this if you're going to leave people."

"I have survived all three of my sisters," he said, "and thanks to Mister Drypto I never married."

I couldn't believe I was saying it, but I was saying it. "All right then. A man has to make his own decisions."

"A man does," Vandoise agreed. "At least I am left that."

"The cave's wired to blow, but I don't think we're supposed to do it today." I had reset and checked the charge myself that morning, and I'd be lying if I said that bag of gold didn't cross my mind a time or two. Well, here was my second chance to do the right thing. "If we are, I'll figure something else out. When do you want me to do it?"

"At sundown," he said. "Right when the sun touches the mountains, you count to one hundred, and then you push that plunger. You hear me?"

"Sundown," I said. "Count to one hundred."

Vandoise caught my wrist as I went to leave him there. "If this dynamite doesn't go off when I want it to, boy, this thing that's going to kill me? It'll have your scent next. You make sure and blow this cave."

"I will," I said.

"All right then." He let go of my wrist. "I may not seem grateful, son, but you are doing me a kindness. Remember that."

I couldn't say anything else to him; my mouth was seized up again. Holding onto the canvas bag, I worked my way around the rocks to a good place to hide the gold. Then I came out and told the foreman that the charges in the cave were all wired. He said all right, we'll check it again and blow in the morning. I started to argue, but then I thought how that would look, and I thought of all that gold hidden in a crack in the rocks. "That sounds good," I said. "We knocking off then?"

There were a few things to clean up, but it was late in the afternoon and everyone was in a hurry to get on home. Right as the foreman was padlocking the shed where the blasting equipment was, I realized I needed an excuse to stay. I'd hitched a ride in with some of the boys from up in Cheyenne, and it was a ten-mile walk.

A friend of mine named Barry called from his old pickup. "You go on ahead," I called back. I jogged over to the truck. "I'm going to look around a bit for arrowheads." My girl in Fort Collins had a younger brother who could never get enough arrowheads.

"How you going to get back to Cheyenne?" Barry asked.

"I'll give you five dollars to come back and pick me up in two hours," I said.

"And beer's on you tonight?"

I thought of all the gold in that sack. "Beer's on me. Give me a cigarette."

He shook me out a Chesterfield and I lit up as he roared away.

I climbed up to a high spot in the old fort and looked out across the plains toward the Medicine Bow Mountains. On the other side of them was a town called Walden. Sometimes I headed up that way to fish in the Michigan River. As I smoked Barry's Chesterfield I thought about that old man, down there in the cave waiting to die, and I almost got down off the rocks and went to tell him I wouldn't do it. But that look in his eye.

He wants to, I told myself, and I spent a long time turning that thought over in my mind, trying to see if it was a real belief or something I was trying to convince myself so I wouldn't feel so guilty when I dropped the plunger.

It seemed real. That look in his eye. *There's something following me that takes death into itself,* he'd said. What kind of something was that?

The sun was low over the mountains. There would be long shadows over the Michigan River, and it was time to break into the blasting shed. I worked the lock with a piece of wire and took the plunger over to a little hollow about a hundred yards from the cave entrance. It only took a minute to wind the wires around the plunger's terminals, and then I just sat there watching the sun settle towards the mountains. There was a wind in the grass, and I imagined I head the voices of all the dead redskins whose ghosts still lived on these plains. One, I said softly. Two. Three.

Over by the cave I saw something, and then in the next instant I thought I'd just gotten grit in my eye. I blinked, rubbed my hand across my eyes. While they were closed, just for a moment, I thought I heard a rattling sound. A clacking on the breeze, like the maracas the Mex girls played sometimes. When I opened my eyes again, there was just a flash of movement by the cave entrance. If that's the old man, I thought, and he's just chickened out, I'm keeping his damn gold. He can just try to take it away. But there was nothing after that first ghost of motion.

Eight-four. Eighty-five. Eighty-six.

A shout came from the cave, but I couldn't understand the words. Then there was another noise, and I don't know what it was, but if I live to be a hundred I don't ever want to hear it again.

One hundred, I said to myself, and depressed the plunger.

Smoke and dust shot out of the cave entrance, and there was a big damned boom even though it was muffled from being underground. Then that whole part of the old fort just sort of slumped a little bit. A couple of the big spires cracked and fell sideways, throwing up more dust, and the sunset caught it all in this brilliant orange, and I sat there thinking that I'd just killed a man. Right then it didn't make any difference that he'd asked me to.

Then I snapped to. Whether he'd asked for it or not, if anybody found out I'd have a hard time explaining myself. I unwound the wires from the plunger terminals and clipped off the curled ends before stashing the plunger back in the shed and locking the door. The boys would take a hard look at everything tomorrow morning, but I'd just tell them that the dynamite had gone off. Wouldn't be the first time that had happened.

I caught myself thinking like a guilty man, and just for a second there I hated myself for what I'd done. But he'd wanted it, I told myself, and it was true, and besides I couldn't undo it. I thought of how Charlotte would get big with my baby, and I thought of the house I'd buy her with all that gold. And he'd wanted me to.

The sack was right where I'd left it, in a hollow at the bottom of a high five-pronged spire. Partway up the spire was a scooped-out spot where you could sit like you were in the palm of a stone giant. You could see a good way out over the plains from there, and if you turned around the mountains were something else.

(7)

The spot we're sitting in right now, Jeff thought. Forty years ago Jarrett Bigelow hid a sack of gold here and killed a man and left him buried under sandstone and graded dirt and asphalt. How many thousand people drive over Vandoise Castleton every day and don't know he's there?

"That clacking sound," Bigelow said. "I don't think I'll ever forget that." After another long pause, he went on.

"The part I always liked about Skyler's story was the way he remembered all of Vandoise's quotes. 'As the poet says,' you know? I've walked around for forty years hearing old Vandoise saying that even though he never actually said it in front of me. And I wasn't there, but I can see that bone monster coming up out of the ground just as clear as I can see my own face in the mirror. I had to pass it on. And—" Bigelow's voice caught, and he swallowed. "I killed a man here, and I guess there's part of me that wanted to confess. Even though he asked me to, and even though I think I did the right thing. Every year less and less people know about the Blackfeet that died here, and every year I'd hear about this or that person I used to know who had died and I would think that I was the only person in the world who knew what happened to old Vandoise. I never told anybody."

Jeff and Cindy looked at each other. He just confessed to a murder, Jeff thought, and he could see Cindy thinking the same thing. Here we are in the middle of nowhere listening to the story of a murderer who is annoyed at us for trespassing on the scene of his crime. I bet he killed Skyler Vasquez, and I bet there never was any bone monster. He probably found some gold, or Vasquez found it, and they argued and Bigelow blew him up in the cave under the old fort. Jeff started to feel around near his feet for a rock, in case Bigelow made some kind of move.

Then, out of the blue, Cindy asked, "Did you marry Charlotte?"

Bigelow nodded. "We were married thirty-six years, until she died a year ago this October."

"And you never told her?"

"No. We had four kids, and now seven grandkids, and I won't tell any of them either. I used that gold to take care of all of them.

I bought land down south of Denver, I put my kids through college in Boulder. And I got a couple of accounts that no one's going to know about until after I'm gone. A little surprise for the grandkids." He cracked a wrinkled smile and stood, accompanied by sharp pops in his knees. "Well. Getting dark. Guess you two ought to get out of here, and stay on that side of the fence next time." He paused for a long time, looking at the sparse traffic on I-25.

"I think about them sometimes," Bigelow said then. "That old boy Vandoise and the monster down there. I wonder if they're really dead, either of them. Wonder if maybe they'll get out some day, and that bone monster'll start chasing the old man again. Seems almost like it ought to happen." He shook his head. "Other times I think I'm just making this whole story sound good, and I killed a man for a bag of gold."

There was a pause, and Jeff thought again of how far they were from anything. Then it passed, and he said, "Wish I'd seen that cave." He was full of imaginings about underground rivers, winding seams that led for miles under the parched prairie. Now it was all dynamited and buried under asphalt. If that story is true, he thought, some archaeologist in two thousand years is going to have one hell of a puzzle on his hands.

"Yeah," Bigelow said. "I wish you had too. I don't know whether you believe me or not," Bigelow went on, "but thank you for listening. Shit," he chuckled, "whether it's true or not, that's too good a story to let die with an old man like me."

"You can say that again," Cindy said.

"This is for hearing me out," Bigelow said, and he held out a hand palm-up. On the open palm rested two gold coins bearing the stamp PIKES PEAK GOLD and the date 1881. "When you two get old, you can be like me and old Vandoise, hanging around out here until some likely-looking kids come along, and then you can pass the story along. Then you give 'em these to make sure they remember."

"We would have remembered anyway," Cindy said.

"Still," Bigelow said, and they each took a coin, and Jeff thought Now we are in it too. This whole story, from the Blackfeet through dueling paleontologists through Vandoise and Sheets and Skyler and Jarrett Bigelow and Mister Drypto the bone monster. Now we're part of it too. Accomplices, perhaps...but no. It was old blood, long soaked into the ground. History, or ghosts. And I guess I was both right and wrong: some stories are buried under concrete out here. But they get out anyway, despite the weight of neglect and age and failing memory.

Jarrett Bigelow touched the bill of his Colorado Rockies baseball cap and trudged through the sand and out of the old natural fort, leaving them in shadow with the faint gleam of gold and the brilliant darkening blue of evening sky.

A Peaceable Man

I have had the privilege of owning a borzoi, which is a lot like having a dog but not exactly the same. The borzoi is refined yet childlike, a lethal hunter who cries if someone sits in his favorite spot on the couch. He is bundled paradox, joy, anxiety, devotion. He exasperates with his stubbornness, enchants with his grace, delights with his buffoonery...but let us not forget that he was bred to hunt down wolves on the steppes.

This is the story I did not tell Detectives Brower and Glenn when they interviewed me the day after Kenny Kazlauskas came over to my house to kill me.

It all started when a violent and larcenous acquaintance of mine named Arthur Czyz discovered that armored cars have to stop at weigh stations. The stations are labeled for all commercial vehicles, so it's not exactly a surprise that this should be true, but in addition to being violent and larcenous Arthur was kind of dumb.

He was, however, possessed of what a Victorian judge might have called animal cunning. So when he found out about armored cars and weigh stations, he knew immediately that he'd found a way to take an armored car. Problem was, he didn't know what that way was.

This is why he had more intelligent friends like me.

Greg, he said to me one day. We were at Otto's Coffeehouse in Allston. I like the college vibe there even though it's a long time since I was in college. Arthur just comes in to see how many of the students get scared of him, plus he likes Otto's coffee and the place is right on Commonwealth Avenue next to one of Otto's early morning stops. Otto drives an overnight pastry and dairy truck, covering Newton, Brookline, and Allston. Into the warehouse in Revere at 3am, out at 4am, back to the warehouse by 8 to reload for the places that aren't open when he starts his first round. He's off by noon if he can avoid traffic, which nobody can do in Boston, a city whose streets still follow the deer tracks widened by the Passamaquoddy Indians back in the day.

I'm usually seated at one of the tables out front of Otto's by seven on any given morning, with Boris standing at my side looking over my shoulder while I read the *Globe*. Borzois don't like to sit, and they're so bony they don't much like to lie on concrete either. So Boris was my clock when we went to Otto's. About the time he got tired of standing around he'd start to grumble and whine. If car engines sounded like howling dogs, a borzoi's whine would be an exact replica of the engine turning over right before it started. *Owrowrowrowrrrrr.*

"Greg," Arthur said.

"Arthur," I said back.

He sat down at the empty chair on the other side of the table. "We could knock over an armored car," he said.

Unlike Arthur, I am not violent. I do, though, confess to a certain larcenous tendency. It keeps me in chai and scones and permits me to begin my days at Otto's instead of behind the wheel of one of the cars that obstructs Arthur's route through Boston every morning.

I set down the *Globe*. Boris sniffed it over, looked at me. I gave him a piece of my scone. His ears shot up when he saw it, but he took it with great delicacy, another borzoi characteristic not shared with more mundane breeds.

"How could we knock over an armored car, Arthur?" I asked. There were no police in evidence, but I didn't like the direction the conversation was taking; although I had no record, Arthur did.

"They have to stop at weigh stations," he said.

"You don't say," I said. "Where'd you hear this?"

He shrugged. "Kenny said something about it."

That put an end to the conversation as far as I was concerned. When he wasn't driving the truck for his father's dairy (and, as I was later to discover, even when he was), Arthur did various unsavory jobs for Kenny Kazlauskas, one of the new breed of organized-crime figure who had popped up in East Coast cities after the breaking of the Cosa Nostra. Kenny K. was sociopathic, irrational, unencumbered by notions of loyalty, and superstitious as a Haitian grandmother—and this last quality had bred in him an intense hatred of yours truly because he thought I was a magician.

I supplemented my illegitimate income with a genuine business as a purveyor of antiques. Boston has antique dealers like Washington DC has lobbyists, and my particular niche was a curious ability to locate and possess items allegedly possessed of supernatural qualities. During the previous ten years, I'd either acquired or brokered the acquisition of a Dale Chihuly sculpture that acted as an aphrodisiac, an Austrian grandfather clock said to confer immortality, a golden cobra from a pharaoh's tomb that animated when its owner's life was threatened, and an antiquated stock ticker that purportedly predicted the market with unfailing accuracy. And many more. The truth is, I never put much stock in any of the stories that accrued around old and valuable things; I'd never seen any evidence of magic, and remained a confirmed agnostic on the subject.

Nevertheless, my reputation, to a brain as paranoid and cocaine-addled as Kenny's made me a prime candidate for burning at the stake. Which in turn made me not at all inclined to do a potentially violent job that might in addition turn out to be competitive with one of Kenny's own plans.

I should have made this clear to Arthur, but he spoke before I could articulate my objection. "All's we'd have to do is make sure that we'd cleared out the weigh station before the armored car got there," he said.

"That and get away afterwards," I amended. "It's not going to work if we leave the scene by merging into traffic on I-95 again, is it?"

"You're the detail guy," Arthur said. "Plans are your thing. I just had this idea. I think you ought to think about it."

"I will," I said, and he climbed back into his truck and drove away in a belch of unburned diesel.

And I did. I thought about it and I decided that like most of Arthur's ideas, it was immensely risky and likely to end badly. I'm a housebreaker by trade. Occasionally I set other things up, but I rarely deal in armed robbery, and I even more rarely deal in jobs that involve armed opponents in public places.

Just to be certain, though—and very much against my better judgment—I started making some inquiries to people I knew in the highway department, and one of them knew someone who knew someone in Maine, and this someone happened to know that there was a gate at the rear of the parking lot of a certain weigh station on a certain state highway in Maine. Installed, it appeared, to preserve access to paper company land that was being cut off by the construction of the highway.

Knowing this was one of the worst things that ever happened to me.

Boris and I camped in the backcountry for a few days, canoeing through northern Maine's beautiful flatwater and watching stars at night. I live in Boston, but I like to get out into the woods. And Boris, despite being a refined animal, had a back-to-nature streak in his heart. He didn't even mind canoeing. I only minded it myself when he tried to stand up in the canoe; when he was a puppy he tipped us a couple of times before I convinced him that we were all better off if he stayed lying down until we got to shore.

It occurred to me while I was poking at my campfire on the second night of the trip that I was looking for an excuse to do the job. Me, quiet and pacifistic Gregory Flynn, contemplating an armored-car heist—and with Arthur Czyz as my partner, no less.

"Crazy," I told Boris, but he was asleep, a white mat on the pine-needled riverbank.

Be honest with yourself, I thought. This is about the Gronkjaer board.

Every so often I become aware of an extremely valuable article that tests my professionalism. I want these items for myself despite the risk possession entails, or perhaps because of it. The Gronkjaer board was one such item.

Like many of the pieces my clients came to me to acquire, this board had an occult history. Apparently a shipping magnate and amateur player had commissioned it in 1844 for his office, and upon seeing it had become so enraptured by it that he had spent more and more time playing the game by himself, falling in love with the feel of the pieces in his hands and with the way the squares gleamed in the lamplight. Soon he was neglecting his business and his wife, and it was not until she committed suicide in 1851 that he realized that he'd allowed his immersion in the game to destroy him. She killed herself by slashing her wrists over the board, and died with the two kings clutched in her hands. He lost his house but kept the board, and executors of his estate eventually found a long and anguished series of journal entries stating that the spirit of his wife had come to occupy it. *It is her revenge upon me,* he wrote. *That for which I abandoned her she now inhabits. I play, and the queen has her face, and the field of battle is as an infinitely variable topology of regret.*

After the magnate's death in 1866, the board had passed through a number of hands, often sold quickly because its owners found themselves playing to the exclusion of all else. The legend about it grew; it was said that when great players took up the pieces, they found themselves replaying their most agonizing defeats. In any case, a long list of broken marriages, suicides, and even murders accompanied the board's history, and the man who approached me to get it for him believed firmly that the board would always contain the spirit of the one person its owner had abandoned to loneliness and death.

This all sounded a bit melodramatic to me, although like I said I've seen some odd things during the course of my career, but I went ahead and started planning the job. Then, the first time I saw the board, in the center of a paneled study on the third floor of an old mansion in Stamford, Connecticut, I realized I wanted it for myself.

If the armored-car job came off, I could buy the Gronkjaer board. Legitimately. I knew it was coming up for auction soon, the current owner being *non compos mentis* and his oldest daughter anxious to sell off the old man's curios before he died and she had to pay estate taxes on everything. Of course I could have just stolen it; exactly such a commission had first brought the board to my attention. After looking into the household security, though, I'd declined the job, and I still wasn't confident I could pull it off. Easier to await the auction.

Except I didn't have the money, which brought me right back to Arthur's proposal and the real reason I was camping in western Maine instead of creeping a condominium in the Back Bay.

Boris grumbled in his sleep, emitting that sound peculiar to the borzoi that resembles nothing so much as the low of a cow. I sat up, looking for shooting stars and wondering whether I believed in the story of the Gronkjaer board.

The next morning, I left the canoe overturned under a stand of pine trees and hiked with Boris along a snaking trail that eventually broadened into a logging road that after some time took a sharp right and dead-ended in an iron gate. NO TRESPASSING, the gate said. STATE PROPERTY. NO ROAD ACCESS.

Boris jumped over the gate—he could clear four or five feet from a standstill—and I ducked underneath it. About a hundred yards further on, the road split. I turned right and twenty minutes later came up to a second gate. On the other side of it was a broad patch of concrete with a small office booth in the middle near the scale.

"Well, what do you know," I said to Boris. He started to trot out onto the lot, but I stopped him. People remember borzois, a fact that is a constant trial to a man in my profession. At times I wished I had gotten a lab or a spaniel. Or a gerbil.

The borzoi, though, is an exceptional animal.

"We'd have to get one guy and use him to get the other guy out of the car," I said to Arthur the next time I saw him.

He sat at the table, spilling my chai. It dripped through the metal curlicues of the tabletop and spotted the sidewalk. Boris strained to get his muzzle all the way to the ground. At home his food and water dishes stood on a little platform, but here in the wilds of Allston he was on his own.

"I was kind of thinking, you know, just overwhelm them with firepower," he said.

"This job works if nobody gets hurt," I said. "Hurting people introduces complications, and raises the possibility that one of us will get hurt as well."

"You keep thinking about it," he said, and got up.

"I'm only going to think for so long," I said, "and then you're going to have to tell me whether you want to go along with it or whether I'm just going to schedule a second-story job over on Charles Street."

Boris sneezed when Arthur drove away. Diesel miasma ruined my chai.

It occurred to me not too much later that we wouldn't even need a car for the job. We could backpack in, do the job, backpack out, and pick up our car at one of the Appalachian Trail lots that dot western Maine's backcountry roads. Easy. But Arthur didn't like it. "Hell, no," he said in front of Otto's the morning I brought it up. "You can't just walk away from a job like that. How the hell do you carry the money?"

"Well, that's the thing," I said. "We couldn't carry all of it. But if we do this right, we'll have enough time to go through the car so we don't end up with a bag of singles. A car gives the police a real handle, something to look for. If the drivers say we walked away, then all the police will have to go on is descriptions of us. And we're pretty ordinary-looking guys, let's face it." This was true, and it was one of the reasons I'd been a successful thief for nearly twenty years. I'd been spotted in the middle of a job maybe half a dozen times, and every time the description given of me was different. People just didn't remember what I looked like.

Arthur, I suspected, was a bit more recognizable, if for no other reason than he was a big man. But the world is full of big men, and if I was planning this enterprise correctly, any searchers would look right through us.

Stores such as REI and Eastern Mountain Sports sell dog backpacks, but a borzoi is such a thin and deep-chested animal that no pack will hang right on him. Because of this, much of the load in my backpack (rented under a name not my own from a Boston University outdoors organization) was dog food. I encouraged Boris to eat hearty while we hiked from the trailhead where I'd parked the rental car (much closer than I'd originally envisioned, it not being clear whether we'd be able to carry both backcountry gear and enough cash to make the job worthwhile) southwest in the direction of our rendezvous with Arthur, who had taken a bus to Portland and from there hitchhiked north and west until he was well into the White Mountains. We were due to meet on the fire road I'd walked with Boris some weeks before.

It was the Monday after July 4th, following a weekend when—Arthur and I hoped—the good people of New England had left much of their money in the small towns of western Maine. The LockTrans truck, we had learned, made a weekly loop through several area municipalities, vacuuming up the deposits of seven small banks, two grocery stores, and the summer resort at the base of Maine's finest ski mountain. I put the over-under on the job's proceeds at just under half a million dollars. Arthur was more optimistic. Neither of us was sure how much of the cash we'd be able to carry. My backpack was spacious, and my gear compact, and Boris would just have to be hungry on the return leg of our journey.

When I made the turn from the trail onto the fire road, Arthur was waiting. Boris trotted up to him and leaned his head into Arthur's crotch, another habit of borzois that people have told me also exists in greyhounds. The action isn't the typical sniffing of a typical dog; the borzoi leans to get affection, and the human groin is perfectly constructed to afford a tall and narrow-headed dog a place to rest.

Arthur stood scratching behind Boris' ears, but the look he directed at me was pure confusion. "What's he doing here?" he said.

"He's our cover. When the police start covering the trails, they're not going to figure that armed robbers would bring a dog."

Arthur looked dubious, and when I had tied Boris to a tree out of sight of the road, he stopped me before we could walk away. "Is he going to be okay?"

A Peaceable Man

Despite his limited intelligence and tendency toward violence, Arthur is soft-hearted when it comes to any animal other than *homo sapiens*. "He'll be fine," I said as I was leaving the rest of Boris's food in a heap on the ground within range of his tether. It wouldn't do to have to leave dog food at the scene of the crime for reasons of space. "He has water, and he'll eat what he wants while we're gone." Which wouldn't be much; Boris was a finicky eater.

We didn't rehearse the plan again as we hiked the final mile or so to the weigh station's rear gate; Arthur and I had done enough jobs together that we knew when we didn't have to beat a dead horse. The plan was simple yet daring; we would overpower the weigh-station attendant and Arthur, wearing his uniform, would wait until the LockTrans truck pulled onto the station lot and then walk out to close the gate. Inside the small office, I (wearing another uniform borrowed at exorbitant cost from a broker in specialized clothing) would flip the switch that toggles the road sign from OPEN to CLOSED. As Arthur walked back, I would come out of the booth to examine the truck's log, apologizing but saying a regulatory change made the action necessary. When the driver or passenger opened the door to give me the log, Arthur and I would draw our guns and get the guards out of the car. They would open the back for us, and we would skate off with however much money we could carry. We would also destroy the security recordings that are standard equipment on newer armored cars.

Then it would be off into the wilderness, and back to Boston. Simple.

It worked absolutely like clockwork. The weigh-station attendant froze at the sight of Arthur's gun, said, "But we ain't got money here," and then fainted dead away. Arthur changed into his uniform and I into mine, and just as we finished our preparations the LockTrans truck pulled off Route 201 and onto the scale. Arthur was already walking out to the gate, and after lighting the CLOSED message on the sign I had no trouble getting the driver to give up first the log and then his and his fellow's guns. Arthur kept the two drivers in the front seat while I popped the back door, destroyed the recording equipment, and stuffed Arthur's backpack with money.

I had filled Arthur's pack and was about to start on mine when, in the distance, I heard the unmistakable *owrowrowrowrrr* of an agitated borzoi.

Things would have been all right. I believe that. It is evident to me. If only Arthur had not leaned out from the side of the truck and said, "Is that your dog?"

I told you he wasn't very bright.

Several things happened at once then. I lost my composure and said, "Are you some kind of goddamn idiot?" and Arthur looked at me with an expression of terrible hurt before glancing back into the front seat of the LockTrans truck as a gunshot sounded and the epaulet on his left shoulder blew away in a spray of blood. As Arthur stumbled backward, he emptied his gun into the truck's passenger compartment.

I was already running. When I got to the back gate, I looked over my shoulder and could not believe what I saw. Arthur had stopped to get his backpack, the one I'd loaded with money, and he was staggering toward the station attendant's car like a GI making the beachhead on Guadalcanal.

The usefulness of Boris as cover would only last until one of the LockTrans guards, if either had survived Arthur's fusillade, mentioned Arthur's inopportune comment. I was a good three hours from where I'd parked the rental, and I hoped that would be enough time to be moving in the car before the police heard about the dog connection. As I hiked, climbing along the edge of a forested gorge with a clear rushing stream at its bottom, I sent up the Thieves' Prayer in Case of an Injured Partner: *Please let him have the sense not to go to the hospital.* Arthur had that much sense, I thought, but you could never tell. People with bullets in them tended to get irrational.

My plan was to get the car and head up into northern New Hampshire for a week or so, maybe Vermont. Pitch a tent, go canoeing, wait for the police to form their initial opinions, then go home and try to make contact with Arthur. Along the way I'd get rid of the clothes and shoes I'd worn to do the job, wrap them around a large rock and drop them into one of the deep lakes that dot northern New England.

A Peaceable Man

My precautions were probably excessive. I'd never been arrested, never even questioned by Boston police. In the aboveground economy, I was just another antiques broker who made his living putting buyers and sellers in touch with each other. We're quiet people, unremarkable. We have museum memberships and we go to the opera. But excessive caution was one reason the police had never had cause to think of Gregory Flynn and larceny at the same time, so I went on being careful and hoped the authorities would go on looking elsewhere when it came to certain unlawful acts committed in the New England states.

In the event, I arrived home six days after the robbery, dropped the car off at the rental agency, and took the Green Line back to my house in Brookline Village. Boris liked riding the T, and he was an unusual enough breed that most fellow riders suspended their natural disinclination to share their commute with a dog.

I knew that someone had been in my house as soon as I opened the door. It's a talent I think all professional thieves have. We've skulked in and out of so many places that we develop a kind of intuition about when someone has been skulking in ours.

The gun I'd carried to do the LockTrans job was at the bottom of Lake Willoughby, far away in the part of Vermont known as the Northeast Kingdom. I owned a licensed .38 automatic, but it was upstairs in my bureau. If anyone was lying in wait for me, they'd have little opposition; I wasn't a fighter.

Boris trotted into the house unconcerned, making a beeline for his water bowl in its frame next to the refrigerator. I went upstairs and checked every room of the house, finding nothing missing or disturbed. To be certain, I opened the floor safe under my bed. Everything I'd left there was still there, and nothing appeared to have been moved.

So why the feeling? In the business I am in, you learn to trust instincts, and my instinct was that someone had been in my house. I thought it over as I watered plants, sorted through the mail, played back the messages from clients on my answering machine. Arthur, maybe? Couldn't be. He wasn't the sharpest pencil in the drawer, but he knew better than to come to my house so soon after a botched job.

I was still mulling it over, still a bit irritated by the sensation, when I opened the *Globe* from the day after the job and saw that both guards had survived. This was a relief, both because it meant that if worse came to worst and the police connected me to the job there would be no murder charge and because I am a peaceable man by nature and my guilt would have been a terrible thing if either of the guards had died.

In the next day's *Globe* I saw that one Arthur Czyz, 39, of Malden, had been found dead in his apartment of a gunshot wound. There were no details, but I assumed the police had found the money from the robbery and were waiting to dot their i's and cross their t's before making an announcement.

The next four editions of the *Globe,* though, contained no such definitive link. Boston police speculated that Arthur had been involved in the job because his wound had clearly been inflicted elsewhere, but they had not recovered the station attendant's car and they had no solid evidence connecting Arthur to the crime.

I looked up from the paper when I heard Boris make that mooing sound. He was standing in the living room, staring into the corner behind an end table, against the wall that divided the living room from the kitchen. I called him and he glanced at me, then went back to his study.

Borzois, I thought. He was probably hearing mice; I would have to get traps again.

That night I dreamed I was sitting in the living room talking to Arthur, who was reclining on my sofa without the slightest regard for the blood that leaked through his shirt and stained the armrest. "Your dog got me killed," he said, and I tried to deny it, but I knew he was right.

I woke up to the thump of the newspaper on the porch. I was on the sofa, the dream still vivid in my mind. Had I walked in my sleep? I never had before. But I'd never had a colleague killed before; perhaps the stress and a bit of lingering guilt were troubling me more than I was allowing myself to realize.

Boris groaned at the door, then whined at a higher pitch when I was slow to get up. I let him out into my small yard and picked up the paper. Again nothing about the robbery except a small notice that both guards had gone home from the hospital and the state of Maine was talking about improving security at weigh stations.

When Boris came back in the house, I said to him, "Arthur says you got him killed." He looked at me, then went into the corner and stared at the wall. He was still there when the police knocked on the door and arrested me for armed robbery and attempted murder.

There isn't much to say about being in prison, although God knows people do say enough about it. My own experience at MCI-Walpole was relatively tranquil; the highlight, if it can be called that, was a scene in the cafeteria during my fifth year. Two of my fellow inmates got into a fight over something and one stabbed the other in the back with a fork. The wounded party leaped away from the table and ran from the cafeteria, fork waggling from just inside his right shoulder blade, and someone shouted out, "Stop that guy! He's stealing the silverware!"

I was lucky, no doubt about it. Being older and innocuous, I wasn't a threat to anyone, and apart from a few perfunctory assaults soon after I arrived, I passed my six years (thanks to a skilled attorney) at Walpole without incident. I read most of what was in the prison library; I tried to keep tabs on my house, which I'd rented to a fellow antique dealer burned out of his own home as a result of a fire in the restaurant below his Charles Street condominium; and I made repeated phone calls to my old friend Karen Garrity, who had volunteered to take care of Boris until such time as I could reclaim him. I never found out who had turned me in, and truth be told I didn't spend much time looking. Revenge was of no interest to me, perhaps because my sentence was the least I deserved for participating in the robbery and getting a man killed. And whoever had placed me at the scene, I reasoned out of a natural faith in humankind, must have had legitimate reasons of self-preservation.

The darkest moment of my Walpole tenure came a year before I was released, when I called Karen to ask about Boris and she told me that he had run away. In disbelief I hung up the phone and cried, only then realizing that he was the only reason I cared about the length of my stay. I was never one of those inmates who loses all sense of the outside world and fears the date of his release, but my guilt over the guard's death allowed me to grow comfortable in this punishment of my own choosing. No family awaited me on the outside, and my friendships were all old enough that a length of time apart would do them no lasting damage. Prison was a limbo I inhabited until a decision was made to return me to civil society, and I only wanted to return because I wanted to see my dog.

That final year passed in a kind of ennui that surpassed even the typical long-term inmate's fatalism. At my parole hearing, I said—honestly—that I regretted nothing in my life so much as my decision to go along with Arthur Czyz and rob an armored car in Maine. Asked about my plans if I were released, I said—again truthfully—that I would like to rebuild my dormant antiques business. I was fifty-one years old and had luckily not had anything in my home that tied me to any other violations of the law, and the parole board released me two months before my fifty-second birthday.

Karen was there to pick me up and drive me back to Boston. We talked about highway construction, mostly, and although I wanted to ask her about Boris I couldn't bring myself to do it. Of course she'd done everything she could to find him, I told myself. But a borzoi is a sight hound; put something interesting in his field of vision and he'll follow it to the next state. They are a valuable breed, too, and I'd spent a number of sleepless nights in my cell wondering if he'd been stolen to be sold. Fitting, somehow, that seemed. Cosmically just. My punishment for my own thievery was having the only thing I cared about in the world stolen from me, and I would never know if he had been sold to someone who cared for him or shot and dumped in a river when the thief found that no one would buy him. There was also the real possibility that he had run away, gotten lost, been picked up by Boston animal control officers, and euthanized at the city shelter. Or adopted, perhaps. I chose to believe the latter. Whatever the case, he was gone, and that was as much my fault as the death of Arthur Czyz.

Then, as we pulled up in front of my house, Karen shut off her car and said to me, "Greg, I have something to tell you."

I waited. She shifted in her seat, fiddled with her keys, and finally went on. "I couldn't tell you this over the phone, but Boris didn't run away. He died."

"He died?" I repeated stupidly.

"I'm so sorry," Karen said. "I just couldn't tell you. He had some kind of stroke, the vet thought, and I had to have him put down. He didn't suffer."

"Boris died," I said softly, more to myself than her, trying the words out on my tongue and reeling as this revelation tore down the barriers of self-serving anguish I'd been hiding behind for the previous year and more. There was no thief, no cosmic justice. Just simple random chance, random as a dog's bark that nearly kills an armored-car guard in Maine.

It is difficult to describe how restorative this was. Agency was granted to me again. No longer did I have the luxury of believing that I was a stone on one pan of some great scale of justice. If Boris had simply died, nine years old with a wandering blood clot, I could believe that I was responsible for myself again.

Karen was still apologizing, and I laid a hand on her forearm. "It's all right," I said. "Better to know. You have no idea how hard it was to wonder." As I spoke, I realized how it must have sounded, and I rushed to correct myself. "I'm not blaming you. I don't know what I would have done in your shoes. You're my friend, Karen. I thank you for taking care of Boris at the end of his life."

We made small talk for a moment after that, agreed to meet for lunch once I'd gotten settled in the house again. Then I got out of the car and walked up my sidewalk and onto my porch to my front door. There was an ashtray on the porch railing; I hoped that Jules had refrained from smoking in the house. My key fit in the lock, surprising me, and the door opened onto my front hall that looked as it always had save for the coats that weren't mine hanging from the hall pegs. In the living room, my couch and coffee table and mantel ornaments were all exactly as I had left them, and the six years I had been gone fell away from me like a dream.

Then I noticed the chessboard in the back corner of the living room, against the wall that separated the living room from the kitchen. Hand-carved mahogany stand, squares done in obsidian and white marble, pieces of the same material. Mother-of-pearl border running around the edge of the board. It was the Gronkjaer board.

An envelope lay in the center of the board. I opened it and read a note in Karen's handwriting: *Welcome back to the world, Greg.*

It was the finest gift I had ever received, and at that moment I was near tears with love and guilt and relief and happiness and grief. I turned to go back to the front door in case Karen hadn't already left, and saw a second note on the coffee table.

Greg, it said. *I'll be back tomorrow to clear the rest of my things out and catch you up on the house (maintenance, etc.). Oh, and I've been seeing Boris in the neighborhood. Karen told me he ran away, right? Guess he tried to come home. I haven't been able to catch him, he always takes off when I go outside, but keep an eye out. I'm sure that when he sees you he'll come right back. Jules.*

You're always standing on one more rug, and it's always a surprise when someone pulls it out from under you.

I didn't mention this to Karen because I wasn't sure whether I wanted to get into the situation that would ensue if she insisted that Boris was dead. Why would she have lied to me? No good reason presented itself, but she had. She must have, unless Jules was mistaken and there was another borzoi wandering through the neighborhood; and given that I'd seen in the flesh exactly one other borzoi in the three years I'd owned Boris, this didn't seem likely. So I let it rest, and instead of confronting Karen went out to look for Boris. I papered the neighborhood with flyers featuring a six-year-old photo, drove from Newbury Street along every side street we'd ever walked on all the way out to the Museum of Fine Arts, sat up nights waiting for the click of his toenails on the porch, but Boris didn't appear. At some point I became convinced that Jules was playing a practical joke on me, and I called him up in a fury. He was hurt, with good reason; Jules wasn't the kind of guy to be cruel in that way, at least not to his friends. "I understand you're a bit strung out, Greg," he said, "but this is bullshit. If I didn't think you were having problems adjusting to being outside again, I'd come over there and kick your ass for you."

This brought me back to earth, and I apologized. He was mollified. We'd been friends too long for a single irrational act to drive us apart. He even offered to cut me in on a job he was and when we'd gotten seated at an outside table I started right in on her. "Karen, why did you tell me Boris was dead?"

"What?" she said. "Because he is."

"First you told me he ran away, though. And Jules told me he saw Boris in the neighborhood, and you know what? I saw him yesterday. He came right into the house, but I left the back door open and he took off again." As I said it, I realized that she would think I was suffering from some kind of grief-induced fantasy—but I had seen Boris, I had felt his head under my hand and brushed his hair from my pants. And I had left the back door open.

"Greg," Karen said slowly. "I know you miss Boris. And I know Walpole wasn't easy on you, and you're still adjusting to being out. And I know I lied to you once about this, but you have to believe me when I tell you that Boris is dead. I was there when the vet put him down. I have the bill." She was looking hard at me, and I could tell that there was no sense pressing the issue. Time to change the subject.

"Thanks for the chessboard," I said. "I meant to tell you before."

"I wanted you to have something," she said. "You've had a rough time, and part of it was my fault. Plus knowing you, I don't think the board will work its curse on you."

I had to laugh at that. She was right. For one reason or another, I'd never married, never had a long-term commitment of any kind. I had no family, no friends outside business circles, no deep emotional entanglements of any kind. This had never been a conscious choice. I'd just always been solitary. In the three years I'd had Boris I'd become more attached to him than I ever had to any human, but at first I'd bought him on a whim, after seeing a borzoi running along the Charles River.

"Mike Bronski came to see me yesterday," I said.

"Don't tell me you're getting back into the business."

"I'm not. And if I was, I wouldn't work with Kenny. The drugs and girls thing is outside my area of expertise, you know? Mike was asking about the money from the armored-car job." She waited for me to go on. "Kenny thinks I know where it is. I'm guessing I have maybe a week before he decides to get someone to work on me and find out for sure. Now don't take this the wrong way, but do you have any idea what Arthur did with the money before he died?"

When I'd been talking about Boris, Karen had looked confused and sympathetic. Now she was just angry. "I cannot believe you're asking me this," she said. "Do you—" She broke off and stared away from me at the passing traffic.

"Karen," I said. "You're my best friend. I don't think you're holding anything out on me for yourself. But you knew Arthur better than I did, and if he had someplace where he stashed job proceeds, you'd know it. If you have your own reasons for not telling me, I respect them; but I'm asking you as a friend who is in danger. Kenny K. is going to kill me if I don't tell him something. That I'm not making up."

She caught the implication of that last sentence, and she didn't like it. More time passed while she watched cars go by. Then after a while she said, "If Arthur had to hide something, it would probably be out at his dad's farm in Fitchburg."

"Thank you," I said, and meant it. "Does Kenny know about this?"

"I'm guessing he's had someone out there looking around, but I haven't talked to Arthur's dad in years. There's no reason for him to tell me if anything has happened."

Nothing had. I called Piotr Czyz the next morning, introduced myself as a friend of Arthur's, and asked if I could come out and speak to him that afternoon. That was fine with him, so after lunch—which I spent looking out the kitchen window for Boris—I drove out of the city through ostentatious suburbs that had been farmland when I'd gone into Walpole. Something about seven-hundred-thousand-dollar houses running their sprinkler systems in the rain gets to me, and the drive out Route 2 had me in a bilious mood for a while, but McMansion metastasis has only begun to nibble at Fitchburg, and by the time I'd found Sunny Hill Dairy I was enjoying the outing. It occurred to me that I could keep driving, go anywhere, forget about Kenny K. and Arthur and the whole damn sordid business, and for the first time I understood—really understood—that I was a free man again.

Forgetting the past six years would mean forgetting Boris, though, and I couldn't do that. No human being worth the name

A Peaceable Man

planning out in Sudbury, but I turned him down. "One time in prison's enough for me," I told him. "This is one guy who is rehabilitated. From now on, I'm an antique dealer."

Which I was, and I took satisfaction from working hard at it and making a legitimate living. I'd been able to support myself dealing antiques for years, but only because much of what I sold had been acquired through nonstandard channels. Now I restricted myself to reputable auctions and estate sales, not wanting to even go near sources that had a whiff of illegality about them. Within a couple of months I was up and running again, and had gotten a storefront's worth of merchandise out of storage and into a tiny space in a coming part of the South End. About this time, two things happened. First, I saw Boris, and second, Kenny Kazlauskas sent someone over to visit me.

Boris appeared in the back yard while I was making coffee at about seven one morning. I dropped my mug on the floor and ran out the back door with coffee squishing in my slippers, and my dog came trotting up to me like he'd just been jaunting around the block for half an hour instead of missing and presumed dead for more than a year. By the time he'd leaned his narrow head into my crotch like sight hounds always do, I was crying, and I led him back into the house wiping away tears and squishing in my slippers and swearing that I would kill him myself if he ever did anything like that again. Then there was a knock at the door, and when I opened it there stood Mike Bronski.

"Greg," he said.

"Mike," I said.

"Mind if I come in?"

"This a social call?"

"Kenny asked me to stop by."

"Then no, I'd appreciate it if you didn't come in," I said. "I'm just out of Walpole, as I'm sure you know, and I'm trying to keep my nose clean."

"Far be it from me to dirty your nose," said Mike. "Kenny just wanted me to drop by, ask if you knew anything about what happened to that money you and Arthur got from the armored-car job."

"Two things," I said. "One: no, I don't. I'm guessing Arthur hid it somewhere before he died. And two: what does Kenny care?"

"Arthur owed Kenny about eighty grand," Mike said with a shrug. "He figures that in this situation, he's kind of next of kin, and since your nose is so clean you don't want to have anything to do with the cash anyway." He looked at me with one of his eyelids lowered just a touch, as if he was gauging the distance between us, and I reminded myself that Mike Bronski had killed six people that I knew of. Most of them had probably seen that look. Kenny K. himself had populated the Mystic River with a number of unfortunate souls who took his money and exhausted his patience. I wondered what Arthur had done to get so indebted to him.

That didn't matter at the moment, though. What mattered was that Kenny had decided he was going to get the money from me if he couldn't get it from Arthur, and I didn't have it. "I'll ask around, see what I can find out," I said.

"You do that," said Mike, still with that heavy-lidded look. I shut the door and turned to see that Boris was gone.

I spent the day stewing over what to do. Kenny K. wasn't the kind of guy who was going to change his mind; if he'd decided I could tell him where the money was, he'd keep turning up the heat until I either told him or he vented his frustration and I couldn't tell anybody anything ever again. For all of three seconds I considered taking the direct approach and just spending the money to have someone take Kenny out. It would have to be someone from out of town, since nobody local would want to weather the storm that would follow, but I could probably afford it. Whether I'd survive the reprisals was uncertain, though, and as I've said, I don't like violence. Even talking to guys like Kenny or Mike made me want to get my teeth cleaned.

So I'd have to convince him I didn't know where the money was, or I'd have to find it and give it to him. Convincing didn't seem likely. Neither did finding out, but that was the pony I decided to ride.

The first thing I did was call Karen. She'd known Arthur longer than I had, and I also wanted to get the Boris thing all the way out into the open. From force of habit, we met at the coffeehouse, which miraculously was still there even after my years in Walpole, would walk away from his dog like that. Even if the dog was supposedly dead.

Time to admit something, I told myself as I parked outside the dairy farm's office and took in a deep manure-scented breath. You don't believe Boris is dead. And if you don't believe Boris is dead, either you believe Karen is lying or you believe your dog has come back from the grave.

I had touched him. I had brushed his hair from my pants.

Piotr Czyz was big and blocky like his son had been, but his bristly farmer's face was missing Arthur's blunt malice. When we shook hands, I was briefly ashamed of the softness of my own palm: the guilty side of the Puritan work ethic.

I suggested we talk in private, and he led me to his office. As he shut the door he said, "Chess player?"

At first I didn't know what he meant. Then he pointed to my tie, a dark green job with knights and bishops all over it. It's one of my favorite ties.

"Not really," I said. "Coffeehouse player, maybe. Mostly I just admire the game, and the people who are really good at it."

He nodded, hand still on the doorknob. "The only people who ever wanted to talk to me about Arthur were police and criminals. You aren't police."

Getting right to the point. "I'm not a criminal anymore either," I said.

A long moment passed while he looked at me without a trace of sympathy in his eyes. "I wish Arthur had lived to say that," he said then, and gestured for me to sit.

We faced each other across his desk, a painted aluminum rectangle that marked him as a man for whom success didn't mean flash. "I was in on the armored-car job with Arthur," I said. "And I'm going to be up front with you and tell you that it might be my fault that he was killed."

I was ready to tell him the whole story, up to and including Boris' fateful bark, but he cut me short. "It was Arthur's fault that he was killed. I got old a long time ago waiting for it to happen."

It might have sounded like he was letting me off the hook, but I knew better. What he meant was that I had no business wasting his time with false guilt. This shook me a bit; Arthur and I had never been friends, but hadn't I mourned him? Or had I only been feeling sorry for myself because his stupid idea had bought me six years in Walpole?

"You're probably right about that," I said. "And if I get killed now, it'll be my fault, but I'm still trying to avoid it."

"I don't know where the money is," Arthur's father said. I waited. "You're not the first to ask, and I'll tell you what I told the other guy. I hadn't seen my son for two years before he died, and he hadn't been out here for a year before that. And he damn sure couldn't have made the drive with a bullet in his lung, and if he had come here with that goddamn money I'd have told him to burn it or else I would."

A deep flush crept across Piotr Czyz's face as he spoke, and I knew that whatever he'd said, he hated me for coming out to his farm and reminding him of how his son had died.

I stood. "Mr. Czyz, I'm trying to stay alive. I don't mean to throw this in your face."

"I hope you do stay alive," he said from behind his desk. "But it's not up to me."

I drove back to Boston wondering what to do next. The dairy had been a long shot, so I wasn't really disappointed that it hadn't paid off. Still, I now had one less option to avoid Kenny K.'s bone saws, or concrete Keds, or whatever other killing methodologies his Mafia-fevered brain had latched onto. This was trouble.

Things only got worse when I walked into my house and found Mike Bronski watching television in the living room. "You are one crazy faggot," he said without taking his eyes off the screen, where motorcycles were jumping over piles of dirt. Mike was under the impression that all antiques dealers were homosexual, a stereotype that just makes me tired.

I still had the gun upstairs in the safe—my one parole violation—but Mike and I both knew that if I took off fast in any direction, he'd make me wish I hadn't. So I stood where I was and said, "What makes me crazy, Mike?"

He shook his head as if I'd disappointed him. "Aren't you smart enough to know when not to play dumb? Jesus."

"Humor me. Why am I crazy?"

"I didn't think you could train those kinds of dogs to attack," Mike said. "I give you credit for that. What is it, an Afghan?"

"Borzoi. Russian wolfhound."

"Whatever, the goddamn thing was fast. Came right out of Kenny's hedge when he went out to get the paper this morning. I was just leaving, and wham here comes this white fuckin blur out of the fuckin hedge." Mike started to laugh. "Like nothing I ever saw. It marked Kenny up pretty good before I put a foot in its ribs, and then it took off like a track dog. I took a couple of shots at it, but…" he shrugged. "You know how many broke-down greyhounds I popped in the last ten years? Every one of them, I wished I could get a nice target rifle, set it up and let that dog run. Okay, dog, you and me. I miss, you're free. Instead I took 'em to the dump, bang, left 'em there for the gulls. And now here I am with this Russian dog hauling ass across Kenny's yard, and all I have is this." He took a snub-nosed revolver out of his belt and laid it on the coffee table. "Didn't seem right."

He turned the television off and stood. "Some dog you got there, Greg. I admire a good dog. Wanted to tell you this before I pass along a message from Kenny. He called me once he'd gotten stitched up, said you got balls. Said you can keep the money if you give him the dog."

On his way past me to the back door, Mike clapped me on the shoulder. "Helluva dog. Truth is, Kenny's scared shitless of it. Thinks it's magic, the crazy sonofabitch. One of us'll be by tomorrow."

After he left, I stood staring blankly at the revolver on the coffee table, trying to make sense of the whole thing. Kenny K. lived in a gaudy neo-Colonial house in Hingham, for God's sake, a good fifteen miles from my house, and the only thing Boris had ever attacked in his life was a stuffed yak I'd given him when he was a puppy. Now, at nine years old, he'd become a pointy-headed assassin? It was almost easier to believe that he'd come back from the dead.

Completely at sea, I grabbed hold of the one question I knew I could get answered. I called Karen.

She didn't sound happy to hear from me, and I think she almost hung up when I asked her what had happened to Boris' body.

"You can't go dig up his grave and see if he's in it, Greg," she snapped. "I had the vet take care of it."

The initial deception I could almost understand; it's hard to break bad news to people when other things have made them vulnerable. But this hurt.

"Do you know what they do with dead dogs?" I shouted into the receiver. "They pile them in a goddamn dump truck and throw them in a landfill to rot, Karen! You couldn't even spring for the hundred bucks to have him cremated while you were lying to me so I could lie awake in my fucking cell thinking he'd starved to death in an alley somewhere?"

As I shouted, I noticed that I was looking at the Gronkjaer board, her gift to me in celebration of my release. And just as that registered, I also noticed that I'd been ranting to a dial tone.

It was getting late, and I was going to die the next day, and I couldn't stand the thought that I might leave this world on bad terms with the human being who meant more to me than any other. The only person for whom my feelings rivaled my love for Boris. That sounds strange and unhealthy, I know, but when it came to relationships I'd never played my cards very well.

I went to Karen's house, and when she opened the door I said I was sorry before she could shut it again, and then I said that people are not at their best when dangerous mobsters were going to kill them in the morning, and I asked her if I could come in and talk for a while.

She let me in, and we sat in a kind of fake companionable silence for a while. She was letting me work myself up to whatever I'd come to ask, and I knew it, and I appreciated it. Thing was, I knew what I wanted to ask but not if it was the right question. I had that tense feeling in the back of my mind that something should have been clear to me, that I was seeing things but not the connections between them. Probably just desperation, I thought. Looking for that miraculous way out when of course there wasn't one.

"Karen, when you told me you hadn't talked to Arthur's father in years, what did that mean, exactly?"

"What are you getting at, Greg?"

You get involved with a woman sometimes, a kind of no-questions-asked relationship. For the comfort. Karen and I had once found that kind of comfort in each other. It lasted about a year, then dried up without either of us feeling aggrieved. She'd married since then, a couple of years before I'd gone to Walpole, but some of the closeness we'd once enjoyed...that kind of feeling never completely goes away.

Unless you push it.

When I asked her if Piotr Czyz and Kenny K. had ever done business, I pushed it. Hard. Her face closed up, and I had time to think that she would just get up and leave me sitting there in her living room. She got hold of it, though, whatever she was feeling, and she answered me honestly.

"I used to work for Pete. And Pete used to work for Kenny. He still might. I try not to know too much about them anymore. When I still had the market, Pete would drop product with the milk run. It was all Kenny's—Pete didn't mind moving it, but he didn't want to get involved with buying and selling. Arthur came in every day to pick it up and move it into the neighborhood. He was still close to his father then, but when he started to munch some of the product Pete threatened to cut him out. So Kenny picked him up, got him started collecting from the pony junkies Kenny made book for. And this set Pete off even more. He didn't want his boy getting dirty for Kenny K., but by then Arthur had a habit and the upshot of the whole thing is that Arthur and Pete stopped talking to each other. And Arthur started to like the horses a bit himself. Kenny really owned him after that.

"A little while after that I sold the market to Kenny, and then I got married, and now I don't have anything to do with it anymore."

I remembered when she'd sold the market. The lease on the building had gone way up as Central Square turned hip, and she'd wanted to put her money somewhere easier and cleaner. So she'd told me at the time. And it had been true, but there was a lot she hadn't told me, too. I could feel that omission, like a wedge of regret and stubbornness driven between us.

Working it over in my head, I decided that Pete Czyz had told me the truth when he denied knowing where the money was. He hadn't told me everything, though, and now I had that tense feeling in my mind again, like I should have been able to put together what he'd left out.

Karen quit talking once she'd spun the story out for me, and I could tell she wanted me to leave. On the way home I tried to put it all together, but I kept running aground on the fact that Kenny K. was coming by the next morning and I had nothing to tell him. Add that to the fact that I had possibly endangered Karen by going to see her when Kenny might well have someone keeping an eye on me, and I walked in the front door of my house feeling very much like a man waiting for the noose at sunrise, hoping only that I didn't take any of my friends with me.

Boris was in the living room staring at the Gronkjaer board.

It made a kind of sense, insofar as seeing your dead dog in the living room can make sense. When Karen had bought me the board, she'd put it in Boris' favorite corner, the one he'd always stared into. I don't know if other dogs do this, but Boris had a habit of staring for long periods of time into particular corners, ears at half-mast and head cocked slightly to one side. I used to joke that he was seeing a ghost, but stopped when a client took me a little too seriously. One of the hazards of the business when you deal with items that people think might be magical.

So if Boris was going to come back and stare into a corner, it would be that corner.

"Hey," I said. "You let yourself in?"

He glanced up at me, swept his tail back and forth a couple of times, then returned to his study of the board. It was set up in one of my favorite positions, the ending of Aron Nimzovich's 1923 Immortal Zugzwang. A classic game, one of the great moments in chess history; with only one real attacking exchange, Nimzovich—in twenty-three moves—compressed the board until his opponent Sämisch had no move that wouldn't cut his own throat. That's what *Zugzwang* means. I'd always admired this game more than any of the other famous matches, the ones awarded brilliancy prizes at one tournament or another; there was something supremely satisfying about the way Nimzovich inexorably forced Sämisch to do himself in by allowing him moves that looked perfect but were in fact suicide. Victory through guile rather than brute force. The kind of achievement that appeals to a peaceable man.

Of course, I found myself in Sämisch's exact predicament. I couldn't find the money, and I wasn't about to give Boris up—even if I could have—so every avenue led to me being found dead by a friend once someone noticed that my mailbox was overflowing. I might have run, I guess, but Kenny was rich and Kenny was mean and Kenny was obsessive and in the end he would have found me, I think. Also, I didn't want to run. I was fifty-two and settled, and I could no more imagine a life working in a hotel in Paraguay than I could imagine taking a gun and killing Kenny myself. There are people who say that anyone will kill given the right situation; I don't think this is true. If I had been able to kill Kenny, I wouldn't have been me. Ergo, I wasn't able to kill Kenny.

What I was able to do was pull a chair up next to Boris and the chessboard and sit, quietly, as the sun went down and the room darkened around me. Sometime after dark he turned around three times and lay on the rug next to my chair, and in the room's perfect stillness I felt myself receding. Tomorrow I would die, and one by one all of the things that had occupied my time grew insubstantial and finally disappeared. I sat, alone, with Boris sleeping on the rug and the faint glow of streetlights picking out the crosses on the two kings' heads.

The phone woke me up. It was Mike. "Kenny says I'm supposed to come over if you have the dog."

"What, is he scared of a borzoi?"

Mike laughed. For the first time in our short and unwilling interaction, I felt like he didn't think I was a total loss.

"I don't have the dog," I said.

He didn't ask whether I had the money. "Okay, Kenny'll be there in an hour."

The phone went dead, and I put my hand down at the side of the chair. Boris was gone.

An hour.

I decided I would die clean, and went upstairs to take a shower. Thirteen minutes, including getting dressed again in my favorite corduroys and a sweater I'd had for thirty years. I spent three minutes thinking about whether I should leave some kind of note for Karen. I was leaving the house to her. She wouldn't move into it, would in fact sell it as soon as my will cleared probate, but she would appreciate the gesture. Forget it, I decided; no note. Everyone who knew me would eventually find out what had happened. I didn't care.

The truth of that struck me. I didn't care. I didn't care that Kenny Kazlauskas was at that moment on his way over to my house to kill me because I didn't know where Arthur had hidden the money. Why? Because I was helpless. Without options or avenues of escape. Kenny was coming over because that's the kind of person Kenny was, and I'd let him do it. I'd let him walk right into my house.

I. Would. Let. Him.

"Jesus," I whispered, and understood everything. Sometimes you think you're playing white, and it turns out you've just been seeing the board from the wrong angle.

The Gronkjaer board was heavy, but it scooted across the rug without any of the pieces falling over. For some reason that seemed important. When I'd gotten it far enough out of the corner that I could step around behind it, I looked for a long moment at the painted-over cover of the milk chute set into the wall. Arthur had spent his entire working life driving a delivery truck for his father's dairy; where else would he have stashed the money if he wanted me to find it?

I couldn't pry the door open with my hands, so I got a screwdriver from the junk drawer in the kitchen and gouged the paint out of the hinges, then worked the tip under the edge of the door and popped it loose. When it opened, bundles of money fell out onto the floor.

Arthur, you were a better guy than I ever gave you credit for, I thought, and was humbled even as pure exaltation swept through me at the realization that I was going to live. Kenny would show up, I'd give him the money, and we'd all forget about the whole thing. The scope of my life, just then constricted to a few minutes, suddenly ballooned out to years again—I would live! I'd grow old!

Most of the bundles of cash stayed jammed in the chute until I scooped them out. By the time I'd cleared the space, the pile was heaped around my feet and I felt like Scrooge McDuck. A small piece of white paper fluttered out of the chute to land on the mound of bills. It was a note. *G,* it read. *Your dog got me shot, but I don't blame him. If I was a dog I would of barked too. See ya after I get doctored up.* There was no signature.

My throat felt tight, and the wash of conflicting emotion brought me to the edge of tears. It's hard to realize that you've been so wrong about someone who's dead; how do you make it right?

Kenny walked in the front door without knocking. He shut the door behind him and stepped into the living room, not showing a gun yet. "Let's have it," he said.

A double arc of stitches curled through his left eyebrow and across that side of his nose. There were more in his ear, and I could see the edge of a bandage sticking out past his shirt cuff. I resisted the urge to comment. It was one thing to be utterly stoned on the knowledge that I'd just been given a cosmic get-out-of-jail-free card, whether through plain magic or just the odd swirls of probability that always cropped up whenever large amounts of money were dislocated from their proper flow; it was another thing entirely to mock a man who would be looking for an excuse to kill me whether I had what he wanted or not. And Kenny was not at his most agreeable: his pupils were contracted to pinpricks, his hands shook, he was blazing with cocaine and scared to death.

I'd taken a couple of steps out into the room as Kenny came in. My chair and the Gronkjaer board blocked his view of the corner, and I took care to stand in the gap between them.

"You tipped the cops to me, didn't you, Kenny?" I said.

He grinned. "Fuckin' A right, I did. I got a right to find out where my money was, and you couldn't work no voodoo bullshit on me from Walpole. It didn't work, hey, if at first you don't succeed, you know?" His eyes were snapping all over the room.

"So let's have it. You don't have it, you know what? They used to press people under stones until they admitted they were witches. I got a big pile of rocks out at a quarry in Stow. You give me the money, they get broken up into road gravel."

"I got it," I said, and gestured behind me.

The table wasn't quite where I thought it was, I guess, or something else was going on, but as I moved my arm the side of my hand brushed the white king where he stood cornered on h1. The king toppled, bouncing on the edge of the table and falling to the floor.

And Boris came out from behind me, head low and upper lip curled back from his teeth.

I'd say that I was as surprised as Kenny, but it would be a lie. His face actually went white, instantly, as if the blood had been vacuumed from his body, and when his mouth fell open a kind of whine came out. Reflexively he reached for the gun in his waistband, but before he could get it out Boris sprang.

A borzoi is a large dog, but he seems larger than he is. Boris stood about even with my hips, and when he stood on his hind legs he could rest his front paws on my shoulders, but the most he ever weighed was about eighty-five pounds. Every ounce of that is muscle, though, and centuries of breeding for the hunting of wolves has made borzois whip-fast and amazingly agile. Boris caught Kenny just as Kenny's hand found the doorknob, and if the door hadn't come open I can't help but believe that Boris would have killed Kenny dead as...well, dead as Boris, right there on my living room rug. But the door did come open, and Kenny threw Boris off long enough to get out of the house, breaking the screen door off its latch as he went. Boris followed him, and as I ran after the two of them I heard Kenny's screams trailing away down the street. When I got out onto the porch they were out of sight. I looked up and down the block, saw no ectoplasmic borzoi and no panicked gangster. Not even an astonished neighbor to make me believe that what I'd just seen was real. Kenny's Eldorado sat parked in my driveway and I was seized by an irrational certainty that some kind of error had been purged and made right again.

The Gronkjaer board, I thought. The one who loved you, and whom you abandoned.

A Peaceable Man

The next morning, bright and early, there came a knock at the door. I was delighted to see that my visitors did not number among them Mike Bronski, even though they were cops and therefore unwelcome.

"Brower and Glenn," I said. "Come in."

They did, and sat. We'd known each other in a professional capacity for six years or so—they were the detectives who'd put me in Walpole.

My natural instincts tend toward courtesy, but I knew from prior experience that it would be wasted on these two. They were both colorless and patient men, ill at ease when they weren't working or talking about work. So I got things started. "Yes, that's Kenny K.'s Eldorado in my driveway," I said.

"Oh good," Brower said. "He's being forthcoming."

Glenn chimed in. "Kenny says you sicced your dog on him. Twice. Most recently yesterday."

"Detectives, you know Kenny isn't a rational man."

"Did you sic your dog on him?"

"My dog is dead," I said, and believed it—really believed it—for the first time. "He died about a year ago."

Back to Brower. "Do we have to take your word for that?"

"I can get you the receipt from the vet. It has the word euthanasia on it, if that's specific enough for you."

"So we found Kenny around the corner, practically catatonic and dog bites all over him, and you don't know anything about that," Brower said.

"Even though his car is in your driveway," added Glenn.

"Did Kenny tell you why he was here?" I asked.

It was a weak effort, not even enough to get Brower to crack a smile. "Why don't you tell us?" he responded.

"He said my dog had attacked him at his house in Hingham," I began. "Which is, as I'm sure you know, a damned long way for a nine-year-old borzoi to go just to bite someone, apart from the fact that Boris was meek as a lamb, couldn't track if his life depended on it, and had never been to Kenny's house before." I paused, hoping the ridiculousness of the whole situation would impress itself upon them. "Plus, as I mentioned, Boris is dead. Maybe some dog did bite Kenny; his face was stitched up when he came here. He said he was going to kill me if I didn't give him both the dog and the money from the LockTrans job."

Glenn arched an eyebrow. "And you said?"

"I don't have my dog any more, and I don't have the money either."

This was true. There's a no-kill animal shelter in the South end that has a 24-hour lobby full of cages where you can drop off strays. I'd gone there the night before and stuffed an old nylon duffel bag full of the LockTrans proceeds into one of the cages. A mournful beagle mutt had licked my fingers through the wires of his own prison. If he hadn't been wearing tags I'd have taken him home.

"You don't have the money," Glenn repeated.

"Whatever Arthur did with it, it's gone."

"So why did Kenny think you had it?" Brower again.

I shrugged. "Who knows why Kenny thinks anything? Come on, Detective, Kenny's got a thousand-dollar-a-day habit and he's been convinced for fifteen years that I'm some kind of sorcerer. Did he tell you that?"

They weren't ready to let it go, I could see that. After a short pause, during which I assumed they were telepathically arranging who would speak next, Brower said, "Sure, Kenny's delusional, and the coke ate through his septum into his brain in about 1987. But he keeps good track of his money."

"If he thinks this money is his," I said, "it's because he put Arthur up to the job."

Brower and Glenn looked at each other. "You remember Greg here saying this at his trial?" Glenn asked his partner.

"Don't think so. Greg, did you forget to mention this at your trial?"

I kept my mouth shut. They weren't done squeezing, and I wasn't going to waste my one bullet until they were.

"We know Kenny put the bug in Arthur's ear," Glenn said. "And we all know that it wasn't going to stick with just your testimony anyway. So what we're wondering is, is there anybody else you might have just remembered was involved?"

I took a deep breath. I only had one thing to give them, and I wasn't sure it would be enough, and down in the pit of my stomach where the old criminal me still lived I felt the rolling uneasiness

A Peaceable Man

of the snitch who knows he's going to turn and can't do anything about it. It's a kind of guilt unlike any other.

"You're not going to hear me say anything about Piotr Czyz," I said.

Detectives Brower and Glenn didn't say anything while they turned that over in their heads until they'd satisfied themselves that I'd really said what they thought I'd said. Both of them stood. I stood with them. "I want to be out of this. As of now. Forever."

"Far as we're concerned," said Brower. Glenn nodded. They shut the door behind them when they left.

I could have left Piotr out of it. He'd lost his son, after all. Thing was, though, that when he'd told me Arthur was responsible for his own death, it was a cheat. And it almost worked; I was so dumbly grateful for absolution that it almost didn't occur to me that Pete Czyz might have been working that gratitude to steer me away from himself. That was part of what I'd figured out as I stood there looking at the chessboard waiting for Kenny to show up and end my life.

I had helped to kill Arthur, and Kenny Kazlauskas had helped to kill Arthur, and Arthur had helped to kill himself. But Piotr Czyz had set his son on that road the first time he'd had Arthur load cottage-cheese tubs filled with cocaine into the GMC TopKick Arthur drove around metro Boston. Somebody's always to blame.

Still, I could have kept my mouth shut. Who was I to judge the truth of Pete Czyz's grief?

I learned loyalty late in life. It's not a lesson that comes easily to a thief. I'd meant it when I told Pete Czyz that I wasn't a criminal any more, and that was why I couldn't let Pete walk away from the setup that had killed his son. Arthur Czyz hadn't been much of a friend, but in the end he was loyal. For a human being, that's not too bad.